I0788938

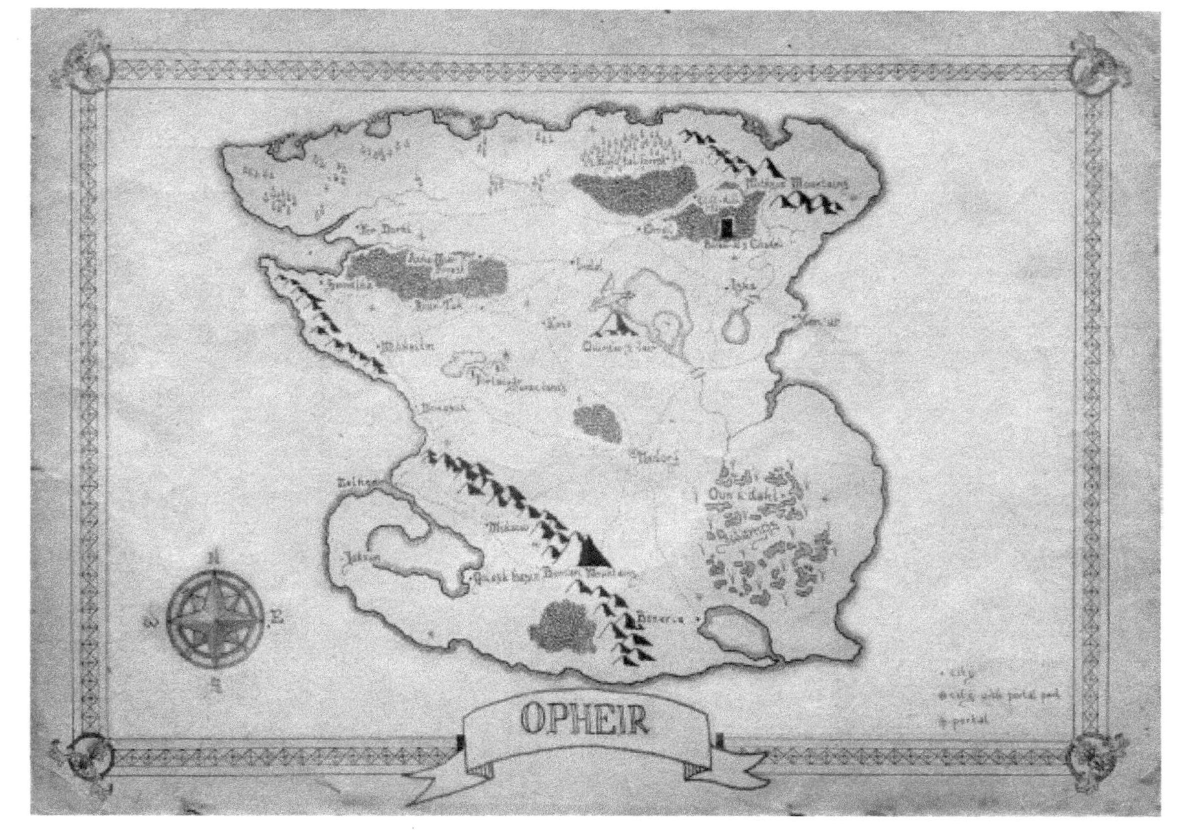

OPHEIR

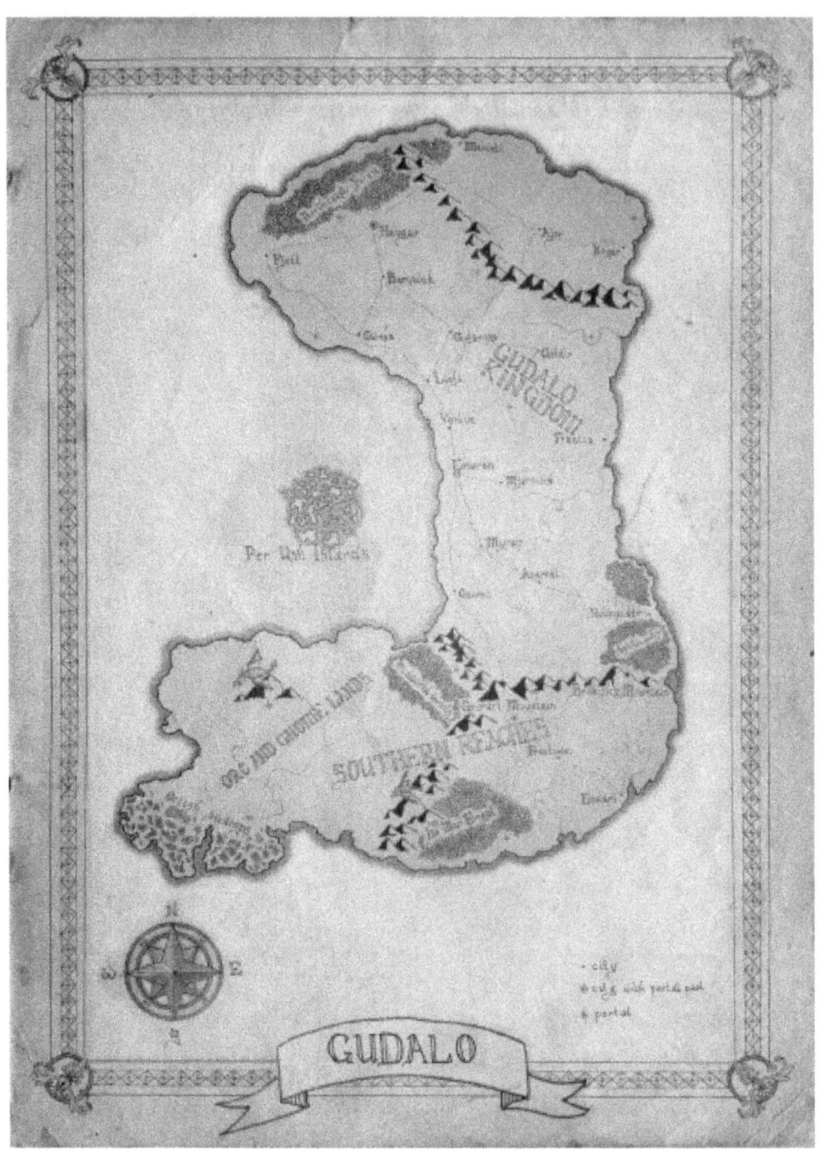
GUDALO KINGDOM
Per Ush Islands
ORC AND GNOME LANDS
SOUTHERN REACHES
N
W   E
S
city
city with portal pad
portal
GUDALO

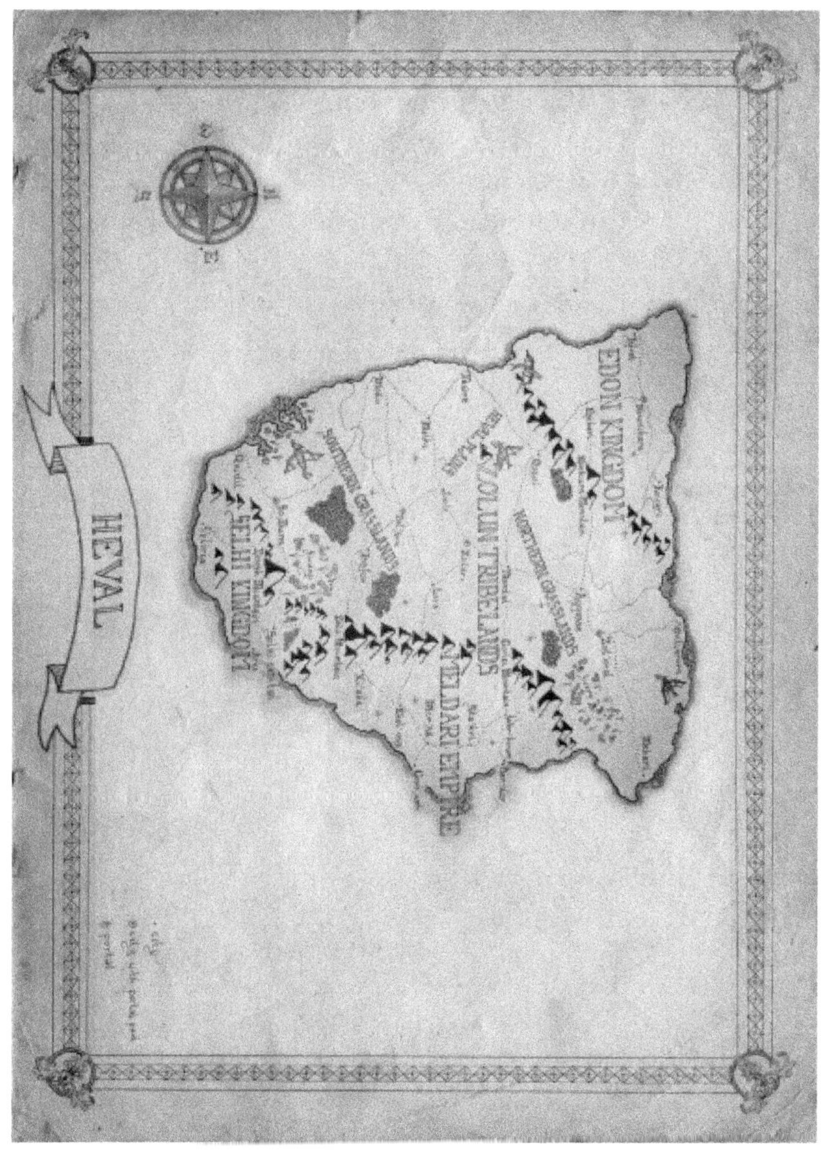
HEVAL
EDON KINGDOM
OLUN TRIBELANDS
MELDARI EMPIRE
NORTHERN GRASSLANDS
SOUTHERN GRASSLANDS
KINGDOM

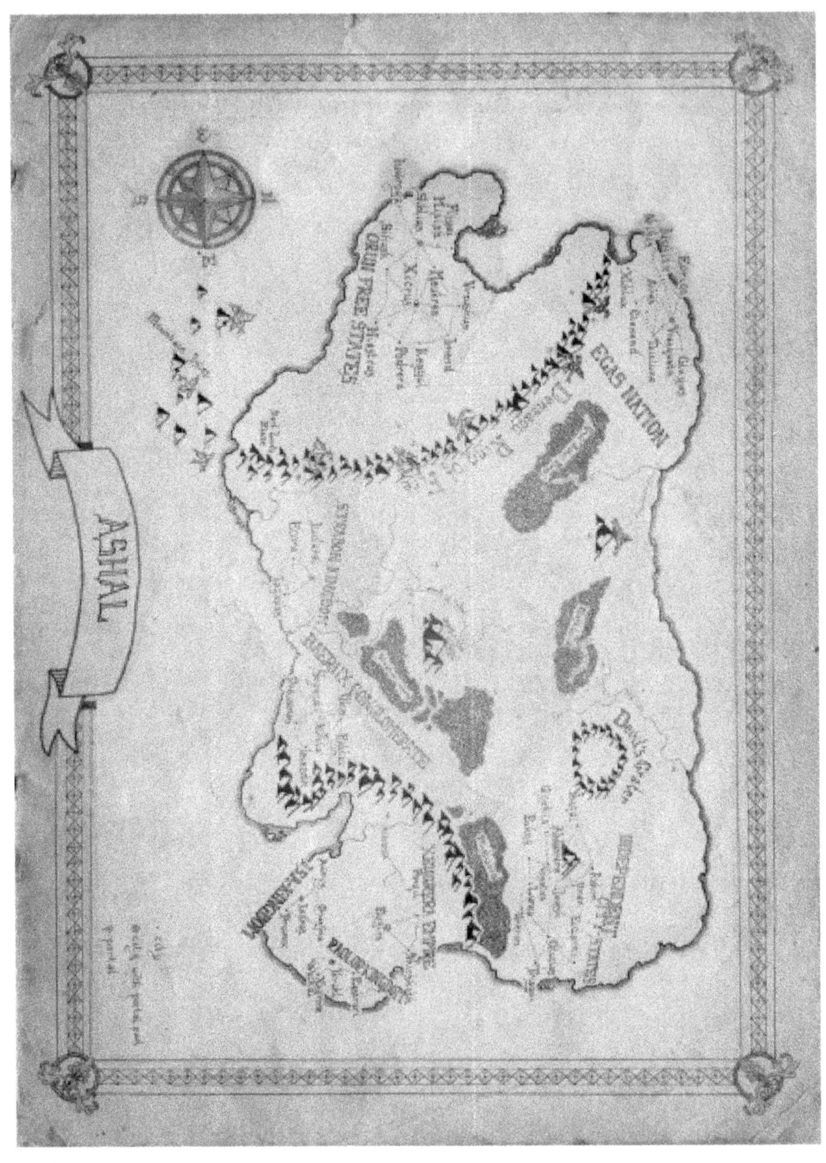
ASHAL
OUUI FREE STATES
EGAS NATION
DEVIL'S GARDEN

Want a bigger map of Emerilia and the continents? Check out **http://theeternalwriter.deviantart.com/**

Character Sheet is located in the back of the book for reference.

Emerilia

This is Our Land

Prologue

Lezar looked over the Demon Horde as it progressed. They were highly resistant to most diseases and poison, but that didn't mean that they were unaffected by it.

The Demon Horde was slow, most of them dealing with cramps and stomach flus that they had seemed to catch over the last couple of weeks.

Lezar smiled as the afternoon turned to night. Hidden amongst the Demon Horde were his own DCA soldiers. It had been easy for them to get into the camp.

The Demon Horde didn't care who walked beside them; they just weighed whether it was worth stabbing them for what they had or not. The Demon Horde was growing in strength, due to their uncaring murder of one another to take another's belongings and food or to eat them.

"Tonight's the night." Krenua stood beside Lezar.

"That it is," Lezar said. "I am surprised that it has taken the Horde so long to start making leaders. If either of the plans are pulled off, then it will be the beginning of the end."

"It does feel good to have a purpose once again. When seeing the Demon Horde, I can understand why the trust that we've built up within the Devil's Crater Army is so useful. Without it, we wouldn't be much better than the rabble down there," Krenua said, a look of disgust on his face.

Lezar grunted in agreement and took one more look at the advancing Horde. Some were trying out their ability at flying, but it took time to understand how to do it properly. It also made beginner fliers vulnerable. It was easy to throw a rock at a new flier and bring them to the ground, stunned and weakened for another attack. Only the strongest Demons, those who had grouped together, or were just plain stupid, tried out flying.

"Without their aerial abilities, we're going to be able to bleed them on the ground. Their loss of mobility is going to be essential for completing this. Make sure that you target the winged ones first."

"There are only a third of them with wings—most of which have wounded wings. You can see the winged ones starting to group together as we had within our own horde when we crossed these plains. You and your brothers were the first of us to learn how to not only fly, but to fight while flying," Krenua said.

"Exactly. Wings give them mobility and advantages. Tonight, we'll take out the leaders among the Demon Horde. The more chaos within their ranks, the longer it will take them to reach Devil's Crater and the more we can bleed them." Lezar's stony features turned into a cold, *pleased* smile.

"I'll head down to the rest of the groups waiting. It will feel good to cut these ingrates down a bit." Krenua looked over the two million-strong Demon Horde. His heart beat fast, a mix of excitement of battle and the fear of death that followed it.

"Good luck, Krenua. Bring me their heads." Lezar held out his arm.

Krenua braced forearms with the general. "We'll sow the ground with their blood," Krenua promised.

Lezar nodded.

Krenua headed down the hill that they were using to watch the slowing Demon Horde getting ready to make camp for the night.

Krenua jogged through the forest, his footfalls light as he made nearly no sound in his movements. It was only through his mini map that he was able to find the Demons assigned to the mission, every one of which from Lezar's brigade.

They had traded their service clothes for rags in most places. For this mission, the Beast Kin were held back, as a very last resort. For this to go off without a hitch, the Demon Horde would have to think that their leadership was killed from within.

Krenua waited and looked over his interface, checking the linked scouts who were updating the map constantly with where the Demon Horde's people were.

The Demons who had already inserted themselves into the Demon Horde camp also ran updates on certain high-value targets.

Dusk turned into night. Demons tried to hunt food down. Brawls started between the hungriest. With no meat to be found, the Demon Horde was not averse to killing their own and cooking them for sustenance.

Still, the DCA waited. The night came and the biggest fights came and went. Darkness descended as the Demon Horde started to fall asleep. The night's air smelled metallic, telling of the victims who had already fallen.

"Go," Lezar said over the brigade-wide channel.

The Devil's Crater Army started to stand up in groups and headed into the Demon Horde's camp. They looked like hunters who were just coming in late. Around fifteen thousand of the DCA soldiers were part of the operation. Facing over two million other Demons, it was hard to figure out that they were part of the same group.

Krenua waited for his group's turn. They moved forward, relaxed and muttering among themselves as they got closer to the camp.

"Hope that there's some damn meat to be had in the camp," Krenua said as they walked.

"Well, if there isn't, then we'll have to make some of our own," another said with a bloodthirsty smile.

"Look at these idiots—more scared of one another than of the creatures that should be in this area." Ilia shook her head.

The camp seemed to be formed into a sort of arena: Demons around the outside, with the interior empty except for those brawling. The Demon groups had their backs to the forest as they watched their fellows they thought of as a larger threat than the natural beasts.

Krenua shook his head, agreeing with Ilia's observation. "Easier for us," Krenua said, as they moved toward the marked targets. "Spread out so we don't look like a group."

They moved apart. A Demon made a pass at Ilia, slapping her ass. Her sword took off his arm; his leering smile turned into a howl of pain before she slit his throat. He made choking noises, causing three other Demons to draw their crude stone weapons and move up to help. Their faces showed looks of shock as they saw blades suddenly emerging from the Demons' chests.

The DCA left the dying Demons.

It's pretty messed up that we're kind of killing our younglings. They were made from the same base as us, though they're pure destruction. The Dark Lord's perfect tools: they're dumb, strong, and loyal as long as they're fed. Simple fact is that they're coming to destroy my home and do that sadistic fuck's dirty work.

"What are you doing?" a large Demon said as Krenua walked past him.

The Demon didn't feel anything as Ilia's blade cut out the tendons in his knee, dropping him down before she took his head off in a powerful blow.

"Killing you," Krenua said, not feeling an ounce of guilt as he moved into the sleeping area. Other groups of DCA moved into the area at the same time.

Krenua walked under a low-hanging tree to see three Demons wrapped in their wings, sleeping around a tree. One of them looked around, her hand resting on her weapon.

Krenua didn't give her time to react, putting his blade through her eye and into her skull.

She slumped to the ground. Krenua dispatched another Demon a second after; the third rustled in his sleep but didn't rise.

Krenua made sure they would never wake from their slumber. The rusty smell of freshly spilled blood made Krenua's stoic expression turn into a grin similar to Lezar's.

DCA who had been hidden within the Demon Horde moved on their targets. Fifty thousand Demons died in a few short hours. Not a large number compared to the mass of Demons, yet nearly every one of them had been the strongest of the Horde. Potential leaders and groups were quashed in a night, while the most aggressive ones were left alive.

"Pull back. Good work," Lezar said. The DCA melted back into the forest.

Krenua stayed up the few hours left until morning, watching the Demon Horde camp. Before night turned into day, movement started to fill the camp. It seemed that word had been passed. By the time the sun had risen, the remaining groups, the bottom feeders and the more aggressive ones were pulling themselves together.

Krenua watched as a battle played out in the middle of the camp. The open area in its center turned into a gladiator pit.

The Demons would probably level up but without leadership and their mistrust, it was like the first days they came to Emerilia. It was a free-for-all.

"We kill fifty thousand; they kill nearly two hundred thousand. That's what I call a strategic advantage." Lezar watched the scene with Krenua.

"What do we do now?" Krenua asked.

"Nightly raids; I want to fan the flames. The more time we hold them back here, the longer Efri gets with his traps. I want them disorganized, sleep deprived, and unwilling to trust one another when we hit them." Lezar looked to Krenua.

"I'll see to it." Krenua nodded and looked back to the camp one more time. *Once they clear Efri's traps, then they'll be at Devil's Crater and the real battle will start.*

***

Josh watched the interface in front of Florence disappear. For a few moments, there was nothing. Then, the drop pad's runes lit up. There was a flash of light as the drop pad had disappeared. In its place was a teleport pad. A control terminal sat on top of it.

Everyone looked around, as if stunned by what had just happened. It didn't seem as nearly ground-breaking as they'd thought.

Josh knew that with time, this would change. It wasn't having the teleport pad that would change Emerilia; it was what they did through the teleport pad.

"Get the control terminal off and put it in the control room," Florence said.

Two Stone Raiders grabbed the terminal, moving it off to the control room on one side. The entire area around the teleport pad had been made for speed and efficiency as well as defense. They wanted to be able to control what went through the teleport pad immediately.

The teleport pad hummed with power; the Stone Raiders' hands went to their blades.

A portal opened, showing Lucy on the other side.

"Well, it looks like it worked. Congratulations." Lucy smiled at Florence.

"I didn't think that it would there for a bit." Florence laughed.

Lucy stepped from the guild hall and out into Verlun. The portal closed behind her.

"Ah, just had to ramp up the excitement!" Josh said.

"Yeah, ramping up the excitement has nearly turned me into a nervous wreck," Lucy said dryly.

"Well, anyway, I have to get back to planning out a fight. I'll see you ladies later," Josh said, seeing that they were eager to catch up.

"Fine, go have fun. We'll get your supplies sorted out." Lucy waved Josh away like some annoying mosquito.

Josh grinned and headed for the control room, where the teleport pad's controls were. As much as he was excited by the things going on in Verlun, when he thought about the impending war that was going to happen at Devil's Crater, he couldn't help but feel more excited.

Fellox's hundred grand is as good as mine! What the hell can they do that compares to an entire war between two different groups of Demons with Beast Kin thrown in? Bloody hell, it's nerve-racking, it's nuts, and it's bloody brilliant!

***

"What?" Geswald held his pipe in his numb hands.

"From the sources that we have, we're getting reports that the Stone Raiders have installed a teleport pad at their new headquarters in Verlun. They are starting to talk to local businesses. We believe that it was put into place a few days ago. With their standing treaties with other nations for fighting on their behalf, their network is expanding rapidly," Pete said.

Geswald looked at the man blankly. His eyes moved around the office he sat in but didn't settle on anything. "What kind of monsters are they that they can buy a teleport pad? Where did they even get the drop pad from?"

Pete cleared his throat. Geswald's eyes focused on him again.

"We have heard rumors of a member of the Stone Raiders being a Dwarven Master Smith. I think that is how they were able to make it. Three days ago, there was another teleport pad connected. This one in a town called Cliff-Hill. It's an insignificant place, but the only place in Opheir other than Nadorf. They are connected to a Human city, Omal, as well as an Elven forest, Kufo'tel, and the Mithsia Mountains. Trade goes through the village, where they have large smithies and a ceramics factory. I have been looking into these factories and the smithies through the connections in the traders' guild. They're owned by the same person, Dave Grahslagg, the reported Dwarven Master Smith. He has multiple patents on different items and it seems that he is responsible for using all of the smithy and ceramics factories' income to buy a teleport pad," Pete said.

"So, the Stone Raiders basically bought *two* teleport pads in as many days. They call a Dwarven Master Smith one of their people and they can somehow get goods from somewhere on a near-constant basis?" Geswald sat back in his chair, feeling much older.

The guildmaster was right. I've never seen a guild have this kind of power before.

"We need to cancel all plans that we have with the Stone Raiders. They are not a group we want to anger. We can maybe pressure them in some way, but direct confrontation will lead to nothing," Geswald said firmly, relieved that he had been held back from his hasty attack plan he'd made just a few weeks ago.

"Yes, master," Pete bowed, wincing as he said the next sentence. "Lord Esamael received the same information as us a few hours before. He sent a message for you."

"Well, out with it." Geswald frowned.

"Lord Esamael, upon hearing that there is a second teleport pad held within fifty miles of his own teleport pad, has expressed his *displeasure* at the current situation. He wants us to do something about them. If we do not, then he will increase the cost of using the teleport pad, as well as taxes, while doing his best to interfere in our businesses. He said it in more flowery language."

"Did he send his message to just us?" Geswald asked darkly. His mind worked to try to figure a way to balance himself between the Stone Raiders and Lord Esamael.

"No, he sent it to a number of merchants and traders. We have already received complaints from a few of them."

"Esamael is a powerful man. His family has owned this town and its teleport pad for many generations. They're more powerful than most kings. Their power is only beaten by the actual King of Gudalo on this continent. Even with no standing army, their ties make them strong indeed. With the new information about the Stone Raiders, we're going to have to tread very carefully," Geswald warned.

"Yes, master," Pete said.

"Send word to the council in town that we need to discuss these latest developments."

"I will see to it personally." Pete bowed before he left the room.

Geswald looked around his office. He had been excited with the thrill of the hunt and his opportunity to show others his real power and crush a group of Players. It would have been *perfect*. Now that he knew of their true strength and pulled back his plans, he was getting forced from another direction to try to carry them out.

I need time to figure it all out, to see a way of keeping Esamael happy while not angering the Stone Raiders too much.

***

Lord Esamael drank wine from his ornate glass. It was handcrafted straight from Markolm. It was worth a small village's income for a year. He didn't really taste the wine that was worth more than a farmer's yearly expenses. Opulence wasn't an acquired taste; it was a standard to him.

He had silver hair and bright blue eyes. His jawline and well-groomed hair would make many girls swoon for him. He was well-built, the physique of a man who took his physical training seriously.

He let out an angry breath as he drank from his glass again. His eyes were fixed on the horizon. In the direction of his gaze lay Verlun. The Esamael family had not gotten to their seat of power through sitting back and letting others walk all over them. They were well versed in the art of backroom deals and non-physical arm-twisting.

Anyone who didn't fall in line, they put them in place with force. They might not have a big standing army, but they controlled the gangs and crime in the region. Accidents weren't all that uncommon.

I will have that teleport pad and I will get those Players to either leave or submit. They might be immortals, but they're still weaker than my own forces and I know where they respawn.

He drank deeply from his cup.

He had issued his orders out to the traders and other groups to start the discreet pressure. If the Stone Raiders didn't take the hint, then Esamael would be forced to take things into his own hands. He was the law here. No one liked being in a cell for months; even the immortal Players usually changed their bodies after a few months.

Esamael turned from the balcony and headed into his castle.

Chapter 1: Eye Opener

Alkao watched as crate after crate of weapons moved out of the teleport pad. The Earth and Dark mages had been hard at work, raising what was going to be the new capital city of Devil's Crater. Alkao had decided to call it Unity. It was meant to show how the Demons and Beast Kin had come together to make a place for them to live together. It was four kilometers wide, with a hundred-meter-wide moat around it. If the city expanded, then more moats would be put out every few kilometers.

The amount of earth that Fornau had moved was simply incredible. The Stone Raiders were only adding to his work. Unity had been on a slight rise; their efforts had turned it into a decent-sized hill.

Homes had sprouted from the ground, creating barracks and defensible structures around the teleport pad that was off center of the city. Administration buildings had been the first things to go up. Homes and shelters had also been formed.

Roads cut through the ground, making a road system for buildings that weren't there yet. Each road was four wagons wide, with a sidewalk. Beneath it, something called a sewer system had been installed, as well as a running water system like what Alkao had seen with the Dwarves.

The Stone Raiders' magical abilities made Alkao shake his head.

"Something the matter?" Anna asked from beside him.

"It's just—seeing all of this. I didn't think it was possible. The work that the Stone Raiders have done to help us. It's incredible," Alkao said.

"You're on credit for the damn weapons, but with the rest of it, it's more just seeing what they can do. It's become something of a competition and it's one way to level up skills they haven't used before. I think most of them are grinding out their builder skill.

There's nothing much else to do until we start tearing the Demon Horde apart." Anna looked over the growing city.

"You've only been here a few days. Aren't you tired from whatever raid you were on? From what I've heard, it wasn't easy." Alkao didn't try to pry at their secrets; it was clear that whatever they had done, they were keeping a secret for someone else.

"Yes, but the Stone Raiders love to challenge themselves. Raiding, being in a fight against impossible odds—that's what we live for." Anna smiled.

Alkao nodded. "I can understand that. As a younger Demon, I was always challenging my other brothers to fight and searching out the hardest of dungeons. There were several times that my bull-headedness got me into trouble." Alkao chuckled and rubbed a scar on the side of his head.

Anna looked amused. "To the Players, this is but a game. Only Dave and Suzy know the truth. The rest of them see this as just *entertainment*; they can die, but they come back again. Sure, they lose a few levels and some gold, but where a POE would swear off fighting after a close encounter with death, they feel the thrill of almost dying, rally and go and do it all over again. If they know they're going to die, you can bet that they're going to charge the enemy instead of sitting back."

"I would not like to fight them in battle," Alkao agreed, looking them over. They were a happy-go-lucky bunch, but the power they demonstrated so easily was amazing; their magic, strength, and prowess in battle was nothing to be looked down on. *They might be mercenaries, but they're well worth the gold.*

Josh walked through the city, headed toward him and Anna. "Alkao, what's up, mate?" Josh grinned. Looking at him, you wouldn't think that he was the leader of the Stone Raiders.

He was a good-looking man with dark-brown hair and a lean build. Although he was built more for speed than strength, the way he walked and the weapons sheathed in the small of his back spoke of his skill as a fighter. His aura suppression was very good, another one of the skills that the Stone Raiders were grinding out.

Alkao couldn't even sense his aura unless Josh wanted him to. Alkao didn't doubt that Josh's aura was nearly as strong as his.

"Josh." Alkao smiled; it was hard to not like the man once you got to know him.

"Sorry I can't chat for too long. I'm supposed to meet the Golden Sabres in Cliff-Hill. It seems that they want to talk about merging their guild with ours and they have some questions. They want to meet there so that the other Players don't see us openly talking and start making their own conclusions. Ugh. I didn't think I would have to worry about press and public opinion." Josh shook his head. "Well, anyways, I'll be gone for a few days, but when I get back, I should have the rest of the Stone Raiders in tow as well as, *hopefully,* the Golden Sabres, rebranded," Josh said with a cocky grin.

"Aren't you scared that they're going to have more spies in their ranks?" Anna asked.

"I am. That is why I'm only taking the established veterans and E-heads of the Sabres. Anyone else, well, there are plenty of guilds out there."

"Bit tough joining standards."

"Yes, but we're not dealing with your run-of-the-mill raids. We need to protect our allies as much as our guild. Having members we can rely on is more important than having thousands of them." Josh's tone became serious.

"You do surprise me sometimes with your rare moments of genius," Anna chuckled.

"Being the one in charge isn't always what it's cracked up to be." Josh shook his head and looked to a grinning Alkao.

"I wish you luck, friend. When you return, hopefully the Demon Horde will have entered Efri's area," Alkao said.

"Poor bastards," Josh said, a massive smile on his face.

Alkao laughed at the look.

"See you later!" Josh waved and headed for the teleport pad.

"Well, I think it's time that we started getting these weapons into the soldiers' hands and see what they can do with real weapons," Alkao said.

"Sounds like a date," Anna said.

Alkao looked to her, a confused look on his face. Her playful smile did nothing to help his confusion.

She led the way to the nearest open area, where soldiers of the Devil's Crater Army were receiving their new weapons.

***

Sparks flew around Dave. Although there were several others working on higher quality blades and custom orders, Dave seemed unaffected by it all. His hand seemed to be covered in Mithril as he pulled out a red glowing piece of metal.

When Dave moved over to an anvil, work seemed to slow as they watched Dave at work. All of them were contract bound to not reveal any secrets they learned at the smithy to anyone else but Dwarven Master Smiths, but they were still fascinated by it.

Dave put the piece of Mithril on the anvil. He pushed his soul energy into the piece of metal, breaking the bonds that held the ingot together. His soul energy moved with his thoughts. The metal turned and formed.

A clay arm seemed to grow from the ground, grabbing another ebony ingot out of the furnace and placing it down on the rough chest piece of the still glowing Mithril. The ebony sheeting seemed to flow almost like a liquid, layering itself over the Mithril. Runes appeared over its surface in short, terse lines. Pieces of sparkling soul gems pervaded the ebony metal. A small ingot of silver came out of the furnace, falling onto the surface of the armor and moving to fill its runes. A sheet of soul gem formed, like the breastplate that was forming, applying itself to the back of it and attaching to the rear ebony metal.

A steel ingot was pulled from the furnace.

Dave was sweating heavily from the effort. His left hand glowed as he placed it on the back plate of the armor, all that was left of his armor. Runes along his arm lit up with power as he drew stored soul energy into himself, relieving the pressures on his chest as he pushed it into the metals he was using. The steel ingots were placed on either side of the armor; one side was pitch-black with glowing soul gem shards looking like stars while the other side was a glowing sheet of a vault-classed soul gem.

Dave destroyed the constructed arms.

The steel ingots flowed over the different sheets of metal and soul gems that had come to form a breastplate. They wrapped around the armor, covering it.

Dave opened his eyes. Sweat poured off him as he looked at the cooling breastplate in front of him. It looked like some simple steel construction. Unless someone had an extremely high evaluator skill, they wouldn't know what lay under the armor.

The smithy was silent, with the apprentices in awe of what they had seen. One of them walked over and handed Dave a cup of water.

Dave nodded his thanks, downing it.

The smith looked over the breastplate. "What is that?"

"It's a replacement. Blew up my last breastplate and I'm going to need a new one for my next battle." Dave looked at the Abscondita armor breastplate and back plate.

His notification bar blinked at him.

Quest: Dwarven Master Smith Level 3

You must craft 10 weapons of S quality with your Smithing Art (Currently 5/10)

Rewards: Unlock Level 4 quest

Increase to stats

His envelope messaging tab was also blinking; he opened it up.

Private Message: Jules

Jules> Just got into town, heading over to your place.

Dave> Be there soon. In the smithy right now. I'll bring Kol with me; do you need anything?

Jules> I'm here already and I'll be good.

Dave> See you in a bit.

"I'll see you lot later." Dave tucked his new armor into his bag of holding before he dismissed his metal glove.

They said their good-byes as Dave got out of his portable smithy and jogged for one of the larger smithies, where Kol was.

"What you in such a rush for?" Kol asked as he arrived.

"We've got you an appointment to keep," Dave said.

"Appointment?"

"For yer damned face!" Dave said.

"You ever heard the part about being respectful to your elders?" Kol followed Dave out of the smithy.

"I can't see you being much of the respectful kind when you were my age. I heard the stories of what you got up to as a kid." Dave smiled.

"Gurren?" Kol asked.

"Who else?"

"Damned grandkids—always ruining a perfectly good and presentable image," Kol harrumphed.

Dave patted him on the shoulder.

"How did the breastplate go?"

"Have a look." Dave pulled it out of his bag of holding. It had cooled considerably while inside the bag. Dave didn't understand how, but it had.

Kol's hands rubbed over its surface as they walked. He tapped it in places, listening to it. "She's a beautiful piece. Might be an idea to make a few more of them, seeing as you keep destroying them," Kol grumbled as he handed it back.

"Good to know you care." Dave grinned and put the breastplate back as they got onto the road toward Omal and Dave's house.

"My next project is working on some rings to augment my Endurance and Intelligence. With this armor, I've got my Vitality pretty much covered unless I run into another damn magic suppressing asshole. If that happens, then I'm going to stay back and hit him with arrows. Otherwise, with my Mana shield and my Health regen on my armor, I'm good to go. That means I can work on my Agility and Intelligence. With rings to increase those stats and Endurance to keep me awake for longer while needing less sustenance, well—I've got my bases covered." Dave smiled to Kol.

"So, you are going to be what? A conjuring warrior?"

"Something along them lines." Dave shrugged.

"Well, that would be one hell of a thing to see."

Ela-Gal and Deia were sparring in front of Dave's house. Esa, Gurren, and Lox were talking to one another and watching the two spar with interest. Jules was checking her bag of holding's inventory on her interface.

"Ah, about time you two showed up. Let's see what we can do!" Jules said, seeing Dave and Kol.

"I don't expect much, missy. Done this too many times for me to get my hopes up." Kol sighed.

"Ah, don't be that way, Gramps," Gurren said.

"Well, let's get this over with," Kol said.

Knowing his house was too small and cluttered with his projects, Dave conjured a large tent with a bed in it to provide Jules a sterile environment and prevent her from running into things as she worked on Kol.

"Better make sure you don't destroy it halfway through and drop my ass on the floor," Kol warned, walking in after Jules.

"I'll try my best," Dave said, following them.

***

"Table please, Dave," Jules said.

Dave created a table next to the bed.

She pulled out various herb remedies, needles, and other medical equipment, laying them beside one another on the table. "I'm going to put you out; then I can get started."

"Damn, you Players are upfront, aren't you? Haven't even got my pants off," Kol said, nervously.

"You can keep your pants on, you old nut." She laughed and put her hand on his forehead. She poured her Mana into his body. Within seconds, he was out cold.

"Now, we move onto the real reason we're here." She cast Detect Wounds. The damage was extensive.

A smile passed over her face as she finally faced a project that she could really devote herself to.

"Hand me the blood bag and the purple-looking concoction. They're in my bag of holding there, which I've given you access to. It's time we got started." Jules pulled off the bandages that covered Kol's face.

It took a force of will for Dave to look at Kol's naked face. It drove home how Emerilia might be fun, but there was the very real possibility for POEs to get hurt or die.

Jules looked to Dave. Her look seemed to ask whether he was going to be okay.

"Blood bag and purple concoction," Dave confirmed. He grabbed the items from the bag of holding next to him. This was his world and his mentor; he wasn't going to back out now.

Thankfully, Jules had already given him permission through her interface for him to access her bag of holding.

Jules went to work, asking for different tools. Dave stayed with her as she went to work. She opened up Kol's face, removing the worst of the damage so she could rebuild it from the inside out.

First, she removed the areas that were burnt the worst around the neckline, exposing the fresh skin underneath. Once that was complete, she used her magic to force Health potions into Kol's face to supply it with the materials she needed to work, using them to bolster her own healing spells

Next, she created the foundation and structure for his face. She rebuilt the bone, creating a scaffolding for his face.

She then rebuilt the muscles and other soft tissues. She placed the basic nutrients that the Health potions would need to form the muscles, fat, and skin tissues. She then recreated his nerve endings, tendons, and blood vessels through her healing magic.

Throughout this process, her interface was open above Kol as she checked and rechecked her progress and the anatomical structure of the different parts of Kol's face.

She moved to the hair, cutting away the scar tissues to allow the healing potions to do their work.

"Now, for the hardest part." She looked at Kol's slowly rebuilding face, which looked like an anatomical model. The basics of the face were there, with the under layers steadily growing and connecting it all together.

With a deep breath, she started using her scalpel on the inside of his ocular cavities, cutting away the scarred and ruined tissues that lay there. She used her different spells to check them and see the damage. It was severe. She drew on the power from the vault-classed soul gem stored in her bag of holding.

Dave let out a sound of shock as the ocular nerves and eyeballs started to form within the ocular cavities.

Jules double-checked the information on her interface's windows that rested in mid-air. Any time her spells deviated from forming something she needed, she would alter the spell to successfully create the complex structures that made up Kol's eyes.

She was panting by the time she finished. Twin brown eyes looked upward as skin started to form across all of Kol's face. The skin followed the now fully formed brow, slowly growing into eyelids that shut over Kol's eyes.

Jules looked over her work, both visually and with her spells that allowed her to see through Kol's face. She applied some more Mana to his face.

Hair started to sprout from his head: eyebrows, eyelashes, and across his face. He looked younger, as if he were just twenty years old with patches of white in his black beard and hair.

"He's quite handsome all fixed up," she said, once again checking him and her work over.

"I'll remember to not tell him that." Dave put his hand on her shoulder.

She looked up to him and saw a thankful expression on his face.

"Thanks, Jules. This...I know it will mean the world to him."

"Ah, well, he helped us out a lot and I owed you a favor or five. Plus, it was a good challenge to see what I can do with mixing modern medical science with magic. Wish this was a reality on Earth." Jules sighed.

"One day, you'll see that what you can do back on Earth doesn't matter all that much."

"What the hell does that mean? Have you been smoking something funny?" Jules smiled.

"No, Doc." Dave rolled his eyes. "Just saying that one day, Earth won't matter because all we've got is Emerilia."

"I know…Josh said something similar when I announced that I was becoming an E-head." Jules rubbed her leg unconsciously. *Being able to stand on two legs and be seen as someone who can do something, not just some invalid—it's the real reason I wanted to help Kol. I could see the same signs of anger and depression in him as I saw in myself before Emerilia.*

"Well, shall we get the others back in here and wake his ass up?"

"The potions and spells should be done shortly. He should be good within a few minutes." Jules put her hands on Kol and used another spell to check her work.

"Sounds good to me." Dave moved to the tent's opening. "Hey, gross stuff is done! Get back in here!" Dave hollered.

***

Kol felt his consciousness return to him as if he had come out of sleep. His face was a bit tight but it was okay. He blinked up at the tent's tapered roof, stretching on the bed, and looked to the people around him.

He stopped midway.

I blinked?

He used his phantom muscles again, darkness falling. He jerked his eyelids open.

"Mirror!" Kol said, not believing it.

Dave handed him one. Kol looked into the polished steel, finding his face looking back at him.

"I have a beard, a nose." He turned to a smiling Jules. "How is this possible?"

"Just needed to put scaffolding in. I guess most people who tried to heal you used straight spells. I used spells and my knowledge of the body to remake the superstructure of your face. Once that was in place, everything else kind of came together," she said.

Kol got off the bed and hugged her. He felt a dampness in his eyes at it all.

He had his face back!

His legs buckled underneath him. Gurren and Dave supported him.

"Damn, what magic did you use? Feels like I got hit by a hammer press!" Kol said.

Jules laughed. Looking at her, Kol could now see the strain on her features and the toll her magic and work had cost her.

"With magical healing potions, they use your own Mana and whatever materials you have in your body to help rebuild you. Makes you extremely tired. Drink this!"

She gave him a green potion he took down in a few gulps. His tongue was no longer a tattered mess as he felt his cheeks; his scarring and gauntness was gone.

He felt energy returning to his body.

"That potion will help you recover Stamina, but you need to eat! Need some weight on those bones to keep you healthy," Jules said sternly.

"Yes, ma'am." Kol smiled. He could actually smile instead of his skin pulling at his face and turning it into a horrifying rictus that would scare most adults away.

Kol held up the mirror to look at himself. "Damn, I am a handsome bastard, aren't I?" Kol looked to Gurren.

"You start bringing ladies round, I'm moving next door," Gurren said.

"You bring enough of them home!" Kol argued.

"But that's different!"

"Hah! We'll see about that, my boy! We need to drink! To eat!" Kol looked to Jules once again. "For you, I will craft you an item of power." Kol smiled.

"Seeing you better is payment enough." Jules smiled.

"Hah! Listen to her! You're getting a damned item of power and you better deal with it, cause I'm not giving the first item of power I can see with these new eyes to anyone else!"

"I'd take his offer," Dave said.

"Fine, you darned hard-headed Dwarves!" She laughed. The rest of the tent was filled with smiles and happiness.

Kol felt his eyes tear up again, laughing and crying at the same time. His eyes fell on Gurren and Dave supporting him. He put his arms around them fully, pulling them to him. "Oh boys, thank you for this! Thank you for all you've done for me and putting up with me."

Dave and Gurren hugged him back.

Kol might not be their real father, but he felt as protective for them as a father might feel for his own sons.

Damn, it is a good time to be alive!

Chapter 2: Make Ready for War

Josh watched as Cassie and her leadership walked out of the teleport pad's portal and into Cliff-Hill.

"It seems that a few things have changed." Cassie looked around the growing town.

"Cassie, good to see you." Josh took her hand and kissed it. They had been having something a few months back before he had disappeared. He hoped that he could rekindle it. Though, he wouldn't do it at the expense of getting the Stone Raiders screwed over.

"You too, Josh," she purred, looking him over.

"Shall we go to your old base you sold us?" Josh asked.

"Certainly. Along the way, we can discuss your terms," Cassie said.

"Something the matter with them?" Josh walked toward the road where wagons waited for them.

"In them, you say that if we join the Stone Raiders, then we are not allowed to stream our feeds in certain circumstances. We can't agree with that; a number of our people make their living off those streams."

"Even without those streams, we are probably making more than any other guild. I don't think anyone has used real currency in months to pay for their E-head costs. With the quests that we have taken on in the past, we have not been able to share any information with any Players or anyone outside of the guild. I can't change the terms. It has happened before and we will probably have quests like it later. In fact, we are running one right now that we are going to hold off on submitting our videos until afterward."

"Josh, those are people's livelihoods, myself included. We can't give those up," Cassie said.

"Okay." Josh shrugged.

"So, you'll agree to change it?" She smiled.

"Nope," Josh said. "This is our guild. Sure, you can join, but we're not going to change the rules that we govern the entire guild with just for you. This has worked for us since the beginning and has continued to do so."

"Josh, you're being unreasonable."

"Cassie, we're not just doing simple quests here. We're doing the kinds of things that could change Emerilia for the rest of the game. They're not just simple raids anymore." Josh held her eyes, hoping to get the point across to her. He saw that most of the Golden Sabres leadership was obviously interested or unsuccessfully trying to appear bored.

"Look, if we can't get past this, then there isn't much point to our discussion. I have things to prepare. The terms that I gave to you are what every Stone Raider gets. We will run our own vetting process that has worked since we started playing. If anyone passes it and still wants to join, we will accept them and train them up, no matter their level. I'm not usually one to boast but this place here, it's nothing compared to our real guild hall. Our real guild hall has a teleport pad all of its own. We've placed two more across Emerilia, and Dave bought the one that you just walked through. We've probably got the most coin and resources floating around on the market. The mage's college and guild have contracts with us for various materials. Our average Player is around level 80. We need more people we can trust. We're happy with our alliance, but it is clear that your guild is suffering right now. After Boran-al, you've tried to rebuild. You went after another portal in Opheir and one in Markolm; both were failures and you couldn't get through. You're still doing tons of quests all over the place, but you're on the decline. It would be a hell of a lot of work, but you could pull yourselves out of your slump. We have our rules for a reason. I really want to share it with you all, but to do so, you need to be part of the Stone Raiders, not just allied with us. I fought beside you at

Boran-al and we opened the Alturaran portal together! Something that no other two guilds have done together! I want to see you guys having fun. I want to fight beside you again." Josh's gaze swept from the Golden Sabre leadership to Cassie.

Their armor was pristine, covered in accents of gold and silver. It made them look like true paladins of Light.

In comparison, Josh almost looked like a beggar. He wore five different pieces of armor that didn't match, but all of them were more powerful than all of their armor combined.

There were two Stone Raiders off at a distance, but they didn't seem worried in the slightest for their guildmaster talking to the strongest members of one of the top ten guilds in Emerilia.

"I really want to fight with you again. However, these rules are there for a reason. If you can't understand it, then I'm sorry." Josh looked away.

"Josh, you're asking us to come into this blind with nothing but promises while hiding from us what you're doing. We don't even know where you were for the last two months on Earth, six in-game!" Cassie said.

Josh winced. He should have dealt with him being out of communication and not being able to tell her everything better. "Well, join us and then we can tell you. Trust me, it's bloody worth it." Josh's grim look turned into a smile as he looked to the teleport pad behind them.

"This game is so much more than I ever thought possible. It's..." Josh let out a laugh. "It's fucking awesome and I want to share that, but I can't. Not now, but maybe in the future. It's a leap of faith, ladies and gents. I won't deny that, but look at what we've done. Do you think that a bloody raid that took *six months* and we still can't talk about it was anything small? You might think you know Emerilia, but we've done things that I never even thought about. Fuck Earth—this is my bloody home and it ain't pretty and it's definitely not straightforward! But, damned if I don't wake up every morning filled with energy, excited for the next fight, the next raid, to check the loot over and get together with the guild and mess around! I can't tell you anything, but I can promise you something. If you join, you wouldn't believe half the stuff I could tell you, and you'd have so much fun that, if you're not already, then you surely would become an E-head." Josh smiled to them all.

"For the next three days, we're free. After that, we're going into our biggest fight yet. Do you want to watch our feeds the week after or do you want to be there in the middle of the fighting?"

***

Deia and Dave sat on their back porch outside Cliff-Hill, looking out over the farms that decorated the land before the cliff. They were nursing tea and just cuddling with each other while both of them had their interfaces open as they read about different things.

Dave looked to his character sheet. It was about time he added more stat points; he'd become used to his changes so far.

"Fifteen into Agility, fifteen into Intelligence, me thinks," he muttered to himself.

Knowledge passed through his mind; he took a glance at his character sheet before he had to start making notes on his notepad.

Character Sheet

Name:	David Grahslagg	Gender:	Male
Level:	28	Class:	Dwarven Master Smith, Friend of the Grey God, Bleeder, Librarian, Aleph Engineer, Weapons Master
Race:	Human/ Dwarf	Alignment:	Chaotic Neutral

Unspent points: 471

Health:	18,800	Regen:	6.14 /s
Mana:	4,130	Regen:	15.75 /s
Stamina:	2,480	Regen:	13.45 /s
Vitality:	188	Endurance:	307
Intelligence:	413	Willpower:	315
Strength:	248	Agility:	269

So, this is what level 28 feels like? It ain't bad at all. Dave grinned to himself.

"Did you just increase your attributes?" Deia asked.

"Ye-up. I want to keep increasing them now that my stats are going to take so long to gain. Makes it easier to get those new classes and complete their quests. Also, it's one hell of a rush." Dave smiled.

Deia shook her head and ran her hand over his stomach. "Mmm, I approve." She winked at him, reached up and kissed him.

She laughed at his expression; he wanted to keep up the kissing, but also wanted to write down what was going on in his head.

"Write down your new revelations. I'm doing some of my own research too." She patted his chest to reassure him and leaned back against him as she continued to use her own interface.

"You know me too well." Dave kissed her head before he wrote out a series of ideas and solutions on his notepad.

There was a knocking noise from the front of the house.

"Come round the back!" Dave and Deia yelled, looking to each other before laughing.

"Damn, are you two mind reading each other?" Josh came around the corner with a big smile on his face.

"Hey, Josh, you want a drink?" Dave asked.

"No, I'm good, but thanks. Was just talking to Alkao a little bit ago, as well as the Golden Sabres." Josh's smile turned into a frown.

"How did things go with the Sabres?" Deia asked.

"Well, it looks like they want to be able to stream. Most of them went into the guild because they wanted to be flashy and make their money off their actions and streams. There are a number of really good fighters in there, but I don't know if they're interested in coming and fighting with us in the muck instead of playing knight." Josh sighed.

"And Cassie?" Dave asked.

Deia shot a curious glance to Dave and Josh. Dave was one of the few people who knew about Josh and Cassie.

"She wasn't happy with it. I don't know what they're going to say. Their guild is dying, but they don't want to admit it. Honestly, I think the 'we're doing awesome ass raids but only Stone Raiders can come got some of them. Others don't want to be going into this on blind faith. There's also the fact that as soon as they announce this, then the Golden Sabres are going to start collapsing. If that is the case, then they want to have something they can point to and say join us here. We don't take everyone and that is a big issue. Really, it comes down to them accepting our guild rules and leaving the Golden Sabres behind completely. They've seen plenty of other guilds have fallen apart, but they can't seem to get it through their skulls that it's happening to them." Josh ran his hand through his hair.

"But, what about Cassie?" Dave drove on. Deia looked to Josh as well.

"I don't know, man. I did kind of just disappear for most of six months, because running everything down under was a full-time job. I want to see if we can get back together, but I don't know if we can while she's in another guild. The stuff we're doing in the Stone Raiders, it's like I just want to go and tell everyone in the world, but I can't because we made a promise. How do you have a relationship when you can't share that?" Josh looked to Deia and Dave, not as their guildmaster but friend.

"Either she will join and you can test it out, or you go your separate ways. When the truth of what we've done comes out, I'm sure that she'll understand. Does that mean you should hold your own happiness back?" Deia asked.

"But..." Josh started.

"Josh, she's a grown woman and you're a grown man. It makes sense that there will be things that divide you; this is one thing that is your entire life. You're driven by it and not sharing your aspirations with someone, keeping this all bottled inside, I couldn't see you enjoying that," Deia said.

"You make sense, but..."

"Where matters of the heart are concerned, you're blind as hell?" Dave said.

"Something along those lines." Josh chuckled and rubbed his face.

Dave and Deia gripped each other's hands, wanting to help Josh, but knowing that he would have to go through this on his own.

"Well." Josh slapped his legs, as if trying to change his state of mind. "We start work in a few days. So, I hope you've got all your business in order! I know you two have been busy, but it's time we showed the world that the Stone Raiders are back and stronger than ever." Josh smiled.

Dave and Deia returned the smile.

"Oh, hell yeah. I need to work on my weapons master class," Dave said.

"I'm still working my way to it too. I'm nearly able to get my assassin class. Just need to get some higher skill in poisons and archery." Josh's eyes slid to Deia.

"I'll help make sure you can hit the broadside of the barn with a bow and arrow." Deia sighed and poked Dave.

"Ow! What?" Dave asked.

"You should work on your teaching skill. You should get the academic class and maybe trainer class."

"Teaching skill?" Dave frowned and looked to Josh, who shrugged.

"Teach other people the skills you have and you get the passive skill of teaching. People understand what you're saying, or trying to present. The trainer class is when you get to mastering teaching, teach more than a hundred people and have mastered one subject to teach others." Deia talked as she worked her interface.

"The academic is for having the librarian class, master the inference skill, and be an apprentice at teaching. Also, you need to graduate some sort of training that requires Intelligence and achieve the rank master in your field. You have the skills and can gain teaching easily enough; also, you're a Dwarven Master Smith, and graduated that, so..."

"Fine. I'll add it to my list of things to do," Dave said.

"Josh, why don't you go for the Guildmaster class?"

"There's a class for that?" Josh asked.

"There's like a class for everything." Deia smiled.

"Well, what do I need?"

"You need to have a guild of over twenty people. You need to make your guild part of every POE guild. We have trader's and adventurer's but we need the mage's guild still. Also, we need to have a guild hall. Then we need to have a vote. If you're elected guildmaster by the guild, then you get it. It doesn't come with stat bonuses, though," Deia warned.

"What does it come with?" Josh asked.

Dave read from her interface. "Guildmaster level 1 provides the people under you with a 5 percent bonuses to their stats. After level 1, there are no more stat gains, but there are things like resistances that are added in for every level afterward."

"Well, we can't rush into a meeting with the mage's guild; they're probably the most powerful guild with their college teaching thousands. Best to leave that for later when we're negotiating from a position of strength instead of when we're hungry and desperate." Josh smiled and stood. "I'll let you two get back to your free time. I'll see you later."

"Come 'round whenever." Dave waved to Josh.

"Well, I do have to try out this drink of yours sometime." Josh smiled. "Thanks for the advice, Deia!"

"No problem, Josh," Deia said.

Josh waved and headed around the house.

"I'll go tell Ela-Dorn she's got two more days. Otherwise, we'll disassemble the darned thing, put it into a cart and ship it through the teleport pad with us," Dave said.

"Okay, and you can teach me about magical coding when you get back." Deia smiled to him.

"I love it when you talk skills—so sexy." Dave kissed her as she laughed.

"Wisdom comes with age," she said as Dave got himself out of the love seat they'd been lying in.

"Always did love me some older ladies." Dave gave a roguish wink before he disappeared into the house.

He stepped into the middle of the magical formation Bob had made. He'd studied the hell out of it, but he just didn't understand how it worked. He hoped that Ela-Dorn's lessons or Malsour's insight might be able to link it all together.

Dave appeared in the command room again. He took the lift down to where the portal storage was.

Ela-Gal waved to Dave sleepily as he came out of a bathroom. "Morning, Dave."

"Dude, it's like nearly noon. What the heck were you doing last night?"

"Oh, I was fighting some of your Stone Raiders." Gal smiled. "They're not bad fighters."

"Ah, that would make sense. I heard people getting scared about the automatons near the town. I had to say they were a project of mine. I wonder what the hell they think you two are doing, hiding in my house. Ela-Dorn hasn't left since getting here." Dave shook his head.

"Ah, she's a passionate woman, whether it be about books or other things," Gal said with a pleased smile.

"Before you ask, I'm not the reason he didn't get much sleep last night. I might be driven, but I'm not deaf...men!" Ela-Dorn rolled her eyes as she looked at a portal that was surrounded by pieces of paper, books, and all manner of items.

"In two days, we're going to Devil's Crater. If you can't figure out a way to get this thing moved, we're going to have to disassemble it in a cart." Dave's face turned thoughtful as he walked around the teleport pad.

"What?" Ela-Dorn asked.

"Well, it's made big enough, so that a wagon could go through it with some space to spare. That makes it about as big as a wagon, just a bit bigger, but really—who pays attention to those things? What if we were to tilt it and make it part of the wagon? Just need to sandwich it between boards. Could pile it with the next shipment of arms going through. Be a pain, but it could work," Dave muttered, mostly to himself, holding his chin as he walked around the portal.

"Dave? What are you talking about?" Ela-Dorn asked.

"Well, if I was to put it into a wagon's frame, then it would just look like a wagon. We load it up with weapons and armor, no one knows the difference." Dave shrugged.

"How are we going to make a wagon to fit this into?" Ela-Dorn asked.

"That part's easy. I'm just hoping that the path down here is still intact and big enough for this."

Private Chat: Bob

Bob> Waypoint added. Good luck. Going to be a pain in the ass hauling that thing up.

Dave> Thanks, Bob!

"Okay, so, we do have a way to do this." Dave smiled.

Chapter 3: Softening Up the Opposition

The Demon Horde was in terrible shape. With random night attacks from the disguised Demons of the Devil's Crater Army, or DCA, and their own internal attacks they pulled on one another, they hadn't slept much in weeks. They were thin from the lack of sustenance in the area. They were more savage and dire than ever before.

Good thing that we're not fighting them yet.

Efri used the spell Heat Vision to see through the forest and to the Demon Horde. The first Demon disappeared into a trap, screaming as it was impaled on spikes under the thin covering.

Others disregarded the screams of pain, charging forward with renewed vigor and channeling a skill that the DCA had been trying hard to overcome: berserker.

Another was hit with spikes that swung down from the tree cover, impaling it. All across the Horde, they encountered traps from every direction. The smell of blood and cries of pain only served to make them run faster, screaming out their battle cries.

DCA Earth mages, both hidden within the Demon Horde and trailing them, had been adding traps all around them, enclosing the entire Demon Horde.

Panic started setting in after an hour. Any direction they tried, there seemed to be traps. The Demon Horde started charging forward, as if they were near the enemy. They screamed and brayed for blood, their hunger and lack of sleep driving them wild.

They only encountered more traps.

Efri frowned. Only a few tried to run away. They were cut down, but they were so few.

"What is going on? Why aren't they pulling back? After all of this, I know we would have started regrouping. Knowing that we were up against an enemy, we'd start making some sort of plan.

Charging straight ahead? What did the Dark Lord do to them?" Efri frowned, biting his lip in thought.

We've only got around two miles of traps. If they just keep running in a straight line, then they'll clear it quickly. Without terrorizing them in the nights and making them slow their pace for the traps, they'd reach Devil's Crater sooner than projected.

Efri pulled up an audio chat with Alkao.

"Efri, how goes the traps?" Alkao sounded cheerful.

"They're running right through them. They're running one behind one another, seemingly out of instinct. A few go down, but the rest keep going. They're going to reach you sooner than we thought. I'm going to give the order to pull my forces back to your keep," Efri said.

"Very well. I'll send word to the Stone Raiders and Lezar. It's time we started using hit-and-run tactics on them."

"Yes, brother," Efri said, angry at himself for his part of the plan for failing.

"This is not your fault, brother. These Demons are twisted. We did not know how they would react, but now we do. Your traps will still weaken them. Now, take your forces to the flank opposite Lezar. You will close in, then attack them from the rear. I trust in you," Alkao said.

"Yes, brother." Some of the tension in Efri's shoulders fell away.

Alkao cut the channel.

Efri opened up his party chat and started to issue commands to his brigade. *My people did me proud; we couldn't have seen this. But, when it comes to finish off these beasts, this Demon Horde will come to fear my brigade's steel.*

***

"Dave, we're moving! The Demon Horde sped up!" Deia yelled as she walked out of the house.

All last night, they had been working to carry the portal up through a tunnel that Bob had made. Dave had done his work and two Stone Raiders with horses had met them, taking the now functional cart from them.

"What's the word?" Dave asked.

"All guild, assemble." Deia closed the door behind her as Dave pressed his hotkey on his armor. It seemed to form over his body.

Deia smirked. A smile grew across her face. *Damn, he looks like he means business in his armor.* She pressed her hotkey for her own armor and walked to Dave. It spread across her, her blades on each hip.

"Well, let's go hunting," Dave said, a devilish grin on his face.

Deia nodded, a wild look in her eyes as they ran through the copse of trees and straight for the training square where the teleport pad was.

Coming down from the Stone Raider compound, Josh led more Stone Raiders in their various armors and weapons to come in behind Dave. After them came carts filled with weapons and armor. Ela-Dorn and Ela-Gal were riding one.

"Dave, could you do the honors?" Josh asked.

"My pleasure." Dave moved to the control center of the teleport pad and punched in coordinates.

Induca and Suzy joined them. A party of fifty people and ten wagons were ready to go through the teleport pad. People watched them as they moved, interested in what had got them in such a rush.

Jules and Esa were the last to join them.

"Good for you to join our little expedition." Josh smiled.

"Sorry, Josh. Was getting a gift from Kol; he made me something." She looked at her necklace.

Dave looked over the necklace.

Necklace of Protection

The first Master level piece Dwarven Master Smith Kol has crafted in twenty years, given to the one who gave him back his sight and his face.

Mana Barrier: 145/145

Increased Willpower +25%

Increased Stamina +25%

Charge: 12,000/12,000

"Damn, those are some nice pieces. Even without my level of Magical Circuit, he's really a master to be able to get those kinds of natural Affinities into the metal, so that it doesn't take a soul gem to provide them all power." Dave shook his head.

"You admiring her necklace?" Deia asked.

"You want one?" Dave asked.

"No, my ring does just fine." She smiled, held up her engagement ring.

Dave gave her a quick kiss.

"Though if we are about to go fight some things, it's probably a good idea for me to put some more points in few more places." Dave opened up his interface and placed another 30 of his stat points: 15 into Intelligence and another 15 into Agility. He'd learned from when he'd gained a whole whack of classes in Alephir. Falling over and hitting ceilings sucked.

Character Sheet

Name:	David Grahslagg	Gender:	Male
Level:	34	Class:	Dwarven Master Smith, Friend of the Grey God, Bleeder, Librarian, Aleph Engineer, Weapons Master
Race:	Human/Dwarf	Alignment:	Chaotic Neutral

Unspent points: 441

Health:	18,800	Regen:	6.14 /s
Mana:	4,280	Regen:	15.75 /s
Stamina:	2,480	Regen:	14.20 /s
Vitality:	188	Endurance:	307
Intelligence:	428	Willpower:	315
Strength:	248	Agility:	284

Dave rubbed his hands together. With his stat points, he wasn't close to being near a level 30. He was close to 340.

"Whoa there—stop leaking your Affinity everywhere," Deia chided.

"Ah, whoops," Dave said, his excitement getting the better of him.

"Looks like saving your stat points up is working out. Sent a shiver down my bloody spine, that's for sure." Josh kept his voice low.

Dave just shrugged with a smile on his face.

He could craft things to deal with his other weaknesses and spells to shore up the rest. He had a respectable amount of hit points. With his Intelligence and Agility, most people seemed slower, especially when he actually thought about it and started using his increased Intelligence and Agility. Well, he'd started to truly challenge Deia in the limited sparring matches they'd had at Cliff-Hill.

Dave was excited to see how his skills and attributes stacked against a horde of Demons.

He fired up the teleport pad. A gloomy room appeared on the other side.

"Move it!" Josh ran through the teleport pad. Everyone followed behind, including the carts.

Cliff-Hill disappeared; in its place, they were in the guild hall's teleport pad control room.

"Push to the sides! We're going right back out to Devil's Crater!" Josh said. Stone Raiders rushed into the teleport pad room, gearing up and falling into groups.

Automatons clunked into the room, following Ela-Dorn and Ela-Gal.

"What is your magic?" Ela-Gal asked.

"Maybe, I'll tell you later," Dave said.

The teleport pad's portal closed. Another one opened, this one showing them Devil's Crater and the beginnings of Unity.

"Move!" Stone Raiders who had been gathering from all over Emerilia into the guild hall now stormed out and into the city.

"Ela-Dorn, Ela-Gal—get your cart unloaded quick as can be; I'll put your time limit before the cart falls apart at fifteen minutes," Dave yelled as he followed the rest of the Stone Raiders.

***

Ela-Dorn and Gal tore the payload off the cart. The driver took it back to the guild hall. Demons gathered the supplies, hauling the weapons crates around with ease. There was a tension in the air.

Ela-Dorn didn't doubt that war was coming to Devil's Crater.

The teleport pad's portal closed behind them.

"Could you connect us to Alephir? We're going to be taking the cart now," Ela-Dorn said.

The two people who had guided the cart quickly unhooked their horses. Automatons took their place, holding the cart.

"We're connected. Have a good one," the Aleph in the control center said, waving to them.

Ela-Dorn smiled back, waving to them as they passed through the teleport pad's event horizon.

She walked over to the group that was hurriedly assembling. The council was coming out and people looked at their councilwoman and her overly large cart with curiosity.

"Where is it?" Hamdir asked.

Ela-Dorn looked at the cart that the automatons were pushing. "Right there." She watched as the time on Dave's construct's time limit reached zero.

The cart disappeared and the portal dropped to the ground. It had been the base of the wagon's cart. Dave had somehow formed an entire cart around it, allowing them to smuggle it out without any questions.

Excited chatter rang out as they all looked at the portal. The Aleph's pursuit for knowledge, the thing that had pulled them together, was symbolized in this very portal. When they were cast out as heretics, it was for questioning the gates of the gods. They had gone on to reverse engineer the teleport pads from the portals.

To them, they were looking at a holy relic.

Behemoths were dropped from their storage racks above the teleport pad. They grabbed the portal and heaved it up.

"Now it's time to figure out its secrets. I'll be at the college," Ela-Dorn said. The teleport pad activated again and the behemoths walked through.

Chapter 4: So, It Begins

"My lord! The Demons are in Devil's Crater." Boran-al came to a knee in front of his lord.

"Good. I thought that they would be too dumb to make it all the way. What are their levels?" The Dark Lord thought of what else he could do with the creatures.

"My lord, I don't mean our Demons. I mean the first generation of Demons," Boran-al said.

Where the Dark Lord's eyes were, purple flames seemed to ignite.

Boran-al shuddered under the pressure of the Dark Lord's aura.

"What?" the Dark Lord asked, his restraint clear.

"I was watching over the Demon Horde. They've been fighting among one another for the entire time. Without there being other beasts to kill and that large fight between all of the larger groups, they've been in chaos. I now think that those attacks were carried out by the rebelling Demons. As the Horde got within two hundred miles of Devil's Crater, they encountered traps, hundreds of them. Giving in to their rage and sensing a fight, they charged forward through the traps—which had to be made by someone. I looked over Devil's Crater and all the keeps have been restored. There are fields of crops being grown and just a few minutes ago, I saw a force rushing from a teleport pad toward our Demon Horde that is slowing down and apparently getting into fights."

"How many of the first-generation Demons are there?"

"At my best guess, maybe four hundred to six hundred thousand." Boran-al coughed under the pressure coming from the Dark Lord.

"Change the second generation's quest and make them capable of seeing one another. I want them to kill anything that's first generation. Get me the strongest of the Horde and I'll give them my blessing. Use your own abilities to enhance them as much as possible. We will crush them," the Dark Lord said.

"Yes, master." Boran-al bowed all the way out of the room. He couldn't even stand fully under his lord's pressure.

The door closed behind Boran-al.

The Dark Lord let out his full aura. Few would know that it was not anger but bloodthirst. "I will take those who dared to try to fight against me and I will crush them wholly in their own home. The Grey God robbed me of their defeat all those centuries ago; he will not take it from me again!" He fell into deep rolling laughter and stood up from his chair. The room seemed to disappear around him as he looked through the clouds above Devil's Crater. Marks appeared, showing where his newer, loyal Demons were and where the forces that had rebelled at him hid.

He laughed and moved his skeletal hand, a trail of Dark power following after it. Although the other gods used their power wells, diminishing it on their creations, the Dark Lord had never been more powerful. "Those Alturarans have their uses. Now is not the time to use my power. Live or die, it will be a spectacle."

The Dark Lord filled with excitement. It had been a boring few years, but now war came; he lived and thrived in war and battle. It was the only thing that made him truly feel alive.

***

The Stone Raiders ran through Devil's Crater, out of the growing city of Unity and down the road that led to Alkao's keep to the northwest. Everyone from the guild who was combat trained and not in the middle of something crucial was with them.

Dave placed a call. "Jesal, it's Dave."

"I got that much from the private chat request," Jesal said.

"I know that you've been experimenting with the aluminum artillery tubes as well as alternate rounds. I'm asking if you could lend them to me," Dave said.

"Why?"

"I'm about to go into a fight against about two million Demons—need some fire support. Also we can see how useful those rounds are," Dave said.

"Where the hell are you that you're fighting Demons? I didn't even know that they were back!" Jesal said.

"I'm in Devil's Crater. The Demons who rebelled against the Dark Lord are here and we're supporting them. I have to ask that you don't start spreading that right now, though. I couldn't share this with you before because the leaders here wanted more time before they dealt with the rest of the world. Right now, we need support; if we don't get it, I don't think we can hold the Demon Horde back."

"So, you want me to lend you the artillery to help the Demons that we fought against centuries ago in the name of the Earth Lord?" Jesal said. "Ah, I'm screwing with you. Fuck the Pantheon—we owe them one. I can send you the artillery and their support people within two hours, if you have a teleport pad."

"We've got one. I'll put you in contact with Lucy; she's running all this support stuff. Thanks, Jesal."

"No worries, Dave. You're always helping others. You have the support of me and the Council of Anvil and Fire. You're one of us," she said, her voice firm.

"Thanks, teach," Dave quipped, trying to bring some levity to the gravity of her words. His body tingled as he truly realized for the first time the kind of power and responsibility that came with being one of the Council of Anvil and Fire.

"No worries, you damned crazy bastard," She laughed.

Dave cut the chat and connected her to Lucy.

They were just reaching the keep. Alkao waited for them in the courtyard, a map in front of him.

Josh ran up. The party leaders moved up with him; the rest hung back and looked on.

"They've stopped charging, but they're just over a hundred and fifty miles from the keep. We've got forces here and here moving to box them in." Alkao pointed to two forces coming in from the sides and rear of the Demon Horde.

"Each brigade numbers fifty thousand; they're also the best armed of all our brigades." Alkao looked at Dave and nodded to him.

Dave nodded back. The sword and shield the Demon Prince used was the one that he had created.

"We've got a hundred thousand in this keep here. We're moving forces through the keep and out along the Demon Horde's flanks to reinforce our forces coming in behind them, which is where you Stone Raiders come in. We're going to start using hit-and-run tactics to thin out their numbers and bog them down. We need you to get us some time, so we can move forces through the keep and out behind them." Alkao gestured from the keep toward the icons showing the Demon Horde.

"The rest of the Stone Raiders have moved out in front of the keep and are ready to engage. We'll join in on your attacks. Have you got those extra surprises ready?" Josh asked.

"We have, with some help from your people," Alkao said.

Dave looked around the keep. There were Demons and Beast Kin all over the place: watching on the walls, checking their weapons, and moving supplies to the keep's walls. Through the keep, there was a constant stream of Demons and Beast Kin marching in cadence with one another. Their boots shook the ground with their steps.

The Beast Kin all had decent armor and weapons. The Demons mostly had decent clothes and good boots, but most had nothing more than tough leather shirts and pants. Most were armed with just crude iron or stone creations, with a few armed with steel weapons.

Thankfully, there were a number with bows and stone-tipped arrows. They were crude, but they'd be effective enough.

Demons flew overhead, carrying Beast Kin in their taloned feet as they glided from the keep down toward the formations that headed off into the distance. The sheer scale of it drove home how big the battle was going to be.

"We'll buy you time to get your people into place and try to mess them up as much as possible," Josh promised, slapping Alkao on the shoulder.

"Thanks, Josh." Alkao nodded, before his eyes bore into Dave's. "Dave, could I have a word?"

"All right, Stone Raiders! Move over here. I want two groups: everyone below level 70 with their stats on my right; everyone above it on my left!" Josh said as Dave walked over to Alkao.

"Something on your mind?" Dave asked, his words terse. He had heard how he'd made his peace with Anna and Suzy. Dave hadn't talked to the Demon Prince since he had called out Dave and been an ass.

Alkao hung his head, looking around as if nervous. "Dave, what I did, what I said—it was out of line. I should have thanked you for your gift. For your help. Instead, I scorned you like some child." Alkao touched the hilt of his sword.

"This blade and my shield have protected me since we last parted. I have never received a gift like them. With your enchantment making me have to take the first hit before I could fight back, it made me think out my actions instead of just blindly charge in. You and your weapons educated me, helped to teach me about restraint, of thinking things through. My journey was not easy, but your weapons protected me. They protected my people and allowed me to get this far." Alkao's hulking mass sunk to his knee as he bowed his head.

"Dave Grahslagg, I did not deserve these gifts, but through them, you educated me in the ways of a leader. You showed faith in me with your work while I repaid it with spite. I now know the people of Emerilia are not the ones who attacked me. Those ancestors are long dead. You have shown me the power of extending a hand in friendship instead of a blade in anger. With this sword and shield, I was able to carve out a future for my people. Without them, then they would have not joined me here." Alkao raised his head.

Dave didn't know what to say. Although he'd hoped that the blade and sword would teach the prideful Demon, it had done more than Dave had ever hoped, teaching him humility and to think before his actions.

"I hope that one day, you might call me friend. Through the actions of you and your friends, you have given the people of Devil's Crater a chance. Nothing could repay that debt."

"Well, getting off your damned knee would help; we're attracting stares," Dave growled. He scratched his head awkwardly and looked around at the people throughout the keep looking at Dave and Alkao.

Alkao smiled and rose from his knee.

Dave studied Alkao. "Keep faith with your people—put them ahead of yourself and never settle. You've got plenty of room to grow and we're all going to need friends. Don't forget that." Dave's tone turned serious.

Alkao bowed his head.

"I have high hopes for you, Alkao. Don't let me or your people down."

"I will do everything in my power to help them," Alkao promised.

"Good." Dave nodded and held out his hand.

Alkao shook it.

"When I get back, you're paying for the damned beers and we'll get those smiths of yours trained up! Lots to do." Dave smiled.

"Very well." Alkao sounded relieved.

"See you in a bit; got some Demon Horde to go screw with." Dave smiled.

He walked over to the Stone Raiders and checked out a blinking notification.

Quest: Survival of the Fittest

Together, the races of Demon and Beast Kin have worked together, making a foothold in Devil's Crater. The Dark Lord who sends his Demon Horde, hardened by a long journey and countless fights, sends them unknowingly into your home.
He wishes to use it to grow his forces stronger. Show him your newfound strength. Rise from the history books that you were cast into and LIVE!
The Devil's Crater Army has requested your aid in destroying the Demon Horde. The Stone Raiders' guild has accepted.
Requirements: Defeat the Demon Horde
Failure: Death of the creatures in Devil's Crater.
Rewards: 100,000 gold to the Guild's treasury
Increased reputation with the creature's of Devil's Crater
Fame/Infamy points
EXP
Rights to use the dungeons and raid events within Devil's Crater and in the Devil's Crater's controlled land.

"Okay, everyone below 70—you're going to be staying here. You will be running support for the DCA. I want you on the walls and hammering the hell out of the Demon Horde when they show.

You've got better gear and better weapons; show them just what the Stone Raiders can do. If you're a POE and above 70, the choice is up to you to come out with us on the raid or to stay here and help." Josh looked to the POEs. A few stepped over to stay in the keep with the lower levels, but most stayed where they were.

Josh nodded to Gurren and Lox, who stood beside the rest of Dave's party that had come from Cliff-Hill. The rest were already out in the forest waiting for them.

"Good luck! Let's get stuck into a war." Josh smiled. "Everyone who's coming, on me. Everyone staying, go and see General Malkur."

With that, Josh turned and ran alongside the Demon and Beast Kin marching columns.

The Stone Raiders followed, their speed faster than flying Demons.

"Anna, Malsour, and Steve are waiting for us. We're going to group up. The plan is to move in varying sized groups. We hit the edges of the Demon Horde, send spells and the like into their center and wreak as much havoc as possible. Then we break off, regenerate and go back in again," Deia said as the stone of the cliffs around Devil's Crater turned into forest, the branches cutting off the sun from above.

The gloom mattered little to them as they ran.

"Check your gear and your hotkey bar. I want everyone with potions ready and a second set of weapons good to go at the least. One ranged, one close, and a second of your primary, just in case."

Dave checked his hotkey bar at the bottom of his vision, applying different Health and increased Stamina regeneration potions. He added a sword to his hotkeys. After the magical suppressor, he'd made sure to keep something ready, so that he wasn't caught off guard.

They were rare creatures, but it was best to be prepared.

"What are these Demons like?" Lox asked.

"They're stronger than Dwarves and pretty fast. Long reach, natural claws, and like to use their teeth. Thankfully, none of them have shown the ability to use magic in any form yet," Deia said.

"They're mostly naked with stone weapons," Dave added.

"Sounds simple enough, but with a force this large...the Dwarves have extensive records on how powerful Demons can be, even without a weapon," Lox said. Gurren grunted in agreement as they continued through the forest. Markers of the rest of the waiting guild showed up on Dave's mini map.

"Hit-and-run, in and out—blast them with everything and then we keep going. We get bogged down and they can start to use their numbers against us," Deia warned.

Anna, Malsour, and Steve met them.

"Anna, Malsour, you've met Gurren and Lox; this is Steve, Suzy's soul bound creature." Deia did the introductions.

"Howdy." Steve smiled and waved to them, swinging his axe as if it were a shopping bag and he was at a mall.

"Damn, you're a big bastard," Gurren said.

"I like this one." Steve laughed.

"What are you, one of those automaton things?" Lox asked.

"Similar, but with more extras, which are a pain in the butt to control. That's why Suzy's controlling me, so I can get my systems working normally and be a nice automaton." Steve smiled so hard, it looked painful.

Dave snorted. "You? A normal automaton? And I'm a damn walrus."

"How was the vacay, dude?" Steve asked.

"Eh, work. Looking forward to knocking some skulls around," Dave said.

Suzy, Anna, and Deia were conferencing with one another. Malsour yawned while Induca joined the others, who stood in a circle.

"Yeah, same here; they turned me into a damned laborer," Steve complained, resting his axe on his shoulder.

Dave sensed Gurren and Lox loosening up; Dave knew that they would like Steve. His attitude was very similar to his other friends.

"The most important thing is that I think I might have figured out the things that we were missing from understanding how the teleport pads and portals work," Malsour said.

"Here we go." Induca shook her head.

"Neeeerds!" Steve loudly declared. Gurren and Lox laughed, grinning at Dave and Malsour.

"You'll be happy to know that I smuggled a portal to the Aleph. They should be coming to us with something soon enough," Dave said.

"Good. I'm looking forward to find out what they know." Malsour yawned again and rubbed his eyes.

"Not sleeping much?" Induca asked.

"He practically raised all of Unity by himself and then made sure that the keeps were all functional. Made a lot of crude metal spears and the like," Steve said.

"Well, at least the DCA will have some more weapons to fight the Demon Horde with," Malsour said.

"All-metal spears are going to be a pain in the ass to use," Lox said.

"You haven't seen the Demons. They *like* the weight of them; most wood just cracks in their hands. Makes them terrible archers, but great spearmen," Steve said. If there was one thing that Steve got serious about, it was fighting.

"How are the Demon Horde looking?" Dave asked.

"Like a bunch of savage a-holes. They're killing one another as a source of food. Looks like because they're Creatures of Power, killing them and eating their meat makes them quite a bit stronger. They're all boasting over level 70. Some of them are even reaching between 100 and 200. They're strong, but they're idiots. Their hunger blinds them and makes them more likely to attack one another. The DCA has been using that, putting in their own Demons to get them all excited and fight one another and then leave them to just slaughter one another. That added with the lack of food in the area. The Demon Horde have lost nearly five and a half million in the time we've been harassing them."

"I'm going to guess their morale is low?" Lox asked.

"You could say. They blame one another for everything; don't trust each other at all. Their largest groups aren't bigger than a thousand, which is nothing in a mass of nearly two million. They don't have battle tactics or magic. No time to learn how to fly with their wings, because it makes them weak." Steve shook his head.

"So, what's the plan?" Dave asked.

Deia and the other girls walked over; Deia answered the question.

"The DCA in their ranks is going to start everything off. They'll keep them fighting one another and confused. Then, the aerial Demons are going to drop in on them from above. Again, get them fighting one another and attacking anything that's in the air, including their own people. As they're in the midst of that chaos, we're going to be using parties in guerilla tactics. Hit them hard, and then fade back into the forest. They get close enough to the keep, we box them in with spells and start hammering the hell out of them at range. We'll be at the front, with the DCA supporting us. That is where the real battle starts." Deia looked to everyone.

Dave nodded. The grim faces of the Stone Raiders were all business; all signs of the partiers who they were in their off time faded away. They had been at Boran-al and the Aleph raid; they were tried and tested.

"If you want to record, you can. Josh is asking that people don't upload what they have until after this is all done." Deia looked to Dave and Suzy.

"Neither of us record this, anyway." Dave shrugged.

"Well, get ready. The DCA are making their move soon," Deia said to the group.

"Stone Raiders!" Josh's voice came through everyone's ears over the guild voice chat. "Well, looks like this thing does work."

Dave could hear the grin in Josh's face.

"We're going in right after the DCA Demons make their move. Remember to trust in your groups. Hit and get out. Don't stay around, and be wary of the Demon Horde charging after you hit them. We've got all these traps everywhere; use them if you need to. West forces move out with Kim; north with me; south with Dwayne. Look after one another and we'll take a little rest after this. And if you've got streams or like recording this, record away. I only ask that you wait until after we've destroyed the Demon Horde before uploading it. Good luck." Josh signed off the guild chat as the three markers of the guild leaders started to move in different directions.

"We're going with Kim—keep together," Deia said.

The Stone Raiders separated out into their different groups, rushing through the forest at inhuman speeds.

It wasn't the speed or the silence that they traveled in that would scare most who saw them. It was the cold smiles on their faces that would make the hardest veterans grip their weapons tighter as they broke into a cold sweat.

These were hunters and they had come for their prey, their game.

Chapter 5: Amid Chaos And Destruction

"Start." Alkao's voice passed through the ears of all his brothers and their commanders.

Lezar watched the map on his interface as he walked with his brigade through the forest.

His people in the Demon Horde started their attacks in bouts. Some would wait for the Demon Horde to react and then work to make the most of the chaos to kill more.

Any time the Horde singled out the DCA soldiers, they rushed into the forest or took to the skies. They took out thousands of the Demon Horde, driving them to attack one another and inspiring chaos in their ranks as the real perpetrators left the Horde.

The Stone Raiders moved through the forest in multiple parties, coming from every direction.

Shockwaves rippled out from the battlefield.

Lezar looked up, seeing the very forest itself moving to attack the creatures that dared move through it. Spikes of metal protruded from the ground and rain seemed to form from nowhere. Lightning cracked and screams yelled out.

Lezar looked to his map. The Stone Raiders were like a train wreck, slamming into the Demon Horde and rushing away, leaving nothing but devastation behind. By the time one party had hit, another two came in from another direction.

"Let's see that the Stone Raiders don't get all of the battle. Let's pick up the pace—make sure none of the Horde makes it through our ranks!" Lezar bellowed over his brigade's party chat.

***

Deia watched the backs of Dave, Gurren, Lox, and Anna as they rushed through the forest. All around them, there were Air creations. Suzy's staff glowed with Mana surging through it as Earth, lightning, and metal creations stomped along.

As they cut through the forest, it was obvious Gurren and Lox had increased their Agility in leaps and bounds. They jumped through the trees and treated it as if it were an obstacle course instead of cursing the non-smooth surfaces.

They came over a rise and looked down onto the Demon Horde, a red, black, and gray mass of seething anger. Their red eyes turned as one toward the party as their muscled bodies constricted in anticipation.

Deia didn't need to say anything. Anna's wind blades whistled through the air. Steve fired bolts from his hand as Dave seemed to punch Mana bolts from his hands.

Induca and Deia released a torrent of flames from their hands while Malsour waved his arm at the Demons, casting a wave of curses and hexes, followed by darklings rushing out of the forest's shadows.

Suzy's creations threw themselves forward. The Air creations tore into the Demon formation while the Earth and metal ones threw themselves forward into the Horde.

Lightning moved like a fish through the Demons, first hitting one group, and then spreading out from there farther and farther, leaving jittery and shaking creatures behind.

The metal creatures finished them off.

The front line of Party Zero slammed into what was left of the Demon Horde's side.

Gurren and Lox used their shield and sword combinations as if they were born with them. Dave's erratic fighting style changed from one weapon to another as he seemed to almost teleport between people. Steve bashed Demons away with his shield, sending them flying and turning more than one into pulp. The unarmored Demons were nothing to his axe, especially now that he had the Strength to wield it one-handed. Anna looked as if she were conducting a symphony of death, walking through her opponents with ease.

"Don't get stuck in too much! Pull back!" Deia yelled, seeing that they were carving too deep into the Horde.

The front ranks turned and they started to carve their way out of the Demon Horde.

Deia and Anna were precise killing machines. Thin blue flames and shimmering Air blades followed the path of their blades, tearing whatever dared to move into their path. Malsour's curses and hexes made Demons fall over, screaming in pain, as Suzy's creatures worked together in terrible synchrony to destroy anything that was within their range.

They were once again out of the Horde. The front melee fighters rushed outward, parting, so that the ranged fighters could get in front of them.

Deia, Suzy, Induca, and Malsour charged ahead.

"We've got Demons following," Dave said.

"I've got them," Suzy said. Some of her Earth creations seemed to collapse to the ground, looking identical to the forest around them.

The party continued to run.

Screams reached them as the creations were tripped, tearing the unsuspecting and surprised Demons apart.

"We're looking good for now," Dave said.

"Okay, let's get some rest and check how it's looking and then get back in there," Deia said. The midday was turning into afternoon.

With our high Endurance, it could be a couple of days before we need sleep. The weaker we make them out here, the less we have to fight at the walls.

"Damn, I didn't think that they would be that," Gurren started.

"Weak?" Suzy supplied.

"Yeah," Gurren agreed.

"Means that your training has paid off." Dave slapped Gurren's back as they ran.

"We can't get used to it. There are stronger Demons in their group and if we get too stuck into their formation like we nearly did, they've got the numbers to swarm us and make us have a very bad day," Deia warned.

Party Zero nodded. They were pleased with their strength, but overconfidence could kill them as sure as being too weak.

***

They'd taken five minutes to down some water, chew on some food, and regenerate their lost Mana and Stamina.

Dave's heart pumped in his chest as he ran. They saw the Demons in the distance, stomping through the forest. Dave formed a bow and fired arrows into the Demons.

The rest of the party opened up with their long-range attacks.

A thundering boom came from above. The entire area became hot as Demons were thrown everywhere.

"Babe, was that your fuel air bomb?" Dave looked to Deia, who looked tired.

"Yeah. Needs some minor fixes though!"

"You're all damned insane!" Lox laughed as he fired his destruction staff.

A firestorm raged through the Demons' ranks as the party paused, firing from a metal wall that rose up. Suzy's lightning and Air creations raced into the Demons, adding to the severity of the firestorm.

"Move!" Deia yelled after a few minutes.

They rushed away again. The mages lay down spells and traps for anything that tried to follow them. They dodged between traps that had been put down by Efri's forces.

"Let's go for another one," Deia said.

They had barely touched all of their Mana reserves, but they didn't have much time before the Demons reached the keep. They altered their path, circling around wide to the Demon Horde's flank.

"Hey, Mikal!" Dave yelled as they passed another party.

"Good hunting, Zero!" Mikal jumped through the trees.

Dave saw what they were fighting next.

"Okay, we're going to come into a valley with the Demons right in front of us. We can lay waste to them, bottleneck them into the valley and really cut down their numbers. Soon as anything makes it up the sides or puts real pressure on us, we can leg it out the back," Dave said, ready to lead the way.

"Okay," Deia said.

Dave jumped. Dropping onto a slope, he rode it on his backside. When he got to his feet at the bottom of the slope, he was in a five-meter-wide valley with waist-high rocks dotting it. He charged toward the mouth of the valley. With his Touch of the Land, he didn't need to look back to see the others behind him.

The valley turned into a narrow path between boulders before opening up to show the Demons. They let out screams as soon as they saw Dave.

"I need to go on a diet. I can't make it through," Steve complained.

"Don't worry, we'll bring them to you." Dave strung and fired his bow. Every arrow dropped a Demon. The rest of the party filed out, adding their own long-ranged attacks.

Deia and Induca's fire corralled the Demons, killing those who didn't follow their created path. Malsour's hexes and curses weakened them or dropped them to the ground in writhing pain.

Anna's wind blades cut down dozens with each swing.

Gurren and Lox fired their destruction staffs, their Mana taking just a few seconds to tear through the Demons.

Dave dropped dozens in as many seconds.

The Demons just don't have any ranged weapons. The only way they can get to us is just inundate us with targets where they've got more than enough of their fellows to kill us. Dave saw his notifications bar blinking at him once again.

Ah shit! I have to train up my other weapons as well. Dave accessed his hypercognition, checking the number that he had killed with his bow. Dave fired faster than any Human should be capable of, simply pulling and releasing on his bowstring as an arrow appeared between his fingers.

"Well, looks like I've got my archery kills." Dave slowed back down out of hypercognition. He had a lot more fighting to do and overusing it gave him a wicked headache.

A vortex of Fire ran amok through the Demon's lines. Again, another fuel air bomb went off. This wasn't like the last, which just tore apart a few dozen Demons. This tore hundreds apart in the blink of an eye.

"Looks like I'm getting a handle on it," Deia said.

Lox and Dave shared a look. Lox's eyes seemed to say *well-she's-your-problem-now.* Gurren's eyes said a different story: along the lines of *holy-shit-is-that-the-Deia-we-know.*

Dave continued to shoot his bow. The Demons had only been pushed back a few hundred feet.

"Shit." Suzy covered her head as a rock slammed into her arm.

The Demons seemed to get the idea, and threw rocks at the party.

"Pull back!" Deia said. Another fuel air bomb, smaller than the last, tore apart the first ranks, putting them into chaos once again as Malsour and Induca cast area effect spells. Induca created what looked like a Chinese Dragon—from back on Earth—made of fire.

Malsour's dome of darkness emitted nothing but screams and fog pouring off it.

Dave watched a tentacle. It seemed to be made of oil; smoke rose from where drops fell from it. The Demon in its grip yelled out and disappeared into Malsour's dome.

Dave filed in after the rest of his party. Steve was on the other side.

The melee fighters spread out along the valley. Deia and Induca climbed one side of the valley to see over them. Malsour and Suzy did the same on the other side.

There was a silence and tension in the air. Everyone was focused on the path that led into their small valley.

Dave rolled his shoulders. His Touch of the Land let him see through the rocks and the Demons beyond. "They've made it to the entrance."

The Demons scrambled through and pushed against the boulders. They must've weighed five hundred pounds each but the Demons had grown with fighting one another to survive.

Dave drew and loosed three arrows in the space of a second, cutting through three Demons and making them drop to the ground.

More clambered over them, rushing toward the party.

Dave's bow dissolved, and then regrew into a sword and a shield.

Anna fired bolts in. Malsour laid down area of effect hexes and curses. Suzy's creations made sure that they weren't creeped up on and stopped the Demons from climbing over the boulders or rushing up the sides of the small crevasse they were in.

Deia rose above them; fire under her feet held her aloft as she let loose with a torrent of fire. It rushed through the path in the boulders and out the other side.

The Demons who had made it into the valley charged the melee fighters. Dave slammed his shield into a Demon's nose. It cried out in pain, looking as if it was in shock at its own injury before Dave's sword flicked out and cut through its neck.

Dave's shield blocked another Demon's claws that raked across it. Dave's blade swung low, taking the Demon off at the knees, before a backhanded slash took off its head.

Creating a spike on its edge, Dave slammed his shield rim first into a Demon, piercing through the creature. It choked, falling back in death.

"Pull back!" Lox might not be the leader of a warband anymore, but he could easily read a situation.

They moved back as one. Steve's attacks tore Demons apart or sent them flying. Anna took out her opponents with easy grace. Lox and Gurren were efficient machines.

Dave was the wild card, switching between varying blades and shields, augmenting them as his blades sunk home. Every time his weapon touched the Demons, another would die. Crushed windpipe, through the second rib just so, nicking the heart and lungs, main artery in the leg, the kidneys, through the ribcage, heart, lungs, temple, brain, eyes: every strike was a critical hit.

The Demons were simple anatomical designs to him. It was just a factor of working himself to end them. They were strong creatures, but the more Dave fought, the more he understood. He understood their bodies, his new power, his abilities and how to become better at fighting them.

They were taller than him, had more reach, but they didn't have armor. Their claws were wickedly sharp but little use against his armor.

"Pull back," Lox called.

Again, they stepped backward.

Dave relaxed. He was facing creatures at around the level 100 mark. It felt as though he could choreograph their movements. His apprehension from before fell away. It wasn't hard to kill them. It wasn't their skill, weapons, or level that scared him, but rather their sheer numbers.

When he was fighting them in controlled circumstances like this, he looked for the most economical way to kill the creatures, saving up his Stamina and Mana for what he really needed.

"Weapons master quest status," Dave asked.

To the side of his screen, the quest showed.

Quest: Weapons Master Level 2

Kill one hundred enemies with every weapon type.

One handed and shield 67/100

Two handed 41/100

Dual wielding 81/100

Archery 100/100

Rewards: Unlock Level 3 Quest

Increase to stats

Dave dismissed the screen. It wouldn't take long for him to get his One handed, then he could focus on his Two handed and Dual wielding.

Even with the obstacles in their way, the Demons were hell-bent on tearing them apart. They didn't know the futility of their situation. The party was only backing up due to the number of corpses around them, making footing difficult.

"Damn, easier than Aleph," Steve said.

"Make sure you don't get cocky." Anna tore a Demon in two with a wind blade. "There are nearly six thousand Demons for every Stone Raider here."

"Well, that sounds like a challenge," Steve said.

"Experience farm," Dave agreed, though the two of them understood that they had their limits. "Suzy must be pleased with the experience she gets off you."

"Nope. Doesn't take any of it. Makes leveling up a lot easier," Steve said.

"Nice," Dave said, the two of them having a casual conversation even as they killed Demon after Demon.

They took scratches here and there but they heavily outclassed the Demons. Dave counted as being nearly four times the Demons' level.

"You've become strong, Dave, stronger than I thought possible in such a small amount of time. Though the Stone Raiders have certainly opened my eyes to a few things," Lox said.

"Yeah, thought you'd be having a bit more difficulty with these guys," Gurren quipped.

"Well, in open plains, then they'd probably tear me apart. However, with this setup, waiting for them one-on-one, it gets a bit easier." Dave ducked and turned the blade pointing out the back of his fist, slamming under a Demon's arm and into their chest before Dave threw them free. The life drained from their eyes.

Dave's strength was incomparable to the Demons on a one-on-one basis. The Demons were just fighting practice that gave the Stone Raiders experience as they fought.

Deia, who had been hovering over the valley, was looking for any big groups of Demons and checked over the boulders and into the large area where the majority of the Demon Horde was. She rode her fire back to the side of the valley. Induca took her spot.

Deia started to chant to herself. It took but a few moments.

Another one of her fuel bombs went off. The shockwave ripped through the forest, throwing trees about, obliterating Demons that were too close, and turning those who were within the blast areas into pulp. Others, outside the blast radius, were tossed like rag dolls due to the extreme power of the explosion.

The sky rained dirt, parts of trees, the forest, and Demons. Thousands of Demons died in the blast.

The flow of Demons slowed through the valley as the melee fighters dispatched them with ease. Those Demons who made it through came through with bloody ears from having their eardrums ruptured, and coughed blood from their pulped insides.

Dave felt as though he was giving them a mercy as he ended them.

"Let's move out—recover our Mana and Stamina and come back again," Deia said.

In the distance, clouds could be seen; lightning rained down from the heavens and smote all who lay below.

The forest creaked and groaned as it followed the instructions of the Stone Raiders' mages. After seeing Deia's powerful magic, they were now showing off their larger attacks as well.

Induca turned the ground into lava, killing any Demon who made it through the valley. Their tombstones still remained, even if their bodies were destroyed.

Steve boosted Gurren, Lox, and Dave out of the valley. Anna called on her wind and glided out of it. Suzy used her Air creations to pull Steve out of the valley.

Once Steve's feet touched the ground, the party started to run, leaving the Demon Horde behind.

Dave glanced at his quest.

Quest: Weapons Master Level 2

Kill one hundred enemies with every weapon type.

One handed and shield 100/100

Two handed 89/100

Dual wielding 100/100

Archery 100/100

Rewards: Unlock Level 3 Quest

Increase to stats

"Come on, I've got just eleven to go." Dave sighed as he destroyed the sword and shield he was using and put them on his belt.

Dave checked his notifications.

Active Skill: One handed and Shield

Level: Master Level 2

Effect: Weapons damage increased by 42%. Defense increases by 21%; shield bash is 10% more likely to stun opponent.

Cost: 20 Stamina

Level 129

You have reached level 129; you have **466** stat points to use.

"What? How the hell are they that much experience?" Dave asked.

"The Demons?" Anna asked.

"Yeah. I gained five levels from killing them," Dave said.

"All of them are Creatures of Power, things that the Pantheon themselves have made. They're considered Legendary beasts. Killing them brings in a ton of experience. We're just getting to them before they've really started to use magic or start flying. A flying Demon charge is pure nightmare fuel. If these suckers were in the air, then it would be hell," Lox said.

"They've been fighting one another, plenty of opponents, all of them strong. Whoever survives becomes the strongest and the fact that their own meat is considered Legendary is an over-the-top hack to increase their strength in the shortest time possible," Anna said.

"Damn." Dave shook his head. *What the hell kind of enemy would we be dealing with if the DCA didn't clear out those high-leveled creatures and weaken them from the very beginning?*

They came to a clearing, well away from the Demon Horde.

"Rest, meditate, get some water and food into you." Deia sat down against a tree.

Dave checked with his Touch of the Land to make sure that there was nothing near them. He took a seat beside Deia and opened his character sheet.

Fifteen into Intelligence, sixteen for Agility—couldn't just leave it at two hundred and ninety-nine. These Demons are stronger than they look and we're not going to be resting very long—ten for Endurance and Strength.

Dave checked over his new stats.

Character Sheet

Name:	David Grahslagg	Gender:	Male
Level:	46	Class:	Dwarven Master Smith, Friend of the Grey God, Bleeder, Librarian, Aleph Engineer, Weapons Master
Race:	Human/Dwarf	Alignment:	Chaotic Neutral

Unspent points: 415

Health:	18,800	Regen:	6.34 /s
Mana:	4,430	Regen:	15.75 /s
Stamina:	2,580	Regen:	15.00 /s
Vitality:	188	Endurance:	317
Intelligence:	443	Willpower:	315
Strength:	258	Agility:	300

Dave worked to adjust to his new strength and power.

"All right, five more minutes and we'll hit them again," Deia said.

***

Malkur and Alkao looked at their interfaces, checking and rechecking the reports from their scouts. Their faces reflected the disbelief of the numbers they saw.

Alkao dismissed his interface and looked out over his keep's walls and at the forest beyond. The progress of the Demon Horde was marked with destruction wrought upon them by the Stone Raiders.

"I never knew that people could become so powerful," Malkur said.

"We are the strongest of the people in Devil's Crater, but they are the strongest of all the Players who visit Emerilia. Don't let their levels deceive you. They're much stronger than they appear," Alkao said.

"They're tearing the forest apart, killing hundreds to thousands of the Demon Horde with every attack! How much stronger could they appear?" Malkur asked.

"They're sitting back, regenerating their lost Mana and Stamina before rushing back in. So far, none of them have been killed. When they join the Demons in real battle, side by side with one another, I have a feeling that this will look but like a mere sparring match," Alkao said.

"How is that even possible? To become so strong in such a small amount of time? What trials did they go through?" Malkur said out loud as darkness seemed to explode out of an area. Rain formed from the sky, turning to ice shards that shone in the late afternoon light.

"It gives us something to strive for, someone to beat. With enough training and work, we can become as powerful as the Stone Raiders." Alkao looked to Malkur.

"Sounds like a hell of a lot of work."

"When has anything we've done been easy, dear brother?"

Malkur laughed. "The hottest fires make the finest weapons."

Alkao looked to Malkur with a curious look on his face.

"One of the crafters I was talking to about blacksmithing, too, used it. It kind of stuck," Malkur said.

"Wise words to live by," Alkao agreed, once again looking toward the forests as ruin walked among it. "They will reach the walls in darkness. We'll make sure to give them a welcome that they deserve," Alkao said.

"There is a contingent of Dwarves with odd Weapons of War who have come through the portal and are making their way to the keep!" a Demon communications officer said.

"They're mine!" Lucy said from inside the keep.

"Well, let them up here—help them if you can," Alkao said.

"Bit trusting?" Malkur asked, making sure no one was listening to them.

"I was once shown how making friends instead of enemies is always a wise choice. I've seen some of the Dwarven Machines of War. If they're here, they don't need to get much closer than Unity to strike at us. I also trust in Lucy and the Stone Raiders. We will fight many enemies before our time is done, but hopefully we will stand among many more allies," Alkao said.

"You've grown up, brother." Malkur smiled, proud of his older brother.

"Well, I had some rather blunt lessons that taught me much more than I thought it would." Alkao smiled.

"'Bout damned time." Malkur laughed.

A pillar of light tore through the forest. Pillars of stone burst out of the tree tops and threw trees away, revealing the mass of Demons still charging for Alkao's keep.

"We have much work to do and not much time in which to do it." Alkao became serious, his smile fading away.

"That we do," Malkur agreed.

Chapter 6: Sleepless Night

"Party Four, I want you to link up with Parties Thirty-Seven and Fifty-One. There's a big group of the Demon Horde looking like they're organizing themselves. I want you to make sure that they don't have the time for it. Sending you a waypoint now," Lucy said.

Although Josh was the overall ground commander, right now he was in the middle of a fight and looking out over his own party. Therefore, command went to Lucy as she coordinated the Stone Raiders. They didn't need much guidance, just when multiple parties needed to coordinate for a specific attack or to separate back into individual parties.

"How are the Dwarves looking?" Lucy asked Jerome, one of her aides.

"They're almost ready. It looks like they've brought some kind of Dwarven artillery, though it appears to be a prototype or something. I've never seen anything as portable; plus, they appear to be made of some unique materials." Jerome shook his head.

"They're twenty feet long. I don't know how 'portable' they are, though. I do hope that they are effective."

In the distant sky, lances of Light suddenly appeared and crashed into the forest below. This stood out because, as night arrived, the kaleidoscope of powers died down. Instead, Dark powers came to the fore.

Lucy checked her interface; the force was under heavy attack. They'd become too complacent and attacked too deep within the Demon Horde, allowing them to overrun them. Three were badly injured, one dead and two with minor injuries.

"Well, at least she knew how to make her death count." Lucy shook her head. The spear attack had been powerful, but it had been all of the mage's power, descending right on her position to save her friends.

"Tell Jules that we've got more wounded coming in. Also, I'm going to need more Demons to pick them up and bring them back," Lucy said.

The aides in the command room immediately initiated their interfaces to forward the orders on.

Lucy noticed Kim's party as it hit the edge of the Demons. Her destruction staff's purple-green energy easily cut through a swath of trees as they did Demons. As soon as the attack had started, it finished with her party running away.

In comparison, Dwayne's party was more like bulls. His party was a group of tanks with only two mages to provide support. They crushed anything in their path, using their shields and swords before they, too, disappeared into the night.

Unfortunately, not all guild members were as lucky. Within the dark, the Demons' natural night vision gave them the advantage against most of the Stone Raiders. They'd also started getting smarter. Having eaten their own dead, they had increased in power even as they marched on. None of them had attempted to try to make a camp. It was as if some force pushed them on as they marched through the forest.

"Lezar and Efri's brigades are bedding down for the night so that they're ready for tomorrow," Alkao said as soon as he entered the command center.

"Good; I believe that we'll see the Demon Horde early in the morning. It would be best that we get them engaged with the keep. We'll soften them up with our surprises. Then, with the rested forces of Devil's Crater Army, we smash them against the walls," Lucy said, with an evil grin.

"Good, simple, easy, and hard to screw it up. Sounds like a plan. What do you need from me?"

"I need Demons to move wounded and supplies to and from my Stone Raiders," Lucy said.

"Done." Alkao looked to one of his aides, who bowed before walking off to pass word.

At that moment, Party Zero's entrance onto the battlefield could be seen by all. Fire erupted into the night with a massive explosion as a small replica of a Dragon made out of flames appeared, followed shortly by shockwaves throughout the area.

Lightning ripped through the skies, backlighting the Dragon as it cast flames from its mouth and burned everything surrounding it.

Lucy stood, amazed, as her arcane sight picked up the sheer energies that couldn't be seen from such a distance. The area around Party Zero looked like a maelstrom of arcane energies.

"Make sure that someone puts Xer on. I have a feeling it's going to be a long night." Lucy looked away from the scene of destruction and back to her interface.

***

Dave's war hammer slammed down on the Demon in front of him, meeting their face and crushing them to the ground.

"Pull back!" Deia yelled.

Dave conjured a wall of spikes around the melee fighters and right through the Demons, enabling Gurren, Lox, Steve, and Anna to turn and run with Dave and the rest.

Dave's Touch of the Land was always active, enabling him to continuously scan for any Demons following them and detect any traps in front of their path.

The party came to a stop after five minutes of running.

"Dave?" Deia asked.

"We're good; doesn't look like anything is trying to follow us." Dave leaned his back against a tree and dropped into a sitting position. He was tired and even with a full Mana bar, he felt mentally drained.

"Everyone, we'll take fifteen." Deia slid down next to Dave.

Slowly, the morning was creeping up. Sunrise came earlier in the north.

No one talked, silently eating their food and drinking their water as they readied themselves for the next fight.

Dave checked his notifications.

Quest Completed: Weapons Master Level 2

Kill one hundred enemies with every weapon type.

One handed and shield 100/100

Two handed 100/100

Dual wielding 100/100

Archery 100/100

Rewards: Unlock Level 3 Quest

+20 Vitality

+10 Endurance

+15 Strength

+15 Agility

+200,000 EXP

Class: Weapons Master

Status: Level 2

Effects:
+40 Vitality
+20 Endurance
+30 Strength
+30 Agility

Quest: Weapons Master Level 3

Complete the Quest: Survival of the Fittest

Rewards: Unlock Level 4 Quest

Increase to stats

Level 146

You have reached level 146; you have **500** stat points to use.

Some of the fatigue faded away as strength seemed to fill Dave's body.

"You put in more stats?" Deia asked.

"Nope, just got my level three for Weapons Master and I've got a level increase to 146." Dave flicked his interface over to his character sheet.

Character Sheet

Name:	David Grahslagg	Gender:	Male
Level:	46	Class:	Dwarven Master Smith, Friend of the Grey God, Bleeder, Librarian, Aleph Engineer, Weapons Master
Race:	Human/Dwarf	Alignment:	Chaotic Neutral

Unspent points: 500

Health:	20,800	Regen:	6.54 /s
Mana:	4,430	Regen:	15.75 /s
Stamina:	2,730	Regen:	15.75 /s
Vitality:	208	Endurance:	327
Intelligence:	443	Willpower:	315
Strength:	273	Agility:	315

"These Demons are damn good for experience," Lox grunted.

"What do you have to do to get the next level of your Weapons Master class?" Deia asked.

"Finish the Survival of the Fittest quest." Dave pulled out a piece of dried meat and rubbed his eyes with his other hand.

"Something the matter?" Deia asked.

"I'm just wondering what other monsters are out there. I took my sweet time before I started leveling up. There must be others who have been grinding their stats and classes this entire time.

Some have to be way more min-max than me and could seriously kick my ass. Holding onto not leveling up until it became almost impossible for me to gain stats any other way was one hell of a risk. Though it has definitely paid off—I can't even handle all of my strength right now. Others have had time to get used to it." Dave chewed on the dried meat.

Deia waited, sensing that there was more he wanted to say.

"What are Players like at the very end of their life cycle?" Dave looked at her.

"What are they like? Well, I haven't really gone to the main areas where Players live, though I've heard stories. Usually, they live in Ashal. There are abandoned cities all over Ashal but many can be reclaimed. The Players usually take them over, fighting in Ashal and going through the multiple portals to the other realms where the beasts of the nether wait. Sometimes, they even build cities on the other sides of those portals, visiting Emerilia only rarely. At the end of their cycle, their power is incredible. It is something that only champions of the Pantheon could compete with. They can't compete with a Dragon, but they can best any other creature. Near the end, they become much more nostalgic and wiser. They are less prone to race from quest to quest and more interested in talking to the POE and taking their time. Throughout the cycle, the amount of E-heads increases drastically until the end. At the very end, they usually start giving off gifts to the POE they've made friends with and making donations to causes they believe in. Then, they seem to disappear as they log off for the last time, never to be seen again," Deia said.

Dave drank water, noticing that everyone was paying close attention to their conversation.

"That said, I have never seen such a rapid progression of Players in any of the previous cycles. We might not be the strongest Players, but I don't doubt that we are the strongest guild. The Golden

Sabres, with members over level 300, are even thinking of joining us," Deia said.

"We're not the strongest by any means, but through everything we've been through, we keep coming out stronger again and again," Suzy added.

Deia cocked her head to the side and opened up her interface. "We've got four more hours until sunrise."

"Well, might as well make it count." Steve sharpened his axe.

The rest of the party started to check their gear over, readying themselves for the next fight.

***

The Dark Lord didn't look up as Boran-al held his head, looking around in confusion at suddenly being pulled into his lord's viewing room.

"When the Horde reaches the keep, I will give my blessing to the strongest." The Dark Lord looked down upon the display of Emerilia beneath his feet. It looked as if he stood among the clouds, looking down on the world.

"Yes, my lord." Boran-al got over his disorientation quickly and took a knee before his lord in what was the middle of the sky.

"There are more of the traitors' forces in the forest. Send out our forces and find them." The Dark Lord didn't look away from the scene below him as the first rays of sunlight started to catch Devil's Crater's highest cliffs and colored the morning clouds red, as if foretelling the battle about to happen.

"My lord, I discovered something interesting when researching what your blessing would do to your Creatures of Power," Boran-al said.

"Speak," the Dark Lord commanded.

"It won't just increase their power like normal beings; instead, it will almost double it."

Purple fire flickered within the Dark Lord's hood as he let out a deep and cold laugh, anticipating what was to come.

Chapter 7: The Devil's Demons

"Move it! We've got the Dark Lord's minions to kill!" Lezar strode through the makeshift camp.

Everywhere, soldiers were checking the little gear they had. The entire brigade, fifty thousand Demons and Beast Kin, moved into their formations. They might look disheveled with only minimal gear, but they were far from the rabble they had been nearly a year ago. They had come so far, it was almost night and day.

Their formations were crisp and clean. They didn't care whether the person beside them was an alligator or a bunny Beast Kin—a red, black, or gray Demon. They were all soldiers of the Devil's Crater Army. They no longer looked out for challenges as they moved. They looked forward together at the enemy that threatened their home.

Lezar, stone-faced, watched the army finish moving into their formations. All their nerves, fear, and anxiety were held in by their courage, dedication, and the silent promise they made to their brothers- and sisters-in-arms standing beside them. They would stand together and face their enemies head on. They would not flinch from their duty and they would do everything in their power to save those beside them.

"Let's go show this Horde how an army really fights," Lezar said over the brigade voice chat. "Fooor-ward!"

With his yell, fifty thousand feet moved forward in sync.

***

Efri watched his soldiers spread out in a line as they advanced forward. His scouts had already pushed out in front to make sure the Demon Horde was where their interfaces showed.

As they moved forward, the Stone Raiders seemed to appear out of the forest like ghosts, waiting for his brigade to come closer.

Thinking over their battles, a shiver ran down his spine. *I hope I never have to face them in battle.*

Kim glided from a hill down to meet him. The rest of the Stone Raiders casually lounged around. Although a few moved toward him with Kim, the others were eating, sleeping, sitting around, and watching the DCA as they moved through the thick forest.

"General Efri, I see that you're looking a little thin in the center. Me and my Stone Raiders could take that area, freeing you up more to your right flank," Kim said.

Efri nodded; he knew his center was thin. Their priority was focused on boxing the Horde against the cliffs and not letting them circle around the cliffs of Devil's Crater to attack from multiple directions, which required a heavier concentration on the flanks.

"If you would, that would help me greatly," Efri said.

"No problem. Besides, in the center, we get the best vantage point to rain hell down on the Horde." Kim's smile nearly made Efri flinch.

"I did not expect your raids to do as well as they did. Nearly seven hundred thousand Demons died." Efri shook his head in disbelief.

"Well, don't be too happy. The ones who survived are stronger than before. Most of them gorged themselves on their dead. Also, their stats make them more comparable to level 150 than level 100 now," Kim said in a serious tone.

"Then we will have to fight them with everything that we have." Efri's tone mirrored hers.

"I look forward to seeing how you do in battle. If you need me, send me a message," Kim said.

"Thank you."

She gave him a smile as she, and her Stone Raiders, moved to reinforce the center of the DCA forces that would be right behind the Demon Horde.

***

Alkao watched as the Demon Horde poured out of the treeline that ended just a few miles from the Devil Crater's cliffs.

For a moment, they stopped and looked up the single flat road that ran from the forest toward Alkao's keep, the sole route between the impenetrable cliffs.

The keep shone as the first of the morning sunlight touched its metal walls. Thousands of Demons and Beast Kin lined the walls, readying their weapons and waiting for the Demon Horde.

The Horde let out a bellowing cry and rushed toward the keep.

"Fire!" the Dwarven artillery commander yelled.

Alkao flinched as the artillery pieces fired. They recoiled along their tracks; balls of pure Mana shot up and toward the morning sun.

Earthen and metal spikes rippled out from the keep and down the side of the cliff. Earth creations that had been hiding in the forest jumped up, tripping and killing anything they could get close to.

Magics of all manner spread from the Stone Raiders' mages: hexes, lightning, Fire, ice, Water, Air, Earth, stone, and metal. Some mages grouped together, enabling them to fire even larger Mana artillery than the Dwarves could upon the Demons.

The Dwarven artillery bellowed again. Although there were only ten of the pieces, they could fire once every ten seconds. This was three times faster than the much more powerful mage's artillery, enabling a tremendous rate of fire.

The DCA was not about to be outdone, and added in their own magical powers.

The Demon Horde seemed *excited* in the face of overwhelming weaponry. Despite the spells landing in their midst and tearing through the Demons' ranks, they kept charging with maniacal grins.

Alkao suddenly felt the very air chill several degrees. His eyes thinned as he heard an unnatural scream tear through the battlefield.

A Demon bashed the ground; its wings clawed at the ground while it held its head. As a black miasma poured from its body, it grew in strength and power. Its aura doubled in its force. As it finally gained control, it turned its red eyes toward the walls. The look within them could only be described as an unquenchable hunger. It launched itself into the air at brilliant speed.

The Dark Lord turned his Creature of Power into his champion! Alkao took a running jump, spreading out his massive wings, and flew into the sky. Malkur and Vrexu didn't hesitate to follow their brother.

The three of them rushed out to meet the champion as it raced over the battlefield.

As Dark magic warped Vrexu and Malkur's weapons, they threw them away and followed their older brother. Alkao tossed his sword back to Vrexu, but kept his shield. The trust in his younger brother's eyes filled Alkao with confidence. Alkao's face turned into a grin as he released his full aura for the battle ahead.

The Dark Lord's champion turned to face Alkao. It proved its rookie flying abilities as it tried to stop and hover; instead, it plummeted a few feet and twisted awkwardly.

In comparison, Alkao smoothly swung around the champion while cutting his speed.

The creature rushed toward him, screaming its anger. Spit trailed down its face, hungry for Alkao's flesh.

Alkao waited, watching the creature as it came straight at him. He closed his wings and dove toward the champion. Alkao slammed his shield into the champion's head, making them tumble.

As they righted themselves, they rushed toward Alkao with blind rage.

A blur cut between Alkao and the champion.

"Thank you." Alkao laughed and flapped out his wings once again to their full length.

The Demon looked at its gut in confusion; he'd been opened up from his hip to his shoulder.

"No problem." Vrexu twirled a sword in his hands, cleaning the champion's blood from it.

From the other side, Malkur's claws cut its neck open, nearly cutting it all the way off. The Dark Lord's champion dropped lifelessly to the ground. Malkur and Vrexu carved through the air to float behind their brother.

As two more familiar screams ripped through the air, Alkao looked to his two brothers.

"Well, let's go hunting, shall we?" Vrexu asked.

"After you, big brother," Malkur said.

Alkao flapped his wings and dove toward the two newest champions of the Dark Lord.

***

Esa looked over the walls of the keep. Destructive magic rained down on the Demon Horde.

Calling it a formation would be a compliment to the milling and raging group that tore into anything in their path. It came with the morning light, shining over the keep's walls. The Demon Horde was a mass of shadow moving beneath the forest's canopy, surging up the cliffs toward the keep and its barriers.

The Demons' agile feet turned the defenses below the cliff into a deadly obstacle course. However, it only took one break in concentration to make them miss their footing or handholds, sending them into the spikes around them.

Great swathes of land were ripped apart by the magical forces in play. It was but a drop in the ocean that was the Demon Horde. One and a half million Demons were no small group. Even as many died, more continued on.

It seemed that new energy filled them upon finally finding their quarry. Champions seemed to be born every few minutes. An aura of power washed over them as they charged toward the keep.

The Horde's magics were finally awakened, out of anger, hunger, and frustration. Runes flared to life along the walls, stopping magical attacks.

"Aerial Demons!" one of the Demon commanders yelled out.

The sounds of wings flapping and gaining purchase in the air overtook even the Dwarven artillery as they recoiled in the keep's courtyard.

Esa felt a shadow pass over her. She looked up to see legions of Demons flying over the keep. Gripped in their hands and feet were round containers. They released their containers down the cliff and into the Demon Horde.

Upon hitting the Demons, the magic stored inside was released. Every type of Mana raged up and down the Demon Horde's lines. It held them for a few minutes. Enraged, the Demon Horde threw anything within reach at the flying Demons, catching a few of the unlucky ones.

A few recovered while others slammed into the ground or exploded as their Mana containers were ruptured.

The Demon Horde pushed forward, rushing over the spikes or using their magics to advance.

"Archers! Ready!" a Beast Kin commander called out. Archers, along the top of the keep's wall and within the courtyard, strung arrows.

"Pull!" Strings were drawn back and bows aimed.

"Reee-lease!" The Beast Kin's bellows were followed by thousands of arrows arcing over the keep's walls and down into the Demons rushing toward the cliff.

The aerial Demons returned to the keep as fast as possible, as they ran out of more bombs to drop.

Archers rapidly drew and fired again; arrows were much more simple and plentiful than Mana bombs.

The Demon Horde cried out in pain as arrows continued to fall from above. Esa continued through with her motions, targeting single Demons and watching as a feathered piece of wood sprouted out of their bodies with each release of her bowstring.

***

"If we continue a frontal assault, the Demons will continue to get slaughtered. Pull back ALL our forces to the forest and find out where the traitors' forces are in the woods. We'll destroy them and go around their cliffs to hit them from different sides," the Dark Lord said.

"Yes, my lord," Boran-al said, now a glorified war-aide as he placed waypoints for the Demon Horde to follow.

Boran-al did as commanded, passing down quest changes to the Demon Horde. It had been ingrained into them to follow the quests that they were given. They thought that they might be able to fill the hunger within them.

It took long minutes before they started dispersing out into the forest, hunting the forces that the Dark Lord believed to be there.

Just over one million Demons were still alive. Nearly half the number that had been in the forests the afternoon before.

Boran-al cursed inside his head as he saw Demon corpses being raised from the dead, now under the control of the Stone Raiders' necromancers as they tore at any of their nearby allies.

***

"Brace yourselves! The Demon Horde's turned back and is heading right for us!" Josh said.

"Shields!" Dwayne called out.

Shield-bearing Stone Raiders moved forward while others held back as they scanned the forest for Demons.

The ground smoked in places, the undergrowth and trees twisted by magic. Demon bodies littered the ground, with tombstones above their corpses. The Stone Raiders cleared out the Demons' inventory, turning the corpses into dust that filled the air.

Dave looked to Gurren and Lox on his left; their eyes scanned ahead. Steve stood on his right as they advanced.

The Devil's Crater Army were spread out, moving through the forest to pin the Demon Horde against the keep's defenses. They pulled their weapons free, moving through the destruction brought on the forest while looking for their enemy.

"They're coming! One mile out!" Dave yelled.

"Buffs and resistances!" Kim barked.

Mages spread the spells over the closest DCA members.

"Archers ready!" Deia called out.

Bows were held at the ready.

"One thousand meters!" Dave yelled, moving up through a crater and looking at the pockmarked forest as they came over a slight rise.

The Demon Horde's mass rushed toward them with everything they had.

"Seven hundred meters!" Dave yelled.

"Archers! Pull!" Deia yelled.

Dave could hear the bow strings go tight with tension.

"Release!"

Hundreds of arrows leapt into the air.

Dave placed his shield in the ground and closed his eyes. The world seemed to slow as he latched onto the magically imbued arrows of the barrage. Runes across his skin lit up in power as the hundreds of arrows multiplied into thousands. A dozen arrows added themselves to every arrow the Stone Raiders had fired.

The wave of arrows rained down on the Demon Horde, collapsing the front runners.

Another barrage of arrows fired overhead. Dave destroyed his previous constructs, making new ones and channeling power through him. Again, the Horde's lines faltered.

Dave gripped his shield tighter; sweat poured from his brow as his legs shook from the effort.

Half of the arrows had conjured extras on the next barrage. His thoughts were disjointed as all of his senses cried out to him.

He opened his eyes, looking at a cluster of five Demons yell out in pain as their bodies seemed to grow. A truly fearsome aura came from their bodies.

"Malsour! Kill them!" Dave yelled.

Dave saw stone racing for the surface, like spears through the ground. They got within five feet before being destroyed.

"They're turning into champions; they're invulnerable during the change!" Malsour said.

Dave regained his feet. His eyes glowed gray under his hood. His face was illuminated by runic lines as runes across his skin flared with life and gray smoke wafted away from them.

"We'll see about that." Dave's voice became deeper and more powerful as he channeled more power through his body.

Spell formations showed around the changing creatures, showing the new input of stats and the shield barrier around them. Although it was a normal barrier, the power that went into it was incredible.

A grin spread across Dave's face. "Well, I'll just have to put that power to use." He let out a deep laugh.

He didn't see the worried looks on those around him. His aura seemed to surge outward, making people shake in fear as he pulled more and more Mana into his body from his armor.

It felt as if they stood next to a Dragon with clear killing intent.

Dave pulled and altered the spell formation; it was clean, as if computer-generated. There were clear inputs and calculations, all of which had been made by the AIs of Emerilia, turning the Dark Lord's commands into actions.

"Today, the gods learn they're not the only ones with power," Dave said as he changed the last rune.

The power that had been going into the Demons was now removed, and rushed toward Dave in a concentrated white streak with black veins. Dave's shield and sword changed in his hands as the power slammed into him. A magical circle appeared below him; magical coding filled it.

Dave slowly started to rise above the ground; power poured off his body.

It felt as though his very body was being torn apart with the power of a god being channeled through him, enough power to change a normal person into a champion of a god. He wasn't just tapping into one, but had redirected all five of them, while sucking the very life force from the Demons who were supposed to gain that power.

His rods covered his arms. At the end, there was a hollow aperture, which started to glow with white light.

Twin streams, identical to the power that was rushing into Dave, projected out of his hands. Pure Mana slammed through the Demon Horde as Dave unleashed the power into their front lines. Dave pushed against the force of the twin streams, bracing himself as the very ground around him was ripped up and thrown away with the forces he controlled.

Nothing survived the streams.

Dave closed his eyes, changing the streams to thin and wide blades that tore through the Demon Horde.

It was all his mind could do to keep changing his armor while redirecting the charge through it and right out of the now linked gauntlet-cannons he wore. The power was immense but it wasn't infinite. Dave let out a cry as the last of the energy stopped. He descended back down to the ground. The magical formation he'd created underneath him left burnt marks on the ground.

His gauntlets turned to rods and returned to his side. He immediately grabbed a Stamina and Mana potion, drinking them both at the same time.

"Ugh, well, damn," Dave said. The glow of his eyes and runes fell away as he looked over the destruction he'd created.

"Archers!" Deia yelled, getting people back into the right state of mind.

Dave looked to his friends, who looked at him with a look of shock. "What? I just took the power from those five bozos becoming champions, funneled it through the armor and then out of my hands. Basically just one big Mana conductor. Pain in the ass fixing up the armor's runes; lots of damn power," Dave complained, grabbing his rods as they turned into a shield and golden sword.

"Are you okay? That's more damned Mana than I've seen since Boran-al," Lox said.

"Yeah. Cause I used the armor, it took all of the force. I've got just a minor headache from keeping the runes the right way," Dave said.

Gurren let out a deep laugh and clapped Dave hard on the back. "Yer a damned monster, but yer our monster. Redirecting the

Dark Lord's very own power! Hah, I bet he won't be doing that again any time soon!"

"Thanks," Dave said with a stupid smile.

"Well, you got us a few more minutes, but our sides have met the Demon Horde and they've got more of those champions." Steve flipped his axe in his hand.

"Don't worry, you'll get your chance soon enough." Dave looked at the Demon Horde rushing toward them still.

In the center, they had been thinned out with Dave's redirection of Mana. To the right and left, they had already made it within a few hundred meters of the DCA.

The DCA's mages let loose with their spells as those without armor used slings to whip rocks at the approaching Horde.

Thousands of magical spells ripped through the forest. The Demon Horde unleashed their own spells, crashing through the DCA's lines. Through the stress of battle, a few of the Demon Horde had awakened their magical gifts.

"Well, thank you, Dave, for that fireworks display. Stone Raiders, I think it's time we got into this fight! Kim, I want your forces providing support to ours and our flanks. Scouts and back-stabbers, we'll be supporting the DCA. Dwayne, make a hole in that Horde, would you?" Josh said.

Orders were barked out as the forces were rearranged within less than a minute.

"Shields, forward!" Dwayne said.

Dave hoisted his shield, advancing forward and toward the Demon Horde that was filling in the sides.

"Flanks, hold!" Dwayne picked out people to stop in position, so that the Stone Raiders made a half circle directed toward the Demon Horde.

"Put your shields down and keep your blades equipped. Use your ranged weapons until they get close!" Dwayne said.

Dave's sword and shield turned into a longbow. He took a moment to look at his blinking notifications menu.

Quest: Defiance

You have foiled the Dark Lord's plans and used his own power against his creations. He has marked you for revenge. There is only one way to stop a god: you must become one yourself.

Requirements: Stop the Dark Lord from hunting you. By any means necessary.

Failure: Restart Character

Rewards: Legendary Item: Dark Lord's Domain

Class: Defier

Stop the Dark Lord from hunting you

New Class: Champion Slayer

So, without the blessing of anything divine, or much more than your weapons and your spells, you took on the Dark Lord's Demons turned Champions. Must be hard to walk with balls that big!

Status:	Level 1
	Relationship with the Affinity
	Dark: Hated
	Light: Neutral
	Water: Neutral
Effects:	Fire: Trusted Friend
	Earth: Angered
	Air: Neutral
	+10 to all stats

Quest: Champion Slayer Level 2

Kill 10 Champions (4/10)

Rewards: Unlock Level 3 Quest

Increase to stats

Increased/Decreased reputation with Affinities

Level 210

You have reached level 210; you have **870** stat points to use.

Dave's fingers itched to put those stat points into his attributes but he couldn't. Doing so would make him more vulnerable than not. With the extra power, he was more likely to mess up his reactions or pass out. He'd had headaches and needed to sleep after he had first unlocked his classes. Putting in more after not sleeping for two days while fighting for most of that time—he needed to wait for the right time; he wouldn't get much time before he collapsed from the strain.

Dave drew an arrow and fired it into the Demon Horde's mass. He took his time, picking the strongest of the Demons he could sense before hammering them with arrows. He was nowhere close to the true archery experts, but he could hold his own.

"Release the minions!" Josh grinned.

Dave sighed at the ridiculousness of the statement.

The area behind the Stone Raiders seemed to shake as Air creations, or summoned Air creations, raced out of the forest, aiming for the Demon Horde.

Fire spirits, atronachs, and creations followed in their wake. Atronachs were faintly Humanoid-like creatures made up of materials associated with a single Affinity. Unlike a summoned caster's creations, these were autonomous by themselves. They needed more Willpower to create one, but they could give a normal caster close-in support when they needed it.

Creations from every material as well as the spirits and creatures that fell under their domains rampaged through the DCA and Stone Raider's lines.

"Protect the flanks; help the DCA," Josh called out. The summoners moved to keep in range of their creations or creatures.

Then, the necromancers' creatures showed their faces: Bone Lords from the Aleph college, undead creatures that they had fought over the last six months. Even the Arch Lich's remaining juggernaut stepped out of the forest and into the desolate plot of land that had been turned into a battlefield between the two forces.

More juggernauts stepped up beside it. They started forward; moving slowly at first, they began to pick up speed.

Dave whooped as the juggernauts shook the very ground with their heavy steps. They were still massive creatures, but it looked as if Jake and his necromancers had not been idle. They were faster than they'd been in the Aleph college.

"Watch your aim!" Deia called out. The rate of arrows being let loose fell dramatically as the archers took their time to make sure that they didn't hit friendly forces.

The juggernauts and other minions of the Stone Raiders worked together to make a second force of nearly three thousand creatures that split in half, headed for either flank.

"Cover the DCA; we can take the Horde straight on. Once the DCA is sorted, we will begin our advance!" Josh said.

The Demon Horde continued closing, even under the constant barrage of ranged weapons.

Efri and Lezar's brigades were caught in a fierce fight across their front lines. The Stone Raiders' attacks were helping but they couldn't be everywhere necessary to stop the Demon Horde.

Dave looked toward the DCA; all up and down their lines, battle raged. They were taking down the Demon Horde; the better weapons and training were paying off. Here and there, the Dark Lord's champions emerged from the forest opposite, rushing toward the DCA. They would pay a heavy price, but the DCA stopped them.

Dave focused back on his own problems, shifting the sword in his grip as he watched the Demon Horde in front of him.

The Dark Lord had not waited. He'd already made half a dozen of the Demons into his champions. He hadn't repeated the mistake of letting them change so close to Dave. They'd been well away, too far from Dave for him to read their spell formations, let alone make his changes.

A streak of black lightning raced over the ground and slammed into Steve's shield. He grunted under the shock as the force pushed him backward; his feet dug two three-foot-long grooves into the dirt.

"Well, someone likes playing with lightning," Steve complained.

"Time we dealt with them the right way." Lox shifted his shoulders under his armor.

The Demons let out their blood-curdling screams of hunger, and put on more speed as they closed to within just a few hundred meters.

Dave waited with the Stone Raiders' line.

The Demons slammed into line at virtually the same time. Although a few Stone Raiders toppled over, most stayed rock steady.

Dave's blade lanced out, slicing both of the Demon's main arteries in its legs. As it roared in pain and blood loss, he sank his blade through its chest and stopped its heart. Finally, he slammed his shield through it, turning its ribcage into mush and hurling it back ten feet, and taking out dozens of Demons behind it. All of that happened within the first seconds of battle.

Even as the Demon flew backward, Dave found his next target and took off its head with a single strike. As a blue highlighted area appeared on the next Demon's side, he sank his blade through its ribs and tore through its vital organs.

Almost without thought, he dismissed the sword so he could bring his shield up. A split second later, it rang with a stone's impact. A mass of metal spikes lanced out from his shield; each point wove their way into a Demon's vital areas. The shield returned to normal as five Demons fell to the ground. Their companions crushed them to death, if they hadn't already died. Dave dispatched all that came near with shield or sword.

There were no words or, even time to talk. He worked seamlessly with his guild mates based on his friendship and their mutual trust.

Dave released his sword as a spear appeared in his empty hand. He threw it over a ducking Gurren, nailing a Demon in the neck and nearly decapitated it as it dropped the sharp rock they'd tried to bash Gurren's head in with.

Gurren didn't hesitate, using the opening to take off another Demon at the knees and punch another with his shield hard enough to make their heart stop.

Dave rocked with a hit; looking down, he saw a patch of ice that had hit his Mana barrier. Conjuring a wall in the middle of the Horde, he made a funnel for the Demons to rush through at two or three a time. Once created, Dave moved to the side, allowing a group of archers to clear out the corridor.

Malsour must've seen, because more corridors suddenly showed up, funneling the Demons and making them more bearable.

However, with their natural strength, it would be but a matter of time until they broke the structures and rushed forward in a wave once more.

"Lucy, waypoint for Mana artillery!" Dave yelled to the support chat, sharing a waypoint he'd laid down a bit back from the corridors the Demon Horde were rushing toward.

Lucy didn't respond with words. Instead, the mid-morning sky seemed to light up with Mana artillery.

Kim's own mages added their own artillery to the mix. Mana slammed into the ground, leaving nothing but tombstone menus. The ground shook as dust and debris was shot into the sky.

"Be warned; DCA Demon flight coming in! Once they've thinned out the Horde some, we're advancing. We're spread too thin; we need to get close to the crater's cliffs so that we can provide mutual support. The mass of the Horde is on its way," Josh said.

"The mass of them? What the hell have we been fighting here then?" Lox grumbled.

"The arse end ones?" Gurren asked.

"Smart arse." Lox chuckled.

Dave smiled as the sky darkened with flying Demons. They dropped spheres, carpeting the already broken landscape.

The bombs came to life, evaporating Demons and sending them flying.

Dave knew that there weren't many of those bombs.

They probably just used all of them to have some hope that we could advance and reinforce one another. If we don't have the right- and left-most flanks touching the cliffs, then the Demon Horde can get past us and start attacking the other keeps or working their way through the cliffs and into the crater. If we don't hold them here, then we'll be fighting a battle on multiple fronts.

Chapter 8: A Call Of Allies

Cassie sat in a chair, looking out over the highest towers of Markolm and admiring the beautiful city that spread out around her. She was in a mirror conference room that mimicked the city of Maphrol, the capital of Markolm and the seat of power for the high Elves.

After Josh and the Stone Raiders had left, Cassie had carried word back to her Golden Sabres in Markolm. The guild was coming apart. People were headed in all kinds of directions: some banding together, others heading out on their own.

Cassie had gathered a large group of veteran Golden Sabres, all agreeing to join their old allies.

She sighed and looked out over the simulated city, trying to push down her nerves. Her mind warred. *Would it be the best or worst decision she had ever made?*

The towers of Maphrol calmed her.

The entire island nation, Markolm, was almost eighty percent Elves. The rest were either adventurers taking a break from Ashal or creatures looking to leave the rest of the world behind. Markolm might not be one of the most powerful countries in Emerilia, yet their functions, their actions and customs were much more advanced than any other country's.

And a big pain in the ass. Cassie snorted and looked out over those same towers, which seemed to glow with a yellow hue. It was said that Maphrol was the city of angels.

Its beauty sure was mesmerizing.

I wonder if Josh would come here with me? She blushed. Her mind betrayed her as she shook the thoughts away.

"Cassie? It's Lucy; what is it?" Lucy asked. She was never one for small talk, but the fact that she hadn't even joined Cassie in her Mirror of Communication conference room was telling.

"I asked to talk to Josh; this is very important," Cassie said.

"Well, he's in the middle of a war right now, so, you've got me," Lucy said.

A war? He did say that he was going to be fighting in something that people would be talking about for months.

Cassie took a breath and looked away from the city. She was staying in Hovulaf instead. It was one of the middling cities that held a teleport pad. Something that was vital to the Golden Sabres as they took trips to Ashal to find dungeons and loot. Right now, she was lying down on her bed, with her guards watching over her as she gave her message and her guild's decision.

"The leadership of the Golden Sabres is disbanding the guild. There are a number of members who are interested in joining the Stone Raiders," Cassie said.

"Send me their names. Those we know of and pass our tests can proceed to the nearest teleport pad at all due speed. We will accept the others we believe to not be spies, but we will have to keep them on limited forums access and information access until we can check them out. After Boran-al, we've gotten rather strict in who we let into the guild," Lucy said.

"I understand. What do you need us to go to the teleport pad for?" Cassie asked.

"Well, we're fighting a damned war and we're going to need some reinforcements. Tag, you're it. Now, send me a list of all those who want to join the guild. You will be in charge of making sure that only the people we say come with you. We don't want any more information than absolutely possible getting out. We also have agreements that will cover all of these things. No one is to be streaming anything when they step on that teleport pad. You can record all you want, but it can't be sent out unless the guild okays it," Lucy said. "Do you understand?"

"I understand." Cassie winced at her own words, not wanting to know how much revenue she was going to lose for the move. The

Golden Sabres was a sinking guild. This was the final nail in the coffin. She wouldn't get much for that.

Though, if even half of the rumors coming from the Stone Raiders were true, then she might be able to keep being an unofficial E-head and go about doing her promotions across Earth.

"Good. Welcome to the Stone Raiders, Cassie. Emerilia isn't anything like you thought it was." Lucy cut the channel.

Cassie went to her guild status.

Current Guild: Golden Sabres

Position: Guildmaster

Guild Dashboard

Leave Guild

Her finger hovered over "Leave Guild." She closed her eyes and stabbed her finger forward.

A new prompt appeared.

Affiliation change

Disclaimer: All guild bonuses will be removed. You must be invited back into the guild to gain membership again.
Do you wish to leave the guild [Golden Sabres]?
Y/N

"Yes." Cassie exhaled as she looked to the floor of the room. Her eyes slowly moved back up to her interface and the new display on it.

Current Guild: N/A

Position: N/A

Guild offers: Stone Raiders

She pressed the [Guild offers] and went on to accept the Stone Raiders' offer of membership. She stopped streaming and her recording before she went to the forums. She wanted to know just what the hell she was getting into.

"Aleph? Demons? What the hell?" Cassie said to herself as she passed through the forums. Her eyes widened as her mind went blank with shock at what she was reading. It was incredible. The adventures they'd been having, all they'd been doing.

Yet, no one knew a damn thing. She opened up a thread about the guild halls, frowning at the Cliff-Hill and Verlun guild halls. Her frown deepened at seeing the third.

She clicked on the Aleph guild hall.

A holographic image appeared in front of her. The guild hall entrance began as a single corridor extending out from one point, growing into dozens of rooms, living areas and different workspaces. Then, the hologram moved faster and faster. It rapidly became obvious that it was more than just a single corridor with rooms; it was an entire city with buildings of all kinds filling into the space.

"I wish I joined months ago," she said out loud. She remembered her conversation with Lucy.

There was a war going on and the Stone Raiders, her guild mates, needed her help. Tonight, the Golden Sabres had died, but tomorrow she would see just what adventures and troubles her new guild had gotten into.

***

Lord Esamael slowly lowered the piece of paper he had been inspecting onto the desk in front of him. Geswald hid his fear well for an old man as he watched the handsome young lord at his desk.

Pete had warned him, but there was no denying the fear that the man brought with him.

Geswald was a powerful man, but in front of Lord Esamael, he was barely more interesting than a servant.

"My lord, to what do I owe the pleasure of your visit?" Geswald lowered himself into a bow while ignoring the two stony guards who looked down upon him as though he were their next meal.

Esamael took his time in responding, which kept the trader's guild chapter head bowed, an act that aggravated the old man's back.

"I have heard that the Stone Raiders are charging less than a third as much for people to go through their teleport pad versus our own. It seems to have created a boom of trade within Verlun. I've also heard that because the banks did not accept their offers, they are working on making their own. Our taxable business has decreased by fifty percent and they are exporting and importing more materials than any other teleport pad in Emerilia. I've heard rumors that they are even starting to facilitate talks with the empires and kingdoms in Ashal for supplies."

Esamael's voice was calm; none of his inner rage showed through. However, Geswald knew the man enough to know that he was furious. One wrong word and he would have Geswald's head.

"While this has been going on, you have levied taxes against them and tried to get the people they trade with to turn against them, with little progress."

Geswald raised himself to standing. "My lord, the peasants believe that they can earn more coin from the Stone Raiders. They have banded together and are working to make more gold. I have heard that your tax collectors are getting more gold than ever before."

"You think this is about gold? This is about *power*, Geswald! This upstart guild comes in here, places a teleport pad within my own territory and they dare to compete with *me*. Teleport pads are not just convenient ways to travel from one location to another; they are dominating power. With them, you can control your land completely. You decide and control who comes into your land and how much money you gain. Without our own people to guard the teleport pad, the king of Gudalo and other interests can move around my territory freely. I know there is a veritable flood of the king's own spies now in my territory. We need to have control of that teleport pad now." Esamael's fist slammed into the table. The heavy wood creaked under his strength.

"Yes, my lord." Geswald bowed once again.

"We are just months away from removing our beloved king from his high seat. We cannot let his spies learn of our actions. If they do, then the king will call for his army and sweep down here before we have time to put our plans into action. I heard you had a plan to attack the Stone Raiders before. I want that plan to be pushed forward. In one month, I want the Stone Raiders' guild hall to be nothing but ashes and a bad memory. They were driven out of Selhi for having a war in the middle of a city. At the same time, target those who sided with the Stone Raiders instead of with us."

Geswald's body shook, not from his aching muscles but in fear. The dice had been rolled and the lines made. He had to pick a side. "I will see to it." Geswald had too much invested with Lord Esamael, the future king of Gudalo.

Unseen to all in the room, a miniature scout automaton sent out an encoded message.

***

Shard shared the recorded video with Florence.

"Well, it was a matter of time until it happened." She looked at her reports. She was currently within the Mirror of Communication guild hall, allowing the two of them to talk freely.

"Are you not going to do anything about this?" Shard asked.

A prompt appeared in Florence's vision. "One second." She read it over.

Quest: Coup in Gudalo

You have received information on a coup being planned by Lord Esamael to remove King Sigaird from power. Will you let Lord Esamael's plans succeed and assist him or warn the king of the plot?

Failure: ???

Rewards: ???

"I will, but we have time and now is not the time to distract the other guild members who are at Devil's Crater."

"What will you do?" Shard asked.

"I will take this recording, share it with the people I have made friends with in this town. I will also send a personal message to the king with this video attached—in three weeks' time."

"Why wait so long? Even if the king was to call his army, it would take two weeks. Another week and a half to reach us..." Shard trailed off.

"When Esamael and Geswald's forces come to us, we'll bury them! We are the Stone Raiders; people have been thinking that we're weak because most of the fighting forces have been gone for going on eight months game time. In Selhi, we were driven out. Here, this is our guild hall. We won't let others push us around and try to bully us." Florence's kind face turned into hard lines. Attacking Lord Esamael would turn the population against them. Though if Lord Esamael made the first move and pushed his forces out for everyone to see, then the Stone Raiders would just be defending themselves and they could go full out on them.

I didn't pick this fight, but we will end it, one way or another. By either defending our hall, or coming back again and again until there is none of them left. The Stone Raiders don't give up, even if we die a hundred times.

***

Ela-Dorn looked at the portal that rested in front of her and her small army of researchers. They might have been asleep for a few hundred years but the light of curiosity shone bright in their eyes, from the oldest masters to the youngest novices.

The covering of the portal had been removed, something that the Aleph had never been capable of before. Every time they had tried, the power had surged within the portal and destroyed the runes and inner workings. Now, it was all laid bare. There was a ring with multiple breaks in it running around inside the portal's protective outer layer.

Multiple metals ran around the portal's length. Odd-looking boxes and all manner of components were at different lengths of the portal's radius.

Saying that it was complex would be an understatement. It was the greatest puzzle known to the Aleph: the power to link across entire planets.

"Well, we've cracked the outer layer. It's time that we start to find out the portal's hidden secrets." Ela-Dorn's words broke the almost reverent atmosphere in the room, mobilizing people.

They had a lot of work to do, trying to compare the notes of the various mages who had gathered information from the portals to be used in teleport pads, with the actual information that they now had in front of them.

The future isn't written in the codexes and textbooks. Those are just the stepping stones we might use in order to achieve even greater things in the future, creating a new path to follow and new textbooks to push our descendants forward with.

With a smile, Ela-Dorn walked toward the portal.

Chapter 9: Hold The Line

"Send our forces along the cliffs. Have them move to attack the other keeps and climb the cliffs into the crater. Concentrate our forces on the Demons' formation outside the keep. We'll force them to play their reserves outside the keep or start hitting them all across the cliffs. They can't have as many forces at their disposal as us. What forces can we send to assist them?" the Dark Lord rattled off, looking to Boran-al.

"We have champions in the south but they're days' travel away. For Creatures of Power, we have some wraiths and spectres, but they're hours away and they will be heavily weakened in the daylight."

"Have our forces concentrate their attack at the weaker flanks near the base of the cliffs. Send the champions we have to those locations." The Dark Lord's eyes traced something racing across the sky. "Alkao, Malkur, and Vrexu."

His eyes lit with malevolent light. They had been his most powerful creations at one time, the seven Demon Princes who stood over all of the Demon Horde. It looked as if they had retained their prince status but they eagerly ganged up on the Dark Lord's Demon Champions. Their fighting abilities in the air and their ability to fight as one enabled them to quickly bring champion after champion to the ground.

The Dark Lord gnashed his teeth. He could feel their power growing from constantly fighting his champions.

"Target those three traitors." The Dark Lord pointed to the three Demon Princes as their latest victim plummeted toward the ground.

Tens of thousands of bodies littered the ground.

The Dark Lord looked down on the destruction with glee.

***

"Does my butt look big with these legs?" Steve asked, driving said foot through a Demon. "Ah, sonuva bitch!"

Dave looked over, seeing Steve shaking the Demon corpse off his foot.

"Suzy, did you have to soul bond with this one? I think it's broken!" Dave yelled.

"Well, we can just melt him down for parts, right?" Suzy yelled back as she threw out a new creation core from her bag. Two Air creations acted like a pitching machine and sent the core flying. It landed in the middle of the Demon formation; five others followed it.

The earth—roots, trees, debris, and all—rose into three short centipede-looking creatures with vines sprouting from their top. The vines lashed out—growing, shortening, and tying down the Demons. The thorns on the vines tore the Demons' bodies open.

"Hey, I was just asking if these legs make my butt look big. You two have been changing out my limbs so much I'm not sure which ones I'm wearing!" Steve complained as he backhanded a Demon across the battlefield.

"Forward!" Dwayne called.

"Hooah!" the Stone Raiders yelled back. All of them had been trained in the Dwarves' way of fighting with the shield.

Dave didn't miss the smiles on both Gurren and Lox's faces. They had loved their time with the Dwarven Warclans. Out here, they were becoming stronger than they would have been in decades of being in the Warclans. They didn't have to care about how they looked; they just had to be the best they could be.

Lox used his incredible strength and blocked a charging Demon. His shield stopped it as though it hit a metal wall. Lox let out a cry; his blade took the Demon's leg off and then flashed out to stab into the Demon's eye.

"Well? Opinions, people!" Steve demanded.

"I don't know. It looks like they're faster and you are more powerful. They definitely look better than that one time you went into battle wearing that thong!" Dave said.

"Hey, I was channeling my inner barbarian!" Steve said, sounding hurt.

"More like your inner lingerie model," Suzy said.

Dave snorted, unable to hold his laughter, as he smashed in a Demon's chest with his war hammer. He then dropped low to take another's legs out and slammed the massive head of the weapon through the creature's head as it hit the ground. Changing the hammer to a bow, he sent three arrows flying and took down three Demons.

"Dave, move right!" Malsour yelled.

Dave did so, giving Malsour an opening. From his hands, Dark bolts ripped free as fast as bullets from a machine gun.

Dave made a war axe, using it to support himself as he crossed his right foot over his left, looking completely relaxed.

"Hey, why does Dave get to relax?" Steve grumbled. "Fore!"

Steve twirled his axe, taking out several Demons before he took a half-step/jump forward, planted his feet, brought his axe low, and slammed into a Demon with a *oh-shit-this-is-going-to-hurt* expression on its face.

Dave put his hand over his eyes as he looked at the flying Demon. "Nice! Not that aerodynamic, though."

"Dave!" Malsour said.

"Fine. I'll get back to work." Dave's war axe turned into a shield and sword as he charged in behind the last bolt of Malsour's Dark magic.

"The Demon Horde is pushing the DCA's flanks, which are still weak since they haven't got a firm hold on the cliffs. Therefore, the Demons are making it around them. We need to push up so that we can push our flanks out more and box the Demons in completely," Josh said.

"Well, you heard the guildmaster. Forward!" Dwayne called out.

The Stone Raiders once again all stepped forward as one. With every step, they pushed back the Demons, who were thinning out. Their forces rushed back toward the cliffs and the weak flanks of the formation tried to box them in.

As the Stone Raiders moved, they were able to support more of the DCA, who also moved forward where they could.

"I hope it's in time before those flanks give way," Lox said.

Dave and Gurren grunted their agreement.

***

"Damned Dark Lord's champions!" Lezar barked as he ducked under a wild slash by a Demon. He punched it in the chest, winding it before his sword opened its stomach and chest.

Small cuts covered his body as he held the line with his soldiers on either side. His left wing shot out, turning him fast out of the way of a rock flung at his head. His right wing shot out; the spikes on the end of the bones stabbed through the rock chucker.

Lezar jumped; his wings flapped to raise him up before they collapsed back into his sides. He landed on another one of the Demon Horde, dropping his full weight to knock them to the ground. He drove his sword through them and back out.

Standing up, he flared out his wings, using his wing spikes to impale a running Demon, once again coating them in blood.

"Move it! It's time we removed the Dark One's blight from our lands!" His brigade took heart in their general's words, pushing forward as he fought a fierce battle among the Demon Horde.

We need to push them faster. Our flanks don't even reach the cliffs; we're too far away and the Demon Horde is getting around us.

Lezar switched to the command party chat. "We need reinforcements." Lezar would have never made such a request before training with the Beast Kin. "Our flanks are open and the Demon Horde is leaking through. Either they're going to hit us in the back or they're going to head for the cliffs. If they get us in the back, then I'm going to need to collapse my lines to watch both directions. If they go to the cliffs, we're going to be fighting on so many different sides that it's going to be a mess."

"Very well." Alkao sounded as if he was deep in thought. "Vrexu, you will support Lezar. Malkur, move your forces to assist Efri. Close the holes in our flanks. Spread scouts out to look for the Demons who made it past our lines. Once we have the Demon Horde boxed in, we'll create fortifications around them and move forces to search and destroy the Demons who escaped."

"Understood," Malkur said.

"On my way, Lezar," Vrexu said.

"Be quick. The longer we wait, the more of those creatures get through," Lezar said.

"Use the support of the Dwarven Mana cannons; they're much more powerful than I thought. I will give half to you and Efri to command. I'll move the Stone Raider forces in the keep who are Players to search the cliffs for any of the Demon Horde trying to get into Devil's Crater," Alkao said.

"A battle plan never survives contact with the enemy," Lezar said.

"Couldn't have said truer words."

Lezar changed to the support channel, beheading a Demon while dodging another's fists and claws. His wing snapped out again, making the Demon reel back with the hit. Lezar stabbed his claws into the Demon's chest and ripped its heart out. He tossed it and jumped backward from a vicious swipe aimed at his head. He took a rock to the shoulder.

Lezar felt his inner anger surge, a hunger to bring pain upon his enemies well up inside him. He let out a shout. His voice turned into an elemental force as Demons were thrown away.

New Spell Learned: Siren's scream
Your very voice commands the powers of Air into a physical form.

"Lezar?" Lucy asked.

Lezar wiped away the notification. *Looks like I have an Affinity to Air.*

"I need those Mana cannons support!" Lezar's sword finished off those who had fallen from his shout. Slowly but surely, his lines to either side were moving forward.

"Change out lines!" Lezar said, seeing the fatigue in the front line's movements. Although they had a massive Endurance and Willpower after the Beast Kins' training, they had been in battle for hours.

The lines switched; the second line fought through the first, their blades and spears taking down Demons from the Horde. It was not without losses. Many of the DCA had laid down their lives in service, giving their lives so that they might hold the lines.

The DCA had brought nearly two hundred thousand into the fight, with another fifty thousand on top of the keep. They might have better training and some of them had weapons and armor, but most were fighting with their hands and in rough clothes. Barely better than the Demon Horde.

They could take down a Demon from the Horde easily, but they were outnumbered nearly four to one. Without armor, they were being cut up by the Demon Horde's claws and teeth.

Fifteen thousand had already fallen. As they got tired, they were falling faster and faster; the Demon Horde pushed forward, without care for their well-being. Many stopped, eating the fallen and letting out their war cries before charging forward.

It wasn't a battle; it was a fight for survival.

Without weapons and armor, it was turning into a fight of who had the more fighters, something that the DCA couldn't win.

His anger pushed him forward as wind gathered around him; a veritable maelstrom rose around him, cutting at his opponents. He moved; his image blurred with speed and he pulled power from his Affinity as he moved through the fray. His eyes searched for the Dark Lord's champions.

Lezar looked around. His lines were falling apart. They might be better trained, but his DCA troopers were fighting with mostly crude sticks, their own claws, teeth, feet, and wings.

The Demon Horde overwhelmed them with numbers and now with the Demons turned Dark Champions, they were no longer the strongest on the field of battle.

Lezar looked to his blood-sworn. They were his most loyal supporters. They had followed him when he had been nothing but a Demon Prince. They were some of the strongest within the DCA and would lay down their lives for him.

He looked to Yorai, the leader of his blood-sworn. He didn't need to say anything as Yorai smiled.

"One last charge?" Yorai asked.

They had been pushed back to the rear of the DCA forces. Being on the front lines would make it harder for them to command and control their forces, to see the overall battle.

Now Lezar's fifty thousand-strong had been reduced to a mere ten thousand. The only thing that was keeping them from running was the people on either side of them, their families on the other side of the crater walls and the knowledge that if they were to run then the Demon Horde would just hunt them down.

"Let us show them the power of blood Demons." Lezar held out his arm, recognizing Yorai as his brother.

Silence seemed to fall around them. The battle dimmed as the rest of Lezar's commanders and friends looked at him with blood-thirsty smiles.

"Let us show them the power of Devil's Crater." Yorai clasped his forearm with Lezar.

Lezar grinned. He allowed his bloodlust, his thirst for battle, free, ready to destroy those who dared to challenge him.

The feeling of invincibility fell over him as his commanders spread out a half-step behind him. His wings flicked out. An immeasurable feeling of ancient power radiated from him.

Lezar opened his eyes as he looked down on the battlefield. He was a Demon, a creation of the Dark Lord. Emerilia's people had hidden in fear of the name, becoming synonymous with death.

Now he looked down on the battlefield. It was like countless others: chaos, bloodshed, people forgetting their morals, their beliefs, doing anything and everything in order to just survive for a few more seconds, to just kill their enemy.

Lezar snorted as he looked at this Demon Horde. They reminded him of himself when he had first entered Emerilia. Wild and untamed, there was no true fighting style; they just did whatever they could to cut and harm.

Behind Lezar, his blood-sworn rose up, behind their leader, their Demon Prince.

"Death!" Lezar yelled out. His voice cracked through the skies. Dark Champions turned to face him and his blood-sworn like bloodhounds finding wounded prey.

They rushed toward Lezar. The same invincibility that filled Lezar filled these Demons.

A flash of light happened in front of Lezar and his blood-sworn. A sword and shield appeared in the sky. Lezar grabbed them, taking their advantages as he let out a yell.

Thank you, Dave.

For months, Lezar had suppressed the innate skill that came with his bloodline, the berserker skill. His muscles seemed to bunch up with unlimited energy. It felt as if he could crush mountains and open seas!

Dark Champions moved to intercept but Kala and the other Beast Kins' fighting styles had been ingrained into Lezar's very soul. The Dark Champions fought with wild abandon; Lezar, in his berserker state, cut his opponents apart with brutal efficiency.

His aura and the other blood-sworns exploded outward, sending the lower-leveled members of the Demon Horde to their knees. The DCA used this opportunity to slaughter those who were disoriented and firmed up their lines.

Dark Champions in ones and twos were torn apart as they met the fliers. More and more of them rushed toward the blood-sworn, trying to overwhelm them with numbers.

The blood-sworn knew that this was meant to be their last battle, their last stand to buy the rest of the DCA time.

I hope what's left of my brigade can be saved. That one thought drove Lezar onward. He felt as the first of his blood-sworn used a skill that only the Demon Princes' blood-sworn had been brought into: Blood Burning. The skill increased someone's combat ability; it would burn up energy within the Demon until they stopped the skill or died.

The blood-sworn turned into a windmill of destruction, tearing through Dark Champions as if they were just wooden training dolls.

Finding none in the sky, they raced to the ground. They cut a bloody swath through the enemy lines.

The Dark Lord had made thousands of champions from the Demon Horde. It seemed as if all of them were now converging on Lezar and his blood-sworn.

One by one, faster and faster, the blood-sworn found themselves in an impossible situation. They burned their blood, their very life force for incredible power. They rushed forward with blood smiles on their faces and their eyes glowing red.

Lezar embraced it; he cried out for it; his blood ached in his body as he unleashed his anger upon the Dark Champions.

The blood-sworn opened up the Demon Horde and the skies, killing thousands before they succumbed to their multiple wounds or burned out what was left of their lives. Some, even missing limbs, continued to do everything to try to kill just one more of the Demon Horde, one more of the Dark Champions.

Yorai and Lezar were the last two left.

"One last time!" Lezar yelled.

"You lead and I will follow," Yorai yelled back.

Lezar recognized the words that Yorai had said so long ago when he had become Lezar's first blood-sworn.

Tens of Dark Champions surrounded them; if someone were to look at them, they would see nothing but Dark Champions creating an orb in the sky.

Lezar and Yorai ignited their blood.

***

Vrexu could do nothing but watch as Lezar and his blood-sworn rode forth into the skies above the Demon Horde, attracting hundreds of Dark Champions. They'd done everything they could to kill the Dark Champions, even ignited their blood, burning away their stats in order to gain strength even if it was for a few more minutes to take down more of the Demon Horde.

Vrexu felt as if cold spikes pierced his heart. He and his forces rushed forward, working to support the DCA and Stone Raiders who lay down from Alkao's keep. He was meant to reinforce Lezar, to firm up his lines.

I was too late, and now my brother is fighting to the end to give me and his brigade time to get sorted out. Vrexu watched as Lezar and Yorai were finally trapped by the Dark Champions.

Moments later, they burst outward, charging side by side. Their shields hit hard enough to break bones and make the Dark Champions cough blood. Their blades were coated in blood; their clothes and faces covered in gore. The blood of others and from their own wounds stained everything a dark red.

They were like Demon gods of war: wherever they went, broken bodies were left behind. They had been caught by the Dark Champions for too long; others had moved in and attacked them from dozens of different angles.

Lezar and Yorai yelled out in pain and anger. Dozens of cuts opened their bodies even as they cut down Dark Champions. Each minute they gained new wounds, weakening them.

A dozen Dark Champions jumped on Yorai at the same time; one tore out his neck with their teeth. Yorai dropped to the ground, unable to move his wings before they were torn off. He killed three more before he fell into the Demon Horde and out of Vrexu's sight.

Lezar let out a primal yell, cleaving through any of those who were near Yorai. Darting downward, he landed on the ground where Vrexu had seen Yorai go down.

Dark Champions fell away under the pressure of the yell. Crude wind blades traced the edge of Lezar's blade; white torrents of disturbed wind streaked behind Lezar's wings.

Maybe there's hope; he seems to know some Air magic! Vrexu could only watch as Dark Champions swarmed to the area, darting downward to fight Lezar.

"Move out and support Lezar's brigade!" Vrexu yelled to his own people over the chat as he landed.

Vrexu made to walk forward, to join the battle, when a cold feeling gripped his stomach. It felt as if his guts had been pulled out and cold water poured inside.

The soul bond. Vrexu's face became hard. All of the Demon Princes had made a soul bond with one another—not that of master and servant, but of family. They always had a rough idea where the others were and they would know when they died.

Vrexu's fist turned white as his fingers popped. He took some deep breaths. His brother might be dead but he wouldn't let this moment go to waste. He had died to give Vrexu and what remained of his brigade a chance to survive. He'd taken the pressure off them long enough for Vrexu's people to get into position.

"Hold the line! We stop them here! Wounded to the rear! Use the Health potions!" Vrexu yelled.

The Health potions were expensive treasures to the DCA, but Vrexu would use any measure to see that Lezar's and his own brigade survived this.

***

Alkao hovered above his keep and looked down on the battle that raged less than a mile from his home.

The forest that had stood for hundreds of years had been turned into a battlefield of churned mud. The once peaceful forest was no more. It was replaced with destroyed bodies, weapons, and the scars from powerful spells.

Alkao watched as the Demon Horde fled through the gaps between the forces trying to anchor the DCA and Stone Raiders' formation to the cliffs.

The sound of wings could be heard behind Alkao. Battalions of Demons carrying their Beast Kin fellow soldiers rose over the keep, and dove over its walls. Holding formation like a living and breaking wave, they descended. Efri and Vrexu led their brigades from the front, passing to the right and left of Alkao as he looked over the battlefield.

He had sent Kala with her brigade to watch the cliffs and to man the other keeps to make sure that no Demons made it into their home. There were only his own forces left in his keep. There were no more reinforcements to be had. The Mana cannons fired; the mages added in their own weapons and spells. Colors and spells continued to erupt across the battlefield.

More of the Dark Lord's champions grouped together, readying themselves for something.

Alkao's forces were still severely outnumbered. There were three or four Demons for every soldier in the DCA out on the field of battle. Alkao's own forces could only watch as the Demon Horde stayed well out of range of their bows and slings.

They were supposed to have crushed the Demon Horde's forces against their keep's walls. Instead, the Demon Horde was keeping their forces pinned down as they sent tens of thousands of Demons through the forces meant to box them in.

I feel the Dark Lord's hand at work here. Everything showed that the Demon Horde was not a bunch of very smart creatures, not smart enough to realize that they were being boxed into another trap.

If the fact that there were multiple champions of the Dark Lord wasn't enough of a hint, the way that they were actually using battle tactics showed through.

The brigades continued to fly over the keep and down onto the battlefield as Alkao started to see icons of his forces blink out.

"Pull back and cover our rear; the Demon Horde's coming from behind!" Efri yelled out.

Alkao gritted his teeth and his eyes glowed red. Vrexu and Malkur were now deploying their forces not only right into the path of the Demon Horde trying to escape the kill box, but they couldn't rely on their support from their other brothers as they were getting pressured so hard that they'd had to collapse their lines to make back-to-back formations to fight the encircling Demons.

"Alkao, my scouts and rangers are moving out to handle what Demons are coming back at us; we'll try to take some pressure off your lines," Josh said.

"Go with speed. I do not know how long they will last," Alkao said.

They had been fighting for hours now, with no rest. There was no room for them to move; they were penned in and panic would start to set in soon.

Fighting an enemy head-on was one thing. Fighting them when there was a possibility that they could hit you in the back was something else entirely. He'd held his medics back in the keep, thinking that the wounded could be evacuated to their position and then healed.

Now flying was an extreme hazard with the Demon Horde hurling rocks and their growing magical powers.

Alkao's claws bit into his hands as he looked at the battlefield. He was outmaneuvered and outnumbered, and he had no more tricks left.

His lines pulled back on one another, doubling up, facing back-to-back to take on the new enemy front. Big gaps showed in the formation that was supposed to enclose the Demon Horde, letting more and more of them circle around his forces and hit them from multiple sides.

The DCA started to fall in larger and larger numbers. The Dark Lord's champions, numbering almost one hundred, a massive cost in power, rushed outward. They slammed into the DCA, sowing chaos, destroying lines, and letting their less-powered brethren through the gaps they created.

Alkao had at one time been an unmatched warrior leading his Demons. His older self thought it was possible, that they could still win. The rest of him, the Demon who had come through the Rebellion, knew that unless his lines started to hold, they would collapse and the battle would be lost. Morale was low, but still they fought with everything they had.

His blood wished for him to join the fight, but his duties kept him rooted to the spot. Alkao looked to the battlefield, feeling an outpouring of pure Dark Mana.

Dozens of Demons stopped in their tracks and screamed in pain, more and more every second.

Alkao watched as tens of Dark Champions were born within minutes. The Dark Lord's champions took to the skies in droves. Their numbers multiplied. One hundred, then two hundred, and then three hundred.

"Shoot them down!" Alkao yelled to the keep's defenders. Bolt throwers, destruction staffs, and spells lit up the midday sky.

Alkao watched as the forces moved toward one another. "All defending forces, take out those Demon Champions!" Alkao pulled a massive longbow from the wall he was on. He drew and released the three-foot arrow that accompanied the monstrous bow.

It slammed through a Demon Champion, continuing over Devil's Crater.

Alkao looked to the Demon Champions who now descended toward Unity and the civilians who hid within Devil's Crater.

"With me!" Alkao bellowed. His wings carried him over his keep as he charged after the Demon Champions.

Alkao felt reassured as he pulled his shield from his back. The Demon Champions were rushing Unity, bombarding the city with their magics and cutting down any they found wandering the streets.

Beast Kin and Demons stood beside one another, fighting the champions, giving their families time to escape and keeping the champions contained for the DCA to arrive.

Alkao let out a cry as he rushed toward Unity. He slammed his shield into a Demon Champion, tossing them off a villager they'd been seconds away from plunging their claws into. Alkao pulled out his sword.

The Demon Champion hissed at him and charged him wildly.

Alkao evaded its claws with ease, taking off one hand and cutting deep through its side. Alkao slammed his shield into them, pulling them from his blade as he ducked and turned and evaded a Demon Champion's wing that had meant to take his head.

Lightning struck Alkao, making him cry out in pain as he dropped to a knee. He lurched forward against his attacker. Electricity coursed through his body, making him cry out. The Demon canceled the spell as it ran through Alkao's shield and into him.

Alkao shoved his blade up and into the creature's chest, turning and pulling it out as a Demon's claws raked his back and wings. His wings flicked out, stabbing the attacker and throwing them. Alkao jumped and pushed off a wall, using his wings to glide over to where his attacker lay.

Several Demon Champions faced Alkao as they walked out from the shadows of rooftops and down the streets and alleyways.

Alkao set his stance. His back and wings hurt from being clawed. His body still shook slightly from the electricity that cramped his muscles. "Come on! Let me send you back to your master!"

They charged toward him. Spit dripped from their faces. They hurled rocks and magic, sometimes hitting one another.

Alkao slammed the rocks away, his arm going numb from the impacts. Fire washed over his shield as Alkao gritted his teeth in pain as the bare metal started to burn his arm.

As the spell stopped, Alkao dodged and weaved from three different champions as shadows fell over them all.

"Protect the general and kill the champions!" Krenua yelled.

Yells came from above as Beast Kin dropped from their rides, rolling upward, and into the champions.

Alkao's Demons came from the sky and landed on their descendants. Their blades and claws flashed as they grouped up on the champions, taking them apart.

Demons and Beast Kin rushed to Alkao's side, finishing off the Demon Champions. They faced them as one front, one army with one opponent.

"Kill them all!" Alkao yelled. New energy filled him as the Dark Lord's champions once again surged forward.

Chapter 10: A Smith's Awakening

Dave watched as the lines started to collapse, to fall and wither. They were getting routed and smashed from every side by the Demon Horde.

I need to do something or they're going to be slaughtered. He couldn't fight this battle for them, but he needed to help them.

I need to arm them!

"Cover me. I have a plan, but it's *really* going to suck!" Dave said.

Gurren and Steve stepped together as Dave rushed backward.

"Dave, what are you doing?" Deia asked over the sounds of battle.

"I'm giving the DCA a fighting chance. I'm giving them weapons." Dave slid to a stop and looked back on the battle.

He opened up his interface and checked his notifications.

Level 215

You have reached level 215; you have **850** stat points to use.

"I hope to hell it's enough." Dave opened up his character sheet and dumped his stat points into attributes.

Character Sheet

Name:	David Grahslagg	Gender:	Male
Level:	115	Class:	Dwarven Master Smith, Friend of the Grey God, Bleeder, Librarian, Aleph Engineer, Weapons Master, Champion Slayer
Race:	Human/Dwarf	Alignment:	Chaotic Neutral

Unspent points: 500

Health:	18,900	Regen:	7.96 /s
Mana:	6,740	Regen:	18.30 /s
Stamina:	2,590	Regen:	15.05 /s

6740-

Vitality:	209	Endurance:	398
Intelligence:	674	Willpower:	366
Strength:	273	Agility:	316

Dave closed his eyes as he confirmed the placement of 350 stat points: 230 to Intelligence—any more and he felt he would collapse. He increased his Endurance by 70 as he felt it was the only way to stay conscious, and 50 to Willpower to actually carry out what he needed to do.

He felt the world seem to slow down around him. He opened his eyes and they shone silver; runes across his body brightened with power. Gray smoke seemed to escape his glowing runes and eyes. His mind whirred with ideas. *So many possibilities: a spyglass, a big rock, buffs.* All would take a massive amount of Mana but it couldn't affect the battles already going on. More likely to kill the DCA than help them.

"Create armor." Dave's voice seemed to carry across the field of battle.

Once again, he closed his eyes. He opened up the Mana sharing function on the Abscondita armor Suzy, Deia, Anna, and he wore.

Magical coding started to form underneath Dave; silver lines carved into the ground, reaching the DCA's soldiers.

A Demon emerged from the forest to attack Dave. An arrow sprouted from their neck as Deia and Malsour watched over him and the rear of the Stone Raiders.

The lines extended through the formations of DCA soldiers. As it passed, simple steel armor seemed to grow over each of the soldiers.

As Dave expended power, the vacuum left in the Abscondita armor was refilled with the energy of the dead's souls. Dave saw the soul power moving in all its glory, his Touch of the Land and increased Intelligence allowing him to take in more information than ever. His eyes might have been closed, but he saw more than ever.

Soul gems appeared on the backs of the steel armor. Soul gems formed in the DCA soldiers' hands and next to their arms, swords and shields grew from them.

Dave used the conjured soul gems like the bottles he had made for Bob. They were given the form of the weapons and armor. They would continuously replenish the armor and keep it running as well as their own conjured constructs until they ran out of Mana. The lines Dave had laid in the ground acted as ley lines, glowing with gray power and channeling nearly all of the Abscondita's power through the lines to charge the soul gems.

Souls that hadn't left now rushed toward Party Zero, absorbed by the armor and funneling it to Dave, who directed them into the ley lines he'd created. Dave let out a yell. The ground around him turned into a tornado with all the Mana. There was so much that it created visible lines from Anna, Suzy, and Deia back to Dave.

His aura seemed to capture the entire area, making even the Demon Horde pause for a moment, stuck in their berserker state.

As people died, that power was captured and distributed, creating new soul gems, forming weapons and armor.

Dave set controls into his armor, feeling his consciousness waning. With the massive point increase, he'd already put tremendous strain on his body. Using his full capacity before he had even gotten used to it, he was on the brink of losing consciousness.

Dave let out a yell to all DCA soldiers and Stone Raiders as smoke poured from him. Soul gems with magical coding imprinted into them, continued to form and encapsulate their wearers, arming and protecting them.

***

Efri looked to his body in wonder as armor seemed to grow from his chest outward across his arms and legs; a sword appeared in his right and a shield in his left that he used to block claws that would have gashed his arm badly. Efri reacted, his blade piercing through the Demon. He withdrew it and looked at the fine steel blade in his hand.

"The more you kill, the longer the weapons will remain!" Dave's voice carried over the Stone Raiders' and DCA's general chat.

Efri felt as his armor started to heal his wounds. Energy filled him once again. "Clean up your lines! Prepare for advance!"

The DCA used the new weapons and armor with brutal efficiency. They had been trained to use the shields and swords, having to revert to their claws and simple makeshift weapons due to their limited number of crafters.

Now, with Dave's conjurations, they were a heavily armed and armored army.

***

Malsour rose a protective cairn over Dave, who had collapsed in exhaustion. His armor still touched the ley line, pouring all of the soul energy into it, continuously feeding the DCA's new armaments.

He looked out over the battlefield as the DCA's lines reformed. The injured pulled themselves up, the minor healing properties of the armor pulling them back together.

The others were systematically blasting the ground from the keep into the DCA's formations.

Vrexu and Malkur's formations started to move, finally able to get a minute to sort themselves out. They marched across the battlefield forest and toward their brother brigades.

Lezar's brigade had barely four thousand left standing; two thousand of them had been pulled back for medical treatment. Efri's forces had fared better: ten thousand of his people had survived, with nearly four thousand wounded.

It was only because Malkur and Vrexu's forces had reinforced the two brigades that there was anyone left. Even they had taken heavy losses, losing nearly fifteen thousand soldiers already to the fierce and brutal fighting.

"We're going to move forward, linking up the other brigades with Vrexu and Efri," Dwayne said.

The cairn Dave was in rose up from the ground; power seeped out of it, through the air, connecting to the armor of the DCA soldiers. The ley line went dark along its length.

Dave's runes were now doing the work; he'd had the forethought to make each part of the system able to rely on itself. His armor worked to power the other soul gems, which obeyed the magical coding inside them to create different items.

The ley line had made it easier for Mana to pass from Dave to the DCA soldiers; now it was just at a much slower rate.

As one, the Stone Raiders and the DCA surged forward, but the Stone Raiders were no longer tethered to them. Now, with their new armor and weapons, the DCA took more risks as they were able to hold their own with some support from the Stone Raiders.

Josh protected their backs as Kim and Dwayne led their forces forward. Lucy was running support with the cannons and mages at her disposal.

Following the line, a metal spider trailed along. To those with mage sight, it looked like ribbons of pure Mana were funneled into the spider and then back out to the DCA.

They were still outnumbered nearly five to one.

The DCA had taken terrible casualties being caught out in the open, with little equipment and their lines so thin they hadn't been able to switch out from the fighting to get some rest.

The combined brigades of two hundred thousand had been brought down to nearly one hundred and twenty thousand.

The Demon Champions were stronger than the DCA soldiers. Only the Stone Raiders and DCA commanders could fight them toe-to-toe. The front line soldiers simply slowed the champions down so that the Stone Raiders and commanders moved to aid them.

Now with their new armor and weapons, they saw a chance. Their training took over as they moved forward. Demon claws found armor instead of thin clothing. The DCA stepped up and pushed back, their lines reforming as commanders yelled out their orders.

Malsour looked to his friends fighting off the Demon Horde in front of him. And the spider he controlled. His eyes thinned as shadows seemed to wrap over his entire body. Waves of power billowed off of him, those around him looked at him in alarm.

He cast hexes on the Demon Horde. They let out wails, clawing at their bodies as growths started to appear. Their bodies succumbed to plagues within seconds.

Malsour conjured steel spears that flew through the air, clearing a path in front of beleaguered DCA soldiers. He had been close to changing into his draconic form in order to try to save the battle. Thankfully, it looked as though it was not needed.

Malsour glanced to the spider.

I wonder what Dave will be like when he wakes up. That aura he was giving off was amazing. The power he held within his hands was incredible.

***

Cassie stepped onto the teleport pad, leaving Markolm behind. She stepped out into the middle of a city under attack by Demons. *No, there are Demons all over the place, attacking one another.*

She watched as soul gems seemed to appear around some of the Demons and Beast Kin. Armor seemed to grow from it, covering them in steel plate; weapons and shields formed from thin air.

The armored creatures worked together, pinning down the stronger Demons.

She consulted her map, seeing that the defending armor-wearing Demons had icons indicating that they were allied. Cassie looked at it all, stunned.

"Just what I expect with the Stone Raiders—two races that we've never even heard of before." Bok Soo laughed and stepped around her. Golden Sabres, recently turned Stone Raiders, marched through the teleport pad and into the city.

She could see far above the city. Demons fought in the sky, showing off their aerial dominance. Her eyes caught onto a massive fortification built into the cliff of the surrounding crater. It was lit up from behind with massive spells and the din of a melee fight.

Cassie shook her head, focusing on the unfinished town she stood in. Beast Kin and Demons huddled in their homes, looking at the golden warriors with hope.

"Spread out! Assist our allied forces!" Cassie said. "Move in groups of four or more!"

"Damn, I didn't even think that there were Beast Kin and Demons on Emerilia. Where the hell did the Stone Raiders get this quest from?" Cassie asked in a low voice.

"We'll find out soon enough." Bok Soo spotted a group of armored Beast Kin and Demons fighting off three large Demons who were completely naked and fighting like rabid animals.

Cassie rushed toward the fight, a smile on her face and adrenaline in her veins. This is what she had come to Emerilia for, not the fame or the glory. For the thrill of it all. To see the unexpected, do the unbelievable and have fun with it.

Being the guildmaster of the Golden Sabres had dulled that. But now, she once again found that fire, the ever progressing fire of a gamer. Never settling for just easy, but always pushing to be stronger. To overcome her obstacles and be wowed by the game she immersed herself in.

This is how you game. This is how you play Emerilia.

Chapter 11: From The Jaws Of Defeat

Deia looked over the field of battle. The DCA's forces, now encased in armor, shone brilliantly in the midday sun. Their lines firmed up, no longer faltering and falling apart. They advanced forward with the Stone Raiders, moving to enclose the Demon Horde within a kill box, making the keep the only direction in which they could flee.

Deia looked to Induca.

"Well, I think it's time that you tried out your real fuel air bomb," Induca yelled.

"I think you might be right," Deia yelled back.

Fire grew from her feet, lifting her into the air so she could see the battlefield. The rocks thrown by the Demon Horde were destroyed by her Mana barrier before they could reach her. Her hair whipped around, catching the sun like moving fire as her eyes glowed deep red.

Below her, spells continued to tear through the battlefield. Mana cannons supported the Devil's Crater Army as they advanced forward, fighting on two fronts.

Deia had a proud smile. With Dave using everything he had left, he'd given the DCA the advantage they needed to overcome the Demon Horde.

Now it's time I did my part.

Power seemed to surge through her body. The very air around her smoked from the heat she gave off.

Time you saw what the daughter of Fire can do. She smiled as she poured Mana into her casting, using her arcane sight and what Dave had told her about spell formations to firm up her spell.

Rings of red light with symbols formed and spun around her.

She pushed her right hand forward, pointing toward the Demon Horde as they were pushed back more and more. Although they had the numerical advantage, their numbers were spread out across the cliff range of Devil's Crater, trying to find an entrance into their ancestral home.

The spinning rings aligned with Deia's hand. "Burn."

A fine mist seemed to appear above the battlefield. The forces fighting one another seemed to take a collective breath.

The mist erupted into Fire, obliterating anything in its path. The destruction ranged from ahead of the Stone Raiders, right through the Demon Horde and toward the keep.

Shockwaves threw the Demon Horde into disarray; it killed some, but it stunned many more.

Deia sighed, relaxing as she saw that her attack hadn't slammed into the DCA forces. She'd made it just strong enough to tear through the Demon Horde, but not too strong to do the same thing to the DCA's lines.

Deia watched as the DCA's lines made use of the attack, moving forward as fast as possible while still retaining their ranks.

Efri and Malkur's brigades finally reached Vrexu's. As one, the remaining DCA soldiers marched forward, cutting back the stunned and wounded Demon Horde.

The ranks covering their rears were reinforced as the U-shaped formation reached the edge of the cliffs, soldiers being moved from the front ranks to the rear. The U-shape solidified till the bottom of the U was only four hundred meters wide, creating a kill zone just wide enough for the Stone Raiders.

Spells ranged down the corridor that now led into the keep.

***

"Now we finish them off!" Kim yelled.

"With me!" Dwayne raised his blade before he cut a Demon down. He started forward at a walk, cutting down those in his path. His walk turned into a light jog toward the Demon Horde's mem-

bers still holding their heads, still trying to recover from Deia's attack.

The Stone Raiders and DCA weren't going to give them time
to recover.

The DCA covered over the rear of the Stone Raiders, killing
anything that tried to hit them in the rear.

Dwayne and the Stone Raiders charged through the corridor.
They used every trick they had left. Kim and her mages cast every
buff they had as the Stone Raiders' line turned into a meat grinder.

Demons fell to their weapons as they charged through.

Dwayne cut a Demon down, turning around it and planting
his shield into another's head. He ducked under a swing; his sword
tore the Demon apart as he continued his charge forward.

He felt invincible with his guild mates.

Strength—from his buffs, from his adrenaline—filled him as
he charged onward with his guild, a savage smile on his face. Just
months ago, these Demons would have torn them apart. Now, well,
now they were as strong as the Demon Champions.

The regular Demons could hurt them pretty badly if they could
get past their armor. The Stone Raiders' time in the Aleph's cities
and facilities had turned them into true warriors.

Dwayne was no longer a one-armed veteran discarded by the
people he had sought to defend and the institution that had turned
him into a war fighter. Here, he was Dwayne Trebault, Guild Lieutenant of the Stone Raiders, the indomitable warrior he had always
wanted to be and trained for. He wasn't weak or broken here. Here,
he was complete, with friends who would do anything for him.

***

Bob looked down over the battle. The Stone Raiders swept up and
through the remaining Demons that had been boxed in by the
DCA.

The Demon Horde was injured, barely on their last legs as the Stone Raiders cut through them with ease.

"Well, there's still the Demons in Unity and the ones crawling through the cliffs and trying to get into Devil's Crater to deal with," Bob said. "Though, I have a feeling that they will do just fine."

His screen changed, showing a Jukal wearing a mass of finery.

"To what do I owe the pleasure, aide to the emperor?" Bob asked.

The Jukal looked annoyed, shaking his large chin as colored water misted over his body. He was obviously used to being deferred to and pampered with small talk by the most powerful members of the Jukal Empire.

To Bob, it meant nothing. He had created Emerilia. The emperor might give him orders through his aide, making it look as though Bob were insignificant. However, they had chained Bob to the place and to his life. If Bob was to ever die, he would come back again and again.

He was the only one who knew all Emerilia's intricacies. As much as the controllers and vetters might question his actions from time to time and give him more rules, none of them would ever become the game master of Emerilia.

"The emperor is quite pleased with the results of the Demon War. He has agreed to your plan for the tournaments, with reviving the other species that have been stored away." The aide was clearly unhappy to be talking with Bob.

"Good, though he's going to have to wait some time. I have other plans that have been put into place to heighten the excitement of this cycle. I will also be extending this cycle for the Players due to the extra content," Bob said.

"*I* will consult with the emperor and see if he deems your *ideas* as worthwhile," the aide said.

"Ah, I don't care if you say they're your ideas. Just piss off and let me do my job." Bob closed the channel. Moments later, the aide was back on the screen.

"Do you know who I am? Do you know who my family is?" The aide inflated himself to bulbous proportions, a clear sign of aggravation and desire to fight.

"Look, I've been around for nearly eight hundred years. What are you going to do? Kill me? I can't be killed, since I am part of Emerilia. You know the power and the ideas that come from Emerilia? Guess who gets ten percent of it? This guy." Bob jabbed a thumb at himself.

"So, who is more powerful here? I would have to say it's me, the ever-living game master. I take orders from the emperor. You might relay them, but you're nothing but another mouthpiece. I've dealt with hundreds of you and others like you, so go and tell the emperor my plans. You don't and I'll redirect the power going to your family's home worlds, pull the patents from you and give them to your rivals for a bargain." Bob pressed a button to close the screen as the Jukal deflated in shock at Bob's words.

"Ugh, I hate politics."

Bob went back to looking over Devil's Crater.

"Well, Dave, you surprised me again, you crazy damned Dwarf!" Bob laughed. His good mood returned. The DCA was forming up again, this time facing outward. Injured were being flown into the keep at best speed.

Stone Raiders moved through the lines of the DCA, using their abilities to sense out Demons from the Demon Horde and cut them down with ranged attacks.

"Looks like Efri is pulling back their forces and Vrexu is ordering Lezar's to the rear," Bob muttered to himself, looking at the nearly twenty thousand soldiers who had survived out of the nearly one hundred thousand who had been on the field of battle.

"Where the hell did the Dark Lord get so much power to convert so many of his Demons into champions?" Bob frowned and tapped his chin in thought as he looked over the recordings. Bob had an idea of what the Dark Lord's power was before he was cut off from overseeing them. Now, he had no idea. Even though it would have been enough for him to do all of the changes, he wouldn't have been left with much left over. Dark was not one to use all of his power.

If Light saw that, then she would attack him heavily.

"She might just attack him to see how much power he has left." Bob sighed, annoyed at the idiots who called themselves the lords and ladies of the Pantheon. "Thankfully, Fire turned out all right and it looks like Water just wants to look out for his people. They're going to be one scary force to deal with if he turns them into champions. Most of them are many times stronger than the Demon Horde. Having their powers doubled by also becoming champions would make them monsters. Light and Earth will definitely start looking to turn their Creatures of Power into champions. The forces under their control could easily double in strength. The peak of Emerilia's strongest just jumped higher once again."

Chapter 12: Far From Done

The Dark Lord looked over the image of Devil's Crater, his smile hidden by his hood. He let out a rumbling laugh. "Well, it looks like we made the first Demons stronger than we hoped." He glanced at Boran-al, who looked confused.

"Wondering why I'm not flying into a rage?" the Dark Lord asked, amused. "Well, I guess it is time that I showed you what I used all the power contained within your citadel for. Give new orders to the Horde and the champions. Have them pull into the cliffs around the crater. See if they can find weaknesses and a way to get into the crater. They are to kill as many as they can. There are still a few hundred thousand left."

"Yes, my lord." Boran-al bowed and worked his interface. His eyes fell to the Bone creations that walked through the carnage of the battlefield.

The Dark Lord saw the look of anger and jealousy in Boran-al's face.

I am impressed with the power that these Stone Raiders have shown. Wherever they have been, they have gained more strength. One of them was even able to use my power of conversion and channel it into a weapon. We have a year and a half until the portals start opening of their own accord. Then Emerilia will be washed with death and darkness.

Boran-al finished his final inputs, following behind his lord. They teleported far away. They looked upon a desert, one that Boran-al had not seen in decades. Crystal formations seemed to move in the distance.

The Dark Lord laughed as Boran-al's eyes widened.

"Yes, your citadel was able to break the barrier between these two planes. Now we are able to harvest more Mana than ever before." *Powering all of my magic that I have been restricted from for too long.*

***

Alkao sent his brigade to chase down the Demon Champions who were fleeing Unity, heading out toward the cliffs of the crater where the rest of the Demon Horde was still free to roam.

He wiped blood from his eye. Krenua and his guard fell in around him. He waved off healers; there were others who needed their help more.

He studied the armor and weapons his people wore. Between the shoulder blades, a soul gem glowed under the steel armor. Another one in the hilt of their swords and in the centers of their shields. The armor looked simple but it had given them the edge that they had needed.

He looked out over Unity. There were smoking craters and broken walls. Bodies littered the street: civilians, DCA soldiers, Demon Champions.

Gold-wearing warriors prowled the streets with the DCA, looking for any champions who might be hiding, using their advanced magics to search them out.

They all said that they were Stone Raiders but it was clear from their expressions that they were learning a great number of things for the first time. Instead of asking myriad questions, they continued their work, looking to keep the people safe first instead of sate their curiosity.

Alkao opened a chat with Lucy. "How goes the battle?" Alkao asked, his voice tight.

"We destroyed what was left of the Horde within our formations. Vrexu, Malkur, and Josh are working on a plan to hunt down the remaining members of the Demon Horde. We're going to start having fresh Stone Raiders who died in the battle coming across in the next four hours or so. They'll be leading the hunt. Most of the Stone Raiders are ready to drop," Lucy said in her no-nonsense manner.

Alkao breathed a sigh of relief.

It was close. Our casualties were heavy, nearly half of our strength killed or wounded. If not for the armor, or the golden warriors, we wouldn't have been able to fight off the Demon Horde and the champions raiding Unity.

Alkao ran a shaky hand over his face, coming away with dirt and blood from a nasty cut on his brow. He had been so close to losing all that he had fought for. It had taken more than a little work and more sacrifices than Alkao could think of right now.

He took a deep breath, trying to bring his body and his emotions under control. They had bought time. They had not yet won the battle. There were still parts of the Demon Horde out there. Any one of them a possible champion for the Dark Lord. They would not be safe until they were all hunted down and destroyed. They might have just escaped total defeat but now was not the time to relax.

"I have a bunch of your fighters here in golden armor helping my people out. They look a bit lost," Alkao said.

"Ah, the new recruits—good. I'll have a talk with Cassie. Once we've got everything sorted out, we can start searching from Unity outward through the crater and then its cliffs. We won't stop until all of the Demon Horde and the threat they pose is eliminated," Lucy assured him.

"Thank you, Lucy. I will make sure that Unity is secure and then I can lead the searching forces from here," Alkao said. "Also, I think it would be best if we all got together for a meeting, try to figure out what our next move is going to be."

"Perfect. I'll contact you with more details." Lucy cut the chat.

***

Suzy looked over Alkao's keep. Wounded lay around the courtyard, calling out in pain. Medics rushed to and fro. People with bad injuries were carried into healing tents, where Jules and her medics healed them up enough to only need healing potions or their armor's natural healing abilities.

Suzy didn't want to estimate how many would have died if not for the healing component in Dave's conjured armor.

Healers were being fed Mana potions as they performed area heals in different areas. Within minutes, people who were gravely injured were back on their feet, looking at their bodies, checking for the grievous wounds they'd gained.

The Demons and Beast Kin assisted. The Stone Raiders' medics had gotten good at putting people back together with the amount of injuries and near-death experiences that the Stone Raiders went through. As long as they killed the beasts in their way, dying was a small price to pay.

Suzy had been concentrating on her creations, first fighting among the Demon Horde. Then she watched the Stone Raiders' backs as some of the Demon Horde had flanked around them, trying to hit them in the rear.

Now they'd been given a minute to take a breath, she could see the destruction the Horde had brought. Nearly a million from the Demon Horde had died, but at the cost of over a hundred thousand inhabitants of Devil's Crater and its army. More than thirty thousand sported some kind of injury, from minor cuts and bruises to broken bones and life-threatening injuries.

The Stone Raiders used their own gear and Health potions to fix themselves instead of taking the bed of a POE. They had all earned a ton of levels; dying might remove some of them, yet they could come back. If they lost any of the POEs, they couldn't come back.

It was simple math: the Stone Raiders chose death instead of losing future allies.

The Devil's Crater Army might not be the most well-armed and armored force, but they were one of the larger forces on Emerilia, with most of their force over level 100.

The Dwarven artillery brought her back out of her thoughts. They bellowed; Mana projectiles raced over the keep to slam into the cliffs around Devil's Crater.

Fresh Stone Raiders and the new applicants from the Golden Sabres rushed up the road leading to the keep, continuing in their mad dash through the keep and out toward Vrexu and Malkur's forces. They would run support to the DCA brigades, using their skills of detect life and their battle abilities to take down the Demon Horde.

There was just a third left of the Horde. With a starting size of two million, they had nearly six hundred thousand still looking to break in at another location.

The battle was far from over. The defense of Devil's Crater had just begun.

***

Oloh Kragr, lady under the mountain Aldamire, looked through the powerful telescopes of her mountain.

She was a handsome woman, with a permanent scowl on her face. Wrinkles brought about from the stress of her position emphasized her age. She wore a simple miner's garb with a war hammer on her hip that glowed with enchanted energies.

Scars covered her arms and her body. She was a miner first, but she had trained as a shield bearer for many years. She just wished to mine in peace but she was ready to defend her home and her people. Over the centuries, Aldamire had become synonymous with the best defended position in Emerilia. It had never been breached.

It was said that millions of Players and POEs had fed the ground around Aldamire with their bodies.

Every so often there was a kingdom or empire that tried to crack Aldamire. Players also did the same. The single mountain rose out of the ground like a spike of the gods. Across it, different positions could be seen. Artillery cannons peeked out from batteries, ready to rain Mana rounds down on their foes.

Dwarven Warclans roved the area around Aldamire, visiting the city-states that surrounded the mountain, trading with them and creating their own group.

Few empires and kingdoms had tried to attack Aldamire in the last decade. The mountain stronghold had become stronger, and also their ties with the cities around them grew stronger. The city-states that lay around Aldamire traded in all manner of items. Aldamire was one of the few places where you could get foodstuffs. Not many people were looking to start farms outside of a walled city when everything wanted to kill you.

These ties had become so strong that they put no thoughts toward attacking one another or Aldamire, creating a symbiotic relationship.

Aldamire had even supported them with the Dwarven Warclans when they had been attacked by other powers or even strong beast stampedes.

Oloh Kragr frowned. The telescope was not pointed at these cities to see how they were doing. Instead, it pointed to the northwest.

Since the morning, the mages had been sensing massive amounts of Mana being used.

The Dwarven artillery corps had reported seeing Dwarven artillery in the area.

A memory seemed as if it was trying to get through; she felt as though she had heard something about this. She opened up her interface and moved through her messages.

Her frown turned into a curious noise as she opened up an old message from the Council of Anvil and Fire.

To Lady Kragr,

One of our Dwarven Master Smiths has warned that you might see some sort of display to the northwest of your mountain in the coming weeks. He says to not be alarmed. If you desire to speak to him, we can arrange that.

-Council of Anvil and Fire

She dismissed her interface, holding her elbow and tapping her chin in thought.

"Bloody kobolds!" She turned and ran from the telescope room, rushing toward the command center.

Her guard rushed after her as the Dwarven spotters looked to one another and shrugged before they scanned the surrounding area, ever alert for a possible attack.

Kragr ran through the halls. People got out of her way.

It can't be possible, but why else would the council be there? She tapped out a message to the council, sending it as she reached the command center. She stopped over the massive map that had been carved into the floor. She stood on Aldamire in the middle of the floor, heading for the northwest of the map. She pushed a table and chair out of the way.

Underneath, there was a puckered-looking crater.

"Devil's Crater," she said to herself, getting odd views from those around her.

She whirled around and looked to the command staff.

"Wake the Warclans. I want them armed and ready to move within the day! I want telescopes focused on Devil's Crater. Get those who can conjure long-range familiars to send them to Devil's

Crater. I want to know what is going on there and I want to know it yesterday! Bring up the defenses. Do not make it visible. All of the cities are looking to us for warning signs if a force is approaching. I don't think anything is coming toward us, and I don't want to freak them out. I'm going to need time estimates on how long it will take our ready Warclans to reach Devil's Crater with minimal supplies!" Kragr's voice snapped. The room turned into movement with her orders.

In other mountains, people might question her orders. This was Aldamire; they were the mountain fortress of Ashal.

When their lady gave orders, they were followed.

Chapter 13: Red Morning, Bloody Night

Josh looked around at everyone in the room, most of whom were all of the Stone Raiders' leadership and Cassie. Alkao and a wounded Efri also stood in the room with them, overlooking a map of Devil's Crater. Icons scattered around it showed where the Demon Horde were reported to be and where the DCA and Stone Raiders' forces were located. Kala, Malkur, and Vrexu were connected through Mirrors of Communication that the Stone Raiders had lent them.

There was a somber mood to the room. Hard faces and determined eyes paid attention to Vrexu's briefing. Many glanced to the empty seat where Lezar had sat in previous meetings. Even as Lezar had died—his body found next to Yorai's, a mound of Dark Champions around him—the Demon Princes continued forward. They were pillars of the DCA and Devil's Crater. They could not crumble now; their brother had given his life for his people and his home. They would not dishonor him in that way.

"As Malkur was saying, with the Stone Raiders able to track down the Demon Horde, the problem is that we can hit one group of them, but once they hear the sounds of battle, five others will join in. It's easy to get swarmed and we don't know when we'll come across one of the champions." Vrexu looked frustrated as his wings moved in agitation. "My people are getting tired and hungry. I'm going to need to pull them back for food, water, and some rest."

"We have the fresh Stone Raiders and our new recruits out there. They should be good for some time. We're getting the last of the re-spawns from the end of the first battle. We can start hunting down the Demons with parties again. We can take up some of the slack but we just can't cover an area as large as what Vrexu and Malkur's brigades can," Josh said.

"We will have rotating aerial patrols of our best scouts. They can carry Stone Raiders with the best eyes and Surveyor skills to cover a larger area," Alkao said.

Josh nodded. Having a greater vantage point with less things in the way could extend the range of certain skills and spells that they were using to track the Demon Horde.

"Efri, combine what's left of your brigade and Lezar's together. You will be the new reserve force. I want your people ready and able to fly to any of the keeps or cliffs where the Demon Horde looks like they might break through. Move your forces to Unity. Vrexu, pull back your forces first. I will have my brigade move out of the keep and break under my and Krenua's command. I will take Vrexu's brigade's area. Krenua will switch with Malkur." Alkao looked to his brothers and his second-in-command, seeing their understanding of his words.

"We will switch off the armor that Dave gave your forces to arm the reserve force and my own that will be moving in the field. We have held against the Demon Horde. Now we need our people fed and rested. The battle to come will be one of attrition. We will box in the Demon Horde and slowly whittle down their numbers. We will take our time. Rushing in will just lead to the deaths of our soldiers."

Josh saw the understanding in the surrounding generals' eyes.

"I volunteer my force to replace Kala's. We can hold the keeps, freeing her to take our place in the field," Malkur said.

"My people are fresh and ready for battle." Kala looked as fierce as ever, even through a Mirror of Communication.

"Make it so," Alkao said. "Any more suggestions or questions?"

No one had any.

"Well, let's get to work," Alkao said.

Officers started grouping together, talking to one another about how to complete their transition. They all looked weary, most with blood still encrusted on their armor from the battles they had already been in.

Josh looked to Lucy. "Is Dave awake?" he asked as they left the command center.

"Not yet. His body is going through a lot of changes with the amount of power he unlocked." She shrugged.

"Creating nearly two hundred thousand sets of weapons and armor." Dwayne shook his head. A proud grin spread across his face. "We're breeding monsters." Dwayne laughed.

The others joined in.

They were doing things that they wouldn't have dreamed of weeks ago. It was only when they were next to the DCA that they'd been able to see how strong they'd become in their time helping the Aleph.

They'd killed hundreds of thousands of Demons in just the space of a day. They had not won the battle but their force of a few hundred had been comparable to twenty-five thousand soldiers, half a DCA brigade.

The others talked among themselves as Josh moved closer to Cassie, his chest tight with anticipation. He pushed those feelings away. They could wait—the quest and the raid came first.

"Well, it looks like you took our invitation." Josh smiled as she laughed.

"You have a lot of explaining to do. I didn't even know that there were Demons or Beast Kin on Emerilia," she said.

"Well, there weren't a few months ago. We helped them out and helped them fulfill their quest so that they could move their people back to Emerilia." Seeing her expression, he hurried on. "A bunch of creatures are coming back to Emerilia. Most of them bad, but then there are others who were almost wiped out because of the perceived threat they were. Like the Demons, Beast Kin, and the Aleph."

"So, you helped bring the Demons, Aleph, and Beast Kin back to Emerilia? How?"

"Uh, well, we kind of are friends and help out this one dude from the Affinities Pantheon." Josh scratched the back of his head, realizing just how odd his position was. *It kind of just piled up, the next thing and then the next until we got to this point. I wonder where this journey will take us.*

"Who?"

"Well, we call him Bob, but he's known as the Grey God, or Neutral. He's kind of the guy who balances the Pantheon and Emerilia, trying to protect the POEs and the game's stability. He's a really cool AI. It's crazy how realistic they got the AIs in this game. Feels like I'm talking to real people most of the time." Josh looked at the stretchers of wounded that filled the courtyard as they came out of the castle within the keep.

"Yeah, they're almost *too* real. It's easy to get attached." Cassie also looked over the courtyard. "So this 'god' gives you really rare quests and helps to bring these races to Emerilia. Are there going to be more of the Demon Hordes?"

"I don't think so, but there are going to be other creatures. You know that there's a ton of lore in the game, right?"

"Yeah." Cassie nodded.

"Well, every single creature that got too powerful, or that seemed to disappear from the world, like the Dragons, or the Demons and Beast Kin—well, *all* of them are coming back. From rogue Dragons and wizard covens to different cultists. Bob says that the angels might even come back," Josh said.

"Aren't the angels good, though? The Church of Light says that they cleansed the world of the Demon scourge," Cassie said.

"Well, the thing is that the Demons you see around you—all of them rebelled against the Dark Lord. They wanted to lead their own lives. They used to number in the millions. A force that covered all of Devil's Crater and could go to war with the other races. They owned most of Ashal.

"The angels fought them all the time. They had higher levels, a better mastery of their magic and they were organized, unlike the Demons. They didn't have the Demons' numbers but with their magic and their ability to work together, the two forces were evenly matched. With the Demons saying that they wouldn't follow the teachings of the Affinities, the Dark Lord lost a ton of power. It also meant that this massively powerful group wasn't losing their power to their lord or lady. They pushed back the angels.

"The Affinities banded together. At this time, they had a very close connection to those who provided them with devotions. All of the races rose up and fought against the Demons. Bob saved who he could but they were wiped from the face of Emerilia. For the angels who had been killing for years, it created a vacuum. They were grand warriors, but the fight was over and there was no one for them to vent their ire on. For a time, they reveled in their power. Then an idea started. As the Demons had fallen into depravity from not having a lord or lady to follow, there were others without faith. They went around converting whom they could. It turned into killing those who didn't have faith. Then it turned into killing those who didn't believe in the Lady of Light. They led a holy war across Emerilia, powerful fanatics who had overcome the Demons themselves. Bob sealed them away, the knowledge about the angels banned. Now they will return and that knowledge is free." Josh shook his head as he followed the other guild leaders toward where the Stone Raiders were waiting, just outside the keep's walls.

"So we're going to fight angels, who are really just religious fanatics who want to destroy anything that doesn't follow their beliefs?" Cassie looked troubled.

"You're damn right we are." Josh grinned.

"You know how insane that sounds, right?" Cassie asked.

"Ah, well, doing the sane thing is rather boring." Kim joined the conversation, passing the Dwarven batteries that were being checked over. Lucy drifted over to talk to them.

"I wish I joined you lot after Boran-al. Everything got political and stopped being a game after that." Cassie shook her head ruefully.

"Well, we've got plenty more things to do, and I know we'll need someone to actually understand what we're doing. Josh is more happy with going off and hunting down Demons than planning," Dwayne said.

"And you don't want to go hunt the Horde down?" Josh asked.

"Never said that," Dwayne said, a smile almost splitting his face. Josh rolled his eyes as Cassie snorted.

"Bunch of meatheads." Kim looked to Cassie for comfort.

"I feel like I'm way out of the loop. I didn't really get more than the fact that we have three different guild headquarters."

"You have much to learn, young one," Josh said, as if he were some wise old man.

"Don't listen to him too much—will hurt your brain," Kim said.

A monstrous aura filled the area. Cassie started to sweat and fell to her knee.

"Guess Dave's awake," Dwayne said as the pressure lessened.

"That was Dave?" Cassie's legs shook and her face paled.

Weird. This aura thing seems to affect how we feel. How do they do that in the simulation? Josh thought.

"Yeah, he's plenty powerful. Party Zero is our secret weapon. Damn scary bunch. I don't know what they were doing at Benvari, but they're some of the strongest Players we have," Kim said seriously.

"How didn't his aura affect you?" Cassie asked.

"After feeling the Lich Lord's aura in the Aleph's college, there hasn't really been anything with an aura as scary as it. Also, it was only for a few seconds. I'm going to get the scouts ready. Kim, gather the parties that are ready for hunting down the Horde. Dwayne, go and check on Party Zero," Josh said.

"Got it." Dwayne nodded and headed away.

"Yes, master and commander," Kim joked with an over-the-top salute, wheeling on her foot and marching off.

Josh headed for his scouts. Cassie hurried after him. For a while, neither of them said anything.

"So, where do we stand?" Josh asked, unable to keep silent.

"You're my guildmaster and I'm your new recruit." She smiled, that excited twinkle in her eye.

"I meant, *personally*." Josh came to a stop and looked at her.

Cassie's face turned serious as she held her chin in thought. "Well, now that we don't have you keeping me in the dark about everything and we're going to be seeing one another more," her eyes narrowed as if a judge passing sentence on a criminal, "you owe me an expensive restaurant, helping me find out a good place to become an E-head on Earth, and we'll see."

"Decided on becoming an E-head?" Josh smiled at her attempts to try to stay somewhat serious and failed.

"Well, after everything that you told me, it makes sense. There are just so many things going on. I should be able to make enough money just from the streaming. I hate all the traveling. All of the time that I'm not in here. Earth just feels so dull compared to this."

"That I can understand," Josh said. His eyes wandered from Cassie to Emerilia, the POEs and the Players. The moons in the sky signaling late afternoon. "There's nothing really like Emerilia." His eyes came to rest on Cassie. She had been looking over the land as well—the forest, the crater, and its cliffs.

She seemed to freeze as they locked eyes. Josh stepped closer. His arm wrapped around her back slowly and pulled her slightly. She moved forward, her hands going on either side of his head. His free hand brushed a stray hair out of her face.

They kissed gently. The stresses and worries that had built within Josh fell away, a tension easing within him. Their lips parted. Their eyes fluttered open, his green looking into her blue.

"Think of that as a deposit for dinner," Cassie said.

Josh laughed as she moved back a few steps, looking around as people whistled and grinned at their display. Josh grabbed her hand, pulling her toward the keep's walls where the rangers and the other people with long-range scouting abilities were.

Chapter 14: The Worries Of Gods And Kings

King Sigaird looked out over the city of Haugr. People went about their work through the sprawling city. *How long will it last before Gudalo will once again be at war? It was easier when it was against those to our south instead of lords trying to gain more power.*

Sigaird rubbed his salt-and-pepper goatee before he rubbed his bald head in frustration. He turned around as the door to his royal office opened.

"Lady Merguine, to what do I owe the pleasure?" He looked to the entrance into his office. The doors closed behind her. The runes around the doors and windows of his office flared to life.

Merguine's smile fell away as she crossed the office's floor.

Sigaird's own glee turned to a frown.

"He's making a move," Merguine said. She didn't need to say who she was talking about.

"What is Esamael doing?"

"With the new way in and out of the Per'ush bay through Verlun's teleport pad, we've been able to get in more spies and get out more reports than ever before. We've even been able to connect to some old spy networks. Esamael's built himself a well-trained force that doubles as the guard for the cities of Osomi, Myrar, Emaren, Mhjarovik, Verlun, Liefl, and Geldir. He has a heavy presence in Gufaross and Owesa that cut off our messages before." Merguine sat in the seat before Sigaird's desk.

"Do we have anything that we can use against him?" Sigaird asked.

"Nothing yet, though with the Stone Raiders having a teleport pad within the city Verlun, he's got a hole in his net. From what we've been able to learn, it seems that the Stone Raiders' Traders are getting pressured from all sides. If they don't give in to letting Esamael rule them, he's going to get rid of them somehow. Even then, he could say that he was protecting the city or something of the like and get praise for driving out the Player guild," Merguine said, clearly not happy with her news.

"We need to find something, a way to show the people who Esamael really is, and then get rid of him. He cares nothing of the people. Only his greed and need for more power drives him. War will bring us nothing but turmoil." Sigaird held his head in frustration. "What have the mage's guild and college said?"

"Nothing. They're making it clear that what happens is our business. If it comes near to touching their members or interests, they will defend themselves. They will also watch over any battle to make sure that the rules of war are followed to the letter," Merguine said.

"Good to know that they are at least reliable in their impartiality." Sigaird snorted.

"Unless we have something to show that he has overstepped his boundaries as the lord of Emaren, then we can say nothing. With the guards, they have just gone through his training camps and then to their different posts. All of it is normal in our own kingdom. We do it with the guard forces for most of the cities around Haugr," Merguine reminded Sigaird.

"I know." Sigaird tapped his fingers on his desk, thinking. "Okay, we'll quietly get some of our forces on active duty moved from the southern border up to near Mhjarovik. If something happens, I want to have people in place to do something about it. Cutting off Esamael from those other city guards in different places will help us out. What information do we have on these Stone Raiders?"

Merguine's pretty face turned pensive. "I'm not sure. We know that they destroyed a guild that made it their job to hunt down other Players and hard-to-reach people of Emerilia. Then, they disappeared without a trace from within Selhi. They seemed to appear in a flurry of a few days, appearing out of teleport pads and then disappearing again. One of their members is supposed to be a Dwarven Master Smith who owns the smithies of Cliff-Hill and the ceramics factory. They're one of the strongest reported raiding parties. They've got good coordination in both large-party fighting tactics and regular party-sized tactics. They also have powerful weapons that they have to get fixed by Dwarven Master Smiths. We have reports of them going to a half-dozen unknown teleport pad locations."

"Where are they now?" Sigaird asked.

"We don't know. They disappeared again within a few days of a bunch of them reappearing after disappearing for six months. They seemed to all be in a hurry. Every member of their guild who could drop what they were doing, did so. I have also got reports that the Golden Sabres Guild collapsed and many of their higher level Players chose to go with their guildmaster and join the Stone Raiders, wherever they might be."

"So, we know barely anything about them. Damned mysteries that have been seen fighting like Demons possessed, then they've disappeared. So, other than being a mystery, can they be a threat to us if they are thrown out of Verlun? I ask in case we are not fast enough to assist them," Sigaird said.

Merguine paused and looked to the side, as if trying to find the right words. It was a few seconds before she looked back at Sigaird, right into his eyes.

"The guild that attacked them in Selhi Capital has been devastated. The Stone Raiders placed a curse upon their very souls. It burned them until they changed their skins. The Stone Raiders would appear in the middle of the night from unknown locations into cities with teleport pads and slaughter all those who had attacked them. The magistrate of Selhi Capital has been removed by the queen for her ban on them. When the leader of the Stone Raiders was turned away and hunted down, some in the Stone

Raiders let out their aura. Even then, they were as strong as, if not stronger than, level 100s. There is no knowing how strong they are now," Merguine said.

"What about their raids? How good are they in large-scale battles?" Sigaird asked, the boy who had been trained in the matters of war as much as state coming through.

"They were the first guild with the Golden Sabres to open a portal to the Alturaran lands. They still hold rights to the portal in Opheir. They fought Boran-al's cultists and a Xelur Demon abomination. Dragons were seen assisting them. I can only make guesses at their abilities, though they seem like a guild that one would be an idiot to try to go up against."

"What do you think Esamael will do?" Sigaird sat back and watched Merguine as his own thoughts swirled around his mind.

"I think that he believes himself much smarter than he really is. He knows how to handle the POE and he is subtle in dealing with the Players. But with a blatant challenge like putting a teleport pad within his lands? He is not the kind of man to take that lying down. He might be smart, but he's smart at fighting and hiding his actions. He is not good at hiding his intent and he's a proud man." Merguine shrugged.

"So, he will attack them and we have to decide whether to tell them or not." Sigaird stroked his goatee. On the one hand, he could keep them in the dark, waiting for Esamael to make a mistake and then sweep in with his army from the south. The Stone Raiders might die but they would come back from death. They might lose their place within Verlun and look for revenge. If he told the Stone Raiders, he might lose the element of surprise, but he might have their gratitude and still have the threat of Esamael waiting for him in Emaren.

If the Stone Raiders found out that he had known something and hadn't told them, there was no telling how they'd react. *They do think that we are some kind of constructs made to entertain them.*

No matter his decision, it could backfire on him. He just needed to look for the best possible solution: one that would lead to the least death, removed Esamael, and reduced the tension within Gudalo.

***

The video stopped. Silence filled the room.

Bob looked to Fire and Water.

"So turning your Creatures of Power into your champions *doubles* their strength?" Water said, not really believing what he was seeing.

"Yes, but I'm more interested in where the hell he got all of that power from. He certainly hasn't been saving it up with everything else he's been doing. I've been going through all the information I have and he's not getting it from Emerilia. I don't know where he's drawing it from." Bob shook his head.

"Maybe he has a tap into the ley lines?" Fire said.

"I haven't found any large disturbances into the ley lines other than the Aleph power stations." Bob spotted Water's brow rising.

"With the Creatures of Power and champions restriction being used, all of the creatures I locked away are now coming out to play. I gave the forces that were actually looking to keep Emerilia peaceful time to come back and regain their former glory. When the Creatures of Power and the champions who have been locked away start roaming Emerilia, we're going to need them to stop the planet from falling into chaos," Bob said.

"All of them?" Water's face paled with the news.

Bob nodded.

"I thought that it was only a few of them." Water looked shocked. "What about the angels?" Water's voice was almost panicked.

"They're coming," Bob confirmed, "though that is a later problem. The fact that the Dark Lord has enough power to make nearly a thousand champions in the space of a day is a problem we need to deal with now. We need to know where he's getting that power and how we can cut him off from it. I can't use my administrative powers, though I can still use my magic."

"This kind of power outlet—maybe he's found a new way of harvesting Dark energy into power?" Fire said.

"Like Dark matter?" Bob said, his voice serious. "The amount of power within Dark matter if he could somehow tap into it would be tremendous."

"With you not having your administrative abilities, can we do anything against him?" Water asked.

"We might not be able to, but maybe the emperor of the Jukal Empire would like to have some more power from Emerilia. We can cite how he has a massive draw of power and then siphon it off as tribute to the empire," Bob said.

"Sneaky, but it could work. With the power levels he displayed, he's more powerful than anyone else in the Pantheon," Fire said.

"We shouldn't forget that we aren't the only ones who would have picked up on this battle," Water warned.

"Earth and Dark have always had a close relationship. The issue with Boran-al made them tense, but now with Dark showing this kind of power, Earth will most likely make amends and they will continue to work together. Do we know what Earth has been up to?" Fire asked.

"He's been building up his Creatures of Power and his champions. I wouldn't doubt that he's spent all of his saved Mana on his creatures and champions. With his aggressive strategy, he's going to gain rewards from his power rather quickly," Bob said.

Fire and Water nodded their heads, knowing the kind of power that came with investing heavily in those who would level up quickly and have such a large Mana pool as to increase the power devotions they gave to their lord or lady of the Pantheon.

Fire and Water didn't keep devotions that people devoted to them, drawing from their Mana and thus training up their Intelligence and Willpower. Although the rest of the Pantheon kept this power, Fire and Water gave the power right back to the POE and Players.

If they were to keep that power to themselves and not give it back to those who gave them devotions, then their power would compete with the Lady of Light and the Dark Lord.

"What will the Jukal Empire do with these new changes?" Fire asked.

"I don't know. They've been watching everything through the Stone Raiders' live implants; they know that the Aleph are back—the Demons and Beast Kin as well.

"From my feelers, it seems that they are excited for everything happening. The emperor could try and get them put away, but it would go against popular opinion. Emerilia keeps the people entertained and not thinking about their lives as drones. Making changes that would piss them off and make them look to the emperor in anger are not likely avenues. It's harder and harder for me to talk to my friends with all of the empire tuning in to try to catch a glance of them. I have to make time while Dave is using the Mirror of Communication."

Fire went a little pale. Bob looked away, so as to not draw Water's eyes.

"You said that we couldn't be watched by the empire, though?" Water asked.

"Well, we don't have the same implants as the POEs and Players. Though any interactions with Players or POEs can be recorded, your Creatures of Power cannot record this information since they're made from your own Mana. We need to start thinking about the kind of information that we want the empire to have and not," Bob said.

"You're scared that they're going to see how powerful Emerilia's residents are and start adding in factors to bring them back down?" Fire guessed.

"Something like that," Bob admitted. "We're going to have some of the biggest fights we know happening. We've got a few months before portals start opening on their own to different lands. Then, we've got a war coming that will either destroy the people of Emerilia or have survivors who are the strongest beings we have ever seen. What do you think that the empire is going to do when the race that tore through their fleets now have power to rival the minders that they put into place?"

"They'll clear the slate and reseed Emerilia," Water said.

"They'll try." Fire's determined eyes found Water's. He nodded in agreement.

Bob saw the fierce stubbornness in the two gods' eyes. A smile passed over his face.

"To quote a very old series: I love it when a plan comes together!" Bob said, getting confused looks from Water and Fire.

Chapter 15: Revelation

Dave woke up in a rush and tossed off the sheets that restrained him, looking for a threat, looking for the impending Demon Horde. He staggered slightly, finding that his perception of time was off once again.

"Dave, aura." Deia's voice slightly was strained.

He pulled back in his aura, suppressing it as he realized that he was in a fort that had been placed at the base of the steep path to Alkao's keep.

"What happened? Did the enchantment work?" Dave's notifications bar blinked at him angrily.

"It worked. All of the DCA fighting with us and up in the keep got those soul gems that made weapons and armor," Deia said in a calming voice. She sat on a chair facing Dave as he sunk back onto the cot.

"Good, good." Dave still felt tired but his mind was a whirlwind. His higher Intelligence buzzed through his mind; information started to bleed through his memories as he made connections and began to understand more.

"Wow, I should have done that from the beginning. I didn't put in the right control system. I would need to have it much bigger to do that, though. Huh. I guess those mega mecha animes might have been onto something." Dave snorted and lay back down as his mind continued to race.

"Dave, are you okay?" Deia asked, her concern clear. Dave conjured wheels under her chair, and slid her chair forward. She let out a surprised squeak as she came to stop next to his bed.

He grabbed her arms, smiling as he pulled her onto him and the cot.

Their armor clinked together.

"Better." Dave sounded content as he wrapped her up in a hug.

Deia rolled her eyes and kissed his forehead.

"Though, the damn armor's in the way. Unless there's something you haven't told me, I think your knee guard is jabbing me in the leg," Dave said.

Deia laughed, relief clear as she gave him a real kiss. Dave returned it and sighed.

"You want to know what happened?" Deia asked.

"One second. Need to write a few things down. Got an Intelligence high from all those stats," Dave said, writing down notes on his interface.

"My Dave, the ever constant crafter," she purred, kissing his cheek and laying on his breastplate. Nothing had gotten through his Mana barrier, leaving it unmarred.

Dave smiled and looked to her. He squeezed her gently with his left arm that was still wrapped around her. She had made him a better man and was willing to deal with his eccentric and quirky ways. He kissed her hair briefly and continued his hurried note-taking.

"I don't know of anyone who had put in over sixty levels of stats into themselves in one go. Why did you do it?" Deia asked.

Dave continued to write as he explained. "I knew that there had to be a way to change the tide of the battle. The Demon Horde was nowhere near as effective as the DCA's soldiers one-on-one. The problem was that the Demon Horde had so many more people. Everyone underestimates the power of even simple weapons and armor. They let the user worry less about little wounds, to take a hit to take down their enemy. A sword will take down someone much faster than claws. I wanted to make weapons for everyone but just straight conjuring them would drain me of power and knock me right out. I put in the Intelligence to slow down my perception of time more, giving me the time to figure out what the hell I could do to conjure as many weapons and armor as possible."

"So, you came up with soul weapons? How do they work?"

"The soul gem has inside it a set of instructions, basically a magical coding of conjuration. I built the cores, allowed our armor to channel power into them and then sent them out to the DCA. I imprinted instructions on my armor to act as a factory for the things. It created the soul gems and I picked out where they went to. Fueled with the power of our armor, the soul gems turned from just looking after themselves to carrying out the magical coding within them. They turned into armor, shields, and swords. If I did it all by myself, then I would have fallen apart. I simply made a very complex set of magical coding on my armor to make magically coded soul gems and then feed power through my armor, kind of like me sending instructions to a 3D printer to make another printer that prints a picture." Dave closed his notepad.

"You're crazy." Deia kissed Dave. "But you're my crazy." She looked into his eyes.

"Wouldn't want it any other way." His arms encircled her in her armor. They kissed once again.

"I'll tell the others that you're up, though I don't think many people missed your aura seeping out. Make sure that you get those notifications sorted out. You've got two more classes you have to pick. If you're good for it, the DCA needs people to help them hunt down the six hundred thousand remaining Demons who are trying to get over the cliffs and into Devil's Crater." Deia rose.

Dave made a complaining noise and pulled her back down to him.

"I'll be back soon enough." She kissed him.

"Uh, fine, better be fast!" He pouted.

She gave him another quick kiss and smiled at him. Dave couldn't keep up his pout anymore, and it turned into a wide grin.

She laughed, getting off Dave and heading out of their tent. "Remember to check those notifications!" she yelled back.

Dave grinned and opened his notification bar.

Active Skill: Inference

Level: Expert Level 7

Effect: 77% increased chance of using moves you've read in books.

Active Skill: One handed and Shield

Level: Master Level 4

Effect: Weapons damage increased by 44%. Defense increases by 22%; shield bash is 20% more likely to stun opponent.

Cost: 20 Stamina

Active Skill: Spell formation

Level: Master Level 1

Effect: You use 25% less Mana and your spells are 80% stronger.

Active Skill: Soul Manipulation

Level: Master Level 4

Effect: Tools you make to manipulate souls and their energy is 90% stronger. Able to use Soul energy to fuel spells. 20% increase to soul energies reserves (can only be used for spells; does not act as extra Willpower points).

Cost: Dependent on creation.

Active Skill: Magical Circuits

Level: Master Level 10

Effect: Upon breaking down Magical Circuits, you understand how they function. 50% Reduction of cost in making Magical Circuits.

Cost: Dependent

You have created a new skill
Upon reaching the mastery of a requisite skill, you are recognized as a master of Magical Coding, a subset of Magical Circuits. For this, you gain the class:
Skill Creator

New Active Skill: Magical Coding

Level: Master Level 1

Effect: You remember every magical code you've made or seen and have and encyclopedic knowledge of the runes you've seen.

Cost: Dependent

New Class: Skill Creator
You have gone beyond regular skills, mastering them in the pursuit for more. You have created a new skill in your endeavors

Status:	Level 1
	+20 Intelligence
Effects:	+20 Endurance
	+20 Willpower

Class: Champion Slayer

Status: Level 2

Effect:

Relationship with Affinities Pantheon:

Dark: Hated

Light: Favorable

Fire: Trusted Friend

Water: Favorable

Earth: Angered

Air: Neutral

+2 to all stats

Quest: Champion Slayer Level 3

Kill 10 Champions (0/10)

Rewards: Unlock Level 4 Quest

Increase to stats

Increased/Decreased reputation with Affinities

Level 217

You have reached level 217; you have **511** stat points to use.

Stat Increase

+1 Strength

+2 Intelligence

+1 Endurance

+1 Willpower

Pick a new class

Upon reaching level 50, you may pick one more class or change your old classes.

Pick a new class

Upon reaching level 100, you may pick one more class or change your old classes.

"Well, okay then." Dave rubbed his hands together as he looked through the all-encompassing list of classes. There were quite literally hundreds of them.

Most of the ones that could be gained by actual work increased the person's attributes levels. The ones that could only be bought with each class had other options. There was Herb Gatherer, or Mine Manager. Each of them got a certain amount of resources from different sources. Leveling them up meant either putting in more class points or spending gold on them.

With Dave's burst of knowledge, he had come up with an idea, one that too many mecha animes and a love for heavy armor had brought about. Added with the functionality he remembered from Rock Breakers space suits, he was going to need a ton of resources.

Then there's the other fact that the Dark Lord has painted a target on my back.

He needed options to deal with whatever the Dark Lord sent. His idea went a long way to doing that.

With a half-second of thought, he grabbed the Miner Manager Class. He used most of his gold to put it to the second class level.

You have earned a new class: Mine Manager

You have become a manager of a mine! Provide more gold to this class in order to increase productivity! Items will be delivered to you once a week.

Status:	Level 2
	Every week you gain:
	10 Steel ingots
Effects:	1 Silver ingot
	1 Ebony ingot
	Chance to get 6 random ores

Happy with that, Dave looked to his character sheet and Affinities.

Character Sheet

Name:	David Grahslagg	Gender:	Male
Level:	115	Class:	Dwarven Master Smith, Friend of the Grey God, Bleeder, Librarian, Aleph Engineer, Weapons Master, Champion Slayer, Skill Creator, Mine Manager
Race:	Human/ Dwarf	Alignment:	Chaotic Neutral

Unspent points: 511

Health:	21,100	Regen:	8.42 /s
Mana:	6,960	Regen:	19.45 /s
Stamina:	2,770	Regen:	15.15 /s
Vitality:	211	Endurance:	421
Intelligence:	696	Willpower:	389
Strength:	277	Agility:	318

Affinity Levels

Dark 241 Light 173

Fire 193 Water 142

Earth 218 Air 172

"Okay, so, I've got one more class. My stats are high as hell and I should get some bonuses once we finish clearing out the Demon Horde. My Affinities are damn high, though my Light is low, especially if I'm going to be fighting the Dark Lord. Ugh, this is complicated."

He continued to stare as a million ideas raced around his brain.

"Okay, first—my attribute shortcomings, I can make up with my armor. Affinity, well, I can conjure something to deal with whatever I face. Unless it's a damn magic suppressor." Dave muttered the last part darkly. "Now our biggest advantage is our maneuverability. To get from one place to another. It's why no Dwarven mountain has ever been conquered. All of them can link to one another, mutually supporting. The portals will open soon and we need to have support ready to go through and smash them up, so we can continue to level up and make the creatures coming out of Bob's freezer have a bad time."

Why do I feel like I'm just trying to support the decision I've already made? Dave chuckled to himself and went down the list, clicking on a class he had seen the first time he checked through the list.

Class: Master Summoner

Filled with the knowledge of creatures from beyond the physical planes and Emerilia's borders, you create links between planes, pulling creatures through and binding them to your will.

It was a class that Dave couldn't work toward and gain in a reasonable amount of time, unlike Suzy. He didn't want it for the soul binding techniques of master and creature contracts. He wanted it to understand more about breaking into different realms and planes.

He chose the class.

You have earned a new class: Master Summoner

You have picked the class Master Summoner.

Status: Level 1

Effects: Soul binding will not fail on creatures thirty levels higher than you.

Able to understand which planes you are connecting to.

+30 Willpower

Dave laid there, looking at it all.

He sighed and switched to view his character sheet and his new Willpower stat.

Character Sheet

Name:	David Grahslagg	Gender:	Male
Level:	115	Class:	Dwarven Master Smith, Friend of the Grey God, Bleeder, Librarian, Aleph Engineer, Weapons Master, Champion Slayer, Skill Creator, Mine Manager, Master Summoner
Race:	Human/ Dwarf	Alignment:	Chaotic Neutral

Unspent points: 511

Health:	21,100	Regen:	8.42 /s
Mana:	6,960	Regen:	20.05 /s
Stamina:	2,770	Regen:	15.15 /s
Vitality:	211	Endurance:	421
Intelligence:	696	Willpower:	419
Strength:	277	Agility:	318

"Okay, well, that idea was a dud." Dave pushed himself upward before he was overcome by a sort of vertigo.

"Ahhh, shheee! Man, this is the worst brain freeze ever!" Dave yelled, gripping onto the side of the cot. Information rushed through his mind—techniques on summoning circles and how to open different planes. A smorgasbord of information seemed to open up within his mind.

It finally dissipated after some time, leaving Dave panting with fresh sweat rolling down his face.

Suzy opened the tent's flap. "What did you do now?"

The rest of the party was behind her. Deia walked past her and into the tent.

"I figured out how to get you a contracted creature." Dave smiled.

"Are you okay?" Deia checked Dave over.

"Yeah, just a lot of information to process. With my high Intelligence, I think I made way more connections than I thought I would. Damn, I have a few ideas of how the portals work, even." Dave looked to Malsour.

"Well, that can wait for now. We're needed to support Kala's forces that are moving into the field. We've got an hour. Everyone, get some food into you and we'll get going soon." Deia looked to the rest of the party.

They quickly moved to their own nearby tents and started working on getting ready.

"Well, I think I need a shower." Dave raised a hand. A small shower appeared on the side of the tent.

"Are you sure you're okay?" Deia asked.

"Come join me in the shower and I'll show you just how okay I really am." Dave winked.

Deia pursed her lips. "Fine, but hands to yourself. We've got work to do."

"Okay." Dave smiled, and then destroyed half of the shower and conjured a bigger shower with multiple shower heads. "Damn, I could get used to this new control. With the higher Intelligence stat, it's so much easier to make complex things."

Deia dropped her armored breastplate on the ground, followed by her shirt underneath.

Dave stopped admiring his newfound skills, instead focusing on the beauty in front of him.

"You can't go into a shower with full armor." Deia's pants dropped to the floor.

"Umm, okay," Dave said, numbly pulling off his armor as Deia glanced back at him. She took her time walking to the shower and turning it on as Dave dismissed his armor.

She looked back at Dave, biting her lip. "You going to hurry up and join me?" She pivoted on her foot, showing off her full figure before she stepped into the shower.

Dave nearly fell flat on his face with the whole new perception of time, but he somehow made his way into the shower. His hands fell on her shoulders, working on the kinks that lay there.

She let out a relaxed groan, moving backward so that she was pressed up against his lower half. Dave's hands worked on her back, edging downward and then snaking across her front. He swept her hair away from the side of her neck and kissed it lightly.

"I said no touching," Deia purred, her hands reaching back to find him.

"Some rules were made to be broken," Dave whispered in her ear, biting it gently.

A message appeared in his view.

Private Message: Kol

Kol> Lady Kragr of Aldamire Mountain wishes to speak to you. It seems that she saw some magical artillery coming from Devil's Crater.

I'll talk to her later!

***

"With what we've learned from the portals, we've been able to come up with a number of different circuits that could reduce the power draw and increase the range of the teleport pads without having to use one to jump the others' signal to get all the way around Emerilia. Of course, we're looking into the magical coding side of things. With Dave's skill, it seems that we will be able to reduce that power draw even further and our corrections will not need to be so strict on short jumps, thus less intensive, unless the other items we're connecting to are way out of alignment." Ela-Dorn took a deep breath as she looked at the council members.

She looked as though she hadn't slept in days and she couldn't give a damn about sleep or anything that got in the way of her research. Hamdir hid a smile behind his hand, knowing the work that it had taken to get her out of the college and to Alephir to report to the council.

Her people were coming out with new ideas and firming up theories. It was one hell of an impressive feat.

"You say over longer distances—how long are we talking?" Frenik asked.

"Well, we can connect to portals right now, but they've been stuck on a singular system. For all of their advances, they're linked to one another. Have one portal here, then another at a different location, put them on the same frequency and link them up. As long as they are given power, then they will connect to one another indefinitely. With the teleport pads, we can connect to multiple different locations, but then we're thinking about differences on a planet. There are a lot less things we have to worry about. The portals' connecting frequencies, which we are still trying to figure out, are pretty difficult, though I would say that we could connect to another portal on some of the closest planets or moons where portals are located." Ela-Dorn shrugged.

A shocked silence filled the room. They all knew of the difficulties that the technicians and academics had talked about with connecting two teleport pads over Emerilia. Being able to do it between entire star systems was a lot to take in.

"Well, it seems that you and your fellows have been rather busy," Hamdir said.

"It's hard to get away. It's so fascinating; we are finally getting an answer to all we've been thinking of," Ela-Dorn said with a proud smile.

"Unfortunately, we can't talk about the portal and all we've learned from it for the entire meeting. First, I must bring a request that Josh of the Stone Raiders has made. He and his forces are fighting with the Beast Kin and Demons of Devil's Crater against the Demon Horde sent by the Dark Lord. Their forces were badly mauled. They're currently hunting down nearly six hundred thousand Demons and Demon Champions around the cliffs of Devil's Crater. Josh has asked for our help in clearing the area."

Before Hamdir could continue, Sela spoke up. "What kind of support do they need?" The usually laid-back Gnome leaned forward, her face serious as she looked to Hamdir.

Hamdir closed his mouth as he looked around the table. "I know that the Stone Raiders have helped us out a lot, but are you sure we want to show ourselves like this?" Hamdir asked.

Koza raised his hand. Hamdir indicated for him to talk.

"The Stone Raiders didn't need to help us, but they did. They've cleared out our cities and facilities, something that we couldn't have done for another few centuries. As you said, we need to look outward instead of just inward. We share a common bond with the people of Devil's Crater. They were banished like us. As we were helped in our time of need, we must help those in the same situation. Anything else and we have failed. I ask what the Stone Raiders need. Me and mine will be proud to support them," Koza said.

As Hamdir looked around the table, he knew the people there. He had served on the council with them for many years as the rest of Emerilia seemed determined to hunt them down before the Pantheon finally found a way into their homes, trying to root them out.

They were no longer the scared people who had hid in fear, thinking that any moment one of the Pantheon's forces would flood their homes, slaughtering all.

They remembered that mind-numbing fear. They knew what it was like to call for allies and have none answer. The Stone Raiders had answered, even when they were at their weakest and most vulnerable. They had come and helped, laying down their lives and their hard-won experience, to come back again and again until they saved the Aleph's homes.

"Josh requests scouts if we can send them. There is a large area where the Demon Horde is spread out. If they know where they are, then they might be able to help deal with it all. There are many wounded; people are without shelter and it is cold," Hamdir said.

"I have passed out the message," Shard said.

Hamdir looked up to Shard, seeing a proud smile on his face. When Hamdir left, he had felt like Shard's caretaker. Now it felt as though Shard were some kind of guiding spirit, watching over those who fell under his protection.

"We can help with most of these military matters." Koza nodded.

"With the new enchanted greenhouses, we can easily spare some food," Meda added. "I know that a few of the healers would also volunteer their services."

"I have maintenance workers who are good at shifting dirt around and making shelters," Sela added.

"My people can help out with building and fixing as needed." Frenik looked to Sela, who nodded in thanks for his support.

"Koza, you go first with the automatons and controllers you need. Liaise with the forces within the crater and see what other aid we can provide," Hamdir said.

"I will see to it immediately." Koza stood and saluted Hamdir.

"Very well." Hamdir nodded to Koza. The Elf Halfling turned and marched out of the room. All across Alephir and the Aleph's facilities, automatons started coming online, storage racks moving as the automaton legions of the Aleph activated for the first time in over three hundred years.

Chapter 16: With Friends Like This

Dave touched the small Mirror of Communication he had looted from a PKP member. As he was watching Deia dry her hair with a directed Fire spell, the tent and she disappeared.

He appeared in the conference room that the Council of Anvil and Fire met at every week.

Waiting for him was a hard-looking woman.

Her eyes locked onto Dave as soon as he walked into the room.

Oloh Kragr

Dwarf

Level 285

"Well, you must have damn Giant's blood in you to be that damned tall." She looked Dave over.

"Nah, just Dwarf Halfling. Guess I got the height from the Human side." Dave took a seat opposite her.

"And the bulk of the Dwarves. You must be Dave Grahslagg, the first Master Smith who isn't full Dwarf. Hope you aren't one of those mutts who just gets their body modified without actually having the strength to back it up." Oloh's eyes narrowed as she studied Dave.

"This is all me, though I don't think that my physical proportions are the purpose of this meeting." Dave gave her a pointed look.

"Well, yer a damned Dwarf, that's for sure. Hate all that flowery talking crap. Right, you been shooting off a ton of magic over in Devil's Crater?" Oloh asked.

"Yeah," Dave said.

"Why?"

Dave thought about trying to keep the information from her. She would find out about it soon enough and maybe he could forge an alliance between Aldamire and the Devil's Crater residents.

"The Dark Lord made a Demon Horde and directed them to walk across Ashal in order to become more powerful. They were supposed to settle in Devil's Crater. You might have heard that in a year or so that there will be creatures that threatened Emerilia's survival coming back from the grave. Well, not all of them were bad people. We helped the Demons who rebelled against the Pantheon and the Beast Kin who disappeared a few centuries ago. They were in Devil's Crater and they weren't going to give it up to the twisted Demon Horde under the Dark Lord. Yesterday, the Demon Horde reached the cliffs surrounding Devil's Crater. We killed nearly one and a half million of the Demon Horde, but there are still hundreds of thousands who escaped death and are now trying to find a way through the cliffs and keeps of the crater to try to finish off the creatures living here."

Oloh looked to Dave, as if analyzing how true his words were. "You swear on yer hammer?" she asked, her voice solemn.

"I swear on my hammer," Dave agreed.

She took a deep breath before letting it out slowly. "Well, damn. That is one hell of a pickle. These Beast Kin and Demons in Devil's Crater, what are they like? Are they honorable folk?"

"The Beast Kin have a code of honor that would make Dwarves give them some grudging respect. The Demons used to be rather wild but now they are finally getting their footing and figuring out their place in the world as not just a roaming horde, but as a race putting down roots," Dave said.

Oloh rapped her knuckles on the table for a bit, looking to the ceiling and thinking.

"Right." She hit her knuckles against the table with finality. "Should I be worried that Aldamire might be attacked?"

"I don't believe so. As the Demon Horde dispersed, what I've heard is they've been trying to find other ways into Devil's Crater."

"So, would be best to keep them there and fight them?" Oloh said dryly.

"I would think so," Dave agreed.

Oloh took a deep breath. "I have two full Warclans and their supporting artillery, mages, and engineers who are ready to move in a moment's notice. I can get them to you in about six hours. I will have four more clans ready to move an hour after that." Oloh's eyes found Dave's.

"Aldamire's forces are yours to command, Master Smith."

For a few minutes, Dave didn't say anything. He had seen some of the power that the Council of Anvil and Fire gave him with the new artillery he'd been lent. Now, he was able to call upon the Warclans of Aldamire to support his cause that the council had given their blessing for.

"Thank you, Lady Kragr," Dave said.

"I know my oaths and trust in the council." She waved off his thanks.

"Still, it is a large risk to fight someone else's battles when you could have looked the other way. As for transport, there is no need for the Warclans to walk when they can use the teleport pads." Dave sent her a message with the information she would need to connect with the teleport pad within Unity.

"Impressive. How did they get a teleport pad?"

"We gave them one." Dave shrugged.

Kragr's eyebrow rose in apparent shock. She let out a little laugh and shook her head. "I've heard stories of you and the Stone Raiders. It seems that the stories weren't as wild as I thought."

***

The teleport pad activated. The Stone Raiders watching the pad and the DCA backing them up immediately went on alert. No one had told them of anyone coming through the teleport pad.

A Half-Elf wearing ebony and steel armor covered in powerful runes and Magical Circuits stepped out.

"I am Council Member Koza. Josh said that he required reinforcements?" Koza asked.

"One second, sir. I will contact him," Matt said. He was one of the crafters who had been learning under Dave while they put Aleph's facilities back together.

"He sends his thanks. He will make sure that word of your arrival is passed around. He asks that you meet him up at Alkao's keep." Matt shared a waypoint with Koza.

"Very well." Koza closed his interface.

As he did so, automatons started jogging out of the teleport pad. Dozens of scouts headed for Alkao's keep.

Koza took off at a jog, outpacing the automatons. Matt watched the flood of creatures.

***

Malkur watched the approaching automatons. They had run out of the teleport pad and through the city in single file. As they exited Unity, they formed into four wide and fifty deep ranks. Controllers, Aleph who commanded the automatons, ran beside their creations. It was hard to tell them apart because their armor was in the same style as the automatons' bodies.

There was something powerful about seeing two hundred creations all moving as one. Their feet made a rhythmic pounding as the first groups of scouts were followed by flying drones that whizzed out over Alkao's keep and searched the cliffs around Devil's Crater for signs of the Demon Horde. Fighter, archer, and finally behemoth formations marched to support the DCA.

Just who the hell are these Stone Raiders? With more training and proper equipment, I wonder if we, too, will have the same impression as these Aleph.

"General, we have reports that the teleport pad is active again. This time, there's Dwarves coming through!" one of the aides nearby said.

Malkur enhanced his sight, looking to Unity as a dark group started to emerge from the city, following after the automatons.

Then the drums started, striking a chill down Malkur's spine. He knew those drums. They were the drums of a marching Dwarven Warclan. He remembered all too easily how the small but bulky Dwarves had used their armor and shields to keep the Demons at bay. They were relentless, never tiring, never upset nor happy.

If there was ever an enemy Malkur never wanted to fight in open plains or attack in defensive positions, it was the Dwarven Warclans.

The drums beat out a tempo as Malkur surveyed the Warclans sub-groups. Blackened steel armor covered every inch of their bodies, turning them into miniature tanks. As they marched, their line never wavered. It was perfectly straight, with the Dwarven shields on their backs, ready to be deployed in a moment's notice.

They moved in units of one thousand shield bearers. Battle mages, engineers, and their war machines followed. Ten square formations formed and marched out of Unity, their steps in time with their war drum adding to the volume.

"When the Dwarves march, the very earth is their war drum," Malkur said.

"What was that?" Vrexu asked from beside Malkur.

"Never attack a Dwarf's home or be the focus of their ire. Those armored bastards will hunt you and grind you into paste." Malkur didn't look away from the moving masses of their reinforcements.

"Maybe they can help teach some of our people? I sure as hell don't want to fight them," Vrexu said.

***

Dave and Josh walked into the command center, glancing at the Mirrors of Communication set up for those who were away.

The three Dwarves, talking among themselves, moved to greet them as they entered.

Their leader saluted Dave. "Warclan Leader Fonrir at your service, Master Smith," he said. The two behind him stood ram-rod straight; one male, one female, both with eyes that Dave knew only too well from other POE veterans.

"Good to meet you, Fonrir. I take it that you got my message on the situation?" Dave asked.

"We did. We have been talking with the Dwarven artillery corps that was deployed here to fill in the gaps. We are ready to be of service in whatever manner you need," Fonrir said.

"Thank you, Warclan Leader," Dave said. Observing the man's manner and way he held himself, Dave felt that the Dwarf knew what he was doing.

A Halfling Elf with Aleph armor stepped up and greeted Josh.

"I am Council Member Koza. I have been sent with military reinforcements. The Aleph look forward to supporting our allies. We are capable of rendering aid in a number of ways." Koza looked to the Demons and Beast Kin in the room. "And our fellow returning races."

Smooth operator, Dave thought, seeing the Elf give a reassuring smile to the Beast Kin and Demon leaders.

"Well, it looks like everyone is here. Let us get started," Alkao said from his Mirror of Communication. "Malkur, could you give us an update on the situation?"

All eyes turned to Malkur.

"General Kala and Alkao's forces are sweeping out along the cliffs of Devil's Crater, hunting down any of the Demon Horde that are left. As night falls, their forces will set camp and wait out the night. The Demon Horde is scattered all across the area around Devil's Crater, looking for ways inside. There are multiple ways through the cliffs and the keeps, especially to creatures who can fly. It seems that the champions are the only ones capable of flying at this point in time. We expect for that to change in the near future. The Stone Raiders are using their varying abilities to track down the Demons, but it is slow work. It will take months to clear the area at our current rate." Malkur glanced to Dave. "Also, the armor and weapons that the DCA are currently using are already starting to dispel. We have more orders out for weapons and armor, but our forces will become much less effective."

Koza raised his hand as it became clear that Malkur was finished.

"Council Member Koza," Alkao said, nodding to the Half-Elf.

"I have brought with me a large number of flying drones and scout automatons. They can look from the skies and the ground to find the Demon Horde. My automatons are good fighters, but they are best at defending positions rather than moving over rough terrain. They could bolster your different keeps' positions," Koza suggested.

"That would be much appreciated. Josh's scouts are leading the hunt right now; he would be the best person to coordinate with," Alkao said.

Josh and Koza nodded to one another.

"I can also help with weapons and armor somewhat. We can produce a large quantity of items of decent quality at very high speeds. The Dwarves' weapons are better, but we can make them much faster," Koza said.

The Dwarves seemed to stand a little straighter with that, eyeing Koza with interest. Dave hid his smile at their antics.

Fonrir put his hand up. "My two Warclans can support your DCA, though I think it might be best if we took the front lines. We're stronger fighting in a formation of just Dwarves. Our artillery can set up in the keeps to provide support. The engineers can work through the cliffs and seal up openings in them, though they will probably need help in getting around the cliffs."

"Our Demons can assist in flying them through the mountains between different trouble spots." Alkao paused and looked to Kala, whose hand shot up. "Kala, you have something to add?"

"Dwarven Warclans are feared throughout Emerilia for their shield walls. I believe we should change up our tactics moving forward. Have the Aleph scout while the Dwarves lead forward with the DCA ranging around the cliffs using the mobility offered to us with our avian Beast Kin and Demons' ability to fly. They can hit small groups of the Demon Horde that the Aleph scouts have found. Any big groups can be ground into a pulp by the Dwarves with the DCA and Stone Raiders in fighting support as the Aleph keep overwatch on the battlefield, making sure no one creeps up on us."

"Use the strengths of each group," Alkao mused, holding his chin as he nodded. "I agree. Tomorrow, we'll link up to put Kala's plan to work."

Chapter 17: Beyond All Seeing Eyes

"So, will this actually work?" Sato asked Edwards under his breath. They stood behind a plexiglass window and looked out into the vastness of space and the stars beyond. A few thousand miles away, a small ship moved into view.

In the observatory, the most powerful and influential leaders of the settlement were in attendance.

They had turned the test into an event. A bar was off to the side, with people wandering around with refreshments and drinks. None of the servers came near Sato and Edwards, deep in their work as their people made it clear that they weren't to be disturbed with food and drink.

"Theoretically; I wasn't expecting this to become some kind of event. Think you could start checking out who told everyone that this thing works? I haven't even started to look at its ability to change the heat pattern of the ship and then the air systems and propulsion systems to make sense with what Dave, Shard, and Bob have given us. Since I don't fully understand the elemental science behind it, I couldn't tell you what is really going on, only a vague idea," Edwards said. To him, science was to be celebrated, but only once it was proved and working, not when he had half of a proto-type.

"So, basically, you have all these building blocks you've slapped together, not really understanding the systems but knowing the function they each provide?" Sato said.

"Pretty much. The science behind them deals on a nano and micron level. It's a real pain in the ass trying to get it all sorted out. The fine controls that are included with the Jukal implants are in-credible. They're the universe's greatest UI/UX system. It adapts to the user, gives some major similarities, but it adapts so fast to their user that it really is like magic. Without that interfacing abili-ty, then the components of this magic would be a highly uncontrollable mess. I wonder why the hell they even went this far with it. The first stages must have been a major pain in the ass to deal with." Edwards tapped his chin with a pen while his thoughts wandered.

"The Jukal originally made it to replace their phones, kind of like an omnipresent servant that made them highly productive. They can be implanted at birth and continuously grow with the user. That's what happens with the Players on Emerilia," Sato said.

"Interesting! So, just like our own holo-bracelets applications. Some smart bugger connected the implants to the nanites and microns and went to town, the implants compensating between the two while using machine learning to turn a sentient creature's thought into reality!" Edwards shook with excitement.

The room's lights dimmed as the vista of stars disappeared and the window zoomed in on the prototype ship. It wasn't much to look at: a metal cylinder with different components across its hull, windows here and there, escape hatches and runes. Runes were carved into the hull and filled with silver running in spiraling and concentric designs across the entirety of the vessel.

"Power source is stable; enchantments are looking good. Ready to begin testing on thrust systems," Captain Adams said, her voice calm as ever. Outside of the cockpit, she was something of a sloth. When she was in the seat, it was as though a switch was flipped and she turned into a model pilot and ship commander.

Blue flames started to project out of the rear of the spacecraft. A simple Fire enchantment, but with a variable output pushing the craft along.

"Inertia compensators are looking good," Edwards muttered in Sato's ear.

The ship was a hybrid of magical and technological capabilities. They didn't want to let on that they were using the tech to update their fleet where they could. Asking about inertia compensators was a big warning light to anyone. Sato might trust Dave, but did he trust a man he'd never met with the lives of all those under his protection?

"Power source is okay; we're burning through a lot, even with the new power storage crystals," Adams said.

"Ugh, you military people—would it kill you to call it Mana?" Edwards cast a frustrated look to Sato.

"It's electricity, just with a different name. Sure, it's weird that it can be held within a soul gem and just how much can be held in a soul gem is impressive, but it's still electricity being stored in a solid-state crystal matrix," Sato said.

"Well, at least you're learning something." Edwards huffed and checked his pad filled with numbers, dials, and all manner of information.

The powerful people drank their champagne and talked in excited voices. Sato made sure to not make eye contact with anyone. He didn't need them talking his ears off.

Captain Adams and her crew continued to try out the different enchantments of the ship, from using the Mana barrier to nudge small asteroids to see whether it did in fact function. Seeing the success of the multiple Fire enchantments, Adams became bolder and bolder in testing.

I swear, she's probably whooping every time the channel's off. Sato smiled, watching the captain fly the ship as if it were a space fighter. The thing was agile as hell. Using her Jukal implants, she just thought of what she wanted the ship to do and the enchantments reacted to her commands.

"How can she use all of those enchantments? Wasn't Dave saying that you need to have a link to them or something?" Sato asked.

"Well, it's through the command seats in the ship. We ran command Magical Circuits from all of the enchantments to their chairs. As long as someone has the Jukal implant/interface, they can control any of the circuits that are connected to their seat," Edwards said.

"Huh, that's pretty smart," Sato said.

"That's why I'm the guy who makes the things and you're the one who tries to break them. Now, shush; we're going to try that stealth enchantment. It's going to take a hell of a lot of power," Edwards said.

"This is Captain Adams. Flight check complete. Ship is running good across the board. Ready to move to testing the stealth Magical Circuit."

Sato felt as if there were an itch behind his eyes as he looked away from the zoomed-in plexiglass window.

"Stealth is active," Captain Adams reported.

There was nothing but space where the window was. A screen to the bottom right appeared as various sensors tried to find the craft. There didn't seem to be anything out there.

"Control, how are we looking?" Adams asked.

"Captain, we aren't picking you up on anything. We've even got people looking for you with just optical, but we still can't detect you," Control said.

For twenty minutes, no one could find the small craft.

"Power source at fifteen percent. I'm going to call it," Captain Adams said.

"Understood," Control replied.

The scene outside the plexiglass changed; the prototype ship was just a few hundred meters away.

Sato felt a thin bead of sweat travel down his spine.

"That's amazing; better than I ever hoped!" Edwards declared, breaking the silence in the room.

People whooped and cheered while Sato grabbed Edward's shoulder, his hand like a vise.

"Is something wrong?" Edwards asked, confused.

"Find a way to detect ships with stealth enchantment as soon as possible. If we can do it, so can the Jukal," Sato said.

Edwards turned toward the window, markedly less excited.

Everything that the people on Emerilia had told them worked. All the technology that the Jukal Empire controlled and knew about for centuries.

Sato was left wondering just how lucky they were to be still alive with an enemy that had, by all accounts, *magical* constructs at their fingertips.

***

Geswald looked out of the large window in his office nervously. It had been a week since Esamael had been in his very seat.

Geswald tried to turn a blind eye to the various people who were found dead across Emaren and Verlun. Esamael's forces were at work making sure that none of the king's spies learned of Lord Esamael's plans.

There seemed to be a tension in the air as armed men and women were moving in from the farms and toward Verlun. The groups might look like a bunch of thugs but by their actions and eyes, they were clearly something more.

Geswald had been following Esamael's instructions. The rest of the group who had started plotting the downfall of the Exdar's Traders now didn't have time to talk, leaving Geswald stuck dealing with Esamael and the Stone Raiders.

He'd placed pressure on those who supported the Stone Raiders, trying to get them to back off. It seemed that they cared little for the trader's guild chapter head's words.

They had seen little of the benefits that the traders in Emaren hoarded to themselves. Now, with the Stone Raiders' teleport pad, they were doing more business than ever before. The Stone Raiders were fair and easy to get along with. They were even talking about making their own bank.

Which is half the problem. The Stone Raiders are known by so many with a large reputation. We don't know what is real and what is fake. Who are their allies and their enemies? There are too many unknowns.

Geswald sighed and sipped his tea.

"The spies will find something to use against Esamael eventually. There is just too much going on for them to not learn of his plots. With a teleport pad that we don't control allowing them into his domain, the network of thugs tracking down spies moving through Liefl and Gufaross is useless. I was a greedy fool to get caught up in all of this, but now there is nothing else I can do. My fate is bound with Esamael's." Geswald blew on his tea again, taking pleasure in the comforting ritual and wisps of vapor coming from the cup.

"Now, there is a true threat. I can see the holes in our plan. Either we continue through and rule Gudalo or we are found out and hung for treason." Geswald snorted, happy for once that he didn't have a family to be ashamed of his actions.

He'd devoted his life to being a master of trade. He'd brokered massive trade agreements. He supplied the mage's college itself with materials that no other person could get in Emerilia. Greed and the ever powerful golden coin had been his reward, never being satisfied.

"Well, time to roll the dice and see what happens."

***

"Your Majesty, I'm sorry to disturb you, but I just received a recording meant for you by a person called Florence Guitterez in Verlun. I think you would be interested in it," Danhald, commander of King Sigaird's personal knights, said as soon as the royal office's doors were closed and the enchantments active.

"Share it with me," Sigaird said.

He opened a recording within the message.

It appeared that he was watching a meeting between Lord Esamael and a well-to-do trader.

Sigaird's eyebrows rose as he listened to their conversation.

"Call the war council, *quietly,* and see if Lady Merguine is within the vicinity," Sigaird said.

"Yes, Your Majesty." Danhald saluted before he turned around and left the king's office.

The information showed that Esamael was planning to attack the Stone Raiders, though it wasn't enough for Sigaird to call on the army yet. Once Esamael moved, then Sigaird could finally put in orders to get the southern army moving to attack Emaren.

Esamael's backing by the lords was high so Sigaird had to be careful about who he shared the information with. Deciding what to do with it was the hardest part. It was clear Esamael didn't have regard for Sigaird, but one misstep and Sigaird could be destroyed by the lords and government without ever having a day in the field of battle.

Sigaird's eyes thinned as he read the last line.

"We will exercise the right to defend ourselves through any means necessary. As we have shown faith with you, I hope that you share that same faith with the Stone Raiders."

Sigaird closed his interface and looked to the ceiling. The message was carefully worded, but knowing about what had happened in Selhi Capital, Sigaird understood what it meant.

"Don't fuck with us." Sigaird felt curious instead of apprehensive at the thinly veiled threat.

"If they're willing to take on the king of a country for messing them about, I wonder what they're going to do to a lord who is trying to kill their people and steal one of their treasured items?"

Chapter 18: Shield Walls And Cliff Walls

"Ugh, all this building is boring," Steve complained.

"Look, we need to make sure that the cliffs around the crater don't have any massive gaps in them, so that we know that the Demons won't be able to get in on foot that way. Then, when we're fighting the Demon Horde, we can pin them against the cliffs and tear them apart." Dave watched as Malsour made a wall a hundred foot across and forty foot tall.

"Yeah, but they're learning how to fly, right? So, how does that help us if they just fly over these walls?" Steve pointed out.

"We're putting wards on them that will let us know when something is trying to fly over the wall or climb it," Dave said.

"Good," Malsour said. The wall stopped growing from the ground, polished to reflect the mid-morning sun. Dave closed his eyes and conjured magical code into the wall. The air above the wall seemed to shimmer a bit, like heat waves off pavement.

"We don't have much more to do. With all of the Dwarven engineers and Aleph mages, we should be done today or tomorrow, then we can go off hunting," Dave said.

Steve wasn't the only one who wanted to be out there and hunting down the Demon Horde. The girls were off providing scouts and support to the DCA who were carrying any of the Demon Horde who took to the skies or were in small parties.

Dave knew that they could deal with nearly anything that got in their way. He also knew that he was the fastest at making magical coding. Combined with Malsour's ability to create rock, they were the best at making walls.

Neither Steve, Lox, nor Gurren had spells or the power to keep themselves flying with the DCA like the girls did, so they tagged along with Dave and Malsour in case they ever wandered into the Demon Horde crossing the cliffs.

Dave closed his eyes, using Touch of the Land that he cast on an almost subconscious level. Now he concentrated on his senses and the massive area that he could look through.

"There's a small group of Demons here, about twenty of them. We could clear them out before moving to the next section." Dave shared a waypoint to the rest of the group.

"Be good to break up all this wall building," Malsour said.

"'Bout time we got to put the blade to some of those bastards," Lox said.

"Woo-hoo! Let's go huntin'!" Steve said, giving a painful attempt at a Southern accent.

"Jump on," Malsour said. A section of rock came free of the ground around him. Everyone got on.

"Steve, don't move," Malsour said.

"I'll do my best," Steve said.

The stone platform shot forward. Dave and the others had to lean into the direction they were going.

"This is what I'm talking about!" Gurren laughed. All of them grinned with excitement.

The stone platform moved over the cliffs, rough valley dips and changes in the ring around Devil's Crater with ease.

"We're less than five hundred meters." Dave changed the waypoint to where the Demon Horde's group lay.

The platform slowed slightly as they turned around a large outcropping of boulders, looking down at Demons who were trying to ascend the cliffs.

They let out a cry, rushing toward the platform. Malsour didn't slow; the platform raced forward to meet them. Some tried to get out of the way; others tried to board. Those who tried to board were met by a metal wall of spikes.

Gurren, Lox, and Steve finished off the impaled Demons. The platform rode over boulders and along the side wall of the valley they were in, coming back at the twelve remaining Demons.

Dave felt the world slow down; his two conjuring rods turned into a bow. His fingers pulled back on the string and an arrow appeared between them.

He drew and released. He didn't need to check the flight of the arrow, already conjuring another arrow as he drew the bow string back again. It followed barely a second after the first.

He saw a Demon try to rise in the air with its wings.

A spear of light flashed across Dave's vision.

Then the platform reached the Demons once again. It lowered to the ground as Steve let loose with the repeaters in his right hand.

Dave's arrows took two Demons split seconds apart. His conjured spell ripped through the air, leaving a sizzling hole through the Demon trying to fly, it plummeted back down to the ground.

Gurren slammed a rock away with his shield. Lox leaped into the fray, stunning one Demon with his shield and hamstringing another. Gurren jumped in after him.

The two of them had changed since Dave had fought at Boranal's Citadel. They were stronger, more sure of themselves. They had the eyes of veterans. Their armor was customized and rougher-looking than that of the Warclans of Mithsia. It was functional. They cared for it but they'd been through many battles, changing their manners and ways.

Steve's hand reformed as he threw his massive axe in his right, taking two Demons down at once. A rune glowed on his hand and on the axe. The axe returned to him. He turned once and slammed the spike on the back into the Demon Gurren was fighting.

The Demon's side was caved in as Gurren had to shake them free of his axe.

"Kill steal!" Gurren complained, as he took out another Demon.

It didn't take long until the remaining Demons were dispatched.

Dave looked around for any more to kill.

"Huh, well, damn, we need to finish off these walls faster." Dave destroyed his bow, spinning one of his conjuring rods in his hand, eager to fight more.

"We should be done shortly," Malsour said.

"Better be. That was only a taster," Gurren said.

Steve made a noise of agreement. Lox shook his head and smiled as he cleaned the black Demon blood off his blade.

There was no time to loot the bodies; they needed to continue onward.

***

Dwayne looked over the moving Warclan and supporting elements. It was an impressive sight. Five thousand shield bearers lined up, marching to meet a twelve thousand-strong Demon Horde.

The DCA were in the skies, protecting them from aerial attacks. The Stone Raiders created a formation off to the left side while the right side of the Dwarves was anchored at the base of Devil's Crater's cliffs. The Aleph scouts and drones were updating the positions of the Demon Horde, with the rest of their members moving to the nearest keeps to help with defense.

The Demon Horde rushed forward as a single screaming mass.

They were met by a howling noise. Dwarven artillery bloomed into destructive Mana above the Demon Horde, tearing down great swathes of the Demons. The artillery continued to fire. Controllers called out changes at the rear of the Dwarf formation. The artillery shells guided onto the biggest groups.

Two people with flames beneath their feet seemed to crackle with Mana.

An eardrum-shattering explosion of Fire swept above the Demon Horde. Demons were torn apart, their inner organs ruptured, or their blood boiled by the heat generated by the two Fire mages' fuel air bombs.

"Damn, I wish I could do that spell," Kim complained.

"Deia and Induca are something else when it comes to Fire spells," Dwayne said.

"Yeah, freaking *awesome*!" Kim smiled.

"Shields!" the Dwarven Warclan's leader called out. The Dwarves' shields slammed together; a ripple of buffs glowed over the connected shields. As the rear ranks connected, those bare coverings of buffs turned into a solid wall of color. Magical Circuits spread over the entire Dwarven formation.

The Demon Horde smacked the Dwarven lines. It was like seeing a truck slam into an armored pylon. Their movement was arrested. Some flipped on top of the shield formation; others got crushed under the press of bodies.

Dwarven leaders called out; swords stabbed forward through openings in the shield wall as the Dwarves pushed forward.

"Clear the front," Dwayne bellowed.

The Demons who met the Stone Raiders had been stopped by the melee fighters. Now the mages unleashed their attack. Spells ran through the Demon Horde, clearing the front of the Stone Raiders' formation.

The Stone Raiders pushed through the weakened and stunned Demon lines. They cut down anything in their path. The Stone Raiders boxed in the left side of the Demon Horde. Dwarves flowed with them.

"Good positioning. Move forward—speed and damage buffs!" Dwayne found himself now at the front of the line moving across the Dwarves' front, flanking the now committed Demon Horde.

"Demon Champion!"

"Focus on it!"

"Need a speed debuff on it!"

"Need heals!"

The Stone Raiders kept yelling out to one another, keeping information flowing as they charged through the Horde's lines.

More and more of the Demon Horde took to the skies, trying to close with their enemies. They were pretty dumb; they didn't realize that they were boxed in and getting hit from two sides. They'd already lost over half of their number. The Dwarves' lines were like a blender, tearing the Demons apart with casual skill. Their stacking buffs and bonuses from working together was an incredible sight to see.

The DCA was there to meet them. They had been able to get more weapons and all of the forces beyond the cliffs had some kind of weapon and buffs. They fought in the air. Their mastery of flight made the Demon Horde's beginning fliers easy to manage.

Dwayne flinched as a bolt of lightning tore into the Stone Raiders' formation.

Heals flew and a Demon turned into a bloody pincushion as archers took down the attacker.

Damn Horde woke to their magic. Friggin' pain in the ass. The spells and the Demon Horde mages weren't that powerful, but it added just another thing to look out for. Dwayne found himself sinking in mud.

Dwarven Earth mages countered the Demon Horde's magic. Dwayne and his line rose out of the ground, still hurling themselves through the Horde.

Dwayne felt the Stone Raiders' frustration building as they got into the rhythm of the battle.

Some of the Demon Horde started to turn and flee but the DCA weren't about to let them escape. Airborne DCA soldiers wielding swords cut down the fleeing creatures.

Dwayne's shield cracked a Demon's head; his blade took the leg off another.

The Horde was strong, but the Stone Raiders were bloodied veterans with more experience and an understanding of teamwork that the Horde didn't have.

Artillery fell silent and spells thinned out. The different allies were too close to the Demon Horde. Any support they provided had a good chance of hurting friendly forces.

Dwayne slowed his advance, taking his time through the Horde to save his Stamina and armor, so it wouldn't need as much repairing later.

The Demon Horde broke, trying to flee and save themselves. The DCA hunted them down. Archers and mages sent spells after them.

"Okay, everyone heal up and we'll group off to the side again," Dwayne said.

"Shields! Switch front rank!" the Dwarven leader yelled. The shields came apart to reveal the Dwarves underneath. The front rank turned; the following ranks walked past them, snapping forward as soon as they were past. This continued until the first rank was the last rank. Healers checked them over, as Dwarves checked their gear and got some water into them.

"Prepare to march!" The Warclan divided into their box-like formations once again, so that they could get through the rough terrain, in smaller, more versatile packets.

"I'm always impressed by the Dwarves. Their coordination, especially among their veteran units, is as scary as it is reassuring," Anna said, beside Dwayne.

"That it is. I keep on forgetting that Dave is a Master Smith with them. I didn't realize how much power came with that. Dwarves always stay in their mountains, so it's hard to know how powerful they really are," Dwayne said.

"Well, a good way to think of it is that the Dwarven Master Smiths are like a senate that has proved themselves through their work and their abilities. They vote on things to lead their people. The president is whoever is leading that council at the time. The lords and ladies who rule the mountains are like retainers that the Dwarven people and the Master Smiths agree to lead them. When the Dwarves go to war, the Master Smiths must give their permission as the Warclans are under their command."

"Damn, that is a lot of power," Dwayne grunted.

"It is, which is why they are not simply elected and the president is only for a month or so. They only deal with large issues; the rest the lords and ladies or other elected people deal with. I think the fact that they hate politicking and really just want to build awesome things makes the whole thing work." Anna shrugged.

"The more I learn about all the lore about Emerilia, the more excited I am. I don't know how the Jukal Corporation did it, but they made one hell of a world here," Dwayne said.

It was Anna's turn to look thoughtful as she studied Dwayne. "One day you'll understand the true extent that the Jukal went to create this place."

Her voice was hard, but Dwayne couldn't help but feel that she sounded almost sad.

"We've got another decent-sized Demon Horde group a few kilometers from you. It looks like they saw the battle and are turning toward you. Kala and her forces are moving through the cliffs to deal with the Demons that got in there," Koza said over the northern clearing force's chat.

"How many in the Horde?" Fonrir, the Warclan leader, asked.

"We're counting twenty-five thousand, though there are other groups joining them. Might be around thirty thousand by the time they meet you," Koza said.

"Shall we make a defensive position and let them throw themselves against us? We can keep a creeping artillery barrage at their rear, pin them to us. Once we thin them out, we can advance, killing them or driving them into the artillery," Fonrir said.

"Sounds like a plan to me. Most of my Earth and Dark mages are off working on sealing the cliffs, so we will probably need some help getting our defenses up," Dwayne said. The POE's AI was incredibly brilliant; their speech tree was incredible. They could remember a great litany of things, making the experience every person had with them different. Just like interactions between real people were.

"We have a bunch of fortification circuits we can use to make walls and other such things," Fonrir reassured Dwayne.

"Perfect. Well, let's get to work then!"

Chapter 19: Time To Step It Up

Steve cheered as Malsour's rock-surfboard crested over the cliffs and started racing them down toward the northern group that was engaged in battle with a group of Demon Horde.

Dave laughed out loud as they flew down the slopes.

Five pillars of golden light ripped through the air, right into the middle of the Demon Horde's lines. The light killed enemies but healed allies at the same time. Dave destroyed the conjured staff that was slowly melting in his hands.

"How are you able to do that and not collapse?" Malsour asked. The two of them were at the rear of the surfboard, away from Gurren, Lox, and Steve at the prow; a small railing kept them from falling off.

"I was going about using the armor's power wrong. I was channeling it through myself and then pushing it into spells. It strained the hell out of my mind. What I'm doing now is making objects; I magically code them to create some effect and tie it to my armor's power source. I just point, activate, and the power goes right from my armor to the conjured item. Instead of painting a masterpiece inside my mind, I'm writing it out. It's not as flexible as spell casting, but it means I can do some really massive spells without having to worry about my mental fatigue." Dave smiled.

"Every time I think I've seen the upper limit of your abilities, you show me something completely new."

"Well, what about this?" Dave's conjuring rod appeared in his hand and a rune glowed on the back of his hand. Runes glowed across his body, his eyes shining. The rod turned into a wand; magical coding covered it.

The air crackled with power as similar creatures to Malsour's darklings appeared.

"Darklings, but how are they in the light?" Malsour asked, astonished.

"I guess they're technically lightlings. I just took their constructs and made them from Light instead of Dark. As fast as darklings, but gather power from the Light instead of the Dark. As your darklings can grow with the consuming of their victims' bodies, lightlings grow with consuming souls." Dave calmly observed the lightlings that spread out among the Demon Horde. The Demons, being Creatures of Power, could hurt the lightlings but they were nowhere as fast as the shimmering half-formed creatures.

Other creations and soul bound creatures appeared on the field of battle, helping the lightlings, forcing the Demon Horde to fight a battle on multiple fronts even as the casters and summoners remained safely behind their defenses.

"Look at that." Steve pointed to a Demon Champion who dove into the Demon Horde, cutting through it, supported by the Stone Raiders' myriad of controlled beasts and the Dwarf's war golems that erupted from the ground.

"Someone must have soul bound the Demon Champion to them," Malsour said, a note of respect in his voice.

"That must've been a hard thing to do," Dave said.

"Probably, but if they were injured or nearly dead, then it makes it easier to soul bind them. Also with the soul binding contracts, it could suppress the Demon's hunger for souls and remove the Dark Lord's compulsions."

"Soul binding contracts help to stabilize the contracted creature. I'm happy Suzy's as strong as she is. Without her, I might have lost my bearing on reality." Steve shuddered.

"Well, now you can stand by us and hunt down this Demon Horde." Lox patted the metal giant's leg.

"Nearly there!" Malsour yelled. The rock platform left the cliff for a bit as they sailed through the air. A pillar came up, grabbing them and pulling them into contact with the cliff once again as they continued to race forward.

"Here we go!" The platform sprouted spikes as it slammed through the Demon Horde's formation closest to the cliff.

Bands appeared around Dave's hands and his eyes blazed with power.

Lox, Gurren, and Steve roared as the platform came to a stop. They smashed into the Demon Horde. Dave turned to face the flanking Demon Horde, cutting one down with a thin blade and throwing an axe into another Demon before he recalled it to his hands. Malsour cleared the way to the Dwarven lines to their right.

The fortifications around the clearing forces lowered as they marched forward. The army of thirty thousand was now barely a third of its original size. Artillery continued to blossom on the party's right, killing anything that moved into their barrier formed from firepower.

"Well, let's see how this goes." Dave released his conjuration rods, letting them float as the conjured bracers started to rotate. The different runes on the metal glowed a brilliant blue.

Light projected from his hands, directed into the Demon Horde. It took but a few seconds. Dave turned and moved. His conjuration rods moved to his belt as he used short bursts, firing the Light cannons on his arms tens of times per second, pushing his higher Intelligence as he seemed to flow through the battlefield. Nothing could touch him as he fired the Light cannons.

It was impressive but it couldn't last as he had to keep stabilizing his bracers, so the conjuration and magical coding wouldn't fall apart. They disappeared, as he came up under an attacker trying to claw his face.

His axe slammed into their back as he turned around and dragged his other axe across their neck. A metal spear slammed through a Demon about to claw at Dave.

Dave pulled his weapons free, using the impaled Demon to launch himself into a Demon Champion. His right axe turned into a golden spear as he launched it at the Demon Champion. Spells from across the Dwarven lines hit the hiding champion.

It barely had time to look stunned as a spear erupted out of its side.

Dave and the rest of his party hadn't stopped running.

Behind them lay the mangled dead and the Dwarven lines that were forming along the cliff face to flank the Demon Horde.

"Forward! Double time!" a Dwarf called out. The Dwarven line opened up their shields and raced forward to join Dave and the rest of the party.

"Arrowhead off the Stone Raiders!"

Dave's spear turned to a sword and his axe to a shield as he blunted an attack with his shield, eviscerating the attacker with his sword.

A dozen Demons charged him. Golden spears of Light appeared around him. They shot forward faster than the eye could see, leaving holes in the Demons. They dropped bonelessly to the ground. A bow appeared in Dave's hands as Steve, Gurren, and Lox charged forward.

They smashed into the rear of a bunch of Demons who were harassing the Dwarven shield wall. They cut through the unprepared and confused Demon Horde with ease. Dave conjured and released arrows at a terrifying rate.

Malsour stood to his side. His curses wiped out whole swathes of Demons, making stone manacles to grab the Demons, spikes to impale them, and dozens of spears.

The Dwarves reached the rear of the party. They'd finished off the stragglers and now pressed forward, rolling up the Demon Horde. The artillery stopped, but now three sides of the Demons were faced by the Stone Raiders and Dwarves.

Some, seeing their chance, made a run for it. The DCA, who had been keeping the Demon Horde's fliers on the ground, now swooped in to kill off those runners.

Dave conjured a shield and sword, moving up with his party as they became the tip of an arrowhead-shaped group of Dwarven shield bearers.

The Demon's ranks thinned through death or running away.

Dave held his blade as he found himself looking at Dwayne. "Not a bad day for a hunt." Dave looked for more things to kill but found none.

"Not at all. I guess the walls are up?" Dwayne looked tired.

"All up and warded. Now we just have to finish off the Demon Horde." Dave smiled.

Dwayne grinned.

"I have a large force of three hundred thousand moving for the southeast keep!" Koza said over the leadership chat. As Dave was the Master Smith who called the Warclans, they were technically under his command, giving him access to the chat.

"I have five thousand in the keep. They're going to need back-up," Malkur said.

"All artillery not firing, shift to cover that keep. Kala, Efri—I want ten thousand from each of you to support the keep. Josh, I'm going to need your Stone Raiders. The remaining forces continue to hunt down the enemy through the cliffs. If we pull back your forces, then we're going to have to just clear through the cliffs again if this force scatters," Alkao said.

"Stone Raiders, disengage and start moving for the keep as fast as possible," Josh said over the guild chat. A waypoint marked the keep.

Dwayne and Dave shared a look for a moment.

"Kill any of the Demon Horde that's left and start moving for the keep!" Dwayne's voice carried over the northern force's chat.

Chapter 20: On The Eastern Front

Deia looked at the Demon Horde that was already starting to peek through the cliffs and trees that lay ahead of the contested keep.

They must've seen the DCA Demons carrying their fellows and Stone Raiders. A screech rose up into the air and the Demon Horde started to run for the southeastern keep's walls. Thousands took to the skies, too many for the DCA to put down.

Artillery fired from all over Devil's Crater, trying to suppress the Demon Horde. The DCA fired their arrows and destruction staffs, trying to kill the Demon Horde in the air.

The flying DCA did everything they could to increase their speed. The Stone Raiders began shooting arrows or casting spells.

Deia increased the Fire on her feet and hands, speeding toward the keep faster. Shooting in the air would only slow her down. Anna, Induca, and Suzy followed her, using their own magics to hold them aloft. Malsour raced along the ground with the rest of their party and nearly half of the Stone Raiders they had been fighting beside. They were already entering the keep's inner doors.

The ladies landed on the walls. Induca conjured a Fire tornado. The rapid heat threw the Demon Horde's fliers in disarray and burned all that met the bottom of its cone.

Anna called upon the wind, enhancing Induca's attack and giving buffs to all within range, increasing their speed and attack damage.

Suzy's bag spilled out cores; they activated, pulling air around them before Suzy's commands sent them charging toward the walls.

Deia used fireballs, sending them careening into any of the Demon Horde groups that got too close for her liking and creating a line of destruction across the ground.

Malsour's metal plate rose like an elevator up the inside of the keep's wall, with a growing set of pillars beneath it. The Stone

Raiders off-loaded as it reached the top, flinging spells that they had been working on. Magic flared across the wall and into the Demon Horde.

It slowed the Horde, but it didn't stop them. There was now nearly four hundred thousand Demons. As the Demon Horde had gained flight, it split the Stone Raider's aim as they fought on two fronts. The DCA flying forces clashed with the Demons above, making the Stone Raiders deal with the ones on the ground for fear of accidentally roasting their allies.

There were just twenty-five thousand of the DCA in the keep, supported by another thousand Aleph automatons and their controllers, half a Dwarven artillery battery, and four hundred Stone Raiders.

Thankfully, they were being supported by other Dwarven artillery around the crater, but that was still under twenty-seven thousand against four hundred thousand. Magic might be a massive force multiplier, but the Demon Horde weren't all charging in a straight line. Many used the cliffs for cover, climbing and flying up them to come down on the keep from above.

And now, a bunch of them had magic. It wasn't enough to take out most Stone Raiders unless it was sustained or they were a champion, but it could kill the other defenders easily enough.

Malsour created a mile-wide trench that was twenty feet long and ten deep, filled with spikes. He hadn't destroyed the top of the dirt, so the only way the Demon Horde knew it was there was by charging over it and dropping through the thin covering layer and into the sharpened spikes below.

"Seal the gate up! Aleph archers to the walls—space out behemoths with other support across the length of the wall. DCA, keep taking down the Demons in the air! Kim, I want someone to alter the cliffs around us so we can see the Demons climbing up them!" Josh's voice cut through the general chat.

Josh's words turned into action. Metal and dirt filled in where the gate into the keep was. The sides of the cliff turned into polished stone, dirt disappearing. Exposed Demons were rewarded with Earth or stone spikes pushing them off the cliffs. They looked like angry porcupines by the time the mages were done.

The Aleph moved into position.

Dave ran off, making boxes that acted as mini arrow factories, pushing out bolts for the Aleph automaton archers and the living forces to refill from.

Deia didn't have much time to watch as she continued to cast fireball after fireball, which exploded when they came into contact with the Demon Horde.

Their most powerful weapons weren't their offensive magic, but their ability to make a Mana barrier. They took two or three hits to take down, providing those behind them with the time to close a couple hundred meters.

The Demons might not be as high of a level as the Stone Raiders, but they were still faster than any natural Human. It didn't take them long until they reached the wall. The defenses were firming up, but the Demon Horde put their claws to work, stabbing them into the wall to begin climbing.

Deia called down a firestorm right at the base of the wall. Demons screamed as they burned. Deia tuned it out, working the Fire to project it down and away from the keep instead of undermine its walls' strength.

Malsour downed Mana potions and pulled power from his amulet that powered the Abscondita armor, telling just how much it had taken for him to transport half the guild and then make the hidden trench.

In Human form, he's only a tenth of his true power. Deia turned away, watching as Induca called down a firestorm on the Demons.

The wall seemed to shine with projections.

"Well, damn, Malsour, you know how to make someone have a bad day." Lox pulled out a bolt thrower as his destruction staff ran out of power.

"Just think of what you would do if you were in their shoes. Now, they won't be able to make it up here without flying or breaking the wall down." Malsour drew from his amulet to restore his Mana.

Deia looked to Lox.

"He put razor blades across the wall. They touch this wall and they're going to get really cut up."

"Damn." Deia winced, thinking of how much that would suck.

More artillery started passing overhead as more of the Dwarven artillery corps got their guns within range and set up.

Deia looked to the air; it was a wild melee of Demons in green and red. The DCA Demons were a terror in the sky, but the Demon Horde had numbers and champions on their side.

Deia didn't dare to fire upward, knowing that she'd kill one of the DCA soldiers more likely than not. She saw a new group rush across the skies from Devil's Crater. She looked to see Vrexu's forces. *We might kill all of those on the ground, but the aerial battle is up to the DCA and that will be the one that decides who holds the ground.*

"Josh, we need to get everyone who can fly and fight in the air up there." Deia saw a Demon Champion tear out of the sky and slam into an Aleph archer, tossing them off the defenses, and tear a Beast Kin's throat out before they could react. They beat their wings, powering away from the carnage they'd wrought.

"Got it. I want everyone in their formations. Any who can fight and fly, report to Deia," Josh said.

Parties broke apart as they rushed to meet with their guild leaders. Dwayne, Kim, and Josh were ready and waiting. Lucy and Jules were splitting the support personnel.

Deia waited for the fliers to gather with her.

The girls and Malsour stayed; there were only twenty or so others who were confident about flying and fighting.

"Okay, we're going to get up there and support the DCA as well as we can. Work in pairs and look out for one another. Things are going to get hectic; you think that you can't handle it, then get back down here. It's going to be messy as hell; nausea and motion sickness could get you killed. We need everyone we can fighting, not getting them killed because they didn't know their own limitations." Deia stared at them all, as if testing their mettle with her glare, hoping that her message got across.

No one backed down. Instead, her words seemed to make them stand straighter, taking up her challenge.

"Okay, let's do this," Deia said. People split up, getting into pairs.

Malsour took to the skies, metal across his lower body.

Deia looked to see that he didn't have a partner.

"Don't worry, he'll be fine. The air is like our second home, after all." Fire ignited under Induca's hands and feet. "Shall we?"

Suzy and Anna took to the skies. Anna seemed to run across the sky as Suzy was followed by a swarm of her creations; two of them covered her body, making her able to fly easily.

Fire appeared around Deia. Her eyes glowed red as she started to slowly rise into the air.

The flames weren't just consoling; they were familiar and she drew new strength from them. Ever since she had found out who her real mother was, she had come to not just use the flames she created, but to study them, better understanding her heritage. Her mother was the embodiment of the very element she used.

Every time she used it, it was as if her mother watched over her.

She looked to Induca. "Let's go burn some things." She increased her magic output, using her armor's power reserves. She had a massive Mana pool, but going through it would make her tired. She didn't want to be disoriented when she was flying.

Induca let out a wild cry, excited to be in the air once again.

Deia's face had a harder expression as a plasma pistol appeared in each hand. She fired and the plasma rounds cracked through the air. The plasma slammed into a Demon Champion, tearing them apart.

Deia dialed down the power. The twin fiery pistols tracked her next target as she unconsciously used her Fire to alter her path, tracking her targets.

Using Fire was second nature to her. She flew through the sky, firing plasma and pressurized fireballs to keep the Demon Horde's fighters at range. Induca rode with her, blades of flame or a Fire tornado surrounding her as she barrelled through their enemies.

Malsour floated in mid-air. The Demon Horde's fighters charged him, only to be met by pebbles he created and sent flying through his assailants at speeds that cracked the sound barrier and one-shotted Demons.

Suzy's creations worked together; one created different air pressures that made their target unstable while a second came in with Air blades to tear them apart.

Anna was elegant as ever as she walked, danced, and flew through the sky. An aura of Air surrounded her.

Deia's eyes were drawn to Anna. *I agree with Dave. It still seems that she is keeping her skills hidden. However, with the Jukal and the Pantheon able to watch our every move, it makes sense to have some hidden tricks.*

Just then, a pillar of golden lights seemed to descend from the heavens above. It swept across the Demon Horde formation. Rapid-fire blessings covered the ground.

Deia turned, averting her eyes from the holy light as they found Dave. He looked over the destruction in front of him. A Beast Kin with a glowing armband shook as they guided a massive beam of light across the valley.

Another group with glowing amulets lay blessings down. Here and there, those using the armbands collapsed from Mana fatigue, going well beyond what their body could handle and passing out.

To many, it would look as if they were powerful mages draining themselves in one go—they were, but Deia knew Dave's magic and she could see the power levels of the Abscondita armor and the fully powered vault-classed soul gems that the Stone Raiders carried. Dave was augmenting the different mages' spells and increasing their power with his conjured items.

His eyes blazed with power inside his hood. Her eyes, empowered by arcane sight, saw the changing formations of the spells, enabling him to alter them in real time to get the most out of them.

That was Dave's strength: augmenting others or himself to incredible heights.

Deia didn't have any more time to look at what was going on with the wall. With the new spells, it looked as if more of the Demons had learned to fly. They rushed away from the main road leading toward the keep and around the cliffs.

"Keep them contained and make sure they don't pass!" Vrexu yelled.

Silver and black flying disks seemed to appear, right as they slammed into the encircling flying Demon Horde.

"I can hold them back for a bit and maybe kill some of them, but it won't last for long," Koza yelled.

"I need cover and somewhere to hide," Induca said on the party chat.

"I can do that." Malsour rushed off and away from the battle; Induca followed him.

Deia knew that they would be doing what they thought best. She didn't have any time to argue with them. She moved and fired as fast as possible. Her rounds weren't as powerful as her arrows. However, her plasma and fireball shots exploded, tearing the Demon Horde's fighters apart.

***

Dave watched over the battle as if he saw it through another's eyes. To him, he could see the spells being thrown by the allied mages and the Demons in the sky.

His Touch of the Land extended all around him to provide a complete picture of the battle.

He altered a spell here, turning it against its creator or making it stronger. He conjured repeaters along the wall. The Aleph fighters jumped into them, filling the air with bolts.

To Dave, the battle was no longer a chaos of melee and fighting. His Inference skill and perception allowed him to predict the actions of the Demon Horde and most of his allies. He was now an ethereal spirit. A touch here, a change there, barely a nudge of magic and the battle started firming up.

Some Demons hurled rocks down on him from above. His Mana barrier glowed blue. Dave didn't even seem to notice or care as he continued to reinforce the allies.

His eyes turned to the skies. It was messier but his higher Intelligence allowed him to remember the lore and books he had read on the Demons and angels' battles.

Well, this is going to be a pain in the ass, but we're weak in the sky. The Demon Horde are getting through all over the place and killing our people. First, we need to have a base that is safe from them. If we have wounded, then they can just target the healers so we can't get anyone back in the fight.

Dave kneeled and his hand touched the stone. Mana rushed through his hand as he had to use his own Mana to create the complicated magical coding.

A blue barrier appeared over the keep, stopping stones and the Demon Horde's spells cold as they hit the shield.

Archers no longer needed to duck because the Demons could no longer reach them.

"Focus on the forces in the sky if you can!" Kim yelled out.

Dave conjured what looked like a locker. Coding covered its sides as Dave staggered to his feet slightly. He started recovering his Mana that he wasn't used to expending yet.

The closet opened to reveal a repeater. Dave grabbed it and put it down among some Beast Kin.

"Shoot them with this!" Dave said. "I need ten people to run more of these things across the wall!" Dave said.

"With the Dwarf!" one of the Beast Kin leaders said. The motley crew followed Dave, finding another repeater being pushed out of the closet-looking factory.

He'd conjured the factory, which was easy enough, making a magical tap from his armor to the factory and feeding it from his reserves instead of his actual Mana. It meant he could make more than a dozen, without keeling over with Mana fatigue.

"Take these and put them out along the wall. They use bolts from the factories I've made across the wall!" Dave yelled at the Beast Kin over the noise.

"Gronel! Take this down to the west side!" the Beast Kin leader said, taking over from Dave, who now looked back to the skies.

The barrier was meant to keep out magic and rocks; it wasn't made to stop people. The Demon fighters were now coming down inside the Mana barrier, trying to kill the defenders.

Dave jumped from the wall; his conjuring rods flew to his hands. His right turned into a sword he planted in the back of a Demon Champion. The creature plummeted to the ground, now lifeless with Dave's sneak attack.

Dave's left turned into a shield as he rolled off the Demon as it slammed into the ground, softening his fall as his sword turned into a spear. A Demon raked at his shield he'd raised high to cover himself. His spear slammed into the Demon and the head exploded into spikes. Dave pulled the spike-covered spear back and turned it into an axe. Dave raised his shield, covering his body to deflect stones that slammed into him.

Using his Touch of the Land, he knew that three Demons were advancing on him with speed. He threw his axe with his right hand, burying it in the chest of the level 215 Demon and turning out of the way of the other Demon's charge.

He recalled the axe, parrying one Demon's claws with his shield. It screeched like nails on a chalkboard as Dave felt the axe return to his hand. It transformed into a needle-point rapier longer than a great sword. He slammed his shield forward, applying a stun effect to the Demon to his front. He turned; his rapier darted out with surgical precision. The second circling Demon looked down, confused by the barely one centimeter-wide wound in its chest before it collapsed. Dave's rapier turned into a great sword.

With his monstrous Strength, he could wield it easily in one hand as he cut the remaining Demon nearly in half. Blood sprayed out, hitting Dave's barrier. He looked around and found a band of Demons who were advancing on the Dwarven artillery.

The Aleph's behemoths came into play. The large lumbering beasts moved with a grace that belied their size, their blows savage and brutal.

Seems like they updated their fighting style off Steve. Dave saw similarities in their fighting styles.

More behemoths and other forces were protecting the healers. A small Mana barrier was erected around the healers' camp. Already, there was a heavy flow of wounded rushing in. The Stone Raiders, Aleph, and DCA healers were pulling people back from the brink of death and right back out into battle at an alarming rate.

An army with enough high-skilled healers would be one hell of a scary thing.

Dave's attention turned to the wall. The Stone Raider melee types, Aleph fighters, and Beast Kin soldiers protected the archers, mages, and those who manned the repeaters.

Dave concentrated, remembering Anna's attacks: the form, the way that the spell flowed, and its true formation. As he slashed his great sword, magical coding flared to life on it; minor changes to its base made it release a hungry howl.

Dave conjured Anna's spell, fueling it with stored Mana.

A blade of wind rushed outward over the heads of those at the wall and through the Demon Horde fighters trying to land on or beyond the wall.

Dave had found that conjuring a spell was easier if he made it within an item. He'd simply taken the two parts of Anna's attack, the spell and her sword's movement, and incorporated them into his sword.

The fight for dominance raged above Dave. He looked up. It was like a war of demi-gods. Thousands filled the sky, clashing in a terrible battle with no true direction.

There was just too many of the Demon Horde. Most kept the aerial forces occupied while others swept down toward the keep.

Dave conjured a bow. Ten Demons, seeing the defiant Dwarf, collapsed their wings, diving in an arrow formation.

Dave's arrows ripped at the very air, letting out sonic booms. His aim was unnerving. Five were dead in as many seconds. The Demons howled out their rage; their prey wouldn't leave the battlefield alive.

Dave took down three more. He conjured metal, sinking it deep into the keep's ground and bracing himself. The final two tried to decapitate Dave with their claws. Instead, they found their hands broken by the Mana barrier that covered his body. Dave dismissed his conjured metal as the two Demons let out angry and pained yells.

His arrows found them before they were able to regain altitude.

Dave turned, letting loose an arrow that slammed into a Demon trying to get around Gurren. The creature was blown off the wall. Gurren waved his sword in thanks, gutting another Demon and tossing them off the wall with his shield.

An aura seemed to cover the area around the keep. Dave's legs shook under the power of it.

A Dragon's roar could be heard in the distance.

Chapter 21: Power Unleashed

Lox lost himself to his training, standing beside Gurren and Steve as they defended their allies. They were being swarmed on all sides by the Demon Horde.

A bellow, the likes of which Lox had only heard one time before, echoed through the forest and over the cliffs of Devil's Crater.

On the ground and in the air, fire seemed to swirl, growing and becoming more solid as magma formed into flame atronachs. They darted through the Demon Horde's airborne fighters, leaving trails of Fire and destruction in their wake.

Gurren growled, kicking a Demon off the wall. It yelled, but rose up again on its own wings and rushed back in. Lox's blade rammed into its side while Gurren came out of his shield stance and took the creature's head.

There was no time for words as they continued to fight with everything they had.

The atronachs numbered in the hundreds and were fighting a valiant battle, but there were four or five Demon Horde fighters for every defender left.

They were cutting them down in great swathes, but there weren't enough of them.

Summoners called on their creations and bound creatures that could fly.

Lox looked upward. Time seemed to slow as the Demons of Devil's Crater and the Demon Horde tore into one another. Stone Raiders, summoned creatures, and any remaining Aleph drones fought fifty meters above the keep, slowly being pushed back by the swarm of Demon Horde.

Repeaters fired along the wall while those manning them yelled at their attackers. Here and there, the Demon Horde picked up one of the people within the keep, hauling them off, dropping them, or cutting them apart in the sky.

The Fire atronachs' flames melted away opposition. Lox let out a yell as he saw a Demon take down one of the repeaters' defenders.

The Beast Kin firing the weapon didn't know what happened as the Demon's claws tore through its chest.

Lox watched as they were thrown off the wall by the Demon while two others impaled the Demon with sword and spear.

There was not an inch of the keep that was not being fought over.

"We can't hold; we need more forces now or we're going to get run over!" Josh yelled.

"I can get more people to you within twenty minutes," Alkao yelled.

"That's not enough. We're going to need defenses down from the keep in the crater. Koza, Fonrir, Malsour—see to it. We will hold them there. Move reinforcements in. I want the POEs to begin evacuating. The Player Stone Raiders can get you a few minutes!" Josh said.

Malsour seemed to drop from out of the sky. Demons swarmed toward him as he walked down the line; pebbles accelerated out of thin air and tore apart as he cleared the walls.

"We can leave the automatons here to help you. As our allies, we give control of them to you," Koza said.

"Thank you, Council Member," Josh said. "Get people organized and out of here! Fonrir, I'm going to want that artillery right on the keep."

"Can do." Fonrir's voice was gruff and filled with grudging respect.

Lox knew of Fonrir of Aldamire, a Warclan leader many veterans were proud to call their own. He would keep his end of the bargain.

"Wounded first, then able-bodied POEs! Stone Raiders, hold the Demon Horde as much as possible. Trap the ground and be ready to pull back outside the keep!" Josh yelled.

"Melee, regroup in the keep's main courtyard!" Dwayne called.

"Battle mages, support melee and pull back to the keep's gate toward Devil's Crater!" Kim coughed. Fire had started to burn anything flammable inside the courtyard. A few mages were tending to it, but most were fighting the Demon Horde.

Lox killed off another Demon as Malsour reached them.

"Going down?" Malsour asked as part of the wall came away and they were lowered down to the base of the wall.

"Move!" Steve yelled to the two Dwarves.

Lox gripped his sword tighter. He wanted to stay with his friends, the Stone Raiders, but he knew that he would just be a hindrance as they'd be distracted in keeping him alive.

"Kill the bastards!" Lox yelled, clapping Gurren on the back as they rushed toward the artillery that was now pulling down their guns and trying to move them.

Gurren and Lox knew the guns from their time as shield bearers. They quickly dismantled them and put their Dwarven backs to the carted weapons. They quickly built up speed, headed through the keep's gate as the battle raged behind them.

Fire seemed to illuminate the late afternoon, once again making light cover the crater.

Lox took a look back to see the flame atronachs spread across the front of the keep. Between them, they made a wall of Fire. The DCA fliers made quick on their escape, rushing toward the fort that was now growing along the road from the southeastern keep to Unity.

The Dwarven Warclan that had been left as reserve within Unity was making quick work of the fortifications.

Lox looked back as the wall of Fire between the arrayed atronachs started to bend.

The atronachs held for a moment, casting spells into the aerial Demon Horde. The Stone Raiders' Players retreated from the fortifications slowly while making a rear guard of under two hundred.

Then, the aerial Demon Horde was just too much.

"Artillery, fire on the keep! Stone Raiders, ready yourselves and draw from the vaults!" Josh barked. Lox could make him out. He stood on a rock outcropping as shadows seemed to coil around him like flames with his twin blades glowing red in their hunger.

The atronachs' wall was torn apart, the atronachs themselves being set upon by the Demons who made it through.

Lox's heart paused as his eyes went wide at the number of Demons who filled the air.

"If you're about to die, get someone to kill you or kill yourself. It's better than giving these Demons some experience!" Dwayne yelled.

"Only use soul bound weapons!" Josh chorused.

"Ready your spells! Let's see what you can do!" Kim whooped.

All across the Stone Raiders' lines, amulets that had been drawing power from the guild members now started to flood their bodies with it. Buffs lit up the battlefield like bonfires, solid sheets of protections and enhancements glowing across the Stone Raiders. Many of the mages started to glow; the very Mana they channeled through their bodies tore them up from the inside.

There were no howls of pain or cries for mercy. The Stone Raiders whooped and cheered. Even now, Lox could see the hungry grins on their faces as they stood in the face of that Demon bulwark.

"Stone Raiders!" Josh's voice tore through the air as a shadow of a Xelur Demon Lord appeared around him. His rallying call sent chills down the spines of everyone who heard it.

One hundred and seventy-three voices rose up to join the battle cry as Mana seemed to become a tangible thing as the Stone Raiders pulled on their vault soul gems.

Chapter 22: Rear Guard

Dave's eyes might have been closed, but his senses were open to the universe around him. He pushed his Intelligence to his limits, using healing to wipe away his fatigue. It was physically harming his body, but he needed it to stabilize and strengthen the dozens of spells that the Stone Raiders had created.

Dave found his own voice rise up with the Stone Raiders'. His runes glowed across his body and bloody red lines appeared at the edges as they couldn't handle the power output.

His body hurt, but it was nothing compared to the pain he felt in Earth's simulation. Also here he was being constantly healed by his armor.

"Fire!" Kim's voice filled with hunger as the ranged battle mages released their weapons.

It was as though the gods themselves had called down magic upon the keep.

The dead rose from their slumber, eager to kill the Demon Horde. Columns of light poured down from the heavens. Rain turned into ice as hard as arrows. Lightning arced across the sky. Barrages of spears and Mana bolts of all Affinities charged through the sky.

Swathes of the Demon Horde were washed away; many Stone Raiders fell unconscious from the Mana expenditure. Malsour was at the rear, creating golems and metal skimmers to pick up those already out of the fight, shipping them toward the growing fort in hopes to save them from dying and losing their gear and experience.

Wind turned the sky into a maelstrom; tornadoes erupted as plasma cannons fired.

It was an awesome display of magical firepower, but there was less than a hundred of them, and nearly three hundred and fifty thousand in the Demon Horde. They took out nearly a hundred and fifty thousand with their opening fire, their spells taking a toll on the Demon Horde.

Seeing their opportunity, the Demon Horde charged onward. The smart ones were able to move around the area where the Stone Raiders' spells were. Most were going too fast or there were too many Demons around them to escape the worst of the spells.

"Melee, support the squishy mages! Summoners, keep our skies clear and make sure nothing gets behind us!" Dwayne barked.

Dave opened his eyes. His hands fell to his rods as a shield and a sword extended from them. He glanced to Suzy, Steve, and Anna on his right, and then Deia and Malsour on his left.

Induca was still hiding from everyone's eyes, conjuring and controlling her flame atronachs to try to bolster the aerial forces.

There was no need for words before they silently looked toward the Demon Horde.

They charged toward the Stone Raiders, eager to rip apart those who dared to stop their feast of souls.

"Stone Raiders!" Dwayne yelled, charging forward.

"Stone Raiders!" A hundred voices rose up as the entire mass rushed forward. Even the battle mages boldly strode forward. None of them cared for their lives, for surviving this. They sure as hell did care about making the most of their attack.

Dave felt strength flood his body, his Agility and Intelligence boosted by buffs and enchantments on his armor. Party Zero rose into the air. Dave jumped from conjured rock to conjured rock as Suzy lifted herself and Steve. Her creations swarmed around her, tearing apart anything that tried to get near their creator. Steve fired the repeater in his right hand and hurled his axe through the sky with his left.

Anna took off like a bullet, spinning so fast as to make a tornado through the Demon Horde. Deia's own blades left trails of Fire and falling Demons in their wake. Malsour was covered in rock below the waist, repulsing against the ground. Darkness covered him; darklings and shadow limbs extended from his shadow and reacted as if Malsour had been born with them. Spears and pebbles flew from around him.

Dave let out a scream as he ran faster and faster. Power charged through his shield and encompassed a great swath of Stone Raiders, protecting them from rocks and spells hurled down on them.

The barrier projected off his shield started to hit resistance, but Dave powered on, pushing his armor and his enhancements as Demon after Demon slammed into his shield, damaging it.

Dave felt as if his mind were in a slowly closing vise as he conjured another shield in his right, bolstering his powers. On the inside of his first shield, a blue rune was fading to red, faster and faster. The vault soul gems continued to power him as spells ripped past him, able to pass through the shield-like barrier, but stopping everything coming from the other direction.

The barrier started to crack and fall apart. It shattered into Mana as it disappeared. In a tiny fraction of a second that Dave could only catch because of his higher Intelligence, a wall of force formed along the area that had been his shield.

Return damage is a bitch. A percentage of all of the attacks that had been placed on his Mana shield throughout the battle was redirected forward, right into the Demon Horde.

Dave fell back while the rest of his party surged forward, taking advantage of the chaos he had wrought. With a push, he followed after them. His body was weary and his mind tired. Twin axes appeared in his hands as he charged along with his party and his guild, right into the Dark Lord's Demon Horde.

***

The Dwarven wards simply needed to be placed on the ground, pulling stone and metal from the ground into walls and parapets.

It was impressive magic, but it couldn't be compared to the scale of magic that the Stone Raiders were using.

Efri's mind was blank as he took in the sight of the Stone Raiders' rear guard. He felt the rush of Mana that was expelled, scared to blink lest he might miss something as spells that would fell the strongest of warriors tore through the Demon Horde.

Efri heard the Stone Raiders' war cry as, instead of holding back, they raced forward.

Ranged weapons, spells: all of them took their toll to drop Demons from the sky. Melee fighters, even if they didn't have the ability to fly, rushed up to the bodies of the falling Demons, using uncanny Agility to bring the fight to the flying forces. Others fought on the ground, turning it into an abattoir. They were half-blurred images tearing through the Horde.

Those who had been rendered unconscious by their spells were carried into the growing fortifications.

The Stone Raiders charged into the heart of the Demon Horde. Bodies fell from the skies. Stone Raiders fell here and there, their death followed by a falling cloud of Demons.

Their lack of fear for death and whatever techniques they are using to gain more power—they're using everything that might destroy themselves in order to harass and slow the Demon Horde. Efri remembered the days that he had gone into battle, eager to spill the blood of his enemies, to savage them and take their energies as his own. He had become strong, invincible in his mind. Now, he saw the error of his ways. He was strong, but nothing like the Stone Raiders' titans who used their own destruction to take down thousands for each death.

Dwarven artillery howled over the crater as the other keeps that were in range and the artillery barrages that had been moved fired on the keep. Many of their shells exploded in the air as they met the Demon Horde.

All of the reinforcing DCA from Unity and the armies that were marching around the outside of Devil's Crater made sure that they cleared out any other groups of the Demon Horde that landed quietly.

People moved with brisk efficiency. A number of them looked off to the Stone Raiders' own battles that raged on just a few miles away.

The last of the forces from the keep rushed in. People were waiting for them to move them into different spots. Artillery wagons were turned, their legs dropping down in the dirt as Dwarves formed dirt and stone around the feet to brace the cannons.

The aerial fighting was chaos. The DCA retreated as the Demon Horde were greeted by spells. There were too many of them in the sky for the spells to take out.

"Repeaters!" Koza barked. Aleph automatons raised their repeater arms to the sky. Arrows started to rise up to meet the Demon Horde. Repair bots moved between the archers and crates filled with bolts.

"DCA, prepare to fly!" Efri yelled.

"Artillery, fire!" a Dwarf bellowed, followed by the artillery cannons firing across their line, bucking with the energies expelled.

"Mages, prepare your spells!" Lucy yelled out from the fort. Dust and debris covered the keep as explosions continued to fill the sky as unlucky Demons met Dwarven Mana artillery.

Still, the Stone Raiders continued to fight, filling the sky with a mash of magics and falling bodies.

The reinforcing Demons landed; their officers and veterans organized them into flying wings. The Beast Kin who couldn't fly or the Demons who were too wounded to fly took up positions behind the Dwarves who were swarming the walls.

Efri rose into the air on his wings, headed to the rear of the fort while he looked down on the men and women who would follow him into battle.

"Many of your brothers and sisters and our allies have laid down their very lives in the defense of our homes. They have aided us in our weakest hours. They are out there now sacrificing everything that they have to try to give us enough time to prepare for the Demon Horde." Efri pointed to the keep. His words fell over the ramshackle DCA in front of him.

None of them looked away from his powerful gaze.

"The Demon Horde has made it inside the crater. They have broken the keep and bring an army to kill your families and eat them! This, this is where we will hold. This is where we will stop the Demon Horde. We will not let our families be their food. We will sow their blood into the fields that our grandchildren will grow crops on for generations to come! Let us show why we had to be locked away for the sake of Emerilia. Let us show them the power that comes with standing beside one another and facing an enemy head on. Let us show that Dark Lord just who we are!"

Roars filled the area behind the fortifications. Over seventy thousand flying-capable warriors looked up at Efri, shaking their weapons.

Efri turned and looked to the destruction that was laid bare in front of the fortress.

The Stone Raiders fell from the skies, fighters from the Demon Horde following them.

"Follow me!" Efri's wings beat as they pulled him into the air.

The other fliers activated their magic or innate physical abilities, rising up into the sky after their general.

Vrexu and Malkur caught up with him, spreading out to either side of him.

"Well, to victory or to death." Efri looked to them all, recalling the old chant that the seven brothers had shared when they went off to fight.

"To victory or death," the others agreed. They rose higher into the darkening sky, watching the massive flying Demon Horde that approached.

Chapter 23: Win Or Lose

Anna watched as Suzy's creations started to fail.

Anna moved to help the summoner as her Air creation started to lose lift and form on her back. Power raged through Suzy; her Abscondita armor removed her fatigue and allowed her to concentrate.

"Summoner's Bastille!" The top of Suzy's staff zoomed into the sky as creation cores fell from her bag. Air creations formed and took flight. They created a swarm onto themselves, their wind blades cutting through Demons that lay around them.

The wind pulled at Suzy's almost-white hair. Her eyes glowed white as she channeled her Air Affinity over all others. More and more Air creations formed and took to the skies, clearing areas around the party as they fought. Suzy's choice to use her last resort move with the staff emboldened them and gave them energy as they pressed forward.

Anna let out a wolf-howl and dove into the Demon Horde. She carved out a path of destruction. She was a master of the wind, second only to the Lady of Air herself. The Demons had barely learned how to access her domain. While she was part of it, her blade howled, starting a song that danced across the skies. It was a song of hunger and blood, one of cold Mithril and cutting wind.

She became a blur moving through the skies, letting loose her shackles.

Dave rested in the center of them all, conjuring rock underneath him constantly, so he didn't fall as he buffed their spells and gear, and conjured amulets and items on them to increase their strength and power.

Deia's swords added to Anna's song with the roar of Fire. The heat of the flame and explosion when the intense heat met Demon superheated their bodies' liquids.

Feeling a disturbance in the air, Anna sent Air blades into a pack of Demons trying to get past her. She hovered there, watching as the people of Devil's Crater took to the skies. Their own army rushed to join swords with the Demon Horde that dared to enter their home.

Pride swelled up in Anna as she returned to her attacks. She had once been Anna of the Beast Kin. They had accepted her, taught her and called her one of their own. She still shared those memories with them.

But now I am Anna, an Air Blade Dancer of the Stone Raiders.

She looked to her side as groups of Stone Raiders here and there ran through the Demon Horde. The forces on the ground had lost nearly half their number but inflicted massive casualties.

The Stone Raiders in the sky numbered less than thirty, and although they hadn't stopped the Demon Horde, they had given their allies time enough to make a fort, to defend their people.

The DCA clashed with the Demon Horde, two clouds of people tearing at one another in a mind-bending display of aerial combat.

Anna fought through another group of Demons, only to find herself in open sky.

"Potions and water! Be ready to hit the Demon Horde again!" Deia said, sounding half delirious as her training spoke before her tired mind caught up to it. "We'll help the forces on the ground first."

The party descended toward the surviving Stone Raiders on the ground. Now, the Demon Horde was clashing with the DCA. It was more likely than not that they'd kill their own allies with a misplaced spell.

Anna fought to control her descent.

"Suzy!" Dave yelled as Suzy lost control over her creations. The cores rained down toward the ground as she and Steve tumbled.

Anna felt power surge through her as she caught Steve and Suzy, arresting their downward plummet.

"Uh, Anna, please don't drop me," Steve said.

"Sounds like you're scared of heights." Anna's words were sluggish as it took all she had to concentrate on the spells she was controlling.

"Well, I didn't realize how high up we were!" Steve looked directly down at the ground.

"Your mom has a way to cure a fear of heights. I think I might be out of Mana." Dave slumped over, unconscious.

Deia grabbed him before he could get more than twenty meters down.

Anna increased her descent, knowing how Mana fatigue could catch up on a person at the worst times.

Dwayne and Kim had been killed, but Josh was mostly alive. He was missing a foot, but his ability to move through shadows with his blades made up for that.

"Group together on the ground; get potions into you and gather your guild mates' packs and gear. Someone, help me grow my damned foot back!" Josh growled. "Feel like I should be on a pirate ship instead of with you bunch of weirdos." His pride was clear in his voice, however much he tried to hide it.

They gathered together. Induca appeared some time later, emerging from the ground as Malsour stumbled on his feet.

All of them looked on the brink of falling over with fatigue. They downed potions and gathered the gear of everyone who had fallen.

As they worked, they watched the Demon Horde and DCA clash.

The Demon Horde was able to flow through the gaps that came with aerial formations, attacking the fort. The Dwarves were waiting for them with crossbows and artillery.

Anna looked at the Demon Horde's numbers. *By Jukal.* Their ragtag group of Stone Raiders had reduced the Demon Horde to nearly a hundred and fifty thousand.

The DCA might be tired from constant fighting, but they were better trained and higher level fighters. They systematically carved through the Demon Horde. With over seventy thousand in the air and another ten thousand on the ground, the Horde was being ground down.

Dave pulled himself up. His potions and armor worked to bring him back to the land of conscious. His groans stopped as everyone watched the fight above the hastily made fort.

Gamers were very good about seeing not only what was in front of them, but how it fit with the bigger picture.

"They're coming apart!" Dave said. The others nodded and made noises of agreement. The Demon Horde didn't know their own numbers in the chaos of aerial battle, sometimes killing their own people without a friend-foe overlay.

The DCA ate through the Demon Horde, attacking from every angle they knew. Here, their skill and abilities shone through as the Demon Horde thinned drastically.

Anna dropped into a squat to watch the fight.

In minutes, the Demon Horde broke, a few trying to get away. Repeaters or the DCA hunted them down. DCA groups set off, hunting down more of the Horde that the Aleph scouts had picked up.

If they grouped together, they could be an issue.

Anna turned to look at the battlefield. There was a sea of tombstones from the keep past her to the fort. The ground in between had been churned up. There were burnt patches, projections out of the ground, and the debris of massive spells and the victims they'd claimed.

The keep had been torn apart, with its walls holed. In places, the stone walls had melted from the Dwarven artillery.

A sea of Demon bodies with the occasional body from another race dotted the terrible landscape.

"Take a seat. I'll see where we're needed." Josh sounded relieved and as tired as Anna felt.

She let herself fall backward and leaned against the side of a crater. She pulled potions from her hot bar for Stamina recharge. She let her Mana recharge by itself. Using the armor to fill it would leave her with a massive headache.

Steve's armored ass hit the dirt as he sat in the rather large crater. "Hey, Dave, maybe next time, you'll stay conscious until the end of the fight?"

"Jackass." Dave snorted and threw a pebble at Steve's armored chest.

Induca fussed over Suzy, sitting on her legs once she confirmed Suzy was okay.

"So, Summoner's Bastille—I guess that was your work?" Deia asked.

"Yeah. Suzy will either wake up in a little or die. That thing really plays hell with your Willpower. Don't worry. If she's not up within a few days, I'll kill her so she can respawn," Dave said.

Anna saw Induca flinch, but then settle down.

"After a few hundred years of being used to dying, having you immortals around is confusing." Induca slumped down on the ground.

"Hey, you're like a few centuries old!" Dave said.

"Yes, but we still have that fear of death. You lot, you run in with everything you have, holding nothing back because you know that you might die but you can come back again. Sure, you want to keep your levels and you'll fight even harder for that, but in the end, death is just a minor annoyance," Induca challenged.

"Different mindset." Deia shrugged.

"Josh!" Steve yelled out.

"What?" Josh replied, flat out on his back a few meters away.

"Nice peg leg!"

A stone rang off Steve's head. He never stopped grinning, unaffected by the rock.

"Arsehole," Josh said, but Anna could tell that he was smiling.

Anna's smile soured at seeing the bodies around her. She closed her eyes, setting a ward that would warn her of anyone approaching or attacking. *How many more battles will there be like this before Emerilia can have peace?* A part of her didn't want to know the number for fear of how high the casualties would be.

Chapter 24: A Better Tomorrow

Alkao's wings flapped as he looked over the battlefield from the keep toward the hastily erected fort. His mind thought back to the battlefields that he had lived on for the majority of his life. The sight of so many dead barely affected him before. Now, he saw the wasted lives of those who could have helped to make Devil's Crater stronger. There was much work to be done, a future that was theirs for the taking and those who had died in front of him had done so, so that future could be realized.

He knew that among the dead it was not just the Beast Kin and Demons. There were Aleph, Dwarves, and POEs who had joined the Stone Raiders.

They came to our aid and died so that we might have a chance to carve out a future, a tomorrow. Now, it is our duty to make sure that tomorrow is better than today. Celebrate what they have given us with their final breaths.

Alkao hovered in the air. The DCA had been three hundred thousand strong, no small number, especially when thinking that most of the people had been level 200s with abilities that would have made level 250s wary.

He let out a heavy breath, slowly coming to step on the ground. The smell of death pervaded his senses. It would disappear after a few days if the resources from those who had fallen were not collected and their bodies started to dissipate back into Emerilia.

His heart was heavy with loss. He had spent months preparing for his people's return. He had spent countless sleepless nights doing everything and anything he could to ready Devil's Crater for their arrival.

They had escaped their demise for centuries, been given hope, created allies and turned from a wandering horde into a true community that cared about one another.

Still, they had not been able to sit by and consolidate their strength. His people had paid in blood.

He looked over the battlefield. His eyes saw the scenes of countless battles. Where his first brother had died. Silent tears left lines down his cheeks.

He gave a sad smile, his eyes itchy as his thoughts filled with memories of Lezar. It wasn't the grand gestures, but the day-to-day things—a smile here, giving Alkao some of his water when there wasn't much to go around—small kindnesses that created everlasting ties between people.

Alkao let out a deep breath. It seemed heavy, as if his own emotions weighed on him. He had been hurriedly called the king of Devil's Crater so that there was someone to be in control and command in Devil's Crater's time of need.

He didn't want the responsibility. He remembered how his brother had charged forward with his blood-sworn. They had sacrificed themselves in order to give those who relied on them time. That was leadership: doing everything you could to lead your people to victory and sacrificing yourself in times of need to save those who look up to you.

In Emerilia, the strong ruled, sending out others to do their bidding. But leaders, they inspired loyalty for stepping out and saving these weaker people who carried out their orders.

I want to be a leader like that, a leader like Lezar was.

He made this promise to those who had laid down their lives for Devil's Crater, for those who were weaker than them, for the idea that these people might gain a future, a future that they were willing to die for.

Alkao stood there for a long time, his inner pain numb within his body as he started to envision a path for Devil's Crater. It was only when someone was so close to death that they were able to truly appreciate life and understand how fragile it was.

His wings extended. He rose into the sky with a few powerful beats of his wings. He turned and headed back toward the fort that was one big aid center dealing with the wounded and letting those who had fought find rest and get some food into themselves.

His blood-sworn followed, not saying a word.

Alkao's mood improved as he came to land outside the temporary fort.

There was a sense of relief in the air, but also sadness. They had won out against the Horde but many of their fellows had died.

Koza found him as he walked the camp, checking on his people.

"We have found the remainders of the Demon Horde. The aerial DCA and the Dwarves are closing in on them. There are just a few thousand remaining." Koza's scouts had tracked down the remaining members of the Demon Horde, marking them for all of the allies to see.

Alkao put his hand on the Elf Halfling's shoulder and looked into his eyes. "I might not have said it before, but thank you for coming to our aid when you did. Without it, I fear the number of my people who lay out on that field would be greatly increased." Alkao gestured to the land beyond the fort.

"Our people are not too dissimilar. Both of us were hunted down like rabid animals because Emerilia was scared of our abilities." Koza shook his head. "The Stone Raiders showed us that there are people out there who are willing to stand beside us. As they stood beside us, they stand beside you. I hope that one day the Aleph and people of Devil's Crater can stand beside one another as friends and allies."

"To that, we can both agree." Alkao extended a large hand.

Koza gripped the offered hand, shaking it. "And then, we can show Emerilia and the gods why they should fear us," Koza said, low enough so no one else could hear.

"The Dark Lord is mine," Alkao said, still holding Koza's hand

Koza leaned in. "As long as we get the Earth Lord."

"Agreed," Alkao said. The two of them shared hungry looks.

Stone Raiders jogged into the fort, looking around. Josh was there to greet them. A number were those who had died near the beginning of the battle. People went off to a tent where their gear was piled up and sorted out.

Alkao and Koza turned to watch them. They came out of the tent as if nothing had changed. Many of them actually had stronger auras than when they had gone into battle.

"They're one hell of a fighting force," Koza said.

"They train without fear. Every attack could kill one or the other, sometimes they do. Even if they die, each time they come back stronger from what they have learned. I saw their display of skill at the first battle at the northwestern keep and could see the destruction they brought down on their enemies here. They push the boundaries of what people should be able to do," Alkao said in a serious tone. He had heard of the power of Players before he had been saved by the Grey God. Hearing it and seeing it was two different things.

"I don't think that we've seen even the full scope of their power. With every day, they get stronger. Can you imagine how powerful they will be by the end of the Player cycle?" Koza said seriously.

"I do not know, but I plan to follow them along that path to power." Alkao touched the sword at his hip.

Koza looked at Alkao with a measuring gaze before slowly turning and looking back at the fort.

***

Bob, Fire, and Water sat around a table, watching the fight for Devil's Crater and what was left behind.

"They're a resilient bunch," Water said.

"That they are." Bob saw a proud smile on Fire's face as she watched the part with the Fire atronachs and Deia's fighting. Even though she was happy with her people's achievements, Bob could see the sadness in her eyes. Losing so many people in a day—it was hard for someone who lived for seeing others become stronger and create their own destinies.

"Not the kind of people to wait around either." Fire stopped her watching and dismissed the screen in front of her.

"They will rebuild and grow their army. This is not the last time that we have seen the DCA, I believe. It's also the weakest I think we will see them," Bob said.

"An alliance between Dwarves, Demons, Beast Kin, and Aleph. It sounds like a group I would not want to deal with." Water, too, had a somber look as his eyes moved to Bob.

"I didn't plan for it, though I won't say I didn't hope it would come about." Bob pulled out a pipe.

"Now, we have the Dwarven tournament coming up," Fire said.

"Yes, it will be quite the fight," Water said.

"I trust that you two will let your people compete, too. We need the best to walk the vaults. While the Players are many, they do not have the numbers to cover all of Emerilia. We will need our own champions armed with Weapons of Power to push back the creatures that will wander Emerilia once more." Bob tapped his pipe on his chair to clean it out.

"With that, we can spread the protection across Emerilia. I will send out word to the mage's guild and colleges across Emerilia. The best fighters from the colleges, guilds, towns, cities, and surrounding areas will be given a free ride to the Dwarven tournament," Fire said.

"I will put up the money for a teleport pad so that my people might be able to compete as well." Water looked to Fire.

"Whatever might come to pass in our future, we will stand to-gether." Bob looked to the two others.

"That we will." Water nodded.

"Two of the Affinities actually working together." Fire smiled. "It makes me wonder what we can do."

"No more reacting, trying to shore up our defenses and countering the others' attacks, but instead empowering our own people to create their own future." Water stroked his beard. "That is a powerful tool."

"Together, we can carve out a path for Emerilia and its people to survive the coming challenges," Bob whispered, as if saying it too loudly might break his dream.

Chapter 25: A Path To Power

Dave opened up his notifications now that everything had settled down.

Active Skill: Inference

Level: Expert Level 9

Effect: 81% increased chance of using moves you've read in books.

Active Skill: One handed and Shield

Level: Master Level 5

Effect: Weapons damage increased by 45%. Defense increases by 22%; shield bash is 25% more likely to stun opponent.

Cost: 20 Stamina

Active Skill: Spell Formation

Level: Master Level 3

Effect: You use 25% less Mana and your spells are 84% stronger.

Active Skill: Soul Manipulation

Level: Master Level 4

Effect: Tools you make to manipulate souls and their energy is 93% stronger. Able to use soul energy to fuel spells. 25% increase to soul energies reserves (can only be used for spells; does not act as extra Willpower points).

Cost: Dependent on creation.

Active Skill: Magical Circuits

Level: Mastered

Effect: Upon breaking down Magical Circuits, you understand how they function. 50% reduction of cost in making Magical Circuits

Cost: Dependent

Created Sub-Class: Magical Coding

Active Skill: Soul Smith

Level: Expert Level 7

Effect: 77% less soul energy necessary for crafting with soul smith.

Cost: Dependent on creation.

Active Skill: Builder

Level: Master Level 7

Effect: Speed and efficiency is doubled. Creations material cost is reduced by 35%.

Required: Tools

Active Skill: Dual wield

Level: Master Level 2

Effect: Attacks are 42 % faster. 10% chance of slowing target.

Cost: 15 Stamina

Passive Skill: Perception

Level: Master Level 6

Effect: If using the correct skills, you will see the hidden details around you. (If using arcane sight, can see arcane trip wires or hidden passages. If using regular sight, can see hidden crevices and loot containers.) 30% chance at better loot.

Active Skill: Two handed

Level: Master Level 2

Effect: 42% armor penetration on target. Stamina costs reduced 25% while fighting. Can use two-handed weapons in one hand at 50% increased Stamina cost.

Cost: 35 Stamina

Active Skill: Sprint

Level: Master Level 6

Effect: Sprint Speed is doubled. Sprinting costs 30% less Stamina.

Cost: 5 Stamina/second

Active Skill: Archery

Level: Master Level 2

Effect: Critical Hit chance increases by 42%. Ranged targets take 21% increased damage.

Cost: 10 Stamina

Class: Champion Slayer

Status:	Level: 3
Effect:	+30 to all stats
	Dark: Hated
	Light: Favorable
	Water: Favorable
Relationship with Affinities Pantheon:	Fire: Trusted Friend
	Earth: Angered
	Air: Neutral

Quest: Champion Slayer Level 4

Kill 100 Champions (85/100)

Rewards: Unlock Level 5 Quest

Increase to stats

Increased/Decreased reputation with Affinities

Level 220

You have reached level 220; you have **521** stat points to use.

"Best put those to use. Getting harder and harder to gain levels," Dave muttered, putting 10 into Intelligence and 25 into Agility.

Character Sheet

Name:	David Grahslagg	Gender:	Male
Level:	122	Class:	Dwarven Master Smith, Friend of the Grey God, Bleeder, Librarian, Aleph Engineer, Weapons Master, Champion Slayer, Skill Creator, Mine Manager, Master Summoner
Race:	Human/ Dwarf	Alignment:	Neutral Good

Unspent points: 491

Health:	24,000	Regen:	9.00 /s
Mana:	7,450	Regen:	22.40 /s
Stamina:	3,060	Regen:	18.10 /s
Vitality:	240	Endurance:	450
Intelligence:	745	Willpower:	448
Strength:	306	Agility:	372

Dave let out a breath, feeling the rush of the new stats. "Always feels good with some high attributes. Time to check those class quests and then I can see about getting the DCA armed and ready for whatever they might face."

Quest: Friend Of The Grey God Level 3

Complete the Quest: Survival of the Fittest

Rewards: Unlock Level 4 Quest

Increase to stats

Quest: Bleeder Level 2

Complete the Quest: Survival of the Fittest

Rewards: Unlock Level 3 Quest

Increase to stats

(???)

Quest: Librarian Level 3

Conduct research that allows you to understand how teleport pads work.

Rewards: Unlock Level 4 Quest

Increase to stats

Quest: Aleph Engineer Level 4

Help build 1 Aleph facility

Rewards: Unlock Level 5 Quest

Increase to stats

Increased access to Aleph College Knowledge

Quest: Dwarven Master Smith Level 3

You must craft 10 weapons of S quality with your Smithing Art (Currently 5/10)

Rewards: Unlock Level 4 quest

Increase to stat gain

Quest: Weapons Master Level 3

Complete the Quest: Survival of the Fittest

Rewards: Unlock Level 4 Quest

Increase to stats

Quest: Skill Creator Level 2

Personally teach 1 person your Skill (0/1)

Rewards: Unlock Level 3 Quest

Increase to stats

Quest: Mine Manager Level 3

Pay 500,000 gold

Rewards: Unlock Level 4 Quest

Increase to mine's output

Quest: Master Summoner Level 2

Open a rift to 10 planes (0/10)

Rewards: Unlock Level 3 Quest

Increase stats

Dave closed his interface. He was still recovering from the battle just a few hours ago, but his higher Endurance meant he didn't need much sleep and his other attributes had him feeling better even faster than he'd hoped.

He wandered out of his tent. His party's tents were in a squared-off U-shape around a cooking area. The flaps were open to let in a cool breeze coming in from the north. Thankfully the bodies were all downwind and people were already looting the bodies. Once they were looted, they would disappear off into nothing.

On Emerilia, very few races actually had anything like burials as bodies would disintegrate after a few minutes without magical enhancement. Only kings and queens or the richest lords and ladies had their bodies preserved long enough for official funerals.

Suzy was still passed out on her cot. Induca was also asleep, spooning with her. Steve was close by, acting as a guardian.

Malsour, Deia, and Anna sat in the stone seats Malsour had made around the campfire.

Dave sat beside Deia.

"You stink," she said as his arm circled her back and she rested her head on his shoulder.

"Is that code for build me a shower please?" Dave asked.

"See, this is why I keep him," Deia said to Anna, who simply smiled.

"Well, I don't know about you all, but I am looking forward to taking some time away from this all once we defeat the remainder of the Demon Horde," Malsour said.

"Ah, time to plan the next part of our adventure?" Dave asked.

"Or vacation from all this damned chaos?" Anna chimed in.

"Well, I have many books and the people of Devil's Crater need some help in putting up shelters and proper defenses. There is also Unity that needs building," Malsour said.

Dave could feel the enthusiasm radiating off his friend. His Affinity was thought of by many as evil and linked to death, and in ways, it was. However, to Malsour and many Dark mages, it was a powerful force of building. Malsour reveled in building things. Creating a city and the infrastructure across Devil's Crater was a dream.

"So, what do you want to do, Anna?" Deia asked.

"I want to make sure that my people are settled in and safe. Once that's done, I think I'd be more than happy to go on another adventure. I have no need to go to the Dwarven tournament." Anna tapped her sheathed blade resting on the bench beside her.

"I think I've had enough of fighting for now. I think spending time at Per'ush might be fun." Deia looked to Dave.

"I'd be interested in visiting a bit, but I've got things I need to take care of in Cliff-Hill—the guild hall, here and with the Aleph college," Dave said.

"Good thing we have teleport pads, so we can meet up with one another." Deia snuggled closer to Dave.

"How could I deny that, babe?" Dave leaned down to kiss her.

She smiled happily as Dave looked back to the others, a grin on his face.

"I think Suzy and Induca might also be interested in the mage's college or somewhere that they can train," Malsour said.

"Well, I'm about this close to figuring out teleport pads. I think if we get our heads together for a bit, then I can figure it all out. Also, part of going to the Aleph college is finding out how the portals work and how I can use that to make summonings easier. Be pretty awesome if we can open up a hall of summoning in the guild hall." Dave smiled.

"A hall of summoning?" Anna asked. All of the party looked to Dave in question.

"Well, we've got more than one summoner in our ranks and getting the best creatures to control strengthens the guild. We're not the biggest guild, but we are still one of, if not the, most powerful guild when it comes to raiding. With more summoned creatures, we can have more creatures around that can bolster our numbers. Imagine having three Creatures of Power like Steve at our backs when we go into a fight. One doesn't need to be a summoner to create a soul binding contract. A summoner can control the beast and then pass the contract on to another member of the Stone Raiders."

"Making it so that each Stone Raider gets one or more creatures that bolster our numbers when we're in a fight." Malsour nodded.

"We need the numbers if we're going to keep heading into fights like the last one we just had," Anna added.

"I wonder what's going to happen when we reveal the footage from this fight?" Deia said.

"I don't doubt that we'll be able to win the contest with the other guild vying to be the best raiding guild in Emerilia. When we do, there are going to be tons of Players who want to join. I know that Bob will also help guide some of the better Players and POEs to us. I wouldn't be surprised if the guild doubles in size, unless we have just too many things going on," Anna said.

"What about the E-heads? I know that we have a lot of them, but do you think more will join us?" Dave asked.

"I think so. With the guild's connections, the Exdar's Traders and the Golden Sabres and the way that the guild promotes people going and learning more about Emerilia and their different ways, many E-heads would be interested in the protection of a guild that will allow them to do as they desire and get involved in events that shape the future of Emerilia. Even if we lose the competition with the other guild for the strongest raiding guild, our guild is the most powerful. We have altered the future of Emerilia in a very real way."

The members of Party Zero looked around, thoughtful.

"With Dave's upgrades and our reliance on fighting techniques over pre-programmed controls, I think that we'll be a match for any guild!" Steve declared. "I have not seen these other guilds, but after all of the growth in the last eight months, you might be surprised by the results."

Steve might act like a goof most of the time, but when he was being serious, it was good to pay attention. With his core, he was one of the three most powerful AIs on Emerilia, superseding the AI that managed the planet, farming it of technology, power, and the entertainment the residents brought the Jukal Empire.

They were stopped by a prompt appearing in everyone's vision.

Quest: Survival of the Fittest

Together with the Dwarves of Aldamire, the Aleph, and the DCA, you have protected the people of Devil's Crater and defeated the Dark Lord's Demon Horde.

Rewards:
100,000 gold to the Guild's treasury
Increased reputation with the creatures of Devil's Crater
The Stone Raiders' Guild are seen as: Allies
You are personally seen as: Trusted Friend
750,000 EXP
Rights to use the dungeons and raid events within Devil's Crater and in the Devil Crater's controlled land.

Dave dismissed the quest and looked to his classes that had leveled up.

Class Quest Completed: Friend Of The Grey God Level 3
Completed the Quest: Survival of the Fittest
Rewards: Unlock Level 4 Quest
+10 to all stats (Stacks with previous Class Level)
+300,000 EXP

Class: Friend of the Grey God

Status: Level 3

Effects: +30 to all stats
Access to hidden quests.

Class Quest Completed: Bleeder Level 2
Completed the Quest: Survival of the Fittest
Rewards: Unlock Level 3 Quest
+10 to all stats (Stacks with previous Class Level)
(???)
+200,000 EXP

Class: Bleeder

Status: Level 2

Effects: +20 to all stats
(???)

Class Quest Completed: Weapons Master Level 3
Completed the Quest: Survival of the Fittest
Rewards: Unlock Level 4 Quest
+20 Vitality
+10 Endurance
+15 Strength
+15 Agility
(Stacks with previous Class Level)
+300,000 EXP

Class: Weapons Master
Status: Level 3

Effects:
+60 Vitality
+30 Endurance
+45 Strength
+45 Agility

The effects of the new stats started sinking in as Dave gingerly took his arm back from around Deia and slowly lowered himself to the ground.

"Another stat boost?" Deia sounded distorted by the slight time difference that was making itself known.

"Yeah." Dave was pretty sure he wouldn't wreck anything in the next minute or so.

Deia also slowly moved to lie down on the bench.

"Seems I'm not the only one," Dave said.

"This crap is annoying!" Deia complained.

Dave snorted. A new notification appeared.

Level 221
You have reached level 221; you have **496** stat points to use.

Dave grinned. With his classes increase, he'd been able to gain more levels. He went to check his character sheet.

Character Sheet

Name:	David Grahslagg	Gender:	Male
Level:	122	Class:	Dwarven Master Smith, Friend of the Grey God, Bleeder, Librarian, Aleph Engineer, Weapons Master, Champion Slayer, Skill Creator, Mine Manager, Master Summoner
Race:	Human/ Dwarf	Alignment:	Neutral Good

Unspent points: 496

Health:	28,000	Regen:	9.60 /s
Mana:	7,550	Regen:	23.40 /s
Stamina:	2,990	Regen:	20.35 /s
Vitality:	280	Endurance:	480
Intelligence:	755	Willpower:	468
Strength:	341	Agility:	407

"So, now you're stuck in one place for more than five minutes, when do you think we should plan to have the wedding?" Deia asked.

"Wah?" Dave asked, surprised by the suddenness of her question. The others laughed as he forced himself to relax and not accidentally use the new stats he hadn't adapted to yet.

Chapter 26: A Time To Build

"Send out the next load." Kol wiped his forehead with a rag. He looked over his forge, actually *looked* at it. To many Dwarves, it might be lacking without the massive bellows and tools that a Dwarven smithy in the mountains might have.

Though he had more orders than he could count and commissions for Master-tiered weapons and items to work on, he constantly found himself closing his eyes when working with the metal, only to open them and not only sense the beauty of what he had made, but to see it.

Those Stone Raiders aren't a bad lot, and Jules has certainly come a long way from being one of the troublemakers to open Boran-al's Citadel.

Kol shook his head, lest the others working in the smithy see his smile.

He jumped on a wagon leaving down toward the teleport pad. Crates filled the wagon, each holding dozens of swords, arrowheads, or spearheads. It was up to the people of Devil's Crater to add the wooden sections.

The ride didn't take long before Kol was level with the teleport pad.

He knew that he was traveling nearly around Emerilia, so thoughts of what he would do if he was stuck there filled his mind. He came up with a number of ways that he'd find his way back to his smithy if the teleport pad didn't work.

Then, the wagon was passing through the teleport pad and he was in the middle of a city. There were clear signs of damage everywhere on the buildings and roads, though the rubble had been cleared away for the most part and repairs were underway. Although it was nighttime in Cliff-Hill, it was early morning in Devil's Crater.

There was an odd mixture of sadness and hope in the air. People walked with their heads down, but nodded at the incoming wagons appreciatively.

The wagons didn't have far to go before they reached a large barracks. It was built like a fortress. A wall around a large open courtyard split into different training areas. Sleeping barracks lay along walls as the main keep was being built.

Square shaped formations of Demon and Beast Kin waited, eyeing the wagons as they approached.

Quartermasters showed the wagons where to off-load their gear. Soldiers of the Devil Crater's Army moved to assist in pulling off the weapons. They opened the boxes, laying them in different areas. Off to the side, there was a small yard where arrow shafts and wooden poles were being fitted with arrow and spearheads.

Kol got off the wagon, seeing that everything was in order. He moved to one of the officers overseeing the whole process.

"Where's yer smithy, lad?" Kol asked.

"Smithy? Uh, I think it's down that way. Bunch of smoke coming out of it all the damned time," the Demon said.

Kol grunted, his eyes thinning. A smithy put out a lot of smoke, but from the Demon's tone, it sounded as if there was a lot more than what a normal smithy might let out into the air.

Kol strolled through the courtyard, watching the DCA square formations. Soldiers filed past tables where weapons had been deposited minutes before. They eagerly took their weapons, treating them as if they were Weapons of Power, not just simple steel weapons that Kol's smithy had churned out en masse.

He paused as he saw levitating carts funneling through from the teleport pad. He didn't need his eyes to understand the carts. His breath caught in his chest as he looked at the carts and the automatons with them.

"Aleph?" Kol whispered to himself in awe. *The ancient race that had been so smart that they had threatened the knowledge of the Pantheon?* Now they walked freely among the people of Devil's Crater.

It had been a shock to learn where his weapons were going, and Dave had said that the Ela's were both Aleph. They certainly had the markings and clothes of Aleph that Kol had heard about, though it was only now, seeing an Aleph cart in working order and their marvelous automaton machines, that he truly believed Dave.

He remembered Dave's odd request to have a wagon team to move an oversized cart.

Dave had brought him in on the secret of the seeder and the portals held within. It was Kol's job to make sure that no one found them while Dave was away.

The cryptic language Dave was using made sense as he thought about it more.

They were moving a portal from the seeder to the Aleph's care. Kol's mind worked on its own. He knew that the Aleph were the creators of the teleport pads and that many believed it was from their learning about portals.

If they were able to unlock the full knowledge that came with the portals... Kol felt energy return to his body, the energy he had felt when his eyesight had returned, a joy that made him want to yell out and jump in excitement for the future and what might be.

Kol continued to watch the carts and the Aleph as they worked. Automatons dropped off crates filled with dozens of swords. They were simple and efficient like Kol's, though with his senses, he was able to see more than most.

"Interesting. They're all practically identical and they're not old. They churned out all of them in a week? How is that possible?" He talked to himself, his eyes closed, not caring for the people who looked at the Dwarf with his eyes closed and muttering to himself.

"They must have one of those factory-like things that Dave was talking about. If they do, then they can probably beat the cost it takes us for the different items." Kol stroked his beard. After the healing, it was no longer a patchy mess but now a decent scruff turning into a thick beard. He continued to look at the Aleph, deep in thought.

"Well, there's nothing for it. While the Aleph control the market for mass-producing items, we will have to focus on making items made for the user. Get Dave to take contracts on higher level weapons, things that are made per person instead of by the group. Imagine what they could do if they could make magical artillery?" Kol stopped stroking his beard for a moment. "I think it's time that Dave, the head smiths, and I got together and started to think about how we could start on adding a factory for certain items."

He pulled up his interface, starting to send messages out as he wandered through the town. Here and there, Aleph in their simple yet comfortable clothes worked to repair old homes and streets.

Kol turned a corner, finding himself face-to-face with a half-dozen warbands.

The war leader made to yell at Kol before he closed his mouth and saluted the Master Smith.

The other leaders did the same, their warbands marching on in perfect silence as their commanders rendered honors.

Kol nodded to them as they passed. He looked a lot different with his repaired face, but the necklace that denoted him as a Master Smith was visible.

Dwarven engineers were talking with a number of Beast Kin and Demons and having a rather large and colorful discussion about the layout of the city.

"Look, whoever made your first damned layout made a damn good job of it. Then, you lot gone and fucked it up by letting people build everywhere. You're going to have people with basements in the damned sewers if you keep building like you are," an engineer yelled.

"So, you want us to tear down these people's homes?" a Beast Kin yelled.

"Look, you either take them down now and then you're well set up for later on. Or, you keep building like you want to live on top of one another and you start having people drop dead from all the diseases. Then, you can't get food and water in and out of the city because your roads look like some kid chewing on sugar cane and then rolled around on a piece of paper with a piece of charcoal in their hands!"

"But, these initial plans, they don't make the best use of the island," a Demon chimed in.

"They might not, but they make it so that you're not stepping on one another, have open streets and sanitation works that actually bloody work!" the Dwarf yelled, slamming his fist on the table.

"Also, these plans are made to be expanded. Look at the roads and the water works. Later on, if Unity gets too big for the island you've made, it can be extended outward with another river to cover it," another Dwarf said.

"How are we going to house all our people on this small island?" the Beast Kin yelled, throwing her hands up in despair.

"You've got seven keeps. Sure, one of them is broken, but it's being fixed. An eighth is being built. They're going to house a lot of people and you can be sure that they're going to hire a lot of people who aren't in the DCA to help with the running of things. Then, you've got the small communes in the different sectors. Got your farmers, hunters, and lumberjacks. They're not going to come back to Unity all the time to just live here. Sure, it's nice to have a home here, but most people who live in a city are crafters and traders. Nearly everyone else lives somewhere else to get away from the mess of cities and make a living. You've got miles and miles of area that people can use to make a living. You might think that you'll have a lot of people in Unity, but I wouldn't doubt more than fifty thousand are going to live here, if that," the first Dwarven engineer said.

"So, what about those people we're evicting? You going to just make them sleep on the streets? We just barely won against the Demon Horde. We have losses to mourn. Throwing people out at the same time is not going to go well," the Demon growled. If not happy with the situation, he was at least placated by it.

"We can have them a new place built within an hour. We're also going to be adding running water to every building. None of that crap in a bucket and bathe from a bucket malarkey," the first Dwarf engineer went on.

Kol smiled to himself as he headed in the direction the DCA officer had pointed.

"Running water in houses? You can do that?" the Demon said, his shock clear.

Kol continued through the streets, showing progress. He reached a part of the city that showed the open and undeveloped ground that more houses, estates, and shops would lay upon. Past it was the untouched lands of the valley.

The early morning sun looked down upon the valley. A small farming land was being prepared. Greenhouses were starting to sprout up. Trees and forests ranged across the land. Kol could hear lumberjacks cutting through trees that rested on Unity, clearing them for the growing city.

The sight reminded him of Cliff-Hill before its roots had been planted and the city built up.

There was but a trickle in the moat around the city, but it was growing in size.

Kol scanned with his senses, finding the smithy he had been looking for easily enough. He frowned. His keen senses already picked up issues with the facility. He passed through a grove of re-planted rare trees but it was little to smooth down his frown.

Smithing was an art to him and whoever was running this smithy was manhandling it badly.

***

The Demon Horde was no more and the people of Devil's Crater could now get back to the task of building up their home. With winter fast approaching, houses were going up every day in Unity. Thankfully, Dave had called upon a number of Dwarven engineers to assist the Unity city planners.

It was quickly becoming clear that they had ignored the plans that Fornau had given Alkao. Demons rarely stayed in one place long and most of the Beast Kin cleaned themselves daily out of their beast habits.

For a bid to make shelters, they'd built everywhere and any-where, something that the Dwarven engineers pointed out would hinder rather than help in the future.

The Dwarven Warclans had all retreated except for one, asking permission to scout the area themselves. Alkao had happily agreed. Lady Kragr had also asked to meet with one of Alkao's representa-tives. He'd sent Malkur to meet with the lady of Aldamire Moun-tain.

It was clear that the Dwarves were feeling them out to talk about a possible alliance between their groups. Alkao did not know what power Dave held with the Dwarves, but it seemed to be enough to gain them audience and interest. The trading head of Devil's Crater had also gone with Malkur to talk to Dwarven traders.

Devil's Crater was now a million gold richer, but it was not an infinite supply. Alkao had issued a stipend to any families who had lost someone in the fighting. Then, there were the weapons on credit from the Cliff-Hill smithies. Although the simple Aleph weapons were cheaper, they didn't have the craftsmanship or the finer abilities of the Cliff-Hill's smithies.

He looked down at the contract on his desk, outlining the needs of the DCA and an open spot for the cost of such armaments. He still needed to find someone to make bows for his DCA. After seeing them in the sky, he knew their best use was for hit-and-run tactics. Finding weapons he could use to amplify their natural abilities would be of great help in the future.

Winter approached and it was already becoming cooler. Alkao had placed massive orders for food, clothes, tools for the fields and lumberjacks and greenhouses. If the trade delegation was successful, he might be able to get more glass for his greenhouses as well as the seeds and implements for growing his orchards and farms.

His DCA were strong with their weapons, and, when fully armed, they were fearsome opponents. Yet, he was unable to shake what he had seen when the Demon Horde had met the Stone Raiders' magic.

Magic gave fearsome power and long range, something that the DCA lacked.

Alkao's eyes drifted toward a request on his desk. "A request to go to the mage's guild to learn the way of magic," Alkao said, resting his elbow on the arm of his chair.

"I didn't think the day would come where we would have our people learning from the mage's guild." Alkao shook his head. He opened his interface, sending orders to the generals, and giving permission to allow people to attend the mage's college. However, only in limited numbers, so that they weren't left with a skeleton fighting force.

The Demon Horde was no more, but there were plenty of powerful beasts in Ashal. Not having a significant fighting force was an invitation to death and despair.

He stood from his desk; the chair creaked as it was relieved from his bulk. His wings flicked to each side, limbering up from being half-trapped in a chair for most of the day. Alkao stepped out onto his balcony, looking out across Devil's Crater. The massive valley was covered in darkness. In the distance, he could see the lights of Unity and the various communes set up in various sectors.

He looked to his keep and could pick out the signs of battle still being cleared away. Mage lights and torches lit the courtyard. DCA forces moved between their posts, looking for any possible threats that might come from Ashal's wilderness. A connecting wall ran between the keeps.

Lights lit up the wall, highlighting a full ringed defense.

Alkao's eyes moved to the gate that led out of the keep's courtyard and into the scarred landscape below where the Demon Horde and the full might of the DCA had clashed.

The arch had become a monument, listing the names of those who had fallen in battle—the battle to protect their brothers- and sisters-in-arms. To protect their friends, their families, and all of those who called Devil's Crater home.

Alkao straightened his posture. Emotions ran through him, heavy and thick. There were no words to express his feelings. Instead, he just gazed upon those names, his mind filled with images of that day and a promise filling his mind.

"We will become stronger than ever before. No more will we be intimidated by the lords and ladies of the Pantheon. We will carve out a future with our allies. Might determines the winner and those who get to make the rules. So, we will become the strongest in Emerilia, so that we can live in peace!" Alkao swore on the names of the dead and his honor as a Demon Prince.

A knock on Alkao's door brought him back to reality.

"Come in." Alkao wandered back into his office.

Dave and another Dwarf walked into the office.

"It is good to see you." Alkao shook Dave's hand.

"You too, Alkao. This is Kol, my mentor. He taught me most of the smithing I know. He also runs the Cliff-Hill smithies." Dave waved to the other Dwarf.

"Demon Prince." Kol shook Alkao's hand.

The old Dwarf might not look like much but his hands and eyes told of a hard worker who had tempered the strength of his youth with the knowledge of the matured.

"Please, call me Alkao. Thank you for coming." Alkao waved for them to take a seat on his couches. They did so.

"As we saw in recent battles, my people need weapons and armor. When you conjured armor on them, they were able to beat back a force nearly four times their own strength. The Aleph can provide us with decent weapons at a cheap cost, as well as magical robes. Their armor is much more expensive and takes a lot of time to custom fit. I was wondering if you would be able to fill in that issue?" Alkao asked.

"Makes sense. The Aleph can make a ton of items at a decent quality through their factory methods." Dave shared a look with Kol.

"It wouldn't take much for us to make and fit full body armor, though doing all of that through the portal is going to be a pain," Kol warned.

"What if we set up a smithy here?" Dave asked.

"Could work out nicely. The smithy here is being run by a Beast Kin who is barely keeping things running. We're going to have to buy out a district and build a whole 'nother smithy to work here. Devil's Crater is a great place for raiders and hunters to use as a base to go out into Ashal to get good loot. We can use the loot and items the different hunters and fighters give us to make some really powerful weapons. We're not good at mass-producing like the Aleph, but we can beat them on a weapon-by-weapon basis," Kol declared.

Alkao hid his surprise. He knew that he needed weapons, armor, and a thousand other things that a smithy could make. Having one not only connected by teleport pad but in Unity would solve a lot of issues.

"Would you work on anything besides weapons?" Alkao asked.

"Well, I think they would be our primary business, at least in the beginning. However, there are always apprentices looking to refine their craft. They can work on items like nails, screws, simple repairs or implements and tools," Kol said.

Alkao nodded, his excitement building. "If I was to deed over to you a portion of Unity, would you be amenable to giving a discount or putting that against future costs incurred by the Devil's Crater government?" Alkao asked.

"We could use it as a debt, though only at cost," Dave said.

"Done." Alkao nodded.

"Have to get with some of the Dwarven engineers to get their estimates of land and usage," Kol said, more to Dave than Alkao.

"Get that sorted as soon as possible." Dave nodded.

A message appeared in Dave's vision.

Private Chat

Kol> Was talking to the Aleph. Looks like we can get cheaper materials for a decent cost out of them. Also with your guild thinking about setting up their own refinery, we could get metals from there. Would reduce our overhead for making the armor and also speed it up. They can roll the metal out into sheets so we just need to cut and form it.

Dave gave Kol a thoughtful look before he turned back to Alkao.

"So, the Devil's Crater government will deed to us a portion of land within Unity that we will use to build a smithy as well as housing for its workers. The value of this land at market prices will be used as a credit to be used in future purchases; that is one agreement. The second would be to make armor for all of the Devil's Crater Army soldiers. Once the second contract is completed, then the smithy located in Devil's Crater will be free to work on any projects they desire. Any other contracts with the smithy will have to be negotiated on an ongoing basis," Dave said.

Contract between Cliff-Hill Smithy and the Government of Devil's Crater

Requirements:	Devil's Crater Government will deed to the Cliff-Hill Smithy a portion of land within Unity at market prices.
Failure:	Loss of standing with the Cliff-Hill Smithies and the Council of Anvil and Fire Cliff-Hill subsidiary located in Devil's Crater will focus on the armoring of Devil's Crater Army before taking on any other contracts.
Reward:	Cost of land deeded to the Smithy will act as credit with the Devil's Crater Smithy location. Gain access to Smithy with possible advancement to Dwarven Master Smith level Gain Smithy within Devil's Crater

"Agreed!" Alkao said with a wide smile. He shook Dave's hand before doing the same with Kol.

"I'll get the land and cost sorted out and start talking to the Aleph, though Suzy will probably be the best with this contract stuff," Kol said.

"Well, she's still out. I think she should be back on her feet tomorrow, but otherwise I know a few people who could help with the contracts and negotiations," Dave said.

"I hate all this negotiating stuff; much easier back in my smithy." Kol growled.

Alkao sighed. "I know the feeling. Managing all of this is a pain in the ass." He waved at his desk with papers and all manner of contracts and reports across it. "Though with it all and meetings like this, we're carving out a path into the future. One where we can stand tall and proud, secured in our own power and ready for the threats that we will face together."

Dave and Kol nodded in agreement. Power ruled on Emerilia. It seemed to be a law in Ashal; as others learned of the Demons, they needed to be ready for the threats that would come from other groups. If they seemed weak, everyone would lay siege to the crater for the resources and security that it provided whoever ruled it.

"I heard that you are thinking about whether to let people attend the mage's colleges?" Dave asked.

"It has been one of the subjects on my mind," Alkao admitted.

"Well, if you need it, I know someone in the mage's college and guild who might be able to make things easier. Having strong mages is essential in any standing army," Dave volunteered.

"Thank you, Dave." Alkao gave a kind smile before he laughed. "If not for you and the rest of your party, I don't think that we would be sitting here. I know that there would be a mere fraction of my people left alive. Your help and your lesson about coming to trust and rely on others—I don't think I have learned a more important lesson in my life."

"Ah, you just needed a good push in the right direction." Dave paused, a smile spreading across his face. "And, I think it's about time we started working on a new shield for you."

***

Geswald closed his interface, his face pale and his eyes unfocused.

The plan had been put into action. Lord Esamael's forces were on the move.

Geswald had followed the lord's orders to the letter. There was no knowing who was under the lord's employ. Down here, Esamael was much closer and more powerful than the king of Gudalo.

The cities around Verlun were on alert, watching the city to make sure none escaped. Those who were loyal to the lord and his allies were poised to take over the businesses and properties of those who supported the Stone Raiders.

Esamael's forces would not just destroy the Stone Raiders' guild hall in Verlun—they'd eliminate any and all who supported the guild.

Geswald rubbed his temples. *I am getting too old for this game of politics.*

If they succeeded, then Lord Esamael would have two teleport pads that he might use to assault the northern cities of Gudalo, bringing them under his control. Once the guild hall in Verlun was taken, then Esamael would begin the assault on the northern cities. Everything was set and ready to go.

Geswald opened his interface.

Private Message: Pete

Geswald> Make sure preparations are ready, no matter the outcome.

Pete> It will be done, my lord.

Either Geswald would become one of the richest men in Emerilia, or he would be a man on the run. This was the game of kings and the dynamics of power.

***

"Why didn't you tell me about this earlier?" Josh sat in the Mirror of Communication guild hall and looked to Florence.

"Well, you were dealing with the Demon Horde and having your concentration split probably wasn't the best thing."

Josh sighed and rubbed his face. "Okay, well, you might have a point there."

"I'm getting pretty pissed with the way that the POEs think they can just run over us," Dwayne grunted.

"Well, then, I think it's time we did some running over of our own," Lucy said.

"Oh, I do love it when you get all cold and scary," Kim, the last member of the meeting, said.

"Sigaird is moving his forces up toward Emaren to try to get to Esamael. At the speed they're going, they're going to be late by three days, two days after Esamael has already moved his forces to the northern cities of Gudalo. The armies of the southern border are going to find a series of fortified cities, closed to them and filled with civilians they're supposed to protect. They're not going to do anything without a royal writ, which is going to be a pain in the ass for the king to give when he's fighting a war across his border cities. The king's got spies throughout his organization. Anything he does, Esamael is going to know about it," Lucy said.

"How do I have the feeling you've known about this for a while?" Josh drawled.

"A lady never reveals all her secrets." Lucy smiled as her eyes were cold.

"Go on," Josh said, feeling she had a lot more to say.

"Esamael plans to hit Verlun, then use the teleport pad there to move his forces into the northern cities and spread them out before Sigaird and his forces know what's going on. He's moving all of his armies hidden as guards and thugs down to Emaren and Verlun, leaving behind just enough forces to hold the cities that are under his control or allied with him. We're looking at two hundred thousand trained, armed, and armored soldiers. I say we deploy scouts around Verlun. Josh and his group move through the city, killing the would-be assassins and fighting forces in the city. We use our forces to build a wall. We hold out in Verlun long enough for Sigaird to get his shit together and send reinforcements through the teleport pad and down to clear out Emaren with his southern army."

"So, we need to hold off two hundred thousand soldiers?" Dwayne asked.

"Correct." Lucy nodded.

"What level are they? How many mages and fighters?" Kim asked.

"We're looking at level 150 to 200. Mages...about half of their force. There are plenty of mage's colleges in the area that aren't interested in joining the mage's guild and following their rules," Lucy said.

"What will Per'ush do?" Josh asked.

"Nothing. They're a neutral force. Unless they're attacked or someone oversteps the rules of warfare they've laid down, they aren't going to get involved. I would think the same with the adventurer's guild," Kim said.

"The trader's guild will file grievances and maybe hire the two other guilds to enforce it, asking for repayment and compensation for attacking their establishments. However, Geswald, the trader's guild leader in the area, is firmly under Esamael's control, so we shouldn't expect much support in that area," Florence added.

"Well, we can do it for a while, but I don't think we can do it indefinitely." Dwayne scowled.

"I swear, you never listen to half the stuff you talk about." Lucy shook her head. "How it must hurt inside those small brains." She gave them a sad, apologetic look for their loss in life.

"All right, smartass, what have you got?" Josh rolled his eyes and smiled at her antics.

"We're not alone. Am I the only one who remembers the agreements we have with over a dozen different groups?" Lucy asked.

"Well, we're allied with a bunch of people, but what do you mean?" Josh asked.

"You're thinking so Earth right now. This is Emerilia, the land of might equals right. The land where we have alliances with the Mithsia, Benvari, and Zolu Dwarves, the Asha-moor and Kufo'tel Elves, the people of Devil's Crater, the Aleph, the cities Cliff-Hill, Epikari, Ossai, Zolari, and Zol'Ord."

"Okay, we get the idea, but isn't that for trade?" Josh said.

"Florence, since we have been trading, how much has those different cities or groups used the teleport pad in Verlun?" Lucy asked.

"I don't know the numbers, but with our extremely low tax on trading between our groups, we have at least half of our traffic coming from them," Florence said.

"Okay, but so, what if we lose the teleport pad?" Josh asked.

"So, what if they lose the millions in potential gold?" Lucy countered.

Josh's mind started to work. *How much is someone willing to fight for their investment? Also there is a part about aiding one another if the other is under threat.*

"So, if we're attacked, we can enact our alliance agreements, pulling in forces from these other groups?" Kim said.

"Bingo. We've shown that we're one hell of an investment. With our teleport pad, helping people in a tough spot, we've proved ourselves. What has Lord Esamael done? If they're in the area, he's demanded so much tax that they can barely make a profit and cares little about the people who pass through his lands, most of them being set upon by 'raiders' who happen to be under the lord's employ," Lucy said.

"Don't forget the power that Dave wields with the Dwarves. I don't know what happens when someone is a Dwarven Master Smith, but I would highly doubt that they would look kindly upon those who would dare to attack one," Dwayne said.

"Okay, say that this works and we can defend Verlun—what then?" Josh asked.

"Oh, I'm not saying we sit back and wait for them. I'm saying as soon as we have proof of them attacking Verlun and someone assaulting our people, we tear them apart. I wasn't kidding when I said I'm done with being attacked. We're not going to just defend Verlun. We're going to tear out Esamael's forces. We're going to arrest or kill them to the last fighter and then we're going to tell the king what he's going to have to do if he wants his country back," Lucy said.

"Well, that'll show Emerilia why you don't mess with the Stone Raiders." Florence laughed.

"Hah! Take over a country—well, that's a new one," Dwayne agreed.

"Imagine the looks on their faces. Ah, serves them right." Kim smiled happily.

"Okay, I agree to this, but the king hasn't been aggressive toward us. By your own words, as soon as he knew that Esamael was coming to attack us, he started moving some of his southern army to attack Esamael. He even sped them up when he got your information. It shows he isn't that callous about our case," Josh said in a measured tone. At his words, the other guild leaders turned thoughtful.

"We can treat him with dignity and respect, but if they try to belittle us like they did at Selhi Capital... Lucy, I want you to figure something out to cripple them," Josh said.

"I can do that," Lucy said.

"Well then, we have some messages to send," Josh said.

***

"Suzy?" Induca asked as Suzy's eyes fluttered open. She pushed her notifications away as she smiled up at Induca.

"Hey baby," Suzy said, finding her lips crushed beneath Induca's before she was pulled into an embrace.

"Oh, calm down, you. I'm fine." Suzy held Induca as she felt wetness on her shoulder.

"I know. It just scared me. You were out for nearly a week." Induca wiped tears away.

"Silly girl." Suzy smiled, touched by Induca's pure emotion.

"Knock-knock. You decent in there?" Deia asked from outside.

"One moment!" Induca wiped away her tears. "Coming out!" Induca held Suzy's hand.

The two of them walked outside the tent and onto a piece of ground that had been leveled out. All over the place, there were markings for where buildings were going to go. Stone foundations were in different places; people wandered around, checking different things. Most of them were Dwarves. Dave stood at a table with Malsour and Kol, looking over plans.

"Suzy, you're up!" Deia smiled and hugged her.

"Sorry that I worried you all. Dave said that the Summoner's Bastille would take a lot out of me." Suzy winced. She already missed her staff. With using Summoner's Bastille, her staff's power had been used up, heavily damaging it and the runes contained within it.

"Well, it's good to see you up and about." Steve rose from where he'd been sitting, patting Suzy on the head with one large finger.

"You been keeping watch?" Suzy asked.

"Well, can't have my slave driver dying on my watch," Steve said.

Suzy smiled at the massive metal man.

"Well, I wish that we could rest a bit more, but it looks like something might be happening in Verlun. Everyone has been told to prepare their gear and be ready to move at a moment's notice," Deia said.

"What's going on?" Suzy asked.

"Looks like some lord or something might try to attack the city Verlun and the guild hall there. Wants to take over our teleport pad," Deia said.

"Sounds like Selhi all over again." Induca shook her head.

"It is what it is: idiots being assholes," Deia said.

The others showed their agreement.

"Well, I have some notifications and things to check over, so, I best get started," Suzy said.

Chapter 27: To A Future Dawn

Lady Kragr stepped from her teleport pad in Aldamire out into Devil's Crater.

Warclan Leader Fonrir nodded to her as she exited. Her personal guard looked for threats.

"Well, this looks like quite the city." She looked over Unity. She had heard reports from returning Warclans.

"We've just started, but we are already proud of it." A Demon stepped forward.

He was eight feet tall, with twin horns, black eyes, and wings that poked out the back of his leather armored jacket. He wore a shield on his back and a sword on his hip.

"King Alkao." She nodded to the Demon king.

"Lady Kragr." He returned the nod.

All of the Demon Princes and the other leaders of Devil's Crater had agreed that they needed to show a united front with the other races, so they'd drafted Alkao to be their king. It was for a set time as they figured out what kind of government they wanted to make, but for now he was the commander of Devil's Crater.

Off to the side, there was a Dwarf and a Halfling talking to each other animatedly as they looked over plans.

Kragr frowned at them.

An Elf Halfling cleared her throat and elbowed the Dwarf Halfling.

"Ah, Lady Kragr, thanks for coming! Good to see you; thanks for all the aid you sent. It got pretty hairy there for a bit. Nothing like some Dwarven Warclans to scare the piss out of your enemy." The Halfling walked closer and held out his hand.

"Ah, the famed Dave Grahslagg," Kragr said, with an unreadable expression on her face as she shook his hand.

"She's always in for a fight," Kol said, entering the conversation.

"Kol, is that you?" She frowned, shocked by his appearance. She'd become used to the scars and deformation from his accident.

"I do remember a time when I was in Aldamire for a few dozen years. Are you sure your memory isn't starting to fail?" A smile spread across Kol's face.

"Hah! Well, whoever's been prettying you up had their work cut out for them! Seemed to fix that ornery, old grouchy ass mood too!" She laughed and clapped Kol up in a hug.

Kol slapped her on the back, laughing in her ear. "Good to see you, too, Oloh." Kol released the hug.

The teleport pad opened up behind Kragr. Everyone turned to look as automatons started walking out. A man walked with them, followed by an Elf and an Orc.

The man walked out from the crowd, wearing steel and ebony armor similar to the automatons. Silver filled the runes.

Hamdir

Level 195

Elven-Dwarf

Dave got a goofy smile on his face as he waved at the new party.

"'Scuse me!" Dave wandered over. The Elven Halfling joined him, greeting the Orc and Elf, being introduced to the Elven-Dwarf.

"So, I guess the Aleph really are back in Emerilia? I know that the council said that we should prepare ourselves for a lot of changes in the coming future. I just didn't think that it meant people and races of myth coming back." Kragr looked to Kol.

Kol looked to Alkao and then Kragr. "Dave knows more about what is coming, but I do know this. Our alliances of today will be tested with the battles of tomorrow." Kol's eyes bored into Kragr's.

Alkao made a noise of agreement.

"Well, we have much to discuss," Kragr said.

The Aleph party moved over to them. Dave and the Orc were talking to each other off to the side. A man had joined them. The three of them talked about spatial coordinates and event horizons. The Elf man and Halfling seemed amused by their talks and were instead discussing fighting techniques. The last of the party with the armored Aleph tilted his head in greeting.

"Lady Kragr, King Alkao, I believe we have much to discuss," Hamdir said.

"Indeed, Council Member Hamdir." Alkao looked to the man. "I thank you for all that you have done for my people in the shadows and the way in which you, and Lady Kragr, answered the call of my people, both Demon and Beast Kin, without hesitation. Know that if you ever need our aid, you have it." The Demon looked to them both.

Kragr remembered the reports she'd heard about the ferocity with which the Demons and Beast Kin fought. *Once they have proper weapons, armor, and the training that Emerilia can offer them, they're going to be one hell of a fighting force.*

"There is a place nearby that we can discuss the future in more depth." Alkao waved for them to follow him.

***

Once Lady Kragr and King Alkao moved to continue their talks, Party Zero had taken the teleport pad back to Cliff-Hill, finding themselves at Dave and Deia's cabin as they decompressed from the fighting.

"Okay, we'll have dinner ready in a few minutes." Dave kissed Deia's head and passed her a hot tea before he sat down next to her.

"Ugh, damned PDA!" Suzy said, trying to look disgusted as she rested in Induca's arm.

Malsour laughed from his seat on Deia and Dave's porch.

"Says the person who can barely keep her hands off her girlfriend," Anna said.

"Well, at least I can admit who I like and I'm not afraid to show it." Suzy looked to Induca.

Induca looked down at her pouting partner. "You suck!" Induca laughed, giving her a quick kiss.

Deia nestled into Dave.

"What are you talking about?" Anna asked, looking a bit flustered.

"I'm thinking she's talking about Alkao," Malsour said, not looking up from his book.

"Uh, well," Anna said.

"The girl doesn't know her feelings yet," Deia said. "You've just got to go in there and claim him."

"Don't mind me, just sitting here, prized hunk of Dwarf," Dave muttered into his cup.

"My hunk." Deia looked up to Dave.

Dave narrowed his eyes even as his lips fought to form a grin. "Fiiine," Dave said, dragging out the word as if he was reluctant to admit it.

They all settled into comfortable silence, looking out over the side of Cliff-Hill where Dave and Deia's house was located.

Lady Kragr, Hamdir, and Alkao were still in talks. A basic alliance had been agreed to and already trade agreements were being passed all over the place. It had taken considerable effort on Deia, Induca, and Anna's part to get the others to come back to Cliff-Hill and just relax. Dave and Suzy were still catching up on everything going on with the factory and smithies. Now that they had another smithy starting up in Devil's Crater, they had a whole 'nother set of problems to deal with. They were also making deals all over the place with the people of Devil's Crater, and the Aleph.

Deia snuggled in close with Dave, her fingers entwined with his arm that rested over her. He was a driven and focused man. Where most would find it annoying, she didn't mind. She knew he cared for her deeply, but once he found a task needing his attention, he'd tackle it with everything he had.

Deia was proud of her man.

Malsour had been busy ripping down buildings that had been put in the wrong place. He'd built half of Unity by himself: roads, sewers, water systems. With everything Deia knew, she shouldn't have been shocked by his power anymore, but it was hard.

"So, you heading off for Per'ush tomorrow?" Dave looked to Deia.

"Yeah, want to see my mom and dad," Deia said.

"I wish I could come—just with everything..." Dave frowned.

"I know, babe. Don't worry. I'll be fine." Deia kissed his hand.

"You sure?" Dave asked.

"I'm sure, I'm sure. I know how excited you are about all the opportunities that you have. We don't need to be next to each other all the time," Deia said.

Dave didn't answer, just kissing her head. "Thank you," he whispered.

Deia felt the relief in his voice. He loved her, but what he did would not only bring his smithies to an entirely different level, it would connect and help multiple different races.

"I've also got to see about admission for the Demons, Beast Kin, and Aleph. We don't have long until whatever Bob's kept locked up starts showing up," Deia said.

"Hey, I'm trying my best here!" Bob appeared on his recliner.

"Dad," Anna said in a dangerously low voice as her eyes thinned.

"Baby girl?" Bob gulped.

"Did you know what I found out from Kala?" Anna said, her voice deceptively calm.

"Uh, well, Anna, you know that I'm a rather busy person. It's difficult to keep track of everything." Bob's eyes moved around wildly, as if trying to find a way to escape.

"You forgot to tell me they had been pulled out of cold storage for *six months!*" Anna growled.

"Well, umm, I remembered in the end!" Bob smiled, as if that fact made up for his other wrongs.

"You have dozens of AIs and you can't remember one little thing!?" Anna shook her head and smacked her forehead with her hand.

"Epic facepalm," Dave said. "Bad timing?"

Anna snorted as Bob gave a weak smile.

"Sorry about that. I was dealing with some other things. I just, well...you know how I am." Bob shrugged, a guilty look on his face.

"You'd lose your nose if it wasn't attached." Anna laughed. The rest of the party smiled and nodded their heads.

"Pretty much!" Bob laughed, stood from his seat, moved to Anna and held her hands. "I also forget to say a lot of things, like just how proud I am to hear you call me Dad."

"You soft-skulled Gnome." Anna knelt and hugged her dad.

Bob returned the hug with his small Gnome arms.

"Well, would you prefer if I was a wolfkin?" Bob's body went through a change. He rose in height; ears sprouted through his hair as a male wolfkin with a gray tail, fur, and hair looked at them all.

"Well, bit more regal than being a Gnome," Dave commented.

"Oi, no comments from the peanut gallery!" Bob shook his finger at Dave. A smile appeared on his face, showing his sharp teeth.

"Bit more elegant," Anna commented, looking Bob over. "Wouldn't you want to be Human, instead? You know, I hear Air likes Humans more."

"I told you that in confidence, and I have no idea where that little trickster is. She's drumming up something, of that I'm sure. Just don't know what." Bob tapped his lips in thought.

Deia smiled at her friends' antics.

"Well, as I am running out of time, let me say this." Bob looked to them all. "Thank you, for all that you've done. You've gone above and beyond what I thought you were capable of. I have a soft place in my heart for different groups that the Jukal tried to wipe out. You were able to give the Aleph, Beast Kin, and Demons a future. You've struck a great blow to the Dark Lord with killing his Demon Horde, though there are many more challenges to come. Rest, recuperate, and prepare yourselves for the challenges to come. It will not be easy, though you have started one of the strongest alliances I have ever seen, one based on mutual trials and tribulations that have turned into an inspiring friendship. I will continue to watch over you and guide you as I can."

Bob looked over them all, his eyes holding every single one of their eyes.

If it was not for him, then none of them would be alive. Humanity would just be the rogue groups that had fled far away to not attract attention from the Jukal Empire, barely eking out a life in the darkness of space.

He had guided them to events and groups that could change the future of all Emerilians, both those who were POEs and those who believed they were Players.

Deia felt pride and hope well up in her chest. The opportunities that lay before them were tantalizing.

Bob looked at his interface. "All right, got to go. My five minutes are up. I'll see you all later." Bob smiled and disappeared from Dave and Deia's porch.

***

Dave hugged Deia before the teleport pad.

"So, what would you think about expanding our house?" Dave asked.

"Last-minute question much?" She laughed. "Uh, I wouldn't be against it, but I want to see the plans first. We're going to need more rooms for all of the friends we have staying over. Also running water instead of you conjuring a shower every time. We're keeping the porch and it needs to be warm in the winter."

"Okay, I can work with that. I'll talk with Malsour and I'll see what we can come up with."

"Okay. Make sure you don't overwork yourself or else I'll come back here and kick your butt myself," Deia promised, poking his large chest.

"Very well, my dear!" Dave grinned and kissed her.

She turned and pulled her cloak tight. It was getting cold in the north. Winter was on its way and letting everyone know it.

The teleport pad flared to life, showing mages milling around and the enchanted and magical buildings of the mage's college perched atop the floating islands of Per'ush.

Dave waved to Mal and Fire, who waited on the other side, the latter hidden in her disguise as a librarian.

Deia passed through the teleport's event horizon. She appeared on the other side. The teleport pad closed as another event horizon opened. Materials and smiths walked through, heading into Unity. Malsour and Anna waved their good-bye, headed through the teleport pad and out onto the other side.

As they walked through, Kol walked out to the waiting Dave.

"Ugh, terrible trade!" Dave shook his head, smiling, as he greeted Kol.

"What was that?" Kol asked.

"Just said bye to Deia and now I have to look at your ugly mug."

The two of them looked around for a cart that would take them up to Cliff-Hill's smithies.

"Sorry I'm not more gentle on the eyes," Kol growled.

Dave laughed and clapped Kol on the back. "How is the smithy in Devil's Crater; you been talking to Frenik about materials?"

"Yeah, though we've got a meeting with him tomorrow to go over the fine details. Suzy said she'll be free. I know that you want to fix her staff," Kol said.

The two of them jumped on a cart. The team master made noises at the horses, which pulled them up Cliff-Hill's main road.

"Well, most of the staff is still intact. Just a matter of fixing up the runes, maybe modifying it a bit. For my Dwarven Master Smith class, I've got to build a couple more weapons to get the next level. I was thinking of making weapons for the Demon Princes and Alkao. They're the DCA's best fighters and giving them Weapons of Power will show off our smithing abilities and make those who follow them interested in getting weapons from us," Dave said.

Kol pulled out an amulet and turned it, so that the enchantments lined up and the sound around them seemed to fall away.

"We have a meeting to attend with the council tonight. They wish to discuss an alliance with Devil's Crater. They're in one hell of a spot with nice dungeons within their walls as well as mine shafts and other things. They also want to pick your brain about the Aleph. Be ready for a long meeting," Kol warned.

"Well, we're burning sunlight then! We're going to have to work two times as hard to get those weapons ready!" Dave smiled, excited by the challenge. It had been too long since he had smithed and he was eager to get back at it.

"You know most people take weeks to make Weapons of Power?" Kol said, a proud smile on his face.

"Ah, well, just have to start some friendly competition." Dave winked.

"Damn cheat of a Smithing Art!" Kol laughed and turned the amulet, so the enchantment was broken and they could once again hear the hustle and bustle of Cliff-Hill.

"Things sure have changed." Dave looked around the growing town.

It was on the cusp of being a city. The teleport pad was the only one in Northern Opheir. Being so close to Ashal, trade was now staying in the north instead of venturing south. Trade was booming in Cliff-Hill and it showed in the rapid growth of houses and the main market square that Dave could hear from the smithies and factories.

"It's the look of progress; not everything can stay the same forever," Kol said ruefully.

"Too true." Dave sighed.

"Did you know that we're now exporting to the Egas Nation and Orun Free States? Farmers are claiming land all over the place, driving the adventurer's guild to build a place here to run all of the contracts for labor, clearing fields and hunting down animals. With the high-leveled creatures around here, we're getting quite a few adventurers from Ashal visiting for fun. It was a good idea keeping the taxes low. That teleport pad is operating nearly all hours of the day. Had to hire on our own guards now that Cliff-Hill is growing up," Kol said.

"I heard that a number of people from Ashal are thinking of using Cliff-Hill as a base of operations for their supplies or second homes?" Dave looked to Kol.

"If they've got the coin, they're doing it. Cliff-Hill might be in the middle of a rush of purchases and building, though it doesn't show any signs of slowing down. We are one of the most peaceful areas within cheap teleport pad range of Ashal. The Elves don't trust many who aren't their blood. Gudalo has large taxes on their teleport pads. Between us and the teleport pad at Verlun, I say that we're moving two-thirds of the POEs who go between Ashal and other countries."

"You said that we have hired our own forces. I gather that the Mithsia Warclans have returned to their territory?" Dave asked.

"Yes. The mayor has agreements with them, as do a number of businesses. We're technically a free state, paying taxes to them just within their territories. Nadorf and the Kingdom of Opheir might have something to say about that later when the teleport pad gets really established. If we were to call for aid, there is a full barracks stationed at the wall that separates Kufo'tel and Mithsia from the rest of Opheir. There is one Warclan to patrol the wall and do customs. Another to back them up if they need it or come to our aid if we need it. There are more Warclans that look after the patrolling of the large separating wall and hunt down beasts that could be an issue, and raid dungeons and other locations within the wall." Again Kol used the amulet. "I've been checking into the reports from the Warclan leaders. They say that their clans are stronger than they've been in decades. After four months, the clans rotate out to different mountains, keeping them fresh and learning more about Emerilia. It's costly, but with Bob putting in the odd appearance and the military types agreeing, the Council of Anvil and Fire are willing to spend the soul gems and Mana on it."

Kol turned off the amulet again.

"Also, Zel will probably track you down. After he learned about the new smithy in Devil's Crater, he wants to put up another factory in Wer'Koum in the Meldari Kingdom. He says that there is a ton of clay there. He can have massive pits there to gather the materials and work it, shipping it through Gorlei Mountains and down to Sia'kri. They're both massive consumers of the ceramics for cooling during the day and heating at night."

Dave smiled, looking at all that was Cliff-Hill, knowing that it would change and rapidly. It was energizing to be around people driven to succeed, bouncing off one another to push forward.

"First, we build some weapons, then we'll deal with the rest of this nonsense," Dave said.

"I can barely remember a time when all I had to worry about was making swords. I miss those days." Kol sighed.

Chapter 28: No Going Back

Deia hugged her mother and father, a big smile on her face.

"Not so hard," Mal warned.

"Why?" Deia looked between Mal and Fire.

Fire blushed as Mal wrapped his arm around her shoulders, a proud smile on his face.

"Well, you don't want to hurt your sibling," Mal said.

Deia's eyes went wide as she looked from Mal and Fire to Fire's belly.

Fire smiled and leaned into Mal.

"I'm going to be a big sister?" she said in a rushed whisper.

"It looks that way." Fire beamed. "I thought it was hard for you Elves to knock someone up, but this one here is an anomaly."

"Okay, I might be a few hundred years old, but still don't want to hear about my dad's prowess in bed!" Deia grimaced.

"What, aren't you and Dave looking to have a kid?" Mal asked.

"Ugh, so not the conversation I was thinking of having." Deia held her face in embarrassment.

"Come on, tell your mother." Fire grabbed Deia's hand.

"Can we go somewhere that's not out in public?" Deia asked.

"We do have that meeting to go to," Mal reminded Fire.

"Okay, we walk and talk and you tell me about all you and Dave have been up to. I can only see so much and most of the time, it's you and the two who are supposed to watching over you getting into trouble," Fire chastised as the teleport pad connected to a different island.

Mal got the two women in his life moving, pushing them through the teleport pad as they talked.

"Well, we're engaged to be married, but we've been using contraceptive magic so that nothing can happen. With all that's going on, we don't think now is the time to start raising a family. Plus, we don't know what would happen to the baby if I was to die in battle and respawn. I might have to just stay out of the fighting altogether if I was pregnant," Deia said as they stepped onto a different floating island.

Fire put her arm in Mal's as they walked. "Sensible, but what about the wedding?"

"Elves' engagements can take a decade before being confirmed," Mal said.

"Ugh, you bunch of pragmatists!" Fire complained.

"Well, we live for a long time. We want to be sure that the person we marry is the one we want to stay with forever. Elves mate for life." Mal gave Fire a deep look.

"So, are you two going to finally tie the knot?" Deia asked.

"Uh, well, we don't think that now is the best time." Fire grimaced.

"She's scared that the rest of the Pantheon's going to find out and then try to use me and you against her," Mal said.

"Oh, they can try." Deia smiled. Her eyes crackled with power as they seemed to be living flame for a few moments.

"See, I told you she has your temperament," Mal said with a pleased smile, looking between the two of them.

"Well, I hope she has your ability to study without sneaking off into the studying cubicles," Fire shot back.

"That sounds like a good idea." Mal looked to Fire.

Fire smiled, biting her lip.

Cough, "still here..." *Cough* Deia coughed. Fire and Mal didn't look repentant at all as they looked away.

I'm never going to see a library the same way. Deia shook her head.

"It's clear that you're going to be fighting against people and groups that are larger and more powerful than you. To that end, it's about time you learned some spells that can fully utilize your power," Mal said.

"I just finished fighting off the Dark Lord's Demon Horde," Deia complained, looking to Fire.

"Don't look to me. Who do you think's going to be your teacher?" Fire smirked.

"I'm going to be learning Fire spells from you?" Deia said, excited.

"Yes, but we're going to have to go somewhere else for that. You both have a few people to meet," Fire said.

Mal gave her a thoughtful look, but wasn't able to ask her anything as they reached a massive compound with a metal tower reaching up into the heavens.

Fire led them through security and wards to a magical elevator that brought them to one of the highest points in the tower. Scribes and mages of the highest ranks wandered the halls. They reached an office, where a secretary was waiting. Four golems stood in the corners of the room.

"The arch—ah, Mal!" The secretary broke out into a smile as she looked up.

"He's buried in paperwork, but I know he'll make a minute or two for you. Just make sure that Alamos doesn't find out." The secretary activated an enchantment that released the security wards on the door.

Mal smiled, nodding to her, and held the door open for Deia and Fire.

"Oh, um, hello. What are you—Mal! What's going on? Who are these fine ladies?" Jelanos put down his pen and adjusted the glasses he wore.

"Hmm, seems your wards are still decent enough." Fire changed out of her glamour as a librarian and into an outfit of red leather.

"Lady of Fire!" Jelanos's smile became even wider as he walked around the table and hugged Fire.

"Hey, not so hard." Mal fell into the role of protective father.

"I think the baby will be all right." Deia hit her dad.

"What?" Jelanos pushed himself away and looked at Fire and then Mal. He adjusted his glasses and looked at Fire. "Ignil?" His eyebrows rose.

"About time you figured it out!" Fire broke out into a wide smile.

Jelanos's jaw dropped as he looked from Mal to Fire and then over to Deia and then back again. The similarities between all three of them were easy to see.

"Close your mouth, else you'll attract flies," Fire chided.

"Remember when we were in Tawre...looked the exact same." Mal laughed.

"Well, uh, what?" Jelanos said, at a loss for words.

"Ignil was one of my pseudonyms when I was a little younger and bored, desiring to travel the world. It's where I met you, Alamos, and Mal. There was a little bit more to why I disappeared than Mal and I had a fight." Fire looked to Deia, a mix of emotions on her face, finally settling into pride and happiness.

"You're a demi-god of Fire." Jelanos shifted his gaze to Deia and looked her over.

"I just found out a few weeks ago," Deia confirmed.

"I think that some explanations are in order, and I don't know about you all, but I'd like to sit down instead of standing around," Fire said.

They talked and chatted well through the day. Mal and Fire secured Deia access to everything that she could want, as well as for her party.

"I have to say that as a fellow adventurer from the mage's guild, some of the things that I have been hearing about the Stone Raiders just seems impossible." Jelanos looked to Deia.

"If we could tell you half of the things that we've seen and done, you'd think I was insane." Deia held up a hand, stopping Jelanos from asking more. "I and my guild have agreed to not share what we know until the parties we were working for agree to it. That said, I know that there are some people who would be interested in learning from your institute."

"Well, I do like a mystery." Jelanos smiled and rubbed his hands together.

"You only like a mystery if you get a chance to pull it apart and find the truth behind it," Mal argued.

"Same thing, right?" Jelanos laughed.

"Well, Deia and I need to be somewhere. I'll leave the two of you to talk," Fire said.

"Don't overexert yourself." Mal rose.

"Oh, shut up, youngster. I can look after myself." Fire swat him lightly.

"You might be as old as this college but you've only had one other kid," Mal pointed out.

"And many more to come." Fire gave him a kiss.

Deia found the ceiling very interesting at this point as Jelanos let out a laugh.

"Deia." Fire held out her hand. Deia took it as Mal stepped back from Fire and Deia.

A spell formed around them. The room disappeared and Deia found herself in a cave that had been turned into a home. Mage lights kept it bright. There was an edge to the cave, with red light seeping in from below.

Deia looked out over the lip of the cave.

"We're inside of a volcano?" Deia looked at the heat rising from the volcano floor below. The heat might have killed others, but to a demi-god of Fire, it was rather nice.

"Welcome to the Densaou Ring of Fire, and my home," Fire said. There was a beating of wings as a massive face as big as a bus appeared.

"This one must be yours; she has that same stubborn streak as you, Mother." The Dragon had an amused look on its face as it grabbed onto the side of the volcano and looked at Deia and Fire.

"Don't try and scare her, Denur," Fire tutted, unable to hide her smile. "Deia, this is your older sister Denur."

"You've raised some fine children in Induca and Malsour. I am pleased to call them friends," Deia said.

"I am glad, sister. I do not think that they even realized how much they would become entrapped in the world at large. They quite enjoy their guild and being in a party with your rather *colorful* friends." Denur smiled.

"She wants to grill you about Suzy." Fire took a seat.

"Now she's going to be all guarded, Mom; ask when there's no suspicion!" Denur pouted, before sniffing and leaning her head forward. "Mom, there's something different about you."

"You didn't tell her?" Deia looked between her new sister and mother.

"Well, I have been rather busy and well, I haven't been home in a while," Fire started.

"She's pregnant!" Deia declared.

"Oh! Another sibling! I do get so jealous of my young having so many brothers and sisters and yet I've only met mine! Another one!" Denur's expression could only be expressed as glee.

"Well, at least I know that they'll be well protected." Fire smiled as she looked at her two daughters.

"That's a given." Deia crossed her arms as Denur looked over her shoulder, giving her mother a fierce glare.

Fire laughed at the scene. Tears ran down her cheeks, in happiness and mirth.

Denur and Deia shared a look and shrugged.

***

Josh sat in the city of Zol'Ord at a table across from Gimel, leader of the Fellox Guild, and sipped tea while Cassie ordered pastries.

"So, are you ready to put up your videos and see what the Emerilia community says?" Gimel asked. A number of the guild's leaders grinned, clearly expecting to win.

Josh smiled and put down his tea. "All right. Gimme one second. Gotta send it out to my guild. On the count of three?" Josh opened up his interface.

Cassie came over and sat next to Josh. She started to pull apart a sweet pastry after she put another in front of Josh. "Can I put up my video yet?"

"Doing the countdown," Josh said in a calming voice.

Cassie let out a whoop and opened her interface.

"So, on three. Ready?" Gimel smiled.

"Ready." Josh's finger hovered above the send button for his messages.

"One, two, three!" Gimel stabbed his finger forward. Josh did the same. Cassie started typing things out on her interface with one hand while eating with the other.

Messages zipped across Emerilia as interfaces opened up all across the world. Streams that had been dead for months now had a mass of new content. The Stone Raiders had been challenged and they were returning the challenge.

"May the best guild win." Josh held out his hand.

Gimel shook it and grinned. "Well, no matter the results, I'd be interested in doing a raid with the Stone Raiders."

"Damn, beat me to it—was gonna say the same thing about the Fellox. We're having a little break now but I think that we're going to be up for some raiding and portal opening soon enough." Josh leaned forward, an excited glint to his eyes.

"Portal opening, huh?" Gimel said. The others of Fellox listened intently. The Stone Raiders and Golden Sabres had been the first to unlock a portal. Now the Golden Sabres had collapsed, but a ton of their veteran Players were looking to join the Stone Raiders.

"If you're game." Josh grinned and sat back, as if it was no big deal.

"Well, maybe I can help you out with that." Gimel stroked his manicured goatee.

"You'll be the first guild we call." Josh held out his hand. Gimel shook it; those who had heard of it looked excited at the possibility of the two strongest raiding guilds grouping together.

Josh knew that Cassie would be reporting it on her blog and video stream.

"Holy!" one of the Fellox guild members said, their interface taking up all of their attention.

"What you watching?" Gimel asked.

"Stone Raiders videos," the guild member said, not looking up. Gimel opened his interface.

"Thanks for the pastry. What you want to do now?" Josh asked.

"Well, we do have a guild city to build," Cassie said with a wide grin. Now that the Stone Raiders had been given some breathing room, there were just so many things that they needed to do and possibilities to snatch up.

"Lucy probably has a whole bunch of people she wants us to check over from the Golden Sabres. Now we've got time to vet them properly." Josh stood and held out his hand to Cassie; she took it and stood.

"Wait, are these Demons and Beast Kin?" Gimel looked to Josh and Cassie with wide eyes.

"That they are. If you want to check out Devil's Crater, then you need to go to Cliff-Hill. It's the only teleport pad other than our guild's that will allow you to access Devil's Crater." Josh smiled.

Gimel just looked as though he'd had his mind blown.

"See you later, Gimel. Not many guilds keep their challenges classy." Josh tipped an invisible hat at the guild leader.

"Damn, I hope we can go on a raid like that together one time." Gimel laughed and shook his head.

Josh shrugged. "Definitely a possibility."

Cassie put her arm in Josh's as they walked out of the café and headed for the teleport pad.

Josh checked his interface that was beeping at him with incoming messages. He checked it, finding Lucy's right at the top. He laughed to himself and closed it.

"What was it?" Cassie asked.

"Seems that our recruiting has blown up. Lucy's going a little crazy with all the requests." Josh snorted.

"Yeah, she wants all the information I have on every person who applied from the Golden Sabres. I guess I should do that." Cassie sighed.

"Hmm, well, there is a lot of traffic around the teleport pad. We could go check out the shops." Josh looked to Cassie.

She pursed her lips, an amused look in her eyes. "You want to see me in a dress, is that what you're saying?"

"I want to see where this goes now that we can tell each other everything without guilds in the way," Josh said, smiling even as his eyes were serious.

Emerilia might be a game to some, but to Josh it was his world and his guild was everything to him.

"I'd like that." Cassie moved a bit closer, her voice low and scared but hopeful. She wasn't the brash Cassie that many knew, but the woman underneath who was scared to be burned by a man she cared for.

Josh turned her so she was facing him; he pulled her to him so fast she couldn't react and planted his lips on hers.

She melted against him, her hands on his chest.

They stepped back, looking into each other's eyes after a minute.

"Supposed to buy me dinner first!" She hit his chest.

"Ah, damn. Well, I'll do that later."

"Good!" She slapped his butt.

He grinned and moved faster than she could react, throwing her over his shoulder and running down the street.

"Ah! Put me down!" She half yelled-laughed as Josh started to run faster, using his skills to run between two walls. People pointed and watched in shock as he disappeared over a roof. Cassie yelled the entire time.

****

Geswald stepped out of his heated carriage. He walked between lines of Lord Esamael's guards, who stood on either side of the carpet that led to the lord's grand hall.

There were a number of nobles and people of standing in the crowd who walked down the carpet. They greeted Geswald and made sure to let him pass as he walked through them and into Lord Esamael's estate.

The weather was turning cold with the quickly approaching winter. Pete appeared at his side. His aide had gone on ahead, acting as Geswald's representative. The secretaries and aides got together before messaging their patrons to push ahead talks on Lord Esamael and his allies' plans.

Lord Esamael greeted Geswald with open arms. "Lord Geswald, it is good to see you! I hope you are keeping well." Esamael smiled and hugged the older man.

"Oh, you flatter me, Lord Esamael. I have been in fine health!" Geswald smiled as a servant took away his heavy outer cloak.

"Good, good! We shall have to get together later and have some fire whiskey to your health." Esamael smiled. The expression did not reach his eyes.

"Of course, Lord Esamael. You honor me." Geswald smiled, tilting his head in acceptance of the invitation.

"I must go, as I have many others to greet. I will talk to you later." Esamael departed.

Geswald practically heard the sighs of the ladies and the approval of the older lords and barons in his treatment of Geswald.

Geswald was the second most powerful man in Lord Esamael's estate and as such, he was greeted and talked to by all people of note. Geswald laughed, passed stories and words of thanks, as well as a reprimand here and there, all of it under the guise of conversation and small talk. In Emaren and the surrounding towns, no one conducted business without his agreement, or without giving him his payment.

Geswald's eyes might not be what they used to be, yet he still saw the groups that disappeared from time to time. He glanced to some, looking away quickly.

They were the generals and supporters of Esamael. Officers who had been in charge of leading bandit raids and those who hid their forces as city guards across Gudalo were given their orders.

Dinner parties—who would suspect the true devious nature that lays behind them?

It was much later that he was invited to meet with Lord Esamael. He made his excuses and went to meet the lord.

He stood on a balcony; a large fur covered him as he drank some fire whiskey. A servant put another cloak on Geswald; another handed him a cut glass from Markolm with fire whiskey inside.

The servants retreated as Esamael pressed a button on the balcony. A cone of silence surrounded the two of them.

Geswald sat at the small table on the balcony and sipped from the fire whiskey.

Esamael's amenable mask fell as he downed half of the fire whiskey in one gulp. "Due to unforeseen circumstances, we are going to have to change our plans. I have been talking to my generals and my spies. It looks like Sigaird is not a complete oaf. We have to tread carefully. The Stone Raiders seem to have returned with a great number of goods. The mage's guild and college are buying from them more and more. I have also heard from the Players that the Stone Raiders have apparently fought alongside Demons and Beast Kin. I do not know the validity of these sources, but it has become clear to me that taking out the Stone Raiders will not go unnoticed, as I had hoped." Esamael took a seat.

"What is the new plan?" Geswald asked.

"Do all you can to put pressure on the allies of the Stone Raiders in Verlun. Drive them into the ground and build alliances that will harm the Stone Raiders' allies. A city that sells foodstuffs is not that popular in winter. We shall make them see that siding with us will bring them monetary benefits that the Stone Raiders won't give them." Esamael looked to Geswald.

"I can do that, but the mage's guild and college brings in a mass of buyers. I have also heard that they are buying up foodstuffs and shipping it to unknown places. Maybe it is to these Demons and Beast Kin?"

"Do what you can to disturb that. If they are allies, then we want to put a wedge between them..." Esamael looked to Geswald like a wolf would watch its prey.

Geswald nodded and sipped from his drink. "What is the plan to get rid of them?"

"General Loughbreck controls our forces to the north. It will take days or weeks for our northern forces to reach Haugr. It will only take him a few days to assemble the forces from our northern alliances and take them to Verlun. The city guard and forces in the area of Verlun will weaken them. The army will tear the Stone Raiders apart, capture the teleport pad and give us two teleport pads to gain access to Haugr," Esamael said.

Geswald didn't ask how Esamael knew that the teleport pad in Haugr would be open to Verlun and Emaren leading an assault into the kingdom's capital.

"I can soften them and their alliances up," Geswald said.

"Good. We will wait until spring. The strongest fighters will be at the Dwarven tournament. The Stone Raiders and many warriors from Haugr will undoubtedly go to test their mettle. We will take Verlun and all of Gudalo under our control." Esamael looked off into the distance. A cold smile spread across his face as he twirled his glass and the fire whiskey in his hand.

"To victory," Geswald said.

"To victory." Esamael raised his glass and drained the contents.

Chapter 29: Gifts And Plans

Dave and Kol trudged into the Council of Anvil and Fire's meeting.

"Hah, look at these two bastards. Did yah even sleep last night?" Quino laughed.

Kol made a grunting noise as Dave tiredly opened up his interface and sent a message to Quino before they slumped into chairs. He didn't have the energy to explain it to Quino.

"Well, seems that some people have been burning the late-night coal," Jesal said from where she sat at the top of the table, overseeing the council.

Dave raised his thumb in agreement, yawning as he rubbed his face with the other hand.

Quino muttered to himself excitedly. Endur kept trying to look over his shoulder to see what he was looking at.

"Okay, on to this week's matters," Jesal said. "Demons and Beast Kin have returned to Emerilia. It seems that both groups have settled into Devil's Crater. They were attacked by the Dark Lord's new iteration of Demons. They defeated them with the assistance of three Aldamire Warclans. Lady Kragr has entered limited trade agreements with Devil's Crater. Information has been sent out to all of you on this incident. Please vote on if we should look into creating an alliance with the peoples of Devil's Crater or wait."

The vote passed quickly. Dave and Kol couldn't vote on it as they had vested interests in Devil's Crater.

"We will look to create closer ties with Devil's Crater, allowing Lady Kragr to create a mutually defensive alliance with the government of Devil's Crater," Jesal said. "Second, the Aleph have returned to Emerilia. They came to the aid of the Stone Raiders and people of Devil's Crater. They worked alongside our clans. They have not formally talked to us. Lady Kragr has talked to them and believes that they are receptive to a possible agreement, possibly even an alliance."

Dasano raised his hand. He was the oldest of the Dwarven Master Smiths and rarely spoke but his wisdom held weight.

"You have the floor, Dasano." Jesal nodded to the aged Dwarf.

"Many said bad things about the Aleph but they were very similar to our own people. They looked for answers. As we look to create wonders out of metal and stone, they looked to find answers to the magical mysteries of Emerilia. I heard stories of my great-grand-father when the Aleph would make wonders that no one could understand. How they created the teleport pads and automatons that made the greatest Dwarven smiths envious. The Aleph people had been cast out from their societies and in turn built one of their own. We sat back and watched as they were culled, too scared to act. As my great-grandfather regretted doing nothing all of his life, I hope to put his spirit to rest. The Aleph are the brothers, sisters, daughters, and sons of our forefathers. Together we are much stronger than apart," Dasano said in a calm and deep voice. Every Dwarf listened to his words.

"We shall put it to a vote," Jesal said.

Dave couldn't vote, as he again had vested interests.

"At this time, we will allow for trade agreements to be continued. We will look into the possibility of an alliance at a later time. Mountain lords and ladies may make their own judgments on alliances with the Aleph," Jesal announced. "Okay, next thing: the artillery we've used has proved itself. We have notes back from the artillery corps as well as adjustments to be made but it seems that their rate of fire was nearly tripled and the amount of time they could fire for was increased by four times. After updates to the test-bed prototype, I think that it would be feasible to melt down the old artillery once they are replaced with the newer versions. The military council agrees with this assessment. Anyone have votes against?"

"Are we going to be doing it on a one-for-one swap? Are we going to be giving entire clans new artillery or just transitioning over?" Sola asked.

"It takes more time to make these new weapons and they are more expensive. So, we'll be working with one Warclan at a time to swap out their artillery pieces one by one," Jesal said.

"No issues here," Sola said.

No one else said anything or made to raise their hands. With all the foreboding future predictions, none wanted to arm the Warclans with anything but the best.

"Okay, finally the Dwarven tournament. Preliminaries will start in a few weeks. The mage's and adventurer's guild will be running their own. Some towns and cities will also be hosting their own bouts of fighting, within their guards and general populace. This will take a month or two. Then tournaments will start at Dwarven mountains across Emerilia. Anyone who can make it to a Dwarven mountain will be allowed to enter into the competition. Arenas will be built by Dwarven engineers and mages. Plans are finalized and ready. As winter breaks for spring, we will start the tournaments at the mountains. It will take a month before the fighting will move to Gorlei Mountains on the Heval continent. It will take another month to name a winner of the tournament. It will be our job to test the winners and see of their inner workings. If we judge them to be good people, then the Grey God will judge them before allowing them access to our weapons vaults where they will most likely be bestowed with a Weapon of Power," Jesal said.

The conference room was deathly silent. The Council of Anvil and Fire had been watching over the weapons since they had been recovered, made or given to them by the Grey God.

"Everything has been finalized and there should be little to no alterations to this plan. Next we go on to metals, with our new smelters, as well as the Aleph's and Stone Raiders' ability to churn out a number of rare metals, we have a number of contracts to discuss. It has also been brought to our attention that the need for glass panes will increase due to the residents of Devil's Crater making a series of greenhouses. With the knowledge of silicates and malachite that Dave has told us, there is enough glass to satisfy some of these demands and we will have to figure out pricing for it all. The Aleph can also supply glass panes, but it seems that they don't have much production as they are dealing with their own issues."

Felar raised her hand.

Jesal indicated for her to talk.

"I have heard of the Aleph's ability to manufacture a great number of identical items repeatedly. I was wondering if it would be possible to visit the Aleph and trade different information on smithing, smelting, and their factories?" Felar asked.

"I haven't begun to look at that information. I didn't think that there would be so much going on in the month that I took over this position." The Dwarves laughed, others yelling out that she was doing a fine job. "Would you and some others be interested in trying to set up an exchange of information?" Jesal asked.

"I can do that." Felar smiled.

"Good! Okay, now onto winter preparations."

***

Dave awoke in a corner of the smithy. He stood and stretched, popping things from his rough night of rest. He shook Kol awake, and then opened his bag of holding, took out a pot of Xer and put it into the furnace.

Kol stood up and wiped a coal-stained hand over his forehead, adding to the marks from a long night's work.

Dave looked at the four swords and one shield in front of him. Each was different in their properties, hilt, and magical runes, but the shape of their blade was the same. To most, they would be too heavy for a one-handed wield. Dave had seen the Demons in action; they were much stronger than any creature of comparable size.

He looked to the sixth weapon: a war hammer with a bear's head carved into it. It was as much art as it was functional. Hidden inside the head were magical runes that made the war hammer seem to have frost covering it.

Dave opened his blinking notifications.

Quest: Dwarven Master Smith Level 3

You must craft 10 weapons of S quality with your Smithing Art (Currently 10/10)

Rewards: Unlock Level 4 quest

Increase to stat gain

Class: Dwarven Master Smith

Status: Level 3

Effects:
Allowed access to all Dwarven Mountains and Smithies.
Allowed to take on smithing apprentices.
+30 to all stats
Access to special quests.

Quest: Dwarven Master Smith Level 4

You must craft 20 weapons of S quality with your Smithing Art (Currently 10/20)

Rewards: Unlock Level 5 quest

Increase to stat gain

Dave studied his character sheet.

Character Sheet

Name:	David Grahslagg	Gender:	Male
Level:	122	Class:	Dwarven Master Smith, Friend of the Grey God, Bleeder, Librarian, Aleph Engineer, Weapons Master, Champion Slayer, Skill Creator, Mine Manager, Master Summoner
Race:	Human/ Dwarf	Alignment:	Neutral Good

Unspent points: 496

Health:	24,300	Regen:	9.06 /s
Mana:	7,380	Regen:	22.55 /s
Stamina:	3,090	Regen:	18.25 /s
Vitality:	243	Endurance:	453
Intelligence:	738	Willpower:	451
Strength:	309	Agility:	365

Zel knocked on the door; Dave waved to the man.

He walked in carrying a box of breakfast food.

"Thanks, Zel. You're a blessing," Dave said as the three of them claimed a workbench and started to eat the packed breakfast.

"I see that you two were up banging around all night." Zel looked to the blades.

"Yeah, they might not look like much, but they're powerful weapons." Kol gave Dave a look.

"Hey, better to use Mithril than squirrel it away, and yes, I do know how much Mithril it was." Dave sighed. The pot on the furnace whistled. Dave grabbed the pot out of the furnace with tongs.

Zel gave Kol a look; Kol shook his head and shrugged.

"They're Mithril blades?" Zel looked at them with clear interest. Seeing Mithril was rare; having four blades and a hammer made out of it was a once-in-a-lifetime kind of thing.

"Yeah. Why do you think we had to put them in Kroder snake's sheaths? They'd cut anything else to bits." Kol sighed.

Dave poured Xer into three mugs. "So, I heard that you want to expand the ceramics side of things into Wer'Koum?" Dave grabbed his cup and sat down.

"We've got some decent clay deposits here, but not enough to keep up with demand unless we hire more Earth mages to create it. Wer'Koum has massive deposits no one knows what to do with; they've got a port city, a Dwarven mountain, and are close to our buyers in the Heval Desert," Zel said.

"Okay, I can get behind that," Dave said.

"Also, we've been making a number of the things that you have patents on and selling them. Right now, we're doing the major work on them in the factories and then, for the magical coding, we come over here. I was thinking of making true assembly lines to make the units that are being bought the most. Things like heaters and coolers. Proper showers for everyone, not just inns that Players use," Zel said.

"Have you talked this over with Suzy?" Dave asked.

"Yeah, we've gone over the plans and she's checked it all out. She seems to be onboard with it." Zel crunched some bacon.

"Well, she's better with that stuff than me. It sounds good to me, but she's the one with the mind for that. I'm the dude with about a hundred ideas in every which direction and signs on the dotted line when she tells me." Dave grinned to Zel and Kol's smiles.

"Well, I should have made you deed over your company a lot earlier." Suzy entered the smithy, with Induca beside her.

"Damn, it's nice and warm in here!" Induca got up close to the furnace.

"You two look like you've rolled around in coal for the entire night." Suzy sighed as she looked at Kol and Dave.

"Zel, I looked into Wer'Koum. It's a good place, but Zol'Ord is better. They have more clay that they don't even know about. They're also better for distribution across all of Heval. Their taxes are lower and they've got a ton of Earth mages and low employment rates. We can get the government on our side, reduced taxes, get people employed and keep rolling. If we play it right, all of Heval will be benefiting from us being there. There is the possibility to expand down to Zol'sou as well, due to their teleport pad and their distance from the local swamps and the clay deposits. Everything we need for a thriving factory." Suzy smiled, grabbed a cup from her bag of holding and poured in fresh Xer. "Dave, we're going to have to talk about having a full up-and-running factory. Using people from multiple different trades working together to make production lines. We've got some factory lines with the smithies but they're making just one singular part, like screws. Not complex things like a Muskoka chair, or a shower stall."

Dave scratched his head and sighed.

"Don't worry. I talked to some of the Aleph. It seems that they are interested in the idea of teaching some of our people how to run different kinds of factories. Something of a challenge. I want you and Zel to have a talk with them, see what items and components they can make for us and the items that we're going to have to step up assembly lines for. Building it all ourselves is going to be a pain in the ass. If we can outsource some of it to the Aleph at a cheaper price, it's worth trying out. We scratch their back and they'll scratch ours." Suzy took a sip from her Xer, letting out a content sigh. Her eyes closed in bliss. "Now, that's something for later. You two are meeting the generals of the Devil's Crater Army to finalize the contract for armor. Dave, conjure up a shower." Suzy took a deep drink from her Xer.

"Yes, ma'am." Dave smiled. He could always trust Suzy to keep everything managed and him up-to-date.

Dave conjured two showers and a changing room behind the smithy as Zel and Suzy got to talking.

"Catch!" Dave pulled out a staff and tossed it to Suzy. A screen appeared in front of her face as she studied her staff.

Her eyes went wide as she read the description.

Dave checked the copy of stats he kept.

Staff of Hecate

Forged by Dave Grahslagg, this item has been made for his dear sister Suzy. With it, the very gods themselves shall fear her wrath and accept her judgment. After being broken in the defense of Devil's Crater, it has been rebuilt stronger than before.

Quality: SS

Abilities:

Increased command of all elements making up the staff (+13%)

Increased range of Creations (+25%)

Wielder's Willpower increased (+17%)

Grows in power through use. (+1% to stats of user, stacks with other items)

Summoner's Bastille

Charge: 100,000/100,000

Durability: 345/345

"Told you I'd have it working in no time." Dave stepped into the small changing room. He cleaned himself up, changing into new clothes. Kol did the same.

As they stepped out, the showers disappeared, the conjured water going with it.

Twenty minutes had passed and Suzy was caressing her staff like a lost child.

"Going to go blind from rubbing it so much!" Dave said.

Suzy half jumped, as if fearful that her actions would harm her staff. "Ass!" Suzy growled.

Dave chuckled. "Well, let's go and make a deal." Dave put the weapons and shield into his bag of holding, and slung it over his shoulder.

"Thanks for fixing her staff," Induca said as they walked for a waiting cart that would take them to the teleport pad. Kol and Zel had taken the lead; Suzy followed them in a slight daze, muttering to her staff. Induca and Dave trailed after them.

"Can't have my friends with anything but the best." Dave smiled to Induca.

"I'm so happy I decided to come and hunt down the Lady of Fire's kid." Induca laughed.

"So am I—got two good friends out of the deal." Dave grinned.

"Oh, you charmer." Induca laughed.

"Well, I have my own work to see to. I'll see everyone later." Zel waved to them and headed for his factory.

"See you later, Zel!" Dave smiled and waved, jumping up on the waiting cart.

The cart moved as the horses pulled it down the road and toward the teleport pad.

"Thanks for fixing this up." Suzy held up her staff.

"No worries." Dave grinned.

"First we have the meeting with the DCA, then check on the work happening at the smithy. We're going to hire anyone who wants to learn there. Might even get a few armorers on loan from the DCA. We've got a lot of interest from people who want to be smiths. If you agree, we'll pay the fees for them to come to the smithy, written off as long as they can make it to the apprentice level. After we're done with the meeting and checking on the smithy,

I'm heading for Verlun. You can join if you want, or continue on to the guild hall."

The guild hall that the Aleph had given the Stone Raiders for helping them was simply called the guild hall. The one in Verlun was called Verlun or Verlun hall, same for the hall in Cliff-Hill.

"I think that I'll go to the guild hall. There's plenty to be done there and I have a few ideas for future plans. Kol, you might be interested in it," Dave said.

"A city buried under the ground—sounds just like home." Kol smiled.

"I keep forgetting how many Dwarves are complete recluses." Dave sighed.

***

Anna watched as Suzy, Induca, Dave, and Kol walked through the teleport pad.

"Hey, Anna, what you up to?" Dave asked.

"I'm here to guide you to the meeting. I'm supposed to be a general of one of the DCA brigades, though it's mostly an honorary position because I'm with the Stone Raiders so much," Anna said.

"Where is the meeting being held?" Suzy asked.

"In the main government building." Anna waved to a large building that had risen in the center of Unity. The progress in just a few short days was incredible.

"Damn. Every time I see Earth and Dark mages at work, I have to pinch myself. Houses up in a day? No problem, where do you want the doors and windows?" Dave shook his head.

"Well, you guys have fun at the meeting. I'm going to find Malsour and Fornau. I heard some of my family also came by to help out with the city. They're thinking of making a few mountains nearby," Induca said.

"Don't get into too much trouble." Suzy kissed her girlfriend.

"Knock 'em dead." Induca winked and headed off into Unity.

"So, how's Alkao?" Suzy asked as they started for the government building.

"Ugh." Anna shook her head in frustration.

"What? I'm the only girl here and I need to update the others!" Suzy said, as if she wasn't asking for her own sake.

"He's a fine leader of his people and focused on doing everything he can to help his people," Anna said.

"Booooring. So, you've both been too busy to do anything. We'll have to do something about that," Suzy said with a firm nod.

"What does that mean?" Anna asked in alarm, looking rather flustered.

"Don't worry—Suzy has this covered." Suzy winked at Anna.

Anna rubbed her temples, her tail moving in small, frustrated movements.

"How have things been with the Beast Kin and Demons? It looks like a lot of work has been completed," Dave said.

"We're lucky that Verlun and Cliff-Hill are the only places other than the Aleph where people can get to us. Well, unless they want to try to traverse Ashal." Anna gave them a look that showed her doubt of anyone trying to complete that suicidal task. "The Beast Kin are still teaching for the most part; the Demons who have taken up jobs outside of being soldiers are quickly adapting to their new way of life. They've never had so many options and it's showing. They're still buying up a ton of food from different places. They don't have enough for winter, but with the reward they gained from defeating the Demon Horde and making their home, they should have it covered. Brigades are also off clearing out any monsters that might attack the peaceful folk and marking dungeon locations."

"What about the mage's, trader's and adventurer's guilds?" Suzy asked.

"They've been poking around. It seems that someone has told the mage's guild and they are interested in opening up a guild here with a few magical teachers. They can administer tests to show people what their Affinities are, as well as their strength, for free. Alkao has accepted them and they should have a group arriving in a week or two. It will allow us to find out just what kind of mages we have in the DCA and train them in their talents. The adventurer's guild is excited to come here and set up a chapter. The government is in talks with them, so that the dungeons don't get overused and looking into possibly going beyond Devil's Crater to find more dungeons and the like beyond our cliffs," Anna said.

"Lot of money to be made in a land with so many high-level magical beasts and dungeons without civilization to keep them in check," Kol grumbled.

"It's what made the Demons strong and will strengthen the later generations. Also, with the dungeons within the crater, it will allow adventurers to fight in a dungeon without the dangerous trek to and from it," Anna said.

"Yeah, finishing a hard ass dungeon just to get killed by a creature on your way home—not so much fun. You can find a bunch of people complaining about it on the forums." Dave sighed.

"What about the trader's guild?" Suzy pushed on as they entered the government buildings. DCA soldiers checked them over, saluting as they saw three members of Party Zero.

Dave nodded to them as they passed, getting a respectful half head bow from the ones he made eye contact with.

"What was that about? I didn't think Demons lowered their heads for anything? Nor Beast Kin unless they're weaker or out of deep respect," Dave said.

Anna laughed and rubbed her forehead at Dave's ways. No Jukal would act like him—always asking for praise and deference from all else, even if they had never earned anything but been born into the right species.

"Dave, you practically turned the battle for the northern keep on its head. When the Demon Horde looked like they would crush the DCA, you created armor and weapons that served to keep many of the DCA alive and give them a clear advantage over the Horde. To them, you're a hero, including how the Stone Raiders sacrificed their own lives to try to slow the Horde and kill off as many as possible when they overran the southern keep. We're pretty well respected here, and you have the gratitude of Devil's Crater," Anna said.

Dave scratched his head nervously, unsure of what to say to such high praise.

"I never really thought about that," Suzy admitted.

"You saved the army and the people in this crater. The Stone Raiders are heroes to these people," Kol said. "Should hear the apprentices at the smithy, wanting to make weapons and armor like the venerable Dave Grahslagg."

"Was just helping out." Dave looked to Suzy.

"Yeah, in a big way!" Suzy laughed.

They passed through some more guards. There were people all through the lobby, talking to various people who directed them into the government buildings.

"So, the trader's guild?" Suzy asked for the third time.

"Ah, well, that's an interesting one. Because the Exdar's Traders got their place set up, they're on very good terms with the traders in Devil's Crater, as well as the Aleph. They brokered the agreement between the two parties and are the biggest supplier for food. They basically got everything kickstarted here and got the traders in the area up to speed and gave a number of them loans to start up businesses. Being part of the Stone Raiders adds to their reputation. The trader's guild came over with their people. We have licenses under the trader's guild, so technically we're just extending their reach. They were going to set up a massive chapter house here, but they saw it wasn't really needed. We were pushing along all of Devil's Crater faster than we thought possible. They opened a small place here and they deal with guild issues there. They're rather pleased with all of the taxes they're getting from us on different transactions. We've actually had our rankings as a guild increased with all major guilds for the help we've provided for them. Devil's Crater is an untapped resource and they're thankful to the Stone Raiders for helping them out," Anna said as they reached large double doors with guards on either side. They opened the doors. Anna and the rest were greeted with noise as twelve people lounged around the room.

Alkao sat at the top of the table, talking to his trade councillor. The brothers and Kala were lounging in seats. Efri had his feet on the table while Kala was using quills and pens to show different battle tactics to the generals. There was also Frenik, council member of the Aleph and manager of their mines and forges. Koza was talking animatedly with the generals as well, listening to Kala's show piece. A shrewd looking Orc wearing fashionable rings in his tusks and a high quality robe sat beside Frenik—Oxul, a trader from the Aleph, Suzy's opposite in the talks.

Alkao raised a hand in greeting to the new arrivals and knocked on the table.

The generals' conversation quieted down as they looked to the new arrivals.

"Efri," Alkao said in a tired voice.

Efri's boots dropped to the ground. The large general looked a little shamefaced. "Sorry, King Alkao," Efri said.

"Ah, we're used to it at this point!" Dave said with a grin and a wink at Efri.

"Don't say that. I'm trying to get manners into their thick skulls," Alkao growled, but Anna saw the happiness one has when they greet their good friends again.

Alkao clasped arms with Dave and then Kol, looking impressed with the old Dwarf's grip. "You're strong for someone so old."

"Old? I'll have you know I have barely reached my middle age," Kol grumbled, shooting a glance at Frenik. Frenik rolled his eyes as if to say, "Younglings—what do you expect?"

"Okay, if we might start this meeting?" the Devil's Crater trader said.

"Certainly!" Alkao waved for everyone to take their seats.

Dave shared nods with the generals as Koza and Anna stood off to the side of the meeting.

"We have looked at the contracts put forward by both the Aleph and the Cliff-Hill smithies. We have come to partial conclusions. Looking at your contracts, we are interested in purchasing weapons from the Aleph." The trader nodded to the orcish trader and Frenik. "We have also decided to go with the Cliff-Hill smithies to supply us with full body armor."

The trader proceeded to share messages with the two groups vying for the armament contracts. They talked in private chats, so no one could hear them. It was basically what they had thought would happen; the only difference was delivery times and adjustments to cost.

"These terms are amenable to us." Oxul's voice was deep and flowing, unlike most orcish's grunting manner of speech.

"Thank you. What time can you start delivering on this contract?" Alkao asked.

They had made up an emergency contract to get some battalions armed in case anything happened. This contract was for the entire DCA.

"We can start in about a week, with a firm quota of our production numbers to you in two days," Frenik said.

"Good. I look forward to having my people with weapons instead of just stones and claws." Alkao looked to the other group.

"These terms are acceptable, and match with our previous agreements. We agree to it," Suzy said.

"We can start armoring up your people within the week," Kol said.

"With that, we can draw this meeting to a close," the Devil's Crater trader said.

"I have one more thing." Dave stood and opened his bag of holding. "While one is a leader of an army, they must be ready to lead, as they are ready to fight." Dave pulled out weapons from his bag, throwing them to each of the generals. He threw a war hammer to a grinning Kala and placed a sword and shield in front of Alkao.

"I thought it was time to make you an upgrade." Dave grinned.

"This...this is Mithril." Malkur looked at the textured metal and back to Dave.

"Well, it is a Dwarven secret," Dave said.

"Would be damned impossible to form this much without his cheat." Kol nodded to Dave.

Anna smiled as the Aleph unconsciously moved forward to study the weapons.

"Weapons of Power?" Frenik looked to Kol, getting an affirming nod in return. "How could you do this all in just a few days?"

Kol let out a laugh. "A few days? He made those blades last night! I worked on the war hammer and shield."

The interested faces turned to shock, looking to the grinning Dave and proud Kol.

"I knew that they were master craftsmen, but how much have the master Dwarves changed since we left?" Koza asked Anna in a low voice.

"Kol is a rank seven Dwarven Master Smith; Dave just turned into a level four. The Dwarves haven't changed that much except in the last year. Dave was the first Halfling to ever be admitted into the Council of Anvil and Fire. Since he's been there, he's created a stir. Not only with his techniques but the information he has brought to their council that even I can't compute what the final result will be."

"He certainly has turned the world upside down. I know that Ela-Dorn and many of the Aleph who attend our college see him as an almost holy figure for giving them access to an unconnected portal," Koza said.

"If you think that's something, ask him about the summoner's hall." Anna snorted and shook her head.

The generals gave their deep thanks to Kol and Dave, discussing the weapons with an excited air. Suzy and Oxul were off in a corner, having a rapid conversation. Kol and Frenik were talking to each other about different ideas they had, both of them deeply interested in the other's process.

To Anna, she felt as if she was seeing the birth of one of the strongest alliances in the history of Emerilia.

Chapter 30: To the Guild Hall

Josh stepped through the teleport pad and into the guild hall. Automatons, Aleph from all races, Stone Raiders, Dwarven groups, and people from Devil's Crater were walking around the teleport control room, waiting to go somewhere or admiring the Stone Raiders' guild hall

Josh weaved his way through the crowds, thankful for Cassie, who handled most of the talking and getting them through without making others think that they were ignoring them.

"Damn, you're good at that," Josh said as they left the room.

"A few hundred different events where everyone wants an autograph or you to endorse their brand without going through your manager and you find a way to small talk like a boss." Cassie winked.

Josh laughed and shook his head. He saw Lucy talking to a group of her leaders inside the first housing facility.

"Well, look at you two. Looks like the date was a good idea. Hope you got walls that were a bit thicker than the Cliff-Hill guild hall's." Lucy gave them both a look. Josh grinned as Cassie turned an odd shade of crimson. "Well, I bet that you want to know what's going on here. We've got a bunch of groups who are in Devil's Crater looking for dungeons and helping clear out the nastier animals in the area. Dwayne and Kim are out there. We've accepted three hundred more people to be Stone Raiders. We've got most of them off training in Cliff-Hill, in Devil's Crater, or at the mage's and Aleph colleges. I didn't want to get many more lest we have more recruits than veteran Stone Raiders."

"Makes sense. We don't want to lose our identity with all of these changes," Josh said.

"Good, because we have another three thousand applicants," Lucy said.

Cassie whistled as Josh developed a twitch at the corner of his eye.

"Don't worry—we'll turn this lot into true Stone Raiders quick enough. We've got a lot of open contracts that we need to be finished. I'm going to do half-and-half parties. One veteran Stone Raider party with another new Stone Raider party—get them out there fighting and seeing what it takes to be a real Stone Raider," Lucy said.

"That's a good plan. I know when the Golden Sabres took in a whole bunch of new people, we started having disputes about the proper direction of the Golden Sabres. The older members and the younger ones wanted to do different things and it created tension within the guild." Cassie sighed and shook her head. "Damn shame, but happy to be here now." She looked to Josh and gave him a smile.

Josh returned it before he looked to Lucy.

"In other news, Dave is in. Suzy is here as well, talking to Florence. Verlun is booming right now. We're buying foodstuffs by the ton and selling it off to the Aleph and the people in Devil's Crater, and there are talks to open trading outposts in the Egas Nation and the Orun Free States. They're getting gouged for food and with the difficulty to grow it in Ashal, we can undercut their current suppliers and still make a good profit."

"Also opens possibilities for us to go to their lands and access the dungeons that they know of." Josh nodded. "Damn, this is getting a hell of a lot bigger than I thought it would."

"Yeah, we've got the backing of some of the most powerful groups in Emerilia. We've shown that we're reliable and we can act as a middle ground for everyone. If we were just a group of POEs or Players, then it wouldn't have worked out. We have a balance of both. Makes the groups we're dealing with feel at ease," Lucy said.

"I knew that the Stone Raiders had a lot of friends and were strong, but this is more than just a guild now. It's more like an adventuring empire. You've got alliances with nations and sects that few people gain access to. You've got military might and trading clout. I doubt most people know the full reach of your guild." Cassie shook her head.

"Good, because it's going to need your help." Josh smiled.

Lucy shared in the smile as Cassie's eyes thinned, looking at them both with clear suspicion.

"What are you two thinking?" Cassie asked slowly.

"Well, we thought it would be best to tell you once you got back," Josh said.

"We're getting a lot bigger and while we can manage the fighting and trading side of things," Lucy continued.

"We aren't the best at public relations. We were wondering if you could help deal with the different groups we're allied with?" Josh finished. The two of them stared at Cassie.

Cassie cocked her hip, holding her chin with her hand. "Would I be pulled from fighting?"

"Nope, you fight and do as you want. You could hire people as you want. Both from the traders and the fighting Stone Raiders. Florence is great in dealing with trading contracts but we need someone to talk to those who we not only trade with, but have a mutual defense treaty with," Lucy said.

"You have that?" Cassie's eyes went wide.

"Yeah, we had them drawn up instead of money in some cases. Put us in a better light and opened us up to more raids," Josh said, as if it were of no consequence.

"Those treaties are basically declaring that if you, or any of the signatories, were attacked, you would assist one another, right?" Cassie asked, a confused and slightly shocked look on her face.

"Yes, we wrote them up when we learned of the events that are supposed to start next year," Lucy said.

"I'll take the position. You don't understand how big that is. You could levy less taxes in some places as well as a higher reputation with different groups for your statuses. Like damned children with nuclear codes!" Cassie muttered the last part to herself.

"Told you we needed someone for the job sooner rather than later." Something caught Lucy's eye. "Excuse me, just have to meet with some people from the Council of Anvil and Fire. Seems having just Dave here isn't enough for them to be happy with our contract. I feel that they're just excited to see an Aleph city being built." Lucy sighed.

"Good luck!" Josh waved to her as she wandered away. "Well, talking about Dave—we should go and see what he's done with the rest of the guild hall."

"Just how powerful is Party Zero?" Cassie asked as they walked.

"Well, that depends." Josh looked thoughtful as they walked through the first housing complex. The vertical gardens were growing, lights bathing the area in warm light as Stone Raiders lounged around a tavern that had been made out of a few homes on the bottom floor near the middle of the courtyard. Josh waved to them, looking at another apartment on the bottom floor opposite that was run by the traders, taking in gear to be sold as well as giving out gear and selling different items to their fellow guild members.

There was a relaxed, jovial atmosphere to the housing complex. Like a bunch of friends renting out a house together for the summer and relaxing. People yelled to one another from the balconies above. It was busy but no one was rushing around, taking their time and enjoying themselves.

Aleph and Stone Raiders gardeners used a series of pulleys and seats to move up and down the vertical gardens. Automatons moved goods and items around.

"Well, it seems a lot more alive than when I was last here," Josh said with some pride, waving to a few people here and there. The veterans called out to Josh and Cassie, inviting them for a drink or a mission they were going on. Josh declined, saying he was heading off to find Dave.

They gave directions and extracted a promise for him to join them in a drink at a later time.

"The strength of Party Zero depends on where they are and what they're doing. If one of them is in danger or the guild and their friends are," Josh's eyes darkened, "then nothing could stay in their way. They will tear down the gods and drive armies before them to protect one another.

"Looking at their levels is not an accurate measurement of their abilities. When they're not together, they're two, maybe three times more powerful. When together, they're four or five times stronger. If incited, they're an army onto themselves." Josh frowned. *I don't know how Malsour and Induca did it, but I'm sure that they're related to those Dragons who were at Boran-al. Their aura—the only person similar to it is Deia, and I can never penetrate Anna's suppression. She makes it seem that she's in the high 200s, but the way she fights—I can't help but feel that she's much more powerful.*

Another person might demand to know their secrets but Josh counted them as his friends. He trusted them and their judgment. He wouldn't pressure them in telling him their secrets.

Cassie seemed satisfied with his answer.

"They've come far since Boran-al's Citadel. It's going to be hard to catch up with them." She had a smile on her face.

"Oh, up for the challenge?" Josh smiled.

"Well, it would be pretty fun. Going to need to do some dungeon grinds." She looked to Josh.

"I'll always go dungeon diving with you."

"Oh, so romantic." Cassie snorted as her fingers interlaced with his.

They passed through the second housing complex, which was less rowdy than the first. Crafters were all over the place, talking to one another and looking into the new passages off to the sides of the housing complex. It was a lot warmer in the complex.

Josh looked to the right, where there were two refineries working overtime. Automated carts waited, being loaded up with refined materials and driven to several apartments that had been knocked down to make a holding area for the materials.

They continued through the complex and entered a long corridor that went left and right, with entrances facing forward.

Josh took a right and went to the farthest entrance. The noise of grinding and large machinery could be heard in the background as Dave, Frenik, and Kol talked to one another, pointing at different things in the pitch-black darkness ahead of them.

"Looks like you're up to something," Josh said, making the trio turn around.

"Yeah, making a city. Come look!" Dave said in an excited tone, waving them over.

The lights were turned off, so Cassie held onto Josh's hand tighter. Josh's night vision was in the master levels, allowing him to see in the darkness. It was still hard to see anything at the end of the corridor that extended into darkness.

Lights turned on at random points in the darkness beyond.

Josh's jaw dropped as Cassie breathed in a surprised breath. In front of them was a massive cavern, easily four times longer than the housing complexes that they had walked through and two of them tall, cut out into a cylinder.

Closest to the entrance, an elevator led down to the edge of the city. Miners littered the city, working to cut out more of the city.

Josh watched as a steel box glowed, pushing out a miner. Instead of grinders on its front, it held lasers. It moved forward to help its fellow mining automatons. Automated carts followed it as it started cutting.

"It looks like reverse 3D printing," Josh said. The miners cut out different buildings, giving them shape as they passed.

"Pretty much. Just put in the plans and watch them go. We've got some Air mages and runes working to collect all the dust and debris in the air. Then we've got automated carts that travel to the refineries, break down everything into useful and not. What can be burned is sent to our fledgling power stations down there. I removed the power sources that are in the housing complex. We can run everything on ambient energy collectors I set up and some of the vault-classed soul gems," Dave said.

"How long until we run out of that as a power source?" Josh asked.

"Well, we're working on putting in an automaton factory to help out with the finer detailed work needed in the city. The power source will last for about two months." Dave held up a hand, stalling Josh's angry words.

"We're going to have this power station up in two days with dedicated work. Our Dark mages are down there, making the larger changes. Might even be tomorrow at the rate they're going. They love making things."

"Okay, but how long until we don't need the vault soul gems to keep going?" Josh asked.

"Well, that depends on what you want," Dave said. The Dwarves looked on in interest.

"Explain," Josh asked.

"So, my plan is to make a proper refinery and then another power station. If we have this power station up and running, it will be able to power our housing complexes, build that refinery, keep up miner and Aleph automatons in about a month. If we instead used the vault-classed soul gems, then we could get that done in about a week," Dave said.

"Those soul gems are a limited resource. I really don't want to lose them." Josh looked to Dave.

"Not really. We can recharge them off our guild's amulets. We just up the amount that we draw from people who are off duty, train them in having their reserves reduced. We could fill up a vault-classed soul gem in a day or two. Josh, we can buy more of them from the Aleph and use them as backups for our power stations, added redundancies." Dave gestured to Frenik, who nodded. "Right now, we're filling up our chests of holding with materials that I know Cliff-Hill smithies and the Dwarves would love to buy. Once we have that refinery up, we will *triple* the amount of resources we can process—more for the power station, for trade. With it, we can increase the amount of miners we make and the speed in which we increase the city's size, as well as gain the resources we need to make our own separate power station."

"Separate power station, like the Aleph?" Josh looked from Dave to Frenik.

"The lad doesn't think small," Frenik said. Kol grunted in agreement.

"Okay, so, talk me through everything that's happened so far and I'll decide." Josh sighed.

"I'll leave you boys to it. I have some things I need to deal with. Keep up the good work." Cassie smiled. She glanced at the growing city, shaking her head before she kissed Josh on the cheek and walked back toward the housing complexes.

"Ah, about time you figured out what the two of you were doing." Dave grinned.

"Feels good to finally know where we stand," Josh agreed. "So, now, explain."

"Okay, so, we had that one miner at work and we were having to try to buy more from the Aleph. They don't have any and they're busy working on their own cities and homes. I used my abilities to create a small factory that makes an upgraded miner."

"Wait." Josh held up a hand and stopped Dave. "So, you're powering that entire factory?"

"Okay, well, I had a sort of breakthrough when we were fighting at Devil's Crater. I was conjuring things and imbuing them with my power. At Devil's Crater, I realized that I could make the rough designs of the conjured item. Then I create a power tap from the conjured item to my soul gem. The conjured item was powered by the soul gem, rather than me. It meant I could use a tenth of my power on conjuring—then the costs of keeping it active and using it went to the soul gem instead of through me. I made the factory down there, attached it to the power grid and it draws from that, instead of me. As long as it gets power, then it can keep the other miners going. If that was to be broken or its reserve power source goes out, then the miners would have their own internal conjured soul gems to use. Enough time without power resupply and they'll fall apart," Dave said.

"I was wondering how you were able to do all of those powerful attacks and then you weren't even tired after," Josh admitted, looking at the twenty or so miners that were cutting out the city with their powerful lasers. Carts filled up behind them and added themselves to a backlog of carts headed for the large refinery by a direct tunnel.

"How much are we refining down into usable ingots?" Josh asked.

"We're producing about a hundred ingots every hour or so. We moved from iron to steel because it's worth more and we don't use iron for really anything anymore. We also have a decent amount of ebony, a tiny bit of Mithril; silver and gold are also low. Maybe ten ingots every two hours for all of those ingots." Dave shrugged.

"That doesn't sound like all that much," Josh said.

"With the new refinery, we could put out a thousand ingots an hour. That's possibly an ingot worth of Mithril every four hours, if we can find some good veins of it," Dave said.

"Okay, I just finished talking to Florence." Suzy sighed, entering the conversation. "Hey Josh, have fun on your vacation?"

"Yeah, I did. Dave was just getting me up to date on everything that's going on," Josh said.

"Oh, good." Suzy smiled to Dave.

"What did Florence say?" Dave asked.

"She's going to have a look at it. We've got a ton of the materials we need for Cliff-Hill smithies and with your projections for materials the city will need, she believes we'll be fine for resources," Suzy said.

Dave nodded in thought.

"Okay, so, the not many ingots thing. We're getting a ton of ingots. We don't have a forge here, because we scrapped it for more refineries to get really working on the city. All of the Stone Raiders come to Cliff-Hill or a Dwarven mountain to get their weapons worked on. Sure, we can start people working on their craft here, but Kol is a Dwarven Master Smith. Better to have them learn from a master than try to figure it out themselves. We already have a large group of Stone Raiders working for the Cliff-Hill smithies to learn. We can use the ingots to build different things and for that purpose, I think keeping all of the ebony, silver, and five percent of the steel would be a good idea. We can use those for the greater number of facilities. Now, I am biased, but the rest we can trade away. I am the only person in the Stone Raiders who can form Mithril. The Aleph can turn it into big sheets after a lot of work. For all it's worth, trading with the Dwarves is the best," Dave said.

"However, you should make sure that they understand that any and all materials that you trade to them are to be prioritized for repairing their gear. The council turns ingots of value into a commune object, delegated and passed out on a project-by-project basis. With Cliff-Hill, we are outside of that commune, so any resources we get we can use immediately for our own projects instead of Dwarven projects. Meaning if a Stone Raider comes in with a chunk of Mithril, we can use it to fix their Mithril weapon," Kol said.

Josh nodded. It made sense: Cliff-Hill was a business while the Dwarven smiths were a council made to lead their people.

"Okay, moving away from resources. If you had your way, what is your plan with the city going forward?" Josh asked.

"Once we have the power station up and the refinery, we don't make any more miners but create another two power stations as well as vault soul gem reserves. Then we get to make growing areas and fast." At Josh's confused look, Dave continued. "We have to have our teleport pads open nearly constantly to not only add air down here, but cycle the air. The plants love all the carbon dioxide but we need a ton more to keep the air clean. Once we have the farms up, we have the miners cut out the cylinder and start spinning the city. We have the automatons finish cutting out places as we need them. Add in teleport pads and start building a true leyline power station. Once we have that in place, then we can start looking to any more expansions and opening up things, like a summoner's hall."

Josh looked out over the rough shapes that covered the rounded-out cylinder. Miners worked in the distance, their lasers illuminating their bodies as they worked. Josh snorted as he looked out over it all. "So, we're really building a city?" Josh said, his voice a little shocked.

"It's pretty awesome," Dave agreed.

"Fastest damned thing I've seen. I know my people are interested in borrowing some of those miners. We're having something of a population boom and we're looking to expand," Frenik said.

"Well, I think we can work something out," Suzy said.

"Is this anything like the space stations you made back on Earth?" Josh looked to Dave.

"How did you figure out who I was?" Dave asked.

"Well, Suzy Markel—not a regular name and she does have the same face." Josh smiled.

"Was bound to happen sometime," Suzy said.

Dave snorted. "Well, I added in air locks to the entire place. We're deep down here. If there's a fire or someone attacks, I want a way to shut down areas. I'm also working on a type of canister to hold air in an emergency. Can't be too safe."

"It sounds like you have everything in hand. Okay, I'll ask for people to up the amount that they are bleeding off from their Mana, so that we can keep the soul gems charged. Could you update me every week or so, and let me know if you need anything else? In the meantime, I think I'll have a talk with Florence and see how everything is going with her." Josh clapped Dave on the back.

He made to turn around, pausing as he did so. "If you don't mind me asking, how are you able to play so much? I heard you two are doing a ton back on Earth at the same time?"

"That is a question for another time." Dave's smile turned into a dark frown. "Hopefully, a day much further in the future."

Chapter 31: Train Like You Fight

"Good! Good!" Denur barked as Deia drew in more ambient power from the surrounding area.

Fire felt something clench in her heart, in her very gut.

Deia started to rise from the center of the volcano, pulling in more and more ambient power from the surrounding stones and lava. Her hair whipped around like living flame. Her eyes closed in concentration, a whirlwind of Fire circled her.

Fire stepped through the angry air that howled in complaint at the Mana and heat that spread through the volcano.

She's going to be dangerous, Fire thought with pride, looking at her daughter.

Fire hadn't realized just how strong Deia was. She had been limited by her spells, using her knowledge of Earth and Dave's lesson on spell formations to create more powerful spells.

Her raw power was nearly unmatched, other than by Dragons and the gods themselves. With her Fire spells, she was nearly as powerful as Jelanos, Alamo, and Mal. The three of them had instincts of battle mages and the spells and smarts of century-old men who had been fighting the things that went bump in the night.

Dragons from the Densaou Ring poked their heads through the different holes in the volcano, all of them looking at the Lady of Fire's daughter and the queen of Dragons' sister.

Fire felt her body tingle. The Mana ignited within her, wanting to be released. She calmed herself, a smile on her face as her own hair whipped in the air and her eyes glowed with inner power. *In another time, I would have given in to that desire.* She shook her head, reminiscing about her older self.

Deia called upon the molten core of the planet. Heat rose, slamming through the base of the volcano; the cooled base of the volcano turned to magma shooting up fifty feet. Fire barely noticed the few thousand degrees Celsius that came with being inside an active volcano.

She looked to her Dragons. They looked mildly impressed by Deia's work.

"Hah! We'll have you popping these volcanoes like nothing soon enough, sis!" Denur whooped as she flew around inside the volcano.

"I only got it fifty feet. How is that at all impressive?" Deia looked at the Dragon.

"Most would be panting or passed out at this point. The fact you aren't shows that you know your limits and don't want to use all your Mana in one go. Sure, you've got another four hundred feet to go, but with some refinement and a bit more juice, you'll get it easy," Denur said.

Deia started to come down to rest on a ledge.

"We don't have time for that. Come on. You said that armor allows you to save some of your Mana—put it back in you. In a fight, you're going to be using everything you have. So, let's give it everything you have. Back in the center!"

Deia moved over to the center of the volcano again.

"Ulka, could you fix the bottom, just how it was before?" Denur asked.

The black Dragon seemed to glow slightly. The temperature in the room dropped as the top of the magma pool below turned to a stone plug.

"I'm going to get some books, Denur. Let me know when you're done," Fire said.

Deia either didn't hear or was too focused on what she was doing.

Denur nodded to Fire and then looked back to Deia.

Fire disappeared in a flash of heat, smiling at her two girls working together.

***

Malsour looked at the fields in front of him. Gelimah and Fornau had been interested enough to come and join him in turning Devil's Crater into a true city.

It had taken Gelimah a few weeks to get his butt into gear and over to Devil's Crater, but the recluse only liked one thing more than his treasure and that was building.

He happily whistled, wandering through Devil's Crater. Roads formed behind him. Magnificent houses were created with a gesture of his hands. Each he made was different from the last, incorporating what Malsour taught him.

The information on the different housing needs, including sewers, water systems, heating and the rest, were the bribe to get his brother out of his mountain home.

Now all of them stood in what was going to be the location of a new keep.

"Let's begin, shall we?" Malsour looked to his brother.

"I was only waiting on you," Gelimah said, somehow forgetting the three hours that he had debated Malsour's techniques with him.

Malsour chose to say nothing. He extended his reach down to the bedrock that lay deep below the cliffs that rose around Devil's Crater. From that bedrock, he pulled metal from beneath; weaving it into the rock, he fused them together into a solid base. Rock was compacted and used, metal extruding through it to add strength to it.

Gelimah banished and cleared out an area through the cliffs to create a path through the sheer cliffs, working through where the keep would lay. He cleared out the peaks in the area as Malsour's foundation formed. A shining block of granite with metal moved out of the stone like live snakes. The foundations met with the path through the cliffs. Walls grew upward along the foundations; granite created a polished surface, bowing out to make mages' balconies. Stairs ran up the walls and doorways formed. Twin gatehouses with overlooking arrow slits and holes for a destruction staff looked down upon the entry to the large stone doors.

Malsour weighted the doors so that a man could easily open them, but when locked they would drop down into holes, creating a five-ton stone wall.

Two stories of walls, overlooking the surrounding peaks, finished off in simple crenellations of a castle, continued to grow.

The keep was two hundred meters wide and a hundred deep. Away from the gates and the road that meandered through, a barracks and the keep's castle grew. It was a rounded rectangle with a large area out front for the forces in the keep to train and keep busy. Walls of granite with metal reinforcement created a mess hall, armory, large defensive doors, and a waiting area for units going on duty or ready to reinforce their friends. The floor above held the main barracks, with a large sleeping area and bathrooms. The top floor was an upright cylinder instead of a rounded square. Metal weaved into the second floor's roof. Here, artillery could be mounted with spotters on top of the tall, round third and fourth floors. Stairs wound up the floors on the outside, with doors and windows for the defenders to look out in any direction. Offices for the leaders of the keep were on these two floors.

The whole thing took up two-thirds of the keep, ready to house two companies of DCA soldiers.

Malsour added in overhangs for the walls and a sewage system running through the granite and metal foundation to run down inside the mountain before coming out away from the road that led to the keep.

Cisterns were added to the castle as runes flowed across the inside of the massive walls. Another series ran through the foundations: a place for a soul gem with connecting runic lines in the top of the castle's tower and another hidden in the deep foundations.

Malsour ran walls out of the keep, high over the peaks, creating solid foundations once again as they extended to the walls on either side. They were perfectly level, allowing for soldiers to run and move easily across the wall. Malsour grew overhangs over the walls. Soldiers weren't the most attentive if they were getting rained on.

Malsour and Gelimah panted as they finished their work.

Malsour looked over the barracks. "Damn. Well, I bet anyone who is stationed here is going to be pretty happy."

"I do take pride in my work," Gelimah said, happy with what he'd done. There were not only runes to keep the place defended but more to regulate temperature. Another to have a breeze coming through, so that it wouldn't stink in the castle. He'd also added a small plot to the side of the castle, right near the rear of the keep. With an Earth mage, they could get some dirt in the plot and grow some fresh food for the soldiers to eat. A small pen was located next to it, for animals. Coming back from patrols, soldiers would look forward to a fresh meal prepared in the keep.

"Okay, the walls are decent but they were rushed, most of them are just simply remolded peaks. We need to fasten them to the bedrock so there's little chance of movement. Seems everyone was doing their own thing, so we need to go around, straighten everything out into just one style of wall" Gelimah smiled, it was a daunting task, but it had been so long since he had a project that allowed him to flex his magical muscles. "Well let's get started!"

"Okay," Malsour said. "I'll root the foundations into the bedrock if you banish the peaks around the wall and standardize the layout of the walls. I see you've been looking at the other's runes with your heating, cooling, and Air runes."

"Well, when you sent me that book by Dave, I did get rather interested by the concept and his magical coding skill. Brilliant! I was finally able to make that thing I was telling you about!"

"The Yacozi?" Malsour said.

"Jacuzzi, yes!" Gelimah said, his excitement not even slightly dulled by Malsour's inability to remember the name.

Malsour smiled, as the Mana depleted headache creeped in. Raising an entire keep and a barracks with just two people was not easy on the Mana usage.

The more I use it, the stronger I'll be with it, Malsour thought as Gelimah rambled on. In power and strength, Malsour might be the strongest Dragon other than his mother with all he had gone through with the Stone Raiders.

Still, he had been shown that not even a Dragon's power was absolute.

***

Dave looked around the seeder's bridge. Nothing had changed since he'd last brought Ela-Dorn and Gal to the portal storage. He moved to the elevator, taking it to a slightly scarred and burnt room.

"Well, looks a bit worse for wear with all the experiments Deia and I put it through." Dave smiled as he looked at the different soul gems that were suspended in mid-air by glowing runes beneath.

He checked over his Magical Circuits in the room, wiping them clean by conjuring over them and removing the conjured item. Once they were all cleared, he started conjuring into the metal of the room. For his next experiments, he was going to need some more powerful shielding.

He created an inward Mana barrier as well as power taps for the barrier to the vault soul gem he'd left charging off the wide area runes collecting free Mana. The barrier appeared around the center of the room, containing Dave and whatever destruction he might create.

Dave pulled out a piece of steel Dragon scale armor. His eyes glowed silver as his Touch of the Land allowed him to see into the basic makeup of the armor. He laid it down on a workbench and looked at it.

"Well, I'm decent in close combat, but long range, not so much. That redirection thing I had with the gauntlets was pretty cool. Though it's overkill for anything but a massive army and it kind of gives away my position." Dave continued to look at the armor. "Okay, I'm decent at throwing a spear and if I add in those explosive shafts, then it would get caught or hit something and then explode. I could make it optional if I wanted to take someone down quiet or just blast an area. Though, sometimes I won't get enough time to throw a spear."

Dave stood and walked around, eyeing the armor.

"Steel and silver—it's not going to be strong enough for what I need. I'm going to need Mithril and silver; Maybe a core of ebony." Dave tapped his chin in thought, conjuring what looked like a wrist band, not too dissimilar from the bracelets the Dwarves wore to show their time in the Warclans, or whether they were married.

"Okay, so, if I can't always throw a spear, why can't I make one? Just like Malsour's metal spears he sends flying. Though if I modify the spear, I could make all of the power that makes it into a Mana bomb. For that, I don't need a massive spear. I could just have a smaller one—be faster to create and could fire at speed." Dave sat down at his table, pushing the Dragon scale armor away. Nervous excitement filled him as he looked at the simple band in front of him.

"Well, let's get started."

Dave's body started to glow with runes as his perception of time sped up. As he worked, silver runes slowly formed in the lined white surface of the Mithril. He pulled out a soul gem with a variable power output. He activated it; a slight humming filled the air before settling down. The runes engraved into the Mithril glowed with power, creating long lines of magical coding around the band.

He made a quick line of coding under the band, making it float in mid-air. He activated the different runes. A spearhead formed in mid-air, racing across his experimental warehouse and burying itself into a wall.

"Crap." Dave destroyed the conjured spearhead and activated runes around the large warehouse he used for his experiments. He also changed into his own armor.

"That would have been risky with the exploding spearheads," Dave muttered, changing the settings on the band's runes.

Another spearhead launched out ahead of the ring. It slammed into the surrounding Mana barrier. The Mana making up the spearhead turned into pure energy, tearing at the barrier, resulting in a sudden and violent explosion.

"Well, that's awesome." Dave grinned as he looked at the Mana barrier. He closed his eyes, his mind allowing him to think back on what he had seen.

"Okay, so, bit too close to the hand. Put it forward an inch or two—don't want to conjure it inside my own hand." Dave opened his eyes. The runes changed slightly. Another spearhead shot out ahead of it.

"Perfect. Now let's see how fast this thing is."

A dozen spearheads shot out in a matter of seconds. Dave stopped shooting, whooping and jumping around in excitement.

"Okay, now for the full-length spear." Dave activated the band. A spear appeared, parallel with the band's opening.

"Far enough away. Okay, let's give this a try." Dave put his hand in the bracelet. The spear disappeared.

He cocked his hand backward as if he were about to throw. Nothing happened.

Dave continued to move his hand around, trying to find the sweet spot. Finally a spear grew out of thin air, starting in his hand and spreading out into a shaft and spearhead.

"Okay, so, going to need to fix this whole activation thing, but other than that it should be okay." Dave threw the spear and it hit the barrier.

Dave pulled off the bracelet, modifying its command circuit before he put it back on. He cocked his hand back. Another spear started to form. Dave threw it before it had fully formed. It continued to grow in mid-air but quickly fell in height with the added weight.

It hit the barrier but without the power of the first spear.

"Okay, so, it works, but it isn't the best. How about the explosive version?" Dave shifted a band on the bracelet. He held up his hand. A spear grew to full length before Dave threw it.

The resulting explosion made the barrier turn a darker color for a few seconds. Quite the achievement for a barrier powered with several vault-class soul gems.

Dave laughed at his work; he clapped in excitement and did a slight jig.

He held his palm up. Spearheads seemed to appear in front of his hand in a steady stream. They raced across the room to hit the barrier. Explosions thundered through the room as they hit the barrier.

Dave stopped and looked at his bracelet.

He laughed out loud. Realizing how maniacally and evil doctor he sounded, he quickly looked around to make sure no one could hear him before cha cha-ing from side to side, with his face a picture of pure excitement.

"This is freaking awesome!" He laughed, taking it off, and moved to a worktable. He pulled pieces of metal from his bag of holding. He noticed with his senses that someone was approaching. Well, two people were approaching but one was far away, looking at different machines in the seeder.

"Hey, Induca, what brings you to my evil lair?" Dave said, doing his best to look like some slightly mad hermit.

Induca rolled her eyes. "Suzy wanted to look at the portals. I just heard you blowing things up. Thought it would be more interesting."

"Hah! Damn right! I'm the master of blowing things up." Dave smiled from ear to ear.

"I was also wondering if I could buy some rings from you," Induca said.

Dave sat in his rolling chair, holding his scruff. "What kind of rings you thinking?"

"Something to increase my ability with Fire spells. I've realized that while I am a Dragon, I'm not impervious to everything," Induca said, somewhat sheepishly.

"Good, because everyone needs help, even Dragons. Now, I don't know if rings to increase your Affinity would be as helpful as you're thinking. I've always found that increasing my Intelligence was the best thing. We can try out both, though." Dave closed his eyes. A silver band formed, runes covering the interior and exterior.

"Going to need a metal conjuring device and some kind of engraving tools," Dave muttered to himself.

"What did you say?" Induca asked as Dave grabbed the ring and passed it to her.

"I've found that while I can make things by simply conjuring them, having other machines to augment my ability greatly reduces the cost to me. So, if I created a magical factory that could make conjured metals, I could then engrave runes in them with a carver instead of having to channel all of that energy myself. The headaches I get from pouring my armor's energy into my own Mana pool are not fun." Dave sighed, unconsciously rubbing his temple at just the thought of those headaches.

"Well, how much would that cost be?" Induca asked.

"Well, that ring right there cost me roughly one hundred Mana because of my good control, though something like that soul gem based armor—that took nearly fifteen million Mana."

Induca's eyes went very wide with Dave's explanation.

"Now, put the ring on and tell me what you think," Dave said. Another ring appeared in mid-air in front of him. He looked as if he barely noticed it.

Induca put the ring on. She blinked rapidly for a few minutes, looking around as if seeing a whole new world.

"Okay, cast a simple spell to compare between the two rings," Dave said.

She made a simple flame, closing her eyes to get lost in the magic of the simple flame. She opened her eyes once again and took the ring off. "Damn, that was kind of a rush. Next." Induca passed back the ring.

"I make good stuff." Dave smiled, floating the other ring to her. He grimaced after a second. "Damn, that sounds weird—makes me sound like some kind of weird drug dealer, not a smith making a bunch of rings."

Induca smiled at his antics and put the second ring on. Once again her eyes closed and a flame appeared. After some time, the flame fell away.

"So, which one do you like more? Ring one or two?" Dave asked.

"Ring one. It wasn't just that my Fire magic got stronger; it seemed to open up my mind more," Induca said.

"I'll make you up two of the first ring to stack the stats in your favor and a third for a reactive shield," Dave said.

"A shield?" Suzy walked into the room.

"Hey, babe. Find what you wanted?" Induca asked.

"Kind of." Suzy greeted Induca with a kiss.

Dave was happy to see that Suzy didn't think of her sexuality as something to be hidden away from prying eyes anymore. She didn't go out of her way to show it off to others, but at the same time it didn't shame her; it was just a part of who she was.

"Well, Deia, Anna, Suzy, and I all have Mana barriers with our Abscondita armor. You and Malsour don't, which means that if anything is shot at you and you don't know it, then you're going to get hit. I can make a ring that gives you a pretty strong barrier, so that you can cast your own or fight on. It will be hooked up to the soul gem I gave you and I can make all of them soul bound, though it takes a bit of time for me to get that all done with my other projects. I can have it ready in two days. I need to recover my Willpower," Dave said.

"Make it three days. We're off to Verlun," Induca said, her arm around Suzy's waist.

"I can do that. When you two leaving?" Dave asked.

"About now." Suzy started to move for the door.

"Say hi to Deia for me, and try to stay out of trouble!" Dave yelled.

"You have meetings with Ukon tomorrow, and Kol wants to talk to you about hiring," Suzy said.

"I thought I was getting three days off!" Dave complained as Induca and Suzy made their retreat.

"Things changed. See you in three days!" Suzy yelled back.

Dave sighed and looked around his experiment warehouse. His frown turned into a smile as he spun around in his wheely chair. "Still a day down here. Let's see if I can't get some of those programs

I was thinking about started." Dave opened up his bag of holding, pulling out soul gems, as well as different metals, materials, and other items he'd collected on his travels but hadn't had the time or safety measures to play around with.

He pulled up his interface and locked a notepad to the table, so he could make notes on it without it following him around the entire time.

He sorted out his pieces, rolling around with glee. Excitement filled him as he looked over notes he'd had on different materials and ideas he'd come up with. Rubbing his hands, he returned to his main testing space. First he conjured a simple stand and connected it to a power source. It was as if he were guiding the metal into a new shape instead of trying to form it all by himself.

He put it on the table. A blue flame appeared at the peak of the stand. Dave turned a dial along the neck of the burner, changing the power of the flame. He turned the dial low; the flame disappeared.

Dave pushed it off to the side. Next, he built a simple carver. It was a hand-held device with a spinning Mithril tip that could cut through nearly any material, easily engraving runes and magical coding into multiple surfaces. Dave tested it out on an ingot he had. "Okay, might have to make a few of these for the smithies. Be a lot easier than using chisels."

Dave spent the next couple of hours forming a factory off to the side. The production line was just a few meters long. It took half an ingot of steel, a small bit of silver, a lesser soul gem, and a needle worth of Mithril. Placed into different hoppers, they would be heated up, formed, engraved, filled and connected before coming out the other side.

The upfront cost was as high as making twenty of the carvers. Though this could make five of them an hour, requiring nothing from Dave but more materials.

"Using conjured items to create real ones. I feel like I've still just barely scratched the surface of my skill's abilities." Dave looked to the time; he'd spent five hours on the factory. He sent a message to Kol about the carvers, promising to show him one the next day.

Dave stretched in his seat and took a deep breath. "I'd be lying if I said I wasn't dreading this." Dave looked at his forearm and the runes there.

"Dreading what?" Bob appeared behind Dave.

Dave promptly shrieked like a small child and jumped about ten vertical feet from his chair.

Bob laughed so hard when Dave landed that he'd fallen off his chair.

"Oh! I've got to do that more often! It's so hard to creep up on you with that damned spell you're constantly using." Bob wiped away tears that had formed at the corners of his eyes.

"Ass," Dave said, getting his heartbeat under control.

"So, go on. What were you saying before you tried to compete for highest squalling vertical jumper?" Bob devolved into laughter once again.

Dave glared at him as he tracked down his chair, putting it upright and taking a seat, facing Bob.

"Sorry—just, so *loud*!" Bob continued his fit of giggles.

Dave conjured and destroyed one of the chair legs that Bob was in.

"Ah!" Bob fell out of the chair suddenly. His feet went over his head before he landed. He got up slowly, looking at the grinning Dave. Bob smacked his hands against his pants and shrugged. "Well, I guess I might have deserved that." Bob chuckled. "So what you got for me?"

"I've got some alterations to make to the runes I conjured within my body. Though I'm not really sure what is going to happen," Dave admitted.

Bob cleared his throat, as he held up his chair and looked for a way to fix it.

Dave conjured another.

"You not going to destroy this one?" Bob asked.

"Not in the next three minutes," Dave said.

"Boo-yah!" Bob jumped up in the seat, his Gnome body enveloped in the large chair. "Okay, so what are you not sure about with the new runes?"

"Okay, so, with metals, I can put silver into the runes, so that they work better. With my runes, I made very quick impressions in my body. I've had to work to keep them active, something I didn't know until I had increased my Intelligence. What I want to do is not just create impressions within my body, but magical reservoirs, sort of like chakras of Mana. They are not just impressions but part of me that amplify my Mana through integrating into my body," Dave said.

"Do you know how dangerous that is?" Bob asked.

"Very, but I have a secret." Dave smiled.

"What?" Bob's scientific curiosity put him at the edge of his seat.

"I can conjure things within my own body, and I'm also highly adaptive. I would need to internalize something to create a natural Mana retaining ability, so that my runes would just work naturally," Dave said.

"Okay, so, what are you going to use for that?" Bob asked.

"I have samples of Demon, Dragon, Arch Lich, and sprite blood. I have no idea how I could use them, so, I'm going to need to experiment. In the meantime, I can form new magical code across my body to increase my power output," Dave said.

"Okay. If you give me those samples, I can use those and other samples to possibly create something you could use as this medium you want," Bob said.

"You sure?" Dave asked. It would be a lot of work off his shoulders.

"Look, I don't have all that much to do up there, mostly just hang out with Fire or Water, make plans, watch you lot, and think about what we need for the future." Bob shrugged.

"Where do you live, anyway?"

Bob tapped his chin in thought. He pulled out an amulet and tossed it to Dave. "Put that on and I'll show you." Bob smiled, clearly excited to show something off.

Dave pulled the amulet on. It had runes similar to the ones across the seeder that made it nearly impossible to detect. They were so good that Dave had only found the thing because of its complete absence.

"Hold onto your chair." Bob smiled and light enveloped them both.

Chapter 32: A Voyage Into The Dark

"Diana, I can't in good faith send them out there just yet," Sato said to Councilwoman Wong.

"You've done hundreds of hours of testing on those ships. I know that Captain Adams is more than confident in her ship's capabilities. She and her crew are ready and waiting to be used. Edwards informs me that we will have a full refit corvette ready for use in two days. How long will it take for Adams and her crew to get used to and run full tests on the new ship?" Wong asked.

"About two weeks." Sato sighed and looked around Councilwoman Wong's office. As they had come to work closer, he had come to call her Diana. There were few people who knew the stresses he was under, one of them being Diana.

"I can give you three weeks, then we need to start looking around. For too long we've been hiding on the outskirts of this system. We need to show the people that we are pushing forward, not just surviving," Wong said.

"First, I want them to do full system scans, reposition sensor buoys. Nothing big—we show that we're getting out there and it's not too far that if something does go wrong, that we'll be screwed. Then, and only if everything goes *perfectly,* will I send the recon corvette toward the nearest Jukal controlled system. If we can confirm that the telemetry information we have been given by Dave, Bob, and Shard is correct, then we can establish just what threats are around us." Sato held Wong's eyes.

"Okay, okay." Wong held up her hands to placate the leader of her station's military forces. "What about Emerilia?"

And now she gets to her real question. Sato waited a few minutes, collecting his thoughts.

"If everything checks out and we can confirm the accuracy of the information we have with a dozen different points, then I will send Captain Adams to perform reconnaissance on Emerilia. If there are people on the planet, then we will do what we can to aid them as long as we don't endanger ourselves. Bob didn't fully tell us about what is on or around Emerilia, but it seems that there are some kind of defenses in place. If the people of Emerilia ever became a problem, the Jukal Empire needed a way to destroy them. That could be nukes in the mantle, or orbital artillery—we just don't know," Sato said.

"Okay. We just need to show that now we've got these capabilities, we're not going to just sit here."

"Slow and steady—sure, it isn't flashy, but it will keep us safe. Edwards is coming up with more wonders every day and Bob did promise to have a meeting with us next week. There's plenty going on. We've increased our mining, growth of food; we've got technical magic—literally *magic*—at work with our systems. We've never been better," Sato pointed out.

"I know. It's just that if all of this is true, could it be true that there is a whole race of Humans and different subset races—that could be billions of people. We have less than a million here and Dave said that the majority of people were ten to twenty times stronger than normal Humans."

"I know, but think of how strong we'll be in just a decade. We're increasing people's life spans by years every day. The more people we have with these implants and interfaces, the stronger we can become," Sato said.

"You want one of them." Wong smiled at Sato.

"I won't say I'm not jealous because I can see just how my people are benefiting in a big way from it all. Though I understand why I can't get the tech yet." Sato sighed.

"Who would have thought that we could have created super Humans from alien technology?" Wong laughed.

"There was probably some book or comic about it." Sato smiled.

Wong snorted and sighed. "Okay, I'll run interference. You get me those recon corvettes, and get them training. I want Adams to be as ready as she can as soon as she can." Wong stabbed her finger into her desk to emphasize her point.

"I'll have them ready as soon as possible," Sato agreed.

***

Dave appeared in his chair and promptly rolled down a ramp, using his feet to brake himself.

"What the hell?" Dave looked around the rather large and empty room.

"Welcome to my home." Bob changed from his Gnome body into one of a wolf Beast Kin, one that bore many similarities with Anna.

Dave had become used to people changing their appearances; instead, he studied the seat that Bob was sitting on. It wasn't a recliner, but a proper command chair. There were screens, buttons, and all kinds of controls on his armrests. There were three other seats before him and a sloping U-shaped command area.

"This is a command center? Is this the command center of Emerilia?" Dave asked.

"Kind of. It certainly acts like it for me. Though it's really just part of a much larger network. Come with me." Bob walked out.

Dave rose from his chair and looked at the symbols around him. They were written in Jukal; he knew their shapes from the runes that he'd carved into multiple different items since coming to Emerilia. Dave walked through the halls. The lights turned on as they came through. The air was a bit humid but warm.

"Is this some bunker?" Dave asked, feeling enclosed in the halls as he followed.

"You'll see," Bob said in a smug voice.

Bob entered a lift. Dave joined him. They traveled upward through a few dozen levels.

"So, are you going to tell me where we are, and why I'm here?" Dave asked.

"Well, I'll show you where we are because I haven't been able to show anyone this place, ever, really. Also, you're here because I know you can use what I have here to greater effect than I can. Also, you're my backup plan if anything goes wrong." The lift stopped and they stepped out.

"Anything goes wrong?" Dave asked as they stepped into a room. Chairs were all looking outward into a plain metal shutter.

"Want to see one of the best sights in the universe?" Bob smiled and opened his interface.

The shutters moved quickly, opening up to the observation deck Dave was standing on.

"Wow." Dave looked through the thick polycarbide material that made up the observation bubble. The interesting material didn't distract him as he looked down at Emerilia. He could make out Ashal slowly turning around and into Gudalo. Weather systems moved through the air; whites, greens, browns, and blues showed the beauty of the world below. That shining, beautiful and intricate marble rolled beneath as a vista of stars framed the planet.

Dave looked to the sides, noticing cannons, hangars, and anti-fighter batteries. "This is a warship and we're in space?"

"This is an imperial carrier, six hundred years old and works as well as she did the day she was turned into my prison and home." Bob rubbed a seat he stood next to affectionately.

"I should have thought of this. It makes perfect sense—need some kind of fail-safe in place." Dave looked at the monstrous sides of the carrier. It must've been kilometers long and he couldn't see how wide it was with the curved side of the craft.

"The ever-living caretaker." Bob looked to Emerilia as one of the moons and sun appeared in their view, the observatory's glass darkening.

They stood there for a while, just admiring the beauty that they were able to see in their lifetime.

"You know, I had so many people working up in space but I never got up there myself," Dave said.

Bob held his comments, letting Dave talk.

"I always wanted to go into space. I never had enough money for the hotels in orbit, or even the balloons that would take you up for a few hours. Then, when I had enough money for it, I was an uninsurable nightmare if I wanted to go where my people were. I was worth too much to risk going into space." Dave snorted derisively.

"Well, now here I am, actually over a planet. Kind of weird knowing that I will never see Earth. I thought of it as my home, but now I know that Emerilia is. There's a rare beauty to seeing a world from on high."

"It makes one feel protective," Bob added as they continued to orbit Emerilia. "For many years, I deceived myself, thinking of myself as just some kind of preservation nut keeping alive a species for the sake of it. One day I was in here, strung out and tired by it all. I was crying actually and Anna found me. She asked me what was wrong." Bob took a breath. "I said that I was tired of seeing so many of my Humans die."

Bob turned, looking to Dave with his silver eyes. "Do you know what she said? She said 'It's always hardest for parents to see their children die before them.'"

Bob looked back to Emerilia. "That was the day that I realized that I didn't think of myself as some manager of a zoo. I thought of myself as a surrogate father."

They stood there for a while.

"Come, Dave. I have something to show you." Bob moved away from the observation dome. The shutters started to close again as Dave followed Bob.

They took a short ride on the lift and appeared in a hangar. Instead of rows of fighters and smaller craft, there were rows upon rows of shelving and boxes all neatly stored away.

"This is my gift to you," Bob said.

Dave checked a prompt that appeared off to the side of his vision.

Class: Friend of the Grey God

Status: Level 3

> +30 to all stats

Effects: Access to hidden quests.

> Access to the Imperial Carrier *Datskun*

Class: Bleeder

Status: Level 2

Effects: +20 to all stats
Ability to disable Jukal Link

Dave waved the prompts away as he felt as if something was connecting to his mind. "What the hell?" Dave scratched the side of his head.

Bob stopped and turned around. "Oh, that's the *Datskun*'s systems connecting to you. I gave you commander rights to the carrier."

The itch faded away and Dave looked to Bob.

"Think of turning the lights on and off."

Dave did so and the room's lights turned on and off in time with his thoughts. "Okay, that is seriously weird," Dave said.

"Welcome to Jukal technology!" Bob laughed and moved to a box.

"I also got told that I can now disable the Jukal link," Dave said.

Bob paused with his hand on a box. "Yeah, so, when you want to, you can stop the Jukal from watching through your eyes and using systems located within your own body," Bob said.

"Devices in my body?" Dave asked.

"Questions later. Let me show you something cool first." Bob heaved on the door handle of the box. It opened to reveal ingots stacked upon one another.

Dave's eyes went wide with what he was seeing. He picked up one of the ingots, feeling the textures of the white metal in his hands. His Touch of the Land scoured the metal and assured him that his eyes weren't deceiving him.

"All of this is Mithril? This is more than a yearly output of Mithril from all the Dwarven mountains!" Dave said.

"In here, I have the highest quality materials from across Emerilia—from pelts, to wood to metals and soul gems. I've even replicated a few of your vault-classed soul gems." Bob led Dave through the racks.

Dave's senses were pushed out, finding materials he didn't even know of around him. It was more than a treasure trove; it was unimaginable to his mind.

Bob showed off different items he had: weapons that came from every aggressive species, books on their language, entire shelves that recorded species that had been killed off. The history and resources of Emerilia's six hundred years was held in those shelves. They passed through holding areas that might have been filled with food, weapons, parts and fuel for the imperial carrier. They had been stripped away from the ship, giving Bob plenty of room.

Dave followed along, in awe of Bob's collection of resources. "Bob, what is this all for?"

"Well, recording the species that have been destroyed—there is always something to be learned from them. The materials I've kept in order to have something ready if I ever needed it. Though since you're here, I can gift them to you to be used," Bob said, never stopping his stride.

"You're going to gift this all to me? Why?" Dave asked.

"No one can really understand what the coming war will mean or what it will turn into. Dave, when I said that we're fighting for the future of Humanity, I damned well meant it. Emerilia might be changed forever and the Jukal Empire can't see what they've done. They just want to be entertained, given the next thing to talk about with their friends, to make bets on and suck their life away as they live their stagnant, boring lives. These creatures they're letting out are more powerful than anything I have ever known. I can't even compare them to a Jukal company, platoon, or brigade. They've never fought one another and the Jukal see Emerilia as someone else's issue. It's like news back on Earth: you see something and think that couldn't happen to me and go about your lives. Well, here it is going to happen to them and they don't even know it, just blindly wandering forward without a thought to what they're playing with. If we survive all of the armies thrown at us, then we're going to have to survive the aggressive species. If we can do that, then Emerilia's people are going to be stronger than ever. What do you think the Jukal are going to do when they realize any of this?" Bob asked as a new door opened for him.

"Nothing good," Dave said.

"They're going to do everything they can to regain control of Emerilia, through whatever means necessary and then start it all over again."

Dave looked around the new room. His eyes landed on rows of event horizons at the end of the room. Through many, he saw massive warehouses filled with materials and goods.

"You've started the basis of one of the strongest alliances on Emerilia. I need you to succeed and I need the armies that stand with you to be the strongest possible. All of this is for your use," Bob said.

"Bob, those are portals...to other warehouses," Dave said.

"Yes, they are. Didn't you think that I would skim off a few goodies from the seeders? At first, I just wanted to get around easily, doing experiments and getting Emerilia up and running. Then it turned into stocking materials and items for trade or use when they were necessary."

"This is incredible," Dave said.

"Yeah, though how the hell you're going to move this all I leave up to you," Bob said.

"Crap."

Chapter 33: Streamline

Dave appeared back in his experimental warehouse. He started to walk out, but as he looked around, he felt something was off.

"Bob! Need my chair back!" Dave yelled into the room.

A second later, his rolling chair reappeared.

"Thanks, dude!" Dave made to leave again, before he turned around and grabbed the carvers. He put bands of different metal into the burner, conjuring metal over his own hand to protect it. Dave didn't have the time to experiment with the rings. He finished off three rings in ten minutes and put them into his bag of holding. He took off the amulet Bob had given him and put it into his bag as well.

He formed Mithril on his fingers and grabbed a section of Mithril. His runes lit up as his eyes turned to silver. Mithril, ebony, silver, and pieces of soul gems were integrated into the band. Dave put it on his hand, pulling heat from the fused metals.

Dave pointed his palm at a wall; a spearhead exploded on the Mana barrier.

Dave turned one of the three bands that made the bracelet as he started to walk out. He was getting a large Mana headache but he had a lot to do. Dave quickly exited the seeder and sprinted for the smithy. It took him just a few minutes to reach it. He found Kol not long after.

"I thought you were experimenting tonight," Kol said.

Dave looked around, noticing that it was nighttime. With his night vision, the colors of day and night were just slightly off from one another.

"I was supposed to, but now I've got something I need to do. This is a gift for you." Dave pulled out the carvers and put them on a workbench.

"What are they?" Kol asked.

"They're carvers. Spin really fast at one end—will allow you and the rest to engrave metals much easier. I've got a factory making them downstairs. Right now I need to get off to Devil's Crater, then Alephir, and the guild," Dave said in rapid-fire.

"Everything okay?" Kol asked.

"Uh, well, kind of. Just need to make sure that some things are taken care of. Just got a big helping hand on the supplies side." Dave made to leave, paused and looked back to Kol. "Talk to Deia and see if she knows some bow makers. Oh, and we're going to need Dwarves who know how to build artillery, the new titanium artillery. If you can find any of those people, then get me some plans on what they would need to set up a factory. I'll see if I can't get some Aleph to help speed up the process."

"What do we need that all for?" Kol asked.

"The coming war," Dave said, remembering Bob's words when they'd passed through a portal into one of his massive warehouses. *This might look impressive, but the creatures I have in holding take up nearly twenty times the room and are more deadly than anything your current group of Players have ever seen.* The look in Bob's eyes more than his words had gotten across to Dave: Bob was *scared* by these creatures.

It was past time that Dave got to working on making sure Emerilia was ready for what was to come.

"I should be back by tomorrow." Dave opened up his interface as he ran out of the smithy, toward the teleport pad.

"What about the new smiths and Ukon?" Kol yelled.

"Hire everyone you think is worth the investment. I might be back in time to talk with Ukon!"

Dave sent messages to Alkao, Hamdir, and Jesal. It was going to be a busy night, just not in the way he was hoping. Jesal was the first to reply.

Private Message

Jesal> What's up?

Dave> I've just come into a windfall of materials. I can't use them all and I am willing to sell them to the Dwarves, but with the condition that they are to be used for updating the armor and weapons of the Warclans.

Jesal> We've got a lot of projects going on that would need those materials. I know the Warclans are a big priority. Though I can't make that commitment without more reason.

Dave> The Grey God put them under my control. Their purpose is to help the alliance be ready for the coming war.

Dave made it to the teleport pad and checked his other messages. Alkao had replied. He didn't have time to check it just yet.

"Devil's Crater," Dave said to the teleport pad's controller. They nodded and activated the teleport pad.

Unity appeared on the other side and Dave ran through.

Private Message

Jesal> How much materials are we talking about?

Dave> Enough to change all of the Warclans' artillery guns. It's like two decades' worth of all the Dwarven mountains' mining.

Jesal> $#@%! Okay, I'll get talking to people and see what we can come up with. I was going to sleep tonight, you know.

Dave> Ah, sleep is for the weak, didn't you tell me that?

Jesal> Smart ass.

Dave switched over to the other chat as he ran through Unity.

Private Message

Alkao> I'm in the government building. No rest for the wicked, I guess. What do you need?

Dave> Be there in five. Got something to discuss with you to make your fliers much more powerful.

Dave ran to the government building. Soldiers, upon seeing Dave, checked him for illusion magic and then ushered him quickly inside. He was stopped twice more before he made it to Alkao's new office near the top of the tower.

Dave burst in, drinking from his water skin.

"Whew! Good little run there. You got somewhere where I can test out some explosives?" Dave wiped his face with his sleeve.

"Dave, what did you mean in your message?"

Dave saw his messages blinking. He opened it, finding Hamdir had replied. *Got to talk to him next.* Dave moved to the balcony.

"I've got something that might really improve your army, though I don't have much time, so, I need you to come with me," Dave said.

"Well, it'll get me out of this office." Alkao sighed and rose.

"Where are most of your generals?" Dave asked.

"Kala and Vrexu are off in the training area of Unity. Their soldiers will be the first to get your new armor," Alkao said.

"Let's go pay them a visit. Mind giving me a ride?" Dave asked.

"Can't you fly?" Alkao's wings opened up and stretched through the truly massive door that led to his balcony.

"I can levitate for periods at a time—no flying. Though I do know some rather *risky* ways to get around, but I'd rather not use a rocket to get from here to the training ground." Dave smirked.

"Rocket?" Alkao asked.

"Maybe one day I'll show you. Shall we?"

Alkao checked his shield and sword. His wings flapped and pulled him up into the air. His large feet grabbed onto Dave's shoulders and Alkao dove over the banister.

Dave yelled out as they rushed toward the ground. Alkao laughed as he turned his dive into a glide, quickly turning them toward the training area.

"Hey, no interface and fly!" Dave said, seeing Alkao on his interface. *I should have run to the training ground and had Alkao meet us there.*

"We'll be fine." Alkao dismissed his screen.

***

A tired Malkur stretched and yawned. He had been doing paperwork while Kala and her people had the night off. Kala stumbled into the courtyard; she found a medic who healed her of her drinking. She stopped wobbling and headed to meet with Malkur.

"What the heck is it that Alkao wants now?" Kala growled as she got closer.

"Not sure, though we should find out soon." Malkur pointed at the growing flier headed for their training area.

There were multiple fliers in the early hours of the morning, but few were as big as Alkao in the sky.

"Looks like he's bringing us a package." Kala pointed at the man in Alkao's feet.

Malkur squinted, looking at a displeased-looking Dwarf Halfling.

"Looks like Dave came for a visit." Malkur had a note of respect in his voice as he touched his blade. The weapon was the finest that he had ever seen. He couldn't use it in sparring for the advantages it gave him. Having Kala around made it possible to actually train with the blade without fear of cutting the other's weapons.

Alkao came in to land and released Dave, who dropped onto the ground, squatting to absorb the impact.

"Ugh, hate this nature version of flying. Give me a damned plane any day of the week. At least they're trained to do it," Dave muttered, pulling out a disk of metal.

"So, what do you need us for?" Kala asked.

"Dave has a plan for a weapon that our fliers can use," Alkao said.

"Well, everyone can use it. First, just to make sure, you're going to be changing your organization into two main groups: those who can fly and those who can't. Your fighting tactics are not going to be stand-up battles but rather hit-and-run, whittling down the enemy and making their lives hell and any expeditions they make costly." Dave looked to them all.

"Pretty much," Malkur said.

"We will be adding in artillery units, mage units and healers, as well as supply services," Kala added.

"Good, good. Might have some of that artillery ready for you soon enough. In the meantime, I want to show you something that will change the way that your army fights. Do you have a range around here?" Dave asked.

"This way." Malkur waved for Dave to follow him. They all walked toward the archery range.

"So, what is this idea?" Alkao asked.

"This." Dave tapped the Mithril and Ebony bracelet on his arm which had three different thin bands That could be rotated into different positions.

"What does it do?" Kala asked.

"It's cooler when you see it in action," Dave said.

"Show-off," Alkao said.

"Mad inventor with a sense of pride, thank ye very much!" Dave winked.

They reached the archery range. Dave took the piece of metal he had pulled out of his bag of holding and put it behind a target. He adjusted the bands on his bracelet. He pointed his palm at the target. Spearheads sunk deep into the archery target.

Then Dave cocked his hand back; a spear appeared in it and he threw it across the field and into the target, showing his Strength and Agility with actually hitting the target at two hundred yards.

"So, this thing can conjure items?" Kala pointed at the band.

"Yes. It can be powered by soul gems with the right attachments, but that isn't the best part—at least, not for your forces." Dave turned another band on the bracelet. He raised his palm quickly before he lowered it again. A single spearhead flew across the range.

Malkur watched as it hit the target and exploded. The sound of the spearhead detonating rang through the range as everyone looked at the now vaporized target. The plate that Dave had put down was a Mana barrier that had taken the brunt of the blast, leaving scorched marks along the wall where they didn't cover.

"Pretty good, huh?" Dave grinned.

"What was that?" Kala asked, recovering first.

"They're conjured items, made from pure Mana. If I take away the controlling form of the conjuration, it turns into raging and unformed Mana, just like a Mana bolt. Think of all that refined Mana slamming into a target." Dave pointed at the now vaporized target.

He cocked his hand back; a spear appeared in it. He threw it; as it hit the Mana barrier, extending out and around the plate he'd put down, it, too, exploded.

"Okay, I'm not going to lie. That's pretty impressive. So, what are you hoping for us to learn from this?" Alkao asked.

"I can give all of your fliers and the people on the ground these bands—well, not these ones, but ebony and silver ones. The Mithril ones are much harder to make and honestly they're overrated and expensive for what you need. This can give you more than shields and swords in the sky. You can be like fighter planes with dual guns in your hands. Well, spear throwers, I guess. Then, on the chest plates, we can enchant another conjuring band. Instead of having to carry Mana bombs in your claws, with using your bands, your people could carpet-bomb an entire area with their enchanted breastplates. Turn them into a bomber/fighter hybrid." Dave smiled.

"I get some of what you're saying, but guns, carpet bombs, bombers? I don't know what that all means," Malkur said.

Dave sighed and opened his interface. He looked up the history of fighter planes as well as bombers, and then shared it with Alkao and the other two.

"How much will this cost us?" Alkao asked.

"Probably a bit more as I'm going to have to take some of my people away from other tasks. Though the bracelets—I'm going to talk about doing a patent and selling it to the Aleph, so they can produce a lot of them nice and cheap. Also, I'm realizing how few good magical coders there are, so I'm going to be opening a school at the smithy for learning how to do it properly. If I have to code everything myself, I'm liable to break my workbench with my forehead out of boredom," Dave said.

"You'd be willing to teach others such a powerful gift?" Kala asked.

"Look, we're all in this together now. I'm going to be meeting with the Elves, Dwarves, and Aleph to see about really ramping up production. Right now, there's four different groups that are all working on the same things. If we can get you all together and in an alliance, we can start sharing that information and together we can iron out the weaknesses that every group has. Think of it: The DCA as a supporting aerial and ambushing force. Aleph to manufacture, support, supply, and scout. Dwarves to act as an attacking force or a defending one. Elves to act as close ranged support and Stone Raiders to run about like a bunch of idiots with their heads cut off," Dave said, getting chuckles from the others.

It was one hell of an ambitious plan but Alkao nodded.

"I think it is time that we started not only being allies on paper but also in trade and in support. I will send messages to the others to open up our teleport pad to them. We have plenty of space and much that needs to be done," Alkao said.

"Good. Now, I'll be back in...two days? Maybe three? Not sure—Suzy deals with that. I've got to run to some more meetings. I'll get her to write something up about the armbands and the breastplates. Read over the plane information." Dave drew a quick drawing of a stick figure with wings in 3D. On their chest, he put a circle facing toward the ground, and another two on the figure's arms, sending it to the other three.

"I'll see you later!" Dave said.

"Talk soon." Alkao waved good-bye and Dave returned the gesture.

"Well, it sounds crazy, but if we can actually get this to work, it would be pretty effective," Malkur said to Kala.

"Agreed. Going to be a pain in the ass to train them with shields and swords." Kala moaned. "I can just see some idiot shooting their melee weapons while trying to kill someone."

"If Dave is going to get the Aleph to make these new bands, then we might be able to switch the contract from the swords and shields to these bands," Malkur said.

"This is going to cost a lot more than we hoped." Alkao sighed.

"Well, looks like we're going to have to get some of our people to clear out some of the dungeons around here." Kala smiled.

Malkur hid his grin. Alkao wanted to have his forces trained up more in Unity and the keeps before sending them out to fight again. Kala and Malkur were of the school of thought that they had trained enough. The ones going into the dungeons would be given the best equipment. If they came up against something too hard, they could pull back, but the materials and experience would be invaluable to growing the treasury and their force's abilities.

"It looks like you'll get your wish," Alkao agreed.

***

Ela-Dorn had to be nearly carried away from her lab. It was only the fact that it was Dave himself coming that she was willing to leave.

She arrived at Alephir, about the same time that Dave skidded into the room.

"Whoa! Forgot how close that wall is." Dave clicked his fingers and pointed at Ela-Dorn and Hamdir.

"Just the people I want to see! Dorn, I was wondering if you could do me the honor of teaching me and Malsour a few things about those portals. Damn, I should have grabbed him, too, but he's off reinforcing the keeps and the walls." Dave waved his hand. "Hello, Hamdir. Heard good things—good to meet you properly." Dave moved to Hamdir and shook his hand quickly.

"You said that it was vital that we meet?" Hamdir asked.

"Well, okay, so, may have found a way to really improve the DCA's fighting abilities. I have the patent, want to sell it to you guys because you're awesome with factories and we need them all like yesterday. Also, need to talk to you about hiring a bunch of people as consultants and starting up a ton of factories. So, maybe my smithies can make really good weapons but it takes time and all that mess. You guys can step up a factory in a couple of weeks and crank out items over and over again at a high rate. I have a whole bunch of resources and I need help turning them into Weapons of War. The Dwarves can make really good artillery, but, they can't produce it as fast as you can. Sooo, I want to build an artillery cannon, then a factory to make them all, so that we aren't stepping on people's feet. Going to talk to the Dwarves, though you're going to need to make an effort on your side if you want to not only be friends, but allies for what is coming," Dave said.

"Why should we be allies with them?" Ela-Dorn asked.

"Most powerful assaulting force on Emerilia, got more resources than the Aleph, awesome defenses, have close interests, and you're already trading with them. Got the basics for friendship down. Turning it into an alliance isn't all that difficult and I've been talking to Bob. We're going to need one another," Dave said.

"So, that's who lit the fire under your ass," Hamdir said.

"Yep, making a war economy all by myself." Dave smiled before he frowned. "Well, that does sound shitty—not too proud of that, but if we survive then I'll be fine with it." Dave shrugged.

"Okay, so, go through what you want from us," Hamdir said.

"Okay, so, first a bunch of people good with factories. I can build things pretty easily; I just need people who know the right way to build it the first time. I need more people and machines to run these lines and keep up production. I'm talking shields and artillery, maybe other small things to aid in improving people's magical coding. Oh, I'm going to start teaching people how to do that the right way instead of just taking a stab in the dark. Going to need repair bots and utility bots, so that I can have more people in my shop, less of them running around moving things from place to place. Then foundries and teleport pads. We need to set up a network of teleport pads to get from location to location—move supplies, troops, anything we need in days, not weeks or months. When these things start showing up on Emerilia, we need to be ready for them." Dave looked to them.

"That isn't easy. The cost and resources would be immense," Hamdir said.

"I can supply the materials at a reduced cost. I can also help with the teleport pads. I know a few things that could speed up production and decrease costs," Dave said.

Hamdir and Ela-Dorn looked at each other. It seemed alarmist on Dave's part but the Aleph were a paranoid bunch and there was also the chance to learn much and make a lot of gold in the process. Ela-Dorn nodded to Hamdir.

"Very well. We can get into further talks later. I will get some volunteers together to meet with you," Hamdir said.

"Send them to Kol. I'm going to be meeting him soon—he'll know what to do," Dave said.

"So, do you want to know what we learned from the portal so far?" Ela-Dorn asked.

"I do and I know Malsour does too. I have most of the science down but I'm still missing a few dots. Once I do, I can take apart a portal's Magical Circuits and I should understand them," Dave said.

Ela-Dorn let out a shocked breath and covered her mouth. *To talk of such a rare resource and just destroy it for the chance that he might know how the Magical Circuits will work—none of my people would think to do it. He truly doesn't see them as that great of a resource, or just trusts his own insight that much.*

"Also, we're going to need something a bit faster than carts and various creatures. Sure, they're jogging speed for most things but we're going to need enchanted vehicles good for going off roads and supplying our people on the move. Maybe even have the artillery pulled by them, or combine them and the artillery for magical tanks?" Dave shrugged as he opened his interface and sent a wad of files to Ela-Dorn and Hamdir.

He checked the time at the top of his screen. "Okay, talk soon. I'll get Suzy to call you up. I'm off to go and see a banker! Cliff-Hill please, controller!" Dave yelled up into the control booth. Dave was running through an open teleport pad moments later.

Hamdir and Ela-Dorn looked from the pad to each other.

"Well, he seems like a handful. I hope that we don't need all of these preparations he's talking about, but best to have them and not need them. Gives our people something to do as well," Hamdir said.

"I don't think I want to know what he'll be like if he pulls a portal apart and understands how it works." Ela-Dorn shook her head.

"Brilliant men rarely think about their actions until someone else brings light to them," Hamdir said.

"Well, at least we can start learning magical coding." Ela-Dorn looked through the different files: one on bracelets, another on tanks, hovercraft, artillery, and cars.

Ela-Dorn's eyes went wide with the amount of information in front of her. They referenced things she had heard of Players talking about, but she never thought she'd get the actual technical details on how they worked. She squealed in excitement and ran for the teleport pads.

"Send me to the college!" she yelled. A teleport pad came to life as she dashed through, racing back to her lab, sending copies of the information out to a mass of other researchers and added it to the archives.

We live in such exciting times!

Chapter 34: Time To Build

Kol was waiting as Dave ran up to him.

"Hey, phew. That was a night," Dave said.

"What were you in such a rush about?" Kol asked as they walked into the bank.

"Making plans. Hopefully after this, I can be left alone in peace—well, once I teach some people how to do magical coding, you have all the factories up and producing, that kind of thing."

"What?" Kol said in alarm.

"Something the matter?" Ukon stood in the foyer of the bank.

"Nope, just need to check a few things." Dave waved Kol onward.

What is he doing now? Kol thought.

They stepped into Ukon's office.

"So, what can we do for you?" Ukon asked.

"Well, I heard that you put in word for one of your banks to be moved to Verlun—thanks for that. Took a lot of stress off Florence and the people there," Dave said.

"I saw it as a wise investment. Those higher up agreed with me after all the success we've had in Cliff-Hill," Ukon said with a proud smile.

"Good. Then I'm going to be using all of my savings, except this month's wages, to buy higher levels for my mine manager class," Dave said.

"What?" Kol yelled.

"I've got a bunch of resources and materials coming in, and I've got extra gold coming in as well to pay our people. With the higher mine manager level, we can get more materials faster. I was told that you're holding them?" Dave asked Ukon.

"Yes, we do have the materials from the class." Ukon nodded.

"Good. All of those go to the smithies upon arrival. Is there anything else I should know?"

"I feel it is my duty to remind you that Wis'Zel's ceramics factory in Zol'Ord has been finalized and the paperwork for the money to be sent to the landowners has been completed," Ukon said.

"Perfect—less to worry about. Kol, how was the talks with the Dwarves and Elves?"

"I got a large number of Elves who are interested. They've been making bows out in their trees and they have a constant demand but between gathering materials themselves and then having to put them together, they're being pulled in a lot of directions. If we can supply them with materials, a place to stay, money, food and water, they'd be pleased to get working on making us bows. I had a talk with the council about the artillery. It's clear that we're still in the beginning stages of messing around with titanium and their projects were on the high end; they need more cannons and soon. If we can get a line of them operating, then they're willing to send people to help," Kol said.

"Good, good. Looks like you've been busy. I'm going to be teaching our people how to do magical coding so that they know what to do with the DCA armor— made a minor adjustment to it that we can add in. Also, the Aleph are sending over factory people to help us build multiple factories for different uses. I'm thinking we leave them with making vehicles; we deal with armaments, other than the bands, just because they're finicky as hell and quality control is going to be a bitch on them." Dave tapped his chin.

"With all of this buildup, it is going to cost quite a bit," Ukon said.

"Don't worry, I have gold coming in." Dave waved at Ukon.

"Making a new factory, the cost for start-ups like this—it is in the hundreds of thousands, if not millions," Ukon said.

"I've got a few thousand tons of gold coming in. I'm covered," Dave said.

Ukon looked like a fish out of water with his mouth opening and closing.

"What we've got to do with our alliances and the businesses we've built here is to create a war economy." Dave looked to them both. "Here we're going to be taking people and practices from all of the races we're allied and work with, put them together and make the weapons, armor and other accessories we will need to not only fight the enemy but defeat them completely. Oh, and we'll probably be having the factories and a smithy located in the Stone Raiders' guild hall."

Kol sighed as he nodded in agreement.

"Well, I can get that gold pulled for you today, and I will see what I can do about helping you later on," Ukon said.

"I have multiple patents that I will need to submit. I would like the bank to retain copies just to keep the trader's guild loyal. I don't want anyone messing around with them and making items that aren't of the highest quality. These will be weapons going in the field," Dave said.

"Okay, I can talk to our people and make sure we double-check with the trader's guild to back you up," Ukon said.

"Sweet. Otherwise, how are we looking on the business front?" Dave asked.

"For the last few months, we've had profits across the board. With the new contract, we're actually looking at about breaking even with all of the expansion and predicted costs that Suzy has submitted. No need for loans or anything of that nature. You will be running low on funds after today, but as you've told me, that won't be too much of an issue," Ukon said.

"Well, certainly sounds good!" Dave smiled.

Kol grunted, wondering what changes were coming to Emerilia.

***

Dave sent his orders off and grabbed more carvers from the seeder. He replaced a number of charged vault soul gems and the small carver-making factory. He dropped off the factory with Kol, who was actually in the smithy's office, delegating to his shop heads about the massive hiring process they were going to start. As well as the fact that they would be making a factory that would use people from multiple trades to make items, including smiths.

That dealt with, he headed off for the guild hall. He hadn't told Suzy what he'd done yet, letting her have some time with Induca.

Deia said she would be free from her training in a couple of days. Dave was hoping he could have everything ready by then. He hated dealing with all the managing crap, but it seemed he'd gained some skills from his past life.

He stepped through the teleport pad and entered the guild hall. Malsour was there and waiting for him. He'd already talked to Josh, who had given him the okay to start building up factories and the like. He was also on a payment plan because he'd put all of his money into his mine manager class, but he felt that it would pay off.

Quest: Mine Manager Level 8
Pay 20,000,000 gold
Rewards: Unlock Level 9 Quest
Increase to mine's output

Class: Mine Manager

You have become a manager of a mine! Provide more gold to this class in order to increase productivity! Items will be delivered to you once a week.

Status:	Level 8
Effects:	Every week you gain: 1,280 Steel ingots 128 Silver ingots 64 Ebony ingots 8 Mithril Ingots 384 random ores

With the first level Dave gained ten steel every week, which doubled with each level. At level 2, he got one silver each week; it doubled with every level as well. Ebony he got at Level 3 and Mithril was unlocked at level 5.

The upfront cost was immense and it was only because Bob had put the resources of the *Datskun* under Dave's name that he was able to even buy the extra levels. It had cost him 31,500,000 gold. More wealth than most kingdoms on Ashal had access to. For the Mithril alone, it was worth it. Dave would be getting the same amount of Mithril as the Dwarves mined in a week.

Since the Aleph and the Dwarves had talked, the Dwarves agreed to teach the Aleph some manipulation techniques for the different materials, including Mithril, for a large chunk of the stored deposits.

There was simply no other way for Dave to get Mithril other than to try to mine it himself or get it from the guild hall's miners.

With the additional resources, he could put them directly into his smithies or sell them off. Although it was a massive upfront cost, Dave had little use for gold. His patents were making him money and he had paid off his factories in Zol'Ord and his smithy in Cliff-Hill.

His teleport pad was making gold hand over fist and so was the massive contract for armor with the DCA. Gold wasn't as good as silver for filling runes and there simply wasn't enough Mithril for sale for his smithy to use.

Mine Manager was a costly class, but in Dave's eyes well worth it. He watched as the horses pulled the carriage through the teleport pad and brought him into the Stone Raiders' guild hall. Aleph automatons moved with their own loaded cart of materials that the smithy had bought from the Stone Raiders, ready to load the cart up.

"Thanks for the ride," Dave said to the teamster driving the cart.

"Have a good day, boss." The Elf tilted his hat.

"You too!" Dave jumped off and headed through the housing complex. He greeted Stone Raiders and various others in the first housing complex. In the second, there was just Aleph who had been hired by the guild and guild members. Automatons worked tirelessly, moving resources from the refinery and into the warehouse filled with crates of holding.

Dave continued on his way, working his way through the housing complex and to the large corridor that overlooked the growing city. Dave conjured a disk of metal beneath his feet; runes covered it as he floated down to the city street below. He destroyed the disk and headed through the city.

"Hmm, that would be a decent place for a workshop and smithy." Dave wandered through the city and into a large open area that looked like most cities' marketplace.

He conjured a disk, carving out runes on it. Light shot out from it and created a laser that cut through the rock easily. Dave moved the laser around, cutting out a rough room from the stone block that had been cut out by the mining machines.

"Okay, so, we need more automatons. Also going to need more miners and to get this whole thing moving. So, need power. If I can up my sensing power, I can probably scan the area and see the fluctuations of Mana and follow it to a Mana ley line." Dave carved out a rudimentary desk and conjured a rolling chair. The floor was pretty rough but workable.

Dave pulled out soul gems, the size of his torso, and put them off to the side. He pulled out a carver, making runes around them.

"You are so handy!" He talked to the tool. Excitement at just what he was going to do bled through to all his actions.

He pulled out a number of other materials and laid them on the table, pinning windows of his interface to the wall and destroying his conjured laser. He looked over at the walls. It showed the materials in stock, the number of automatons in use and their locations; another, the rate that the miners were working at, then the power levels, air saturation and the like.

"Okay, we need more room, more resources. To do that, we need more miners, more automatons, and more gardens to keep the air in here working. Maybe an enchanted fan or dozen to keep air circulating—got a few, but still a bit stagnant. Also going to need power to keep this all going. So, to break it down: first, power station; second, gardens; third, get this city spinning; fourth, mine our damned brains out!" Dave wrote down his plan on an interface notepad, "sticking" it to the wall next to the other interface screens. It was as if he had a massive wall screen with all his information.

"Feel like I'm a damned stock market trader." Dave snorted and sat down in his conjured rolling chair. Making sure all of his conjured and powered items were hooked up to his varying power sources, he pulled out Induca's rings and put them on.

"Whoa, that *is* a rush." Dave's voice sounded odd with the sudden boost to his Intelligence.

He checked out the rings.

Rings of Smartness

Formed by David Grahslagg, these rings increase the user's smarts.

Quality:	AAA
	Increase user's Intelligence by 15%
Abilities:	Ability to resize
	Soul Bound (not currently bound)
Charge:	100,000/100,000 (10 weeks)
Durability:	70/70

"Well, not happy about only getting a triple A rating—just one rank below S, though," Dave grumbled.

He had found that getting a nice bonus 5% was easy enough, but going higher than that it became harder and harder. Getting to 10% took a heck of a lot more Mana and needed to be made of ebony, not steel. It was only through Dave's magical coding skills and use of silver he was able to get the ring to work at 15%. Any higher and he would need a full day to work on it instead of a few minutes or use Mithril.

Adding in the soul bound ability and resize was relatively easy now that he'd used it for his own armor—made it easier to move in even at a higher expense of Mana.

Dave's Intelligence was originally 738; with the two rings he was boosted to 976.

"Wait, need to do some stat changes. Been a few days since my last, so, shouldn't be too bad." Dave opened his character sheet.

"So, increase Intelligence, bigger base stat. Then up Agility, so I'm not totally falling over myself. Also less hand cramps from all this coding. Hmm, I want to work longer, so, Endurance as well?" Dave only needed four hours of sleep where most needed eight, but he hadn't slept that much in two days and he didn't want to get stopped for much. Endurance also meant he didn't have to eat as much food as a normal person.

"Okay, 40 in Intelligence and Agility because thankfully I'll be sitting in this seat. Add on 50 Endurance because I have the feeling I'm going to need it. The Mana barrier on my armor is good to make up for my Vitality, which is much higher than when I started off." Dave snorted, thinking of how he thought a stiff breeze could possibly kill him.

He removed the rings and looked at his new stats.

Character Sheet

Name:	David Grahslagg	Gender:	Male
Level:	148	Class:	Dwarven Master Smith, Friend of the Grey God, Bleeder, Librarian, Aleph Engineer, Weapons Master, Champion Slayer, Skill Creator, Mine Manager, Master Summoner
Race:	Human/ Dwarf	Alignment:	Neutral Good

Unspent points: 356

Health:	24,300	Regen:	10.06 /s
Mana:	7,780	Regen:	22.55 /s
Stamina:	3,090	Regen:	20.25 /s
Vitality:	243	Endurance:	503
Intelligence:	778	Willpower:	451
Strength:	309	Agility:	405

Dave closed the window, feeling his tiredness falling away and feeling a little less hungry. He carefully pulled out a handful of nuts and berries and munched on them. The time dilation effect was really noticeable now, but it seemed that the increase in Agility was doing its work to make it so he wasn't all messed up.

"Okay, smarter, faster for longer—let's get started." Dave put the rings on again, which boosted him up to 1,029.

Dave made an unintelligible noise. His eyes moved rapidly as he opened interface windows around him, changing different things before he carved out runes on his table and conjured the basics of what he would need to make his plan a reality.

Chapter 35: Madman On The Loose

General Loughbreck looked out over his "guards." Technically, he was the guard captain of Gufaross. In reality, he was the general of Lord Esamael's forces in the northern cities. Gufaross and Owesa made a barrier between Emaren and Haugr.

It was Loughbreck's duty to make sure that none of the king's spies went south to find out what Lord Emaren and his allies were doing. Seeing as Loughbreck not only controlled the guards in both Owesa and Gufaross, but also the "bandits" who lived outside the city, ready to support him if needed, it was easy to make sure that any spies had an unfortunate accident.

He looked to his new orders. Their plan was continuing on as before. When spring and the Dwarven tournament came, Lord Esamael's forces would be moving to take Haugr. Originally Loughbreck was to take his army and assault Barosvik, keeping the forces there pinned down, so that they couldn't support Haugr as Lord Esamael's armies used the Emaren teleport pad to take the city. Now that there was a teleport pad in Verlun as well, the plan was to assault the city, take the teleport pad there and support the forces in Haugr. Once they killed the king, then the other lords and ladies would bow down to them. Those who didn't, they could hunt down and destroy.

The plan had been to take over Verlun and force the Stone Raiders to give the teleport pad over to Lord Esamael. The problem was that the overconfident Stone Raiders didn't care for the lord or his minion Geswald's subtle threats and pressures.

They were pushing out the old and entrenched competition in Emaren with rare and powerful items that they sold to the mage's college while they made alliances and trades with the farmers in Verlun. The traders there were treated as equals by the Stone Raiders.

They supported the Stone Raiders and they'd overcome the ever-increasing number of barriers Geswald and Esamael had put in their way. Still, even with all of that, the Stone Raiders and their farmer friends had figured out ways around it and were making a ton of gold.

Then it was revealed that the Stone Raiders had fought real Demons in Ashal. Loughbreck just thought it was the work of songwriters and tale tellers. There were no Demons anymore and there was no way that a group of four hundred were capable of defeating them. Loughbreck had an army of two hundred thousand at his command, half of them with magical talents. Gudalo, being so close to the headquarters of the mage's guild and college, attracted a large number of proficient mages.

Loughbreck used his interface to send messages off to some of the captains commanding the "bandits," ordering them to move toward Verlun. He also sent messages to the forces in Verlun. He wanted to know everything about the Stone Raiders' defenses. He cared not for economic warfare and whether they would give over the teleport pad amicably.

Lord Esamael has said that we get to keep half of what we find. Imagine the kind of goods that these Stone Raiders have piled in their guild hall

A greedy look crossed Loughbreck's face as he thought of the wealth and prestige he would gain for supporting Lord Esamael.

Once this is all over, then we can do what we should have done a hundred years ago. We can finally rid ourselves of those non-Human creatures to our south and those Dwarves. We'll make it clear that the mage's college and guild are under our control. We can't have the other races gaining power to try to bully us anymore.

*****

Bronx made excited noises as he looked at the glass-blown item in front of him. The Stone Raiders who had found the item had pleased looks on their faces, just imagining what they could get for the piece.

"Could you stop making noises like a damned preening peacock?" Florence smiled. It was odd, looking at the massive man using his large fingers to delicately trace the beautiful lines that formed the simple vase.

The other Stone Raiders chuckled, including the traders who were used to Bronx's idiosyncrasies.

"Sorry, boss. Just, ohh...it's so damned beautiful!" Bronx practically squealed, not caring what it looked like in the slightest.

"We'll put it up for auction for the noble houses. I know a number of different houses and even kings and queens would be very interested in having this," Florence said to the fighters.

"See, I told you it was worth grabbing." A thief-looking character punched a melee fighter with a large shield on his back.

"Okay, your hunch was right," the melee fighter agreed.

Bronx looked like a kid being told that they couldn't take a puppy home from the store.

Florence chuckled as a message pinged on her interface. She hummed to herself as she walked out of the back of the guild hall and toward the front.

She swiped the message away and frowned. She walked through a sound barrier and into the front of the store.

"I demand to talk to your manager. This is unacceptable. I will not have some *Gnome* treating me like a damned copperless beggar," a man in the essential red robe and staff with a glowing red crystal of a Fire mage said.

Ugh. Why do they all have to color-code themselves. Do they not know how easy it will be to pick them out in a fight and know how to fight back against them? Florence moved to Unasli's aid.

"I'm sorry, sir. I meant no offense. I was just stating the price for that particular soul gem," Unasli said.

"Trying to rob me of my gold, you are, with those over-the-top prices! Look here, I will let you off with a warning, but you will have to find a way to compensate me!" The man's eyes thinned, looking down at Unasli, who sat on a high stool to compensate for her smaller stature.

"Hello. I heard that there was something the matter." Florence stepped up beside Unasli.

"Your pet here slandered my name and tried to sell me a soul gem for well above market value to steal some gold for herself," the mage said, not hiding the way he studied Florence.

She hid her shiver, just feeling his eyes trying to look through her clothes.

"One moment." Florence opened her interface to check the recording of Unasli. She trusted the Gnome but she had to make sure that she was impartial to these things.

She got to the part about the customer using rather nasty racial slurs about Gnomes, and then Unasli snapped back just a bit before regaining her cool. The man had gone into a tirade after that.

"Unasli, I can take over this transaction." Florence decided to get the two of them apart as soon as possible.

"Yes, boss." Unasli dropped off her chair, looking like a furious child as she walked to the back. Florence felt some of her parental feelings flare up. Unasli was only fifteen in Emerilia, a POE who had been looking for work after her mother and father had died in a plague a few years back. They'd had enough money to get their daughter healed, but hadn't survived.

"Good—someone knows their place around here. I will take four of your grand soul gems as repayment for the slight on my honor." The mage held an imperious hand out.

"I'm sorry, sir mage, but this is a business and while we are sorry that Unasli lost her temper, it wasn't without some provocation. Please feel free to browse our wares and tell one of my associates when you are ready to order." Florence tilted her head slightly and smiled at the man.

He seemed to have trouble understanding what she had said before veins started to pop out across his forehead and his pale Human features turned red.

"Do you know who I am!" The man's aura surged outward at Florence.

"I don't," Florence admitted.

"I am Mage Adept Research Tolondur of the Forty-Third Island! Son of Lord Gesar! I will not be treated this way!" The mage slammed his staff on the floor. A bloom of flame appeared above his staff. As soon as it appeared, it disappeared. "Prostrate and bow before me, so that I might spare you!" Tolondur declared.

Florence noticed that a squad of eight fighters held their weapons. They didn't look happy about the circumstance, but it was clear that Tolondur was their master.

"Mister Tolondur, I must ask that you please leave our premises. We do not want to fight you and this is a peaceful establishment," Florence said, not even fazed by the mage's aura or his display of power. *I wonder what would have happened if we didn't have the defenses keyed up, so that all Mana not coming from a Stone Raider is absorbed by the vault soul gems?*

"You dare to—" Any words Tolondur was going to say turned into choking noises as the staff he was lowering to point at Florence dropped to the ground and he was forced to his knees.

"Ugh, well, he was a loud one." Kim yawned as she came out the back of the guild hall. "Florence, do you have any nectar of Egun?" She scratched her head idly.

"Yes, I believe we do. Hector knows where it is," Florence said.

"Thanks." Kim yawned again, not showing any strain of putting Tolondur on the ground with her aura alone.

The guards looked from Tolondur to Kim and Florence.

Florence raised her eyebrow; the guards released their weapons slowly. She gave them a nod and stepped around the counter. She touched Tolondur's shoulder; the man collapsed into unconsciousness.

"It seems that Mister Tolondur is under the weather. Could you see that he gets home safely? Could you also inform him that he is banned from our guild hall here and the Stone Raiders and their affiliates will no longer trade with him or his father. We would be willing to discuss possible terms of lifting this ban with Lord Gesar, but for insulting my fellow guild member and my guild, Mister Tolondur is banned for life. Thank you." Florence nodded to the guards.

"Thank you, milady," one of the guards said as the others gathered the noble up.

"Uh, you wouldn't perhaps have any job openings?" the same guard asked in a low voice as he got close.

"You would have to talk to one of the fighters. You can find them at the teleport pad. They will know more on that side of things." Florence smiled. They were probably good fighters and were smart enough to know when to fight and stay their blades. If they were kicked out of Tolondur's employ, well, the Stone Raiders were growing and she needed dedicated guards, not just Stone Raiders taking a break from raiding across Emerilia.

Tolondur was escorted out.

"Ah, the young—so rash," an older and refined-looking gentleman said, walking up to the counter.

A few people who saw the man went big-eyed and talked to their fellow shoppers.

Florence appraised the man.

Alamos Ecanil

Level 310

Human

With her extra senses, she could tell he was a mage, a powerful one. There was a flash of a badge under his robe but she didn't get a long enough glance at it.

"I was wondering if you could help me. I was told by an old friend that you Stone Raiders might be able to get me some of these items." Alamos produced a list and handed it to Florence.

She took the list and checked over the items. Nearly all of them were rather hard to find and she knew of their numbers and stock because of their rarity. "I think we can get most of these items. Might I ask who gave you our name?"

"You know Deia?" Alamos asked.

"Yes, she was one of the people who helped the Exdar's and Raiders unite." Florence smiled.

"Ah, well, her dad is an old adventuring friend of mine and Jelanos." Alamos grinned.

Jelanos...that sounds familiar, important in the—Wait, he doesn't mean the Jelanos? Then Alamos is the second arch mage? Wait, Deia's dad plays this game? But then how does he have a past with the leaders of the arch mage's college and guild?

"Oh, I will have to thank her for that. Might you be Arch Mage Alamos?" She lowered her voice.

Alamos took on an amused look. "Seems that I can still hide under the radar in places. Thanks for not yelling my name out." He winked.

"No problem. If you want to come with me, I can show you these items." Florence held up the list.

"Thank you. That would be great." Alamos looked more like an excitable kid than a venerable mage.

"Florence, we need to reinforce the back room. I think I nearly melted the west wall," Kim said, heading back to her bedroom turned laboratory.

"Use the damn lab in the back!" Florence hissed under her breath.

"Aw, but it doesn't have any heating, or windows!" Kim complained like a two-year-old. She even stomped her feet.

"Cause you keep blowing out the damn windows and you know how to do some enchanting!" Florence hissed back, catching Alamos's amused look as he followed behind them.

Kim made annoyed noises and frowned.

"Didn't you know that Dave is going to be teaching people how to magically code things?" Florence said, getting an idea.

"He is?" Kim perked up.

"Said he's opening up a school in the guild. I think Josh posted it. Best to get there before someone else takes your spot," Florence advised.

"Turn that teleport pad on! I'm going to the guild hall!" Kim took off at a run.

"Don't forget your experiments!" Florence yelled after her, seeing Kim leave out of a door and then run back in and rush upstairs.

"Quite lively in here." Alamos chuckled.

"Ugh, ever since they got back, it's been hectic." Florence sighed. Weaving past appraisal rooms and stacks of different items, she stepped down a wide set of stairs.

Alamos followed. "Yes, I have heard of a number of Stone Raiders joining the college. It seems that they are quite powerful. I have a meeting with the leaders of Devil's Crater in a week. I've heard from the students we've taken on that you are a force to be reckoned with. Even the POEs have been buying recording stones with the videos from the battle of Devil's Crater."

"Miss adventuring?" Florence smiled as she led to an elevator.

"Some days," Alamos said as the lift started downward. "I didn't believe that your storage was so vast."

"Well, we do have a large number of items." Florence smiled. *Don't need to tell him that all fourteen floors underground are filled with wards and traps, that we just use the trader hub the Aleph gave us and a drop pad in the basement to move goods between our guild halls and to our customers.*

After all the information they had been getting from their scout automatons, they were not taking any chances with their goods. Lord Esamael wanted them gone and all signs pointed to him trying to take the throne of Gudalo for himself.

Lucy was the one dealing with that: gathering information, creating contacts, and preparing them for whatever might come.

***

Malsour stretched as he got up in his bedroom; he'd been assigned one at the housing facility. He grabbed a water skin of juice and headed out of his room.

"Hey, Malsour, this is awesome!" Gelimah yelled from the first floor, where he was drinking with a bunch of rowdy Stone Raiders.

Well, that answers why I woke up. "Don't get too drunk." Malsour rubbed his eyes.

He walked to the edge of the balcony; a shadow pushed him over the banister. He controlled the steel in his shoes and the ground beneath him, slowing his descent.

He yawned and rubbed his head as he headed deeper into the guild hall. Gelimah wasn't allowed any deeper but Malsour knew that his brother could see everything that the guild hall was going to become.

Gelimah liked to stay with his baubles and his experiments, much like Malsour used to be. *When did I start thinking of him as a recluse? I used to think of him as the most sane one out of my family.*

Malsour snorted at his own thoughts. He yawned, extending his senses as he did so; he continued yawning but his face turned to alarm at what he sensed. *The heck is going on?*

He saw Josh walking around, talking to Lucy.

"Josh, what is happening in the city?" Malsour asked.

"Not sure. Dave's apparently in there doing something." Josh shrugged. "Said something about needing to speed things up."

"He's also bought a bunch of land and space for factories, smithies, and the rest. Gave Alkao a good price for all the work he's doing," Lucy said. "Well, Suzy was in charge of the negotiations. Though it seemed to be his idea."

"I think you might want to give that to him for free. If I'm right, he's doubled the number of miners out there. He's already cutting out the exterior runners to turn the city on and he's hooking up a massive power system, I think. Can't really get all the runes." Malsour frowned and picked up his pace.

"What? I thought he was just looking for a place to tinker," Josh said.

"I'll check on him, but he's got fourteen vault-classed soul gems all powered up and working on different projects." Malsour had to yell as he was too far away for normal talking and broke out into a jog.

"What the hell are you doing now?" Malsour shook his head, even as an excited grin appeared on his face. *Well, at least one of us has to look like a respectable and upright pillar of society, not an engineering madman!*

***

Dave floated around on his floating spinning chair. It had got annoying on the uneven floor to deal with the rough edges, so he'd add in a levitating ability.

Now he pushed off the walls, humming to himself as he worked with a carver, entering the last rune on the metal box he was working on. He floated back down. He pulled off some melted silver from the burner and poured it into the runes. A conjured blade appeared in his hand. Scraping away the excess, he placed the box down on a table top filled with boxes.

He had been working for hours. His eyes were itchy when he closed them. *Oh, that feels pretty nice. Work to be done, and I need my eyes to be open for that! Well, I kind of do have Touch of the Land.*

Dave floated through his workshop. It had grown since he'd first started. There were multiple different factories he'd set up, from a small repair bot factory, to a factory of miner bots around the size of a dog, and a runner factory.

He floated over to the runners.

"Well, these should work." Dave looked at the metal. The ebony, Mithril, and silver runners would be embedded on the cylindrical walls of the city. They would act like opposing magnets, pushing against one another, imparting velocity onto the city and keeping it suspended. They would turn the city fast enough, so that all of its interior could be used. Their power requirements were large and each of them were as large as a large garbage can. Hundreds would be put all over the city.

A beeping noise drew Dave's attention. He sped over in mid-air toward the noise. Dave checked one of his interfaces.

"Whoa!" Dave yelled, pumping his fist in the air as he spun around in his chair.

"Dave! What are you up to in here?" Malsour asked, from the entrance of Dave's workshop.

Dave rushed over, stopping right before Malsour. "Malsour! Okay, so, I made these boxes—they're basically upgraded magical code of my Touch of the Land spell. Then I made a bunch of repair bots to take them and put them across the city, so we can know what the heck's around us. They're really good and they gather a ton of information. Unlike me, where I use the spell once and see what's in a limited area. These ones send out a continuous pulse, mapping everything around them for as long as they're powered. Really good at it too—found some nice deposits of materials."

"Dave, you're rambling. What are you talking about?"

"Oh, yeah, sorry, got more Endurance, so I wouldn't need to sleep. Anyway. Seems that they found a ley line. Now I need your help in putting together those dots on portals and teleport pad. Once I've got that, then I could maybe open up a hole near the ley lines and we can send miners in to make us a power station!"

Malsour didn't say anything for a while.

"What? Do I have something on my face?" Dave rubbed away anything that might be stuck to him.

"No, just—what is this all?" Malsour pointed to the different machines.

"Well, I needed a few things to help me out and it's cheaper to make factories, so that I don't have to deal with it all the time. These are all conjured, most I engraved again, so it costs less and I can work longer." A repair bot moved out from under a table, carrying a hot cup of Xer.

"Thanks, buddy! Just what I needed." Dave grabbed the cup, about to take a drink.

Malsour took the cup instead.

"Dude, I need that," Dave said.

"Dave, you need some sleep, a shower, and then you can tell me what you're doing," Malsour said in a measured tone.

Dave looked as if he wanted to argue. He looked around and sighed. "Okay, get someone down here to deal with this. I've got everything programmed into the bots for the most part. Thankfully Shard's helping me out on that side of things. Makes things a lot easier."

"Hello, Malsour," Shard said from a speaker above.

"Hey, Shard, you okay by yourself?" Malsour asked.

"I will be able to continue Dave's projects. I have been trying to get him to rest, but as he has become more reliant on Xer, he's refused the need for sleep." Shard sounded exasperated.

"Thanks, Shard. Okay, Dave, let's get you some food, a shower, and then some sleep." Malsour guided Dave away.

Chapter 36: Two Too Alike

Fire appeared in her home. Mal stood beside her, watching as Deia stood on top of the boiling magma of the volcano.

Mal doubted that he could break her concentration, nor did he feel he wanted to with the aura and strength that permeated the air around her.

Denur poked her head up next to Mal and Fire's balcony, her large eyes focused completely on Deia.

"They grow up so fast," Fire complained, resting her head on Mal's shoulder.

He wrapped his arm around her, smiling as he kissed the top of her head. "That they do." He looked back to Deia, using a Mana sight spell, and augmented his eyes to see the Mana in the air, running through Deia and the mountain. He let out a rush of air as he saw the amount of Mana at his daughter's fingertips.

"When did she get so much more powerful?" Mal complained.

"Well, she does take after her mother," Fire said proudly, preening like a cat, looking up at Mal.

"Yeah, you two are troublemakers." Mal kissed Fire before she could say anything. She made to try to break his embrace, giggling like a little girl at his antics.

They parted. Fire relented and leaned against him again.

"Here we go," Denur said, concentrating completely on her sister.

Mana that had been coating the volcano now reacted to its mistress's call. Deia's hair flared up around her; the entire volcano shook as she raised her hands as if they were weighted down by Emerilia itself. The cold core at the bottom of the volcano started to shift and break, the mantle showing fissures and cracks as super-heated magma rolled and shook, excited by Deia's Mana.

More power poured out of Deia. The magma rose itself higher and higher, expanding under the heat Deia was conjuring inside it. With her Mana, she was pushing the volcano to erupt.

She rose up higher. It seemed as if she were dragging the magma up with her. As it became more excitable, the amount of Mana she put into the volcano was staggering. She rose like some angel of fire, her eyes closed the entire time as the volcano responded to her commands.

Fire's arms became tighter. Mal looked over Deia's Mana. She was feeding it outward but her spells seemed to be degrading as the extra Mana seemed to dissipate and run chaotically through the magma or escape into the air. Deia sweat, not from the heat of the volcano, but the level of concentration it took for her to carry out her task.

Mal put up a heat barrier, the temperatures getting too high for his body to completely annul.

Deia let out a primal yell. Her Mana came back under control as she surged upward, forcing the magma up by changing it and driving her Mana to work.

Magma started to exit through holes in the walls.

Mal knew that the outside of the mountain would be leaking magma, or blowing out a hardened flow in an attempt to escape. Deia made it eighty percent of the way up the inside of the volcano.

She let out another yell. The magma pushed upward again but then sagged as Deia's Mana fled her.

She wobbled in air, falling slightly, clearly unconscious. Mal was about to rush forward when he felt the air lurch. Denur easily plucked Deia out of the air with her hand, circling around the inside of the volcano and came back to Fire's balcony.

Denur changed from her Dragon form to her Human form, carrying Deia as her wings retreated and she stepped onto the balcony. "Well, she's going to need some rest after that."

She really does look like Fire in a lot of ways, Mal thought as Denur put Deia down on a couch.

Denur looked to be in her mid-twenties while Deia looked like she was just entering them. They both had the same fiery red hair and eyes. Their bodies were also similar in shape. Deia was taller, with Mal's pointed ears, sharper chin, and almond-shaped eyes.

"She always pushes her limits every chance she can get," Mal said proudly.

"Well, she's growing a lot faster than I thought she would. She keeps on talking about thermodynamics and Earth terminology, but she keeps growing stronger. That said, she needs a break. I think a trip to the mage's guild for some reading, a bit of relaxing might be a good idea," Denur said.

"We can take her with us. I thought that Dave was meeting us tomorrow anyway, so that will work perfectly." Fire smiled.

"Seems like someone approves of the boy," Mal said gruffly, mixed feelings about letting his daughter go.

"I'm not the only one, especially when someone starts opening one of those fire whiskey bottles he was gifted by a certain son-in-law." Fire poked Mal in the side.

"Fine, he's not *too* bad," Mal complained.

Fire rolled her eyes and sighed, looking to Denur, who simply laughed and shook her head.

"Mind if I tag along? It's been awhile since I saw some of my kiddos," Denur asked.

"We'll need someone to carry her." Fire smiled.

"Saying I can't carry her?" Mal asked.

"Saying that you'll start to think of her as a baby again and won't let her out of your sight if I let you carry her!" Fire said.

Mal pouted but didn't say anything.

***

"Ugh, damn. An Intelligence headache is even worse than a hang-over," Dave complained, equipping his armor and laying back down on his bed. The armor worked to remove his aches and pains.

"That happens when someone overloads their brain with enhanced Intelligence and then doesn't sleep for a few days," Malsour said from the living room, moving to the bedroom and sitting in a nearby seat.

"Hey, buddy." Dave grinned at his friend.

"Hey, Dave. I see you've sped up the work on the city." Malsour grinned, passing Dave two rings he'd pried from his fingers.

"Yeah, well, you know me, always impatient. Just building up the infrastructure we'll need here. I want to make the guild hall to be a hub of sorts: food, smithies, weapons training, magical coding—all of it in one place. With the teleport pads, tons of people can reach us and we can reach others. When the war comes, I want this city to be ready to act as a rally point, a place to re-arm and re-supply and be a launching pad from which to send counterattacks at our enemy." Dave looked up at the ceiling, thinking of all he had to do in order to get to that point.

"Well, then I think it's about time you figured out the science behind teleport pads and portals. Don't know when else you're going to be stuck in one place," Malsour said, getting comfortable.

Dave put the two rings on. "Okay, so, I understand how wormholes are supposed to work. You have normal space in a straight line. Then you have a wormhole that folds that space like a piece of paper and you poke a hole through it. You go through one side of that line and out the other, which, when laid down, is a massive distance in real space."

"Good, that's the basics. Now the teleport pads here work a little differently. They not only make wormholes, but they make an area of gravity resistance, the part that takes the most amount of power. The constant force on the universe is gravity. These spells counter the gravity where you want to make a wormhole, taking it out of the normal laws of gravity. It weakens the fabric of space and time. If you're next to a black hole with a ton of gravity pull, spending two minutes there could be twenty years back here on Emerilia. If you take away gravity, you take away the coefficient of time. The teleport pads sync up to one another; they exchange the complete information of their points of origin, basically inverting the two teleport pads. So, when you're entering the teleport pad in Cliff-Hill, the universe, wanting to fix itself, thinks you're actually in Devil's Crater. The teleport pads are like split atoms: what happens to one, happens to the other, much like ansibles that you Humans talked about for long-range instantaneous communications. Two split particles resonate with each other, so that when you walk into one, you walk out of another. Action to one teleport pad means the same reaction in the other. When a teleport pad calls up another, they again resonate together completely, allowing instantaneous transmission between the two," Malsour said.

"Damn, that's pretty smart, and complicated. How the heck were they able to get the teleport pads to harmonize to such a degree?" Dave asked.

"Factories. You saw them—they're all made *identically*."

"Damn, okay, so, with the annulling of gravity, they remove the aspect of time affecting just a small space. Then by attuning the two teleport pads *completely,* they act as ying and yang: what one does, the other does the opposite—one person walks in one way, they come out the other way." Dave nodded, his mind making different connections.

New Active Skill: Teleportation

Well, look at this guy! Long time, no new skills! Now you've earned, wait, what? Ugghh, come on, dude: teleportation, math, numbers, coding, wormholes, space and time... I was thinking it was something cool, like, I don't know, pickpocketing or horse riding? Nope, just want to punch holes in reality! (Hey, there's a cool skill, hand-to-hand man—could be like some of those monk people, all chi, balance and kicking the other man in the balls!).

Level: Journeyman 2

Effect: Understanding of basic teleportation theories and teleportation systems

Dave looked at the skill. It didn't say anything about bonuses or extras.

"Did you finally get the teleportation skill?" Malsour asked.

"Yeah, just didn't get any bonuses," Dave said.

"I think that it doesn't give any bonuses because it's all mental. The realm of teleportation has got to a certain stage and stopped. The portals work forever and don't need to be replaced going from one place to another. The Jukal Empire doesn't like dealing with innovations unless they have complete control over it. With the people of Emerilia knowing more about teleportation, it makes them look weaker. It could also disrupt their carefully balanced economy that keeps them in power," Malsour said.

"Control the flow of information and goods and you can control the people." Dave rubbed his head in frustration.

Malsour nodded.

"Well, then we're just going to have to break that. How is Devil's Crater? Can I borrow you for a bit?" Dave asked.

"Well, Gelimah, my brother, is here, but he's really enjoying making stuff in Devil's Crater. I think he might set up a lair nearby if he can." Malsour smiled.

"Isn't he the one who likes to hide away from the world?" Dave asked.

"Yes, but he also loves to make things, so Devil's Crater is a ton of fun for him. Lots of people with new ideas and tons of room for him to use his magic freely."

"Okay, with him looking after that, I'm going to need your help in turning this cut-out city into a hub." Dave propped himself up.

"What do you need me to do?" Malsour grinned.

"Well, first I'm going to need to talk to Josh about buying a teleport pad and then we're going to make a power station." Dave smiled.

"Damn, you don't think small." Malsour laughed, excited for the challenge.

"Ah, small is boring." Dave stood.

"First, take a damn shower. You smell nasty, dude."

Dave sniffed his pit. "Oh, okay, yeah, might have a point," Dave agreed. "Wait, I've got another notification." Dave clicked the blinking bell at the corner of his interface.

Quest: Librarian Level 3

Conduct research that allows you to understand how teleport pads work.

Rewards: Unlock Level 4 Quest

Increase to stats

Class: Librarian

Through tireless research, you have taken the written word and used it in a practical sense. Beware the nerd who studies: they've got a dozen ideas others haven't even thought of yet.

Status: Level 3

+30 to all stats

Effects: Read 15% faster

Understand 14% more of the information that you read

Dave laughed to himself.

"Something funny?" Malsour asked.

"Kind of cheated my class upgrade. Seems as long as I figured out how teleport pads worked and the theories behind them, I gained a class level." Dave read the new quest.

Quest: Librarian Level 4

Contribute to someone's research topic

Rewards: Unlock Level 5 Quest

Increase to stats

"Having extra classes does make it a lot easier to continue growing in strength," Malsour agreed.

"Well, I would like to get a trader or maybe talking class sometime soon," Dave complained.

"Oh, why?" Malsour asked.

"Easier to deal with contracts, and it's going to be a pain trying to wrestle all the resources of the guild hall away from Josh, so we can get this place running." Dave waved his arms to encompass the city they were in.

Malsour nodded his head seriously. "Maybe we should call Suzy to help us out?"

"You want to interrupt her and Induca's vacation?"

"On second thought, that wouldn't be the wisest decision," Malsour agreed.

"Hopefully he doesn't know all of the resources it's going to take to get this place online."

***

"You want to what?" Josh sounded more tired than alarmed at Dave's words. He'd become used to Dave's eccentric ways.

"I want a teleport pad. We have a ley line that we can tap for power. Malsour can carve out space for the drop pad; I can send through some miners; they start cutting it all out. It's going to take a bunch of power, but it should be a month or two and we can get it up and running everything we have here with energy to spare," Dave said.

Josh opened up his interfaces, going to his treasury pages as well as his buying page. He tapped his chin in thought, looking over the savings the guild currently had.

As much as I want to just save this or invest it into companies and businesses, this city could become one of our greatest assets. If we can get control of more portals and a few teleport pads, we could directly supply anyone entering or leaving a portal.

With most cities being hours or days away, having us just a teleport away would allow us to be the first group people trade with. With Dave and Kol, they can get any weapon repaired and get any supplies in minutes and be back on their way through the portals.

Also, it will make us be able to deploy our forces anywhere with the coming war events.

"Okay, we can do it, though we're going to be a bit short on gold. We need to have power if we want to keep this place going. Let me know when you want me to get it and have the drop pad in the right place," Josh said.

"Can do. Also, with the power output, it will be way more than what we need for a while, so we can probably charge up vault-class soul gems and sell them to nations to supply their magical power needs," Dave said.

Josh knew commodity trading intimately. His old stockbroker mind started to work, thinking about all of the resources that he now had at his disposal. Loading them onto the market in one go could make it crash, but if done right, they could keep the markets stable and still continue to make a good amount of gold and profits.

"You've given me quite a bit to think about," Josh said.

"So, is that a yes?" Dave thinned his eyes. Even Malsour leaned forward, an expectant look on his face.

"Fine, go for it before I regret it," Josh said.

"You won't regret it!" Dave yelled as he and Malsour ran for the door.

"I don't think I've ever seen them move that fast," Josh said into his now empty office.

***

Malsour was back in the city once again. This time, he wore a ring that glowed faintly. It was connected to the sensors Dave had put together. He leaned against a wall and closed his eyes. He reached out with his senses, connecting to the ring.

The world around him seemed to explode into detail.

Malsour looked around with his senses. The sensors were highly detailed in what they saw. Their range grew by the minute, traveling through every medium they found to find more information. Malsour felt tiny with everything he could sense, but he also felt powerful. A god surveying all that was under his control. *Is this what Dave feels when he looks at the world through his Touch of the Land?*

Malsour focused on the ley line that the sensors had found. He remembered how the Aleph power stations were laid out. Dave wanted to alter the power station to get more out of it, but they both agreed to go with what was tried and tested instead of Dave's prototype.

Malsour held an image in his mind of the Aleph power station, moving it around to see the best way it would take advantage of the ley line. After a few minutes of altering, he finally knew where it was going to be.

Malsour placed his hands on the ground, willing his Mana through the rocks, down toward the point he had marked in his mind. His Mana raced downward at first, slowing after a few minutes. It became harder and harder for it to push onward and downward.

Malsour lost focus on time as it moved through different materials under Malsour's control. Finally, just a thread of his Mana reached where he wanted to create a drop pad. Malsour continued to push Mana through the link he'd made. It was painfully slow and hard work, as if he were carving out a letter in Mithril with a mountain on his back.

Malsour grunted and sweated, focused totally on his task. If he were to take a rest, then he would need to make a new path to the drop pad's location. He welcomed the stress on his body, smiling. With the Stone Raiders, he had come to welcome the harder tasks, pushing himself further and harder.

***

Dave had his eyes closed and floated around in his chair in a lazy pattern.

Inside his mind, he was looking at the different spells he had seen battle mages and the Aleph mages using, as well as those he had seen used in the fields of Cliff-Hill.

There was a beauty to the spell formation, a weave through different factors to come to a final creation. Though, to Dave, it felt as if something was missing from the spells used on the vertical gardens. He compared them, looking at how they coaxed the plants to grow more. It was a stimulation of chemicals within the plants that made them grow.

Dave thought back onto fights he'd seen Earth mages using plants. With his near photographic memory, something tugged at the edges of his mind.

A little saying that one of the Aleph gardeners had said: "Although Earth magic is good at growing plants, slow and steady is the way to do it. You've got to let the plant talk to you and tell you if it's ready to grow, and then you only grow it to just before its limit, else it might not give that good of a harvest."

Dave pondered the words.

"Okay, so, plants live off a few things. They need carbon dioxide, water, sun, and nutrients in the ground, so..." Dave smacked himself in the head, groaning at his idiocy. Inside his mind, he was remembering glimpses of plants that had fought for Earth mages. After a fight, they were withered and dead, all of their resources and fuel used up to fight. Earth magic commanded plants, and supplied them with nutrients in the soil. It might draw in more water from the surrounding area, but they were used up in a quick fight. They didn't have the endurance of, say, Earth golems, or Dark mages' metal and stone.

It didn't take that much energy from the Earth mages to command great swathes of forests because they were using the forest's energy.

Dave opened his eyes and his interface, moving to his notepad and the 3D sculpting tool.

"Okay, so, what if we were to supply them with water, the proper light lamps and maybe some fans to keep the air circulating if they have a huge growth rate?" As Dave talked, he added in a sprinkler and irrigation, and then light lamps, altering them, so that they covered the entire area. Fans would circulate air through the area.

Now with a basic structure, Dave looked at the different components that he needed to make magical coding for. The lights needed to be the right wavelengths of light so they wouldn't burn the plants, or give them the wrong light. That was a bunch of researching online and finding the best places to grow crops across Emerilia and comparing farmers' notes.

Then irrigation just needed a simple rune to keep the water moving and a sensor in the soil and air, so that the sprinklers would keep the area at a certain humidity without needing someone there the entire time. He added in Earth runes that would keep the soil nutrient-rich; he added in the ability to alter the composition of the soil's layers and nutrients as well as the growth rate put on the crops.

The air fans were complicated in figuring out the best way to have the air moving over all the crops in a manner that wasn't too fast to blow them over but enough that they would be saturated with carbon dioxide.

"I'm going to need to set up a circulation system that pushes the carbon dioxide into these growing areas," Dave muttered as he looked over the rough 3D sculpted area. It was a basic greenhouse with different systems and magical coding off to one side.

"Later I can maybe try to automate the whole thing, but that will work for now. Have to see what the gardeners and farmers think." Dave sent the plan off to some who he had talked to get a better understanding of what they needed.

He checked on the city's progress. It was about a kilometer wide from floor to opposing floor and four hundred meters deep. It was a ton of work to carve out the different places and although they had a bunch of miners, it still took time. They were also having a problem with the two refineries in the housing complex not being able to handle all of the material going through it, so there was a backlog of materials waiting to be processed.

Dave's smaller miners and repair bots were working on carving out places for the runners in what would be the outside of the city. Once they were in place and the city was five hundred meters long, Dave would start powering the runners and cut out the city with a one-hundred-meter-thick floor. Once the runners took the load of the city, then Dave could start the rotation cycle and get the city turning and open up access to all sides of the city.

"So many things to do." Dave smiled to himself. He reached out through his sensors, taking in the information that they were relaying back. He used them to find what Malsour was working on.

The drop pad was coming along slowly. Hundreds of kilometers away, through compressed stone, Dave wasn't surprised it was so hard for even a Dragon to manipulate.

He opened his eyes from using the sensors and opened his interface to check the building progress of the refinery. "Forty-seven percent." Dave bit his lip in thought. "Well, I guess there is really nothing that I can do right now to speed things up. Everything's in the miners' and repair bots' hands. When the farmers get back to me, I can see about working on that, and Dark mages are better with speeding up forming the different facilities."

Dave looked over to the doorway as Matt, one of the Stone Raiders' artificers, stepped into his workshop.

"Well, I've heard of work driving people up the wall, but never floating up it in a chair." Matt grinned.

"Well, I wasn't able to smooth out the floor and my runners kept on getting caught, plus it's relaxing floating around," Dave said, defending his actions.

"It does look cool. Where do you want these ingots?" Matt asked.

"Place them in the correlating resource hoppers." Dave waved at the factory lines off to the side.

Matt looked at a pop-up before he dismissed it from his screen. Apparently Dave's request had turned into a quest.

"Hmm, I should check my class quests," Dave muttered to himself. He opened his interface as Matt put ingots and materials into different bins.

Quest: Dwarven Master Smith Level 4

You must craft 1 weapon of SS quality, or 50 of S Quality with your Smithing Art (Currently 0/1 (0/50))

Rewards: Unlock Level 5 quest

Increase to stat gain

Quest: Friend Of The Grey God Level 4

Get the Stone Raiders' Guild Hall functional

Rewards: Unlock Level 5 Quest

Increase to stats

Quest: Bleeder Level 3

Get the Stone Raiders' Guild Hall functional

Rewards: Unlock Level 4 Quest

Increase to stats

Ability to disable Jukal Link

Quest: Librarian Level 4

Contribute to someone's research topic

Rewards: Unlock Level 5 Quest

Increase to stats

Quest: Aleph Engineer Level 4

Help build 1 Aleph facility

Rewards: Unlock Level 5 Quest

Increase to stats

Increased access to Aleph College Knowledge

Quest: Weapons Master Level 4
One handed and shield 0/1000
Two handed 0/1000
Dual wielding 0/1000
Archery 0/1000
Rewards: Unlock Level 5 Quest
Increase to stats
Passive skills from other weapons increase from 25% when not equipped to 50%

Quest: Champion Slayer Level 4
Kill 100 Champions (85/100)
Rewards: Unlock Level 5 Quest
Increase to stats
Increased/Decreased reputation with Affinities

Quest: Skill Creator Level 2
Personally teach 1 person your Skill (0/1)
Rewards: Unlock Level 3 Quest
Increase to stats

Quest: Mine Manager Level 8
Pay 20,000,000 gold
Rewards: Unlock Level 9 Quest
Increase to mine's output

Quest: Master Summoner Level 2
Open a rift to 10 planes (0/10)
Rewards: Unlock Level 3 Quest
Increase stats

"Hey Matt, I know you're an artificer, and you know something about magical coding. Would you be interested in learning more?" Dave asked.

"Yes." Matt's head turned around so fast Dave thought he broke his neck.

"Would you say it's a topic of research for you?" Dave wheedled.

"Yeah, sure," Matt said, a confused look on his face.

"Boo-yah!" Dave punched a triumphant fist in the air. "All right, finish up with that and I'll teach you about magical coding." Dave grinned. *If I can teach him, then I might be able to get Skill Creator and Librarian up a level!*

"Be done in a second!" Matt moved much faster to put the ingots from his bag of holding into the various factory hoppers.

Chapter 37: Oncoming Tournament

Geswald looked out over Emaren from his office's large windows. Day had turned into night as he lost himself in his thoughts.

"Sir?" Pete said from the doorway.

"Hello, Pete," Geswald said, his voice as tired as he felt.

"We have got word from some of the people we know who went to Devil's Crater. It seems that the Stone Raiders' videos of them fighting the Demon Horde was right. They've made a friendship with the Devil's Crater inhabitants and are regularly clearing out the crater of wild animals and clearing out dungeons. However, we were not able to get a reading on the strength of the Stone Raiders there. We were able to get some on those who are training in Cliff-Hill. We weren't able to get any information on their other guild hall. We have no location for it and it seems the only way to reach it is by teleport pad. The Cliff-Hill smithies are owned by a person called Dave Grahslagg, a member of the Stone Raiders. They're expanding into Cliff-Hill and another company also owned by Mister Grahslagg is the ceramics factory in Cliff-Hill that is expanding into Zol'Ord." Pete stopped talking, waiting for a reaction from Geswald.

"Anything else?" Geswald knew that even if the Stone Raiders all got killed off, they could come back. They had run away from Selhi after their fight with the PKP Guild and Lord Esamael believed that they would do the same when confronted with his army.

Geswald hoped it would go as Esamael planned.

"It seems that any of the Stone Raiders who desire to join the tournament will make their way directly to the mountains where the tournaments are being held. They have the gold for it and the guild wants to show off their strength." Pete paused, as if wondering the best way to continue.

"Out with it." Geswald looked to Pete, feeling better after knowing that the majority of the Stone Raiders would be far away, unable to interfere.

"Alamos of the mage's college was at the Verlun location. It seems that one of our people we sent to make the Stone Raiders look bad was incapacitated and then escorted out. We could have spun it to make them look bad, but Alamos was in the store and agreed with the Stone Raiders' treatment of the mage. He expelled the man as soon as he returned to the college and made it clear that the mages of the college reflect on their institution. Any behavior that is unbecoming of a mage's guild or college student will be reprimanded and punished accordingly," Pete said.

Geswald's eyes thinned as he took a deep breath in. "Interesting." Geswald pondered. "Seems that the mages support them, and have given them some added protection. Let's see if we can't reach out to those who don't agree with this current ruling. See if we can't use them later. Also, see if we can decrease prices here and make the stores that the mages deal with more appealing than the Stone Raiders' in Verlun."

"Also, the adventuring guild, while they haven't made it public, most of their chapter houses refer to the Stone Raiders as an ally. The Stone Raiders give them a discount and assist the guild but don't pay fees," Pete said.

Geswald snorted.

"With the decreased prices, the adventurer's guild is getting a lot more from the Stone Raiders than they could get with their fees. Also allows them both more freedom."

"I have heard that the trader's guild want to increase their ties to the Stone Raiders as well as Dave Grahslagg's businesses. They assisted with helping the people of Devil's Crater. Being such a new secured village within Ashal, it is sure to grow into a city with both its natural and manned defenses. The fact that there are dungeons within their walls and not too far beyond is sure to attract all manner of people," Pete said.

"Yes, which is making it much harder for me to apply pressure and still not go against what the guild's leadership is telling me." Geswald pinched the bridge of his nose, letting out a loud and frustrated exhale.

"I know it's not my place, but it seems that the Stone Raiders are becoming quite a powerful force in Emerilia."

Geswald let the tension in the room grow.

"It does, doesn't it? I wish we had a way out of this mess, but we're in too deep. Esamael has given us assurances, and based on what the Stone Raiders have done in the past and how they will be playing in a tournament, we should be okay. There are just a few hundred of them." Geswald waved his hand as if it were a moot point. He didn't know the full power of Esamael's forces but from what he had gathered, it was around a half million strong.

More than enough to deal with the Verlun hall.

"They've been recruiting. They've got nearly five hundred in training camps, or being cycled through Devil's Crater for training. Their vetting process is in-depth. We haven't been able to get anyone in and while they don't hire the highest-leveled people, they take on those who are driven and believe as they do," Pete warned.

"Our cards have been played. All we can do now is try to stack the rest of the deck in our favor." Geswald felt more tired now than when he had started talking to Pete.

***

Dave watched as Matt used the carver. His runes were a mess but they were easy enough to read.

With computers, keyboards, and voice recognition, there really wasn't that much of a need to learn how to write with a pen and pencil back on Earth. Maybe it'll be easier for the POEs to get the writ-

ing aspect while the Players can understand the coding method bet-ter—maybe pair them up?

Dave snorted, already starting to plan out the best way to teach his magical coding to others. He'd made a ton of interesting things with his simple magical coding, but there was just one of him. If he could have a dozen coders, he could spread the load out, all of them refining Magical Circuits and coming up with new code.

It could be a magical coding revolution! Dave focused back on Matt's work with a smile on his face.

Matt finished off his final rune, ending it with the Xelur symbol of end. He looked at it, as if expecting it to explode.

"Okay, now let's put it in the test cage." Dave clapped Matt on the shoulder.

"Okay." Matt put it into one of the machines Dave had created to ease his magical coding.

There was a line of code in a box, with four lines of code depicting different corners around the inner box. Matt placed the piece of metal into the inner box.

He pushed a switch on the side of the outer box. It lined up the runes, activating the Mana barrier in the outside box. He turned on another switch; the metal floated.

"Hmm, might be an idea to make a control bracelet, easier than having to conjure runes into my armor," Dave muttered to himself, looking to his spear bracelet. Adding in the ability to turn it on and off and allow someone without the conjuring skill to change its outputs was pretty revolutionary.

Maybe add a higher powered ability to the bomber runes engraved on the DCA's armor? He shook his head, concentrating on the metal band as Matt turned a dial also placed into the table next to the testing station.

The runes below the metal lit up; the runes engraved into the metal started to glow. The magical code didn't store much power but it should be enough to activate it.

"Well done." Dave grinned as the metal vibrated slightly and then settled back down.

"Thanks." Matt took a shuddering breath and grinned nervously. The last ones had blown up rather spectacularly; the runes had not been deep or refined enough and the energy escaped randomly, and there was no power control. The metal had filled with energy and continued going, making it unstable and adding another black mark to the testing station.

"Well, let's see what you've made." Dave smiled. He understood some of the runes but he'd let Matt pick and choose what he wanted to make.

A thin beam of crackling energy extended out from the metal. It was hazy and sparks flew off from it.

"You're losing power from minor problems in the coding. Need to work on your carving skill." Dave studied the item.

Matt nodded, waiting, eager to learn more.

"Also, your shaping is not the best. If you're trying to make a Halo sword, you should have used Aleph and Ooinfa runes," Dave said with a reproving glance.

Matt looked downtrodden with Dave's remarks.

Dave couldn't keep the look up. Breaking into a smile, he excitedly clapped Matt on the shoulder, making the man stumble slightly with the Dwarven power behind it. "But it's a damn sight better than my first tries!" Dave laughed.

Matt broke out into an embarrassed and proud smile.

The metal fizzled and shuddered. The runes were melting slightly with the power going through them. Dave flicked the power off. The sword's five-inch-long Mana blade faded. Sparks ran across it before dying.

"I just got the skill magical coding." Matt looked at a window on his interface.

"Boo-yah! We've got a lot more to do, but Mana sword—I didn't think of that. Pretty cool. Might have to try that out." Dave deactivated the testing station and pulled out the metal.

"It says that I get a bonus in learning magical coding by learning from you because you're the original skill creator," Matt said with clear shock. His shock turned to excitement.

"Much to learn, you do," Dave said in his best wise old goblin voice.

Matt let out a big belly laugh.

Dave joined in before he handed over the metal. A pop-up blurred in his vision.

New Active Skill: Teacher

Well. Hello again there! Looks like you can teach an old dog new tricks! And even old dogs can teach others new tricks... Or something like that...Well, at least, you aren't running around in circles trying to catch your own tail, most of the time. Just boring the hell out of people with your damned lectures! Why did I have to get stuck with this guy? Can I get some adrenaline junkie? I'm calling HR!

Level: Apprentice Level 3

Effect: You can teach people skills that you have prior knowledge of, up to your level of ability. Your students are 5% more likely to understand what you're teaching them. Teaching on subjects you have a higher knowledge on will yield higher results. Teaching skills you have mastered or created give a higher chance for students understanding your lessons.

Dave rolled his eyes; he'd missed whatever weird AI was making up his descriptions. Seemed they were pretty bored. "Maybe I'll meet them one day." Dave shrugged and pushed the pop-up aside, and found two more.

Dave laughed to himself.

Class: Librarian

Through tireless research, you have taken the written word and used it in a practical sense. Beware the nerd who studies; they've got a dozen ideas others haven't even thought of yet.

Status:	Level 4
	+80 Vitality
	+30 Endurance
Effects:	+60 Strength
	+60 Agility

Class: Skill Creator

You have gone beyond regular skills, mastering them in the pursuit for more. You have created a new skill in your endeavors

Status:	Level 2
	+40 Intelligence
Effects:	+40 Endurance
	+40 Willpower

"All in a day's work." Dave felt the rush as his body adapted to the new stats. *Might be an idea to just sit around, do some training with other people than just grind out levels. With more classes, it makes it much easier to increase my stats.* Dave pondered and opened his character sheet.

Character Sheet

Name:	David Grahslagg	Gender:	Male
Level:	148	Class:	Dwarven Master Smith, Friend of the Grey God, Bleeder, Librarian, Aleph Engineer, Weapons Master, Champion Slayer, Skill Creator, Mine Manager, Master Summoner
Race:	Human/ Dwarf	Alignment:	Neutral Good

Unspent points: 366

Health:	26,300	Regen:	10.66 /s
Mana:	7,980	Regen:	23.55 /s
Stamina:	3,240	Regen:	21.00 /s
Vitality:	263	Endurance:	533
Intelligence:	798	Willpower:	471
Strength:	324	Agility:	420

Dave took a deep breath; his eyes and runes glowed slightly with the influx of power. It settled down, Dave feeling refreshed and stronger than ever.

"Okay, so, what did you learn from your first success?" Dave looked to his student.

"I need to work on my carving." Matt winced.

"Well, yes, but what about the coding, the power output, everything and anything!"

"The runes weren't the best made, which was making the power unstable and messing with the coding. I need to refine my carving for that. I can see why you now use so much silver in runes. Their ability to stabilize and help the magical coding work will be a lot of help in larger productions. I also was trying to do way too much. If I had scaled down the output, then I could have sustained the blade for longer. I also thought more about form over function. If someone's hand had been on that blade, they would have been getting a surge of Mana right through their hand." Matt winced.

"Well, you're learning." Dave smiled and slapped Matt on the back. "We've got a long path ahead of us."

Dave's smile flickered slightly, thinking of all the challenges in their future.

And the Players don't even know simulation from reality.

Dave's resolve firmed. He would do everything he could to get his friends and those he called his family ready for what was to come.

Epilogue: A New Pantheon

The Dark Lord waved his hand at the air. The spell took a lot of power, what was worth five months of his old follower's devotions.

Boran-al shivered in excitement at his lord's newfound power. Space seemed to distort, tearing open a hole through it. The Dark Lord walked through the shimmering portal without a care.

Boran-al followed on his heels.

They exited the portal in a dark room. Pitch-black crystal glinted on the walls. It seemed to drink in any surrounding light. Boran-al had been born and molded in darkness; he could see through it easily as they made their way through massive ornate halls, each twenty feet tall and sixty feet wide.

What kind of creatures would make a place such as this? Were these halls made for their size, or because they simply desired it?

Boran-al followed his master without a word.

"As you might have thought, I have been gaining power from sources other than my followers." The Dark Lord sounded excited. "I found a new source of power and devotions, a much more powerful one." Twin crystal doors parted with barely a sound, revealing a shining desert beyond, covered in black crystals like the building they were in.

The tower stretched into the sky, making it hard to see how far the odd crystal desert spread.

"Welcome to Alturara, land of the Alturarans, my new followers." The Dark Lord waved his hand as if to embrace the desert before him.

Boran-al looked down in shock. The crystal desert wasn't a desert at all but a gathering of Alturarans. Their bellows were like a wall of force, their grating and screeching cheers making Boran-al shudder. He smiled hungrily, his eyes filled with greed and malice.

"I used your citadel's power to open a portal to these lands and anoint new champions within the Alturarans. They have gathered a loyal following that eagerly devotes their power for my blessings," the Dark Lord said with pride.

"Master, you are brilliant beyond compare." Boran-al prostrated himself before his lord and master.

The Alturarans weren't just creatures; they were organic life that had left behind their forms to grow into crystals. Using their Dark Affinity, they could easily control their much stronger and powerful crystal bodies.

The Dark Lord indicated for Boran-al to rise after a few moments. Boran-al stared over the balcony. He giggled until it turned to laughter. His eyes wandered over the Alturarans. Among them, massive beasts, taking on various forms and ranging from ten stories tall to forty meters long, moved about.

With this army supplying my master power, nothing will stand in our way!

Emerilia will be continued in Stone Raider's Return.

As a self published author I live for reviews! If you've enjoyed Emerilia, please leave a review!

Hope you have a great Day! ☺

Want a bigger map of Emerilia and the continents? Check out

http://theeternalwriter.deviantart.com/

You can check out my other books, what I'm working on and upcoming releases through the following means:

Website: **http://michaelchatfield.com/**

Twitter: **@chatfieldsbooks**[1]

Facebook: **Michael Chatfield**[2]

Goodreads: **Goodreads.com/michaelchatfield**[3]

Thanks again for reading! ☺

Interested in more LitRPG? Check out **https://www.facebook.com/groups/ LitRPGsociety/**

---

1.   https://twitter.com/chatfieldsbooks

2.   https://www.facebook.com/michaelchatfieldsbooks/?ref=hl

3.   https://www.goodreads.com/author/show/14055550.Michael_Chatfield

Continue on for Character Sheet!

In Alphabetical order
Ankol

Dwarf

Dwarven Master Smith. Smithing Art: Metal Spinner. Lives in Grorart Mountain.

Boran-Al

Lich

One of the Dark Lord's Champions. Works directly under the Dark Lord. Creates Creatures of Power and carry's out the Dark Lord's orders. His Citadel was destroyed.

Alastair Montgoa

Arch Lich aka former Lord Vailyn. Gave up his fellow Aleph to have everlasting life; used the centuries to build strength and knowledge

Barry

Dwarf

    Dwarven Master Smith. Smithing Art-Unknown. Wandering smith.

Cassie

Elf/Human Halfling

Holy warrior. Leader of the Golden Sabres. In a relationship with Josh Giles.

Dark Lord

God

Embodiment of the Dark affinity. Created Demons. Normally an ally with the Earth Lord. Always looking a way to tip the power balance of Emerilia in his favor.

Dasano

Dwarf

Dwarven Master Smith. Smithing Art: Metal Press. Lives in Grorart Mountain.

Akatol Dracul

Dragon

Water Mage. Was the second Dragon, Denur's husband. Went mad and started a genocide, disappeared.

Denur Dracul

Dragon

Fire Mage Hailed as 'Mother of Dragons'. First of her race, a creature of power created by the Lady of Fire. Seen as her daughter. Sister to Oson' Deia.

Gelimah Dracul

Dragon
  Dark Mage. Brother to Induca, Louna and Malsour

Fornau Dracul

Dragon

Earth Mage. Quindar's mate Malsour and Induca's grand-nephew.

Induca Dracul

Dragon

Fire Mage. One of the youngest from the first generation of Dragons. Sister to Malsour, daughter of Denur, aunt to Quindar, great aunt to Fornau. Member of the Stone Raiders and Party Zero.

Kinal Dracul

Dragon

Louna Dracul

Dragon
>   Induca, Gelimah and Malsour's sister.

Malsour Dracul

Dragon

Dark Mage. One of the oldest Dragons in existence, first born of Denur. Deia and Induca's Guardian, Stone Raider and Party Zero member. Brother to Induca. Great Uncle to Fornau Dracul and Uncle to Quindar Dracul.

Quindar Dracul

Dragon
  Wind Mage, wife to Fornau, Niece to Induca and Malsour.

Wokui Dracul

Dragon
    Water Mage

Xednai Dracul

Dragon
One of the first Dragons, had several Dragons. Her son is Fornau.

Gorpal Dunsk

Dwarf

Dwarven Master Smith, lives in Aldamire Mountain, created 3 Weapons of Power - Mace of Fury, Tower Shield, Boots of Smash. Smithing Art: Paint Copy

Earth Lord

God
> Embodiment of the Dark affinity. Created Earth Sprites.

Edmur

Dwarf

Dwarven Master Smith. Had been in the Dwarven War Bands as a Shield Bearer. Former pupil of Quino's Brother to Endur. Smithing Art: Metal's Song

Edwards

Human. Military scientist within the Deq'ual System. Friend of Sato's

Edwin

Beast Kin. Beast Kin representative on ruling council.

Endur

Dwarf

Dwarven Master Smith. Had been in the Dwarven War Bands as a Shield Bearer. Former pupil of Quino's, brother to Edmur, lives in Zolu Mountain. Smithing Art Hammer Blows

Esa

Human

Melee fighter. Member of Mikal and Jule's party. Fought at Boranl-Al's Citadel.

Member of the Stone Raiders. Going out with Jules. Works under Dwayne as a fighter. Being trained for a leadership position under Dwayne.

Lord Esamael

Human.

Lord of Emaren within the Gudalo Kingdom.

Ela-Gal

High Elf.

Warrior living in Aleph, married to Ela'Dorn. Persectued by high elves as heretic.

Ela-Dorn

Orc.

Researcher and professor at Aleph College. Aleph Council Member. Married to Ela-Gal

Fend

Dwarf
  Lord Under the Mithsia Mountains.

Geswald

Human.
    Trader's Guild Chapter head in Emaren.

David Grahslagg

Dwarf/Human Halfling, in-game character of Austin Zane. Dwarven Master Smith, Resident of Cliff Hill, member of Party Zero and the Stone Raider's Guild. Other names: Austin Zane

Josh Giles

Human

Rogue. Leader of the Stone Raiders. Was a investment broker on Earth, became an E-head. In a relationship with Cassie from the Golden Sabres.

Gimel

Human
    Warrior.
    Fellox Guild Master.

Gorrund

Dwarf

Dwarven Master Smith in Benvari Mountain with Jesal, teaching four apprentices. Smithing Art: Blood Bender.

Goula

Demon
: On the Ruling council for Devil's Crater.

Gurren

Dwarf

Shield bearer, member of Dwarven War Band under Lox's command, sent to guide people to Cliff-Hill. Friend of David Grahslagg, Kol's Grandson. Member of the Stone Raiders.

Helick

Dwarf
Dwarven Master Smith.

Kim Isdola

Human

    Cleric/alchemist. Lieutenant in Stone Raiders.

Ishox

Demon
On the Ruling council for Devil's Crater.

Arch-Mage Jekoni

Human/item

Soul bound to Staff of Growing, over 2,000 years old; missing legs. Held within Dwarven Vaults with other Weapons of power.

Jeeves

AI
Made by Bob to assist the Dwarven Master Smiths.

Jeremy

Human
Fellox Guild member.

Jesal

Dwarf

Dwarven Master Smith, Dave's master smith trainer. Smithing art: Nature's Guide

Jules

Human

Healer. Member of Mikal and Esa's party. Fought at Boranl-Al's Citadel.

Member of the Stone Raiders. Used to be an army medic, E-head without legs IRL. Going out with Esa. Works under Lucy as support, leads the healers of the Stone Raiders.

Joko

Dwarf

Shield bearer, member of Dwarven War Band under Lox's command, sent to guide people to Cliff-Hill. Friend and trainer of David Grahslagg.

Deceased.

Anna'Kal

Wolf Beast Kin/Administrator AI24681

Air mage. Originally a program meant to assist Lo'kal with the running of Emerilia. Anna was uploaded to a Player body and inserted into Emerilia. She became emotionally attached with her charges. When the Beast Kin people were wiped out from Emerilia she went into cold storage, waiting for her father to awake her when a chance came to fight against the prison they had created.

Member of the Stone Raiders and Party Zero. Daughter of Bob.

Lo'kal

Jukal

Scientist, created Emerilia. Awarded the position of the Gray God, maintains Emerilia, its people and Players. Other names: Bob, Bobby McMahnon, The Balancer, Gray God.

Kino

Demon
    On the Ruling Council for Devil's Crater.

Kol

Dwarf

Dwarven Master Smith. Gurren's grandfather. Resides in Cliff-Hill. Taught Dave how to Smith. Runs his Smithies. Smithing art: Blind Man's Touch

Lady of Air

Goddess

Embodiment of the affinity Air. Known for causing mischief. Her Champions act as spies and information brokers, tilting the balance of Emerilia.

Lady of Fire

Goddess

Created Dragons, Mages Guild and College. Gave gift of 'knowledge' to the people of Emerilia. Mother to Deia, Lover of Oson'Mal and best friend with Bob.

Other Names: Ignil

Lady of Light

Goddess

Sent Players to kill/capture Dragons to make her own Creatures of Power. Created the race known as Angels. Large rivalry with the Dark Lord.

Lena

Demon
> On the Ruling Council of Devil's Crater. Wife to Vrexu.

Lovan

Dwarf
    Mithsia Mountain Warclan leader

Lox

Dwarf

Shield bearer. Was the commander of the War Band sent to guide people to Cliff-Hill. Friend of David Grahslagg. Member of the Stone Raiders.

Suzy Markell

Human (IRL)

High Elf (Emerilia)

Austin Zane's secretary and best friend. David Grahslagg's best friend and assistant with running Cliff Hill Smithy and Factory. Summoning Mage. Steven's contractor, member of Party Zero and the Stone Raiders.

Max

Dwarf

Shield bearer, member of Dwarven War Band under Lox's command, sent to guide people to Cliff-Hill. Friend of David Grahslagg.

Deceased.

Meda

Dwarf/Elf

Aleph Council member. Deals with the food within Aleph cities and facilities

Melanie

Human
Arch Mage Alamos' Wife.

Melhoun

Water snake made by the Water Lord.
Sealed away.

Mikal

Human

Rogue. Jules and Esa's party member. Member of the Stone Raiders. Friends with Party Zero.

Oson'Deia

Elf/Demi God Halfling

Elven Ranger and Fire Mage. Daughter of Oson'Mal and Lady Fire of the Affinity Pantheon. Resident of Cliff Hill and member of the Stone Raider's Guild, Leader of Party Zero.

Other names: Ouluv'Deia

Penelope

Human
Fellox Guild member.

Pete

Human
>Geswald's secretary.

Queen Farun

High Elf
    Queen of Raolor.

Queen Mendari Selhi

Human
Queen of Selhi.

Quino

Dwarf

Dwarven Master Smith, lives in Zolu Mountain. Trained the brothers Endur and Edmur. Smithing Art: Internal cutting.

Rola

Dwarf

Dwarven Master Smith. Smithing Art Puppeteer. Lives in Aldamire Mountain.

Sato/Communications officer Sato

Human

Lives in De'qual system.

Communications Officer, becomes Vice commander of Deq'ual military forces. Grandfather original settler.

Emperor Talis

Human.

Ruler of the Xeugrera Empire, located in the Ashal Continent.

Tounk

Dwarf

Shield bearer, member of Dwarven War Band under Lox's command, sent to guide people to Cliff-Hill. Friend of David Grahslagg.

Deceased.

Demon Prince Alkao/Alkao Travezar

Aerial Demon

Melee fighter. Commander of the Third Demon Horde and leader of Xerzit lands. Oldest of the five remaining Demon Prince's of Devil's Crater.

Dwayne Trebault

Human

    Melee fighter. Lieutenant in Stone Raiders. Leads and trains the melee fighters in the Stone Raiders.

Venfik

Elf
Lady Air's advisor.

Lucy Vernia

Wood Elf/Human

Lieutenant in Stone Raiders. Spy master, deals with supporting the Stone Raiders and paperwork.

Vrexu

Demon

One of the seven Demon Princes. General in the Devil's Crater Army. Married to Lena, the youngest of the five remaining Demon Princes.

Water Lord

God

Embodiment of the Water Affinity. Created the Mer-People and water creatures. Created the Water Serpent Melhoun. Rival to the Lady of Fire.

Austin Zane

CEO of Rock Breaker's Corporation. Engineer specializing in space vehicles. Background in Astro physics. Other names: David Grahslagg

Wis'Zel

Wood Elf

Bard. Works for David Grahslagg, managing his Ceramics factories in Cliff Hill.

Do you like LitRPG? (I'm going to guess that's a yes seeing as you've come this far) Check out LitRPG society on Facebook!

https://www.facebook.com/groups/LitRPGsociety/

www.ingramcontent.com/pod-product-compliance
Lightning Source LLC
Chambersburg PA
CBHW070645310726
48982CB00001B/418